Grey

pulled h

arms en

Trying

arms on the harbormaster's chest. In studying medicine she'd encountered many naked bodies, men and women both. But all her years of schooling hadn't prepared her for the devilishly attractive man who stood so brazenly before her, watching her every movement. He smiled down at her, his dimple a deep crater in his cheek, as she slipped the shirt away from his wide, muscular shoulders.

His body smelled clean, like sunshine and sea. Fiery tremors shot through her when he jerked her against his chest. Never before had Rachel felt this strange hunger for a man's touch. Never before had she experienced desire.

BRIDE OF THE NIGHT

TENA CARLYLE

ZEBRA BOOKS
KENSINGTON PUBLISHING CORP.

ZEBRA BOOKS are published by

Kensington Publishing Corp.
475 Park Avenue South
New York, NY 10016

First Printing: February, 1994

Printed in the United States of America

Prologue

Winter 1875
Somewhere off the coast of England
Dearest Daughter,

It is with great sadness that I write this letter to you today. My one consolation is that you will receive it, for I've paid dearly for that promise.

I trust, daughter, that at last you will come to understand what has become of your papa. I did not desert your mother as some would have you believe. Those who might have spread such vicious rumors are the same ones I know to be responsible for shanghaiing me.

I pray she is well, although I'm certain my absence has been a trial for her, and I am uncertain if she could suffer the strain of learning of my condition. That is why I write to you. With your sensible disposition and your ability to take charge of a situation, I know you will lighten your mother's burden.

Rachel Thomas turned the pages, feeling the tears well in her eyes. Her parents had been so close. She thought of them now, together again at last.

You must realize how proud your papa is of you. Perhaps I should have heeded your mother's warnings and discouraged your interest in medicine. But in truth, I could not bear to part with the intellectual questions with which you challenged me. Your young mind was like a dried sea sponge—a soft elastic skeleton, free from contaminants and able to absorb knowledge with great ability. These qualities, my Rachel, plus your determination and loving heart, will make you a gifted physician.

Here upon this ship, we are no more than slaves, flesh taken by force to man the vessel, then killed or sold for the turn of a coin. We are as much in bondage as were our African brothers and sisters who not so long ago won their freedom. No man should be reduced to this animal state, to not be allowed control over his own destiny.

You ask . . . why him, a doctor? It is because I openly labored to bring down the men accountable for such heinous crimes against the good citizens of our town. It was to that end I dedicated my energies, and it was that end that brought me here.

The enclosed list contains the names of men I know to be responsible for the rash of shanghaiing in Astoria.

She paused to turn to the last page. On it were the names of three men—names that meant nothing to her, but obviously names she needed to remember. She read on.

I send you this list, daughter, so that you will avoid these men at all cost. These are ruthless, heartless criminals who care for nothing but the profit that the illegal sale of men will bring. They are guilty of murdering a man's soul and should be judged not fit for humanity themselves.

So please, my daughter, I beg of you to grant your father his one wish. In my absence, insist your mother join you until my return. When your schooling is finished, go elsewhere to set up your medical practice, for I have made enemies in Astoria and fear for the safety of my two loved ones. Leave your destination with a man named Taithleach.

8

If God deigns I should again be free, I will come for you both. Until then I shall be at peace knowing you have promised to protect your mother.

Your devoted papa,
Theodore Thomas

Rachel carefully folded the letter and leaned her head back against the wooden rocker, listening to the rhythmic creaking against the fir flooring and the constant drone of rain outside the windows of her front parlor.

Fading daylight cast an anemic glow over the sterile interior of the room. Starched white curtains, free of ruffles, hung at the windows, a meager attempt at softening the white-washed walls and gray woodwork. In the dim light even the framed hand-colored botanical prints seemed faded and dull.

And ignoring the fact that her severe chignon confined radiant mahogany hair, Rachel, in her black serge and starched white apron, felt as gloomy as the climate that surrounded her.

Only the brilliant fusion of color in the rag rug in front of the hearth seemed to mock Rachel's dark mood. Rivaling a Joseph's coat in its pattern, every hue of the rainbow stared back at her as if trying to erase her melancholy.

Four years had passed since the letter had been written and three since it had reached her in Michigan, two months after her mother's death of a broken heart and spirit.

Rachel had finished her schooling—with the highest grades in her class. But she had not done as her father requested.

This small house on Franklin Street was all she had

left of her parents. Released from a promise the letter had extracted, she had come home, refusing to give it up as well. But as her father had predicted, her shingle, hanging where his had once hung, found no patients beating a path to her door.

Was she being shunned by her father's so-called enemies? Or because she was a woman doctor? The reason did not matter. She'd returned with one motive—to take up her father's crusade. She would wipe out the scourge of shanghaiers that plagued the innocents in the port of Astoria. And she had a list of names.

Chapter 1

Astoria, Oregon, 1879

Grey Devlin walked into Baldy's Saloon and Gaming House on Astor Street, propped one seaboot on the brass rail that ran its length, and ordered a shot of bourbon. From his coat pocket he retrieved a coin, flipped it to the barkeep, then grabbed a handful of peanuts from a dish. Turning toward the room, he leaned against the bar and tossed several into his mouth, washing them down with the contents of his glass. To all who looked his way he seemed a man without a care in the world.

A sudden shiver hit his spine, not from the seared path left by the sour mash, but because he felt frozen through to his bones. Cold wind and rain had been gusting off the Columbia River for the better part of the day. Even his woolen underwear and pea jacket failed to keep him warm against the penetrating dampness.

Pushing his yacht cap back, Grey propped his elbows on the familiar bar. He'd been coming here almost daily for the past two months—since he'd been named harbormaster for the port of Astoria. It was a position he'd be proud of under different circumstances, but Grey knew the reason he'd been given the job. He also knew the reason he'd taken it.

Baldy poured another jigger into Grey's empty glass. "Still pissin' rain?"

Grey looked over at the proprietor, whose face and body sported more hair than a hibernating grizzly. "Yep. Enough to drown the fish." The two exchanged understanding grins. In this part of the country there were two kinds of folk, those who liked rain and those who didn't, but for most of the year they all had to live with it.

Grey watched the soft-spoken barkeep rub down the well-waxed counter with a soft rag, more from habit than necessity. The man was proud of his job and even more proud to be on this side of the Bering Straits.

Rumor had it, the fellow had acquired his name, not because he was bald, but upon his initiation into his new homeland. Ten years earlier he'd arrived aboard ship from Russia, and on first seeing the American bald eagle had mistakenly called it a buzzard. The trappers and frontiersmen who heard his blunder immediately christened him *Baldy,* and it had been so ever since.

Upon meeting him, Grey had immediately liked the man and his saloon, which sat near the river not far from the port authority office. The area, known as Swilltown, boasted a saloon on every corner, and often one in the middle of each block. Genteel ladies spoke in whispers of the bawdy goings-on in the area, but they never, ever walked there.

Choosing Baldy's over the countless other saloons

that dotted the area between Fifth and Tenth Streets, he would stop by for a drink and friendly conversation before making his way up the hill to Miss Purdy's Boarding House where he let a room. Today was no different.

"Seen Tully?" Nodding toward the barkeep, he scanned the room for his friend.

"Ain't been in today yet. My guess, it's too cold and damp for the old salt."

"It would take more than the elements to keep Tully inside," Grey replied. "He takes to this bone-chilling weather like a salmon swimming home to spawn. It's in his blood."

"Now I know the man's veins are filled with ice water." The barkeeper moved to the other end of the counter to wait on another customer, leaving Grey alone with his drink.

Grey removed his jacket and hat and placed them on the bar beside him. Catching his reflection in the mirror, he used his fingers like a comb and raked the flattened strands of blond hair into obedience. Satisfied, he concentrated on the customers in the room.

Astoria was a wide-open town. With its own river and seaport, it was the high spot between San Francisco and Seattle, with a night life that rivaled none. Gambling, drinking, and whoring were commonplace, and from what Grey had witnessed over the past weeks, Baldy's happened to have some of the finest-looking females in Oregon.

A piano, badly in need of tuning, plinkety-plinked a melody that bore no resemblance to the original score. But the off-key notes lent themselves to the ribald atmosphere and seemed to make the many seafaring souls who tarried there feel right at home.

Once more, Grey scanned the room through the mirror. His interest piqued at the feminine apparition that appeared on the stoop leading to the rooms where the ladies of the evening practiced their trade.

As Baldy made his way back to the near end of the bar, Grey nodded in his direction. "Who's the new gal?"

"Chinook's her name. A friend of Opal's out of San Francisco. When she comes into town for a visit, Opal lets her work the floor, same as the other gals. If Opal's happy, I'm happy. The ladies belong to her."

Chinook, Grey thought, as he positioned himself to study the woman who still stood on the platform. Her hair, as pink as the Pacific salmon whose name she bore, hung halfway down her back in a cascade of curls, and her eyes were straight on him.

He averted his gaze to keep from staring, then, as if drawn by a magnet, looked back into eyes that were focused strictly on him. He was no man's fool. The woman in green satin was sending him "come hither" signals from across the smoke-filled room, and the candid invitation provoked a surprising tightness in his loins.

In response he wondered if, as her name also suggested, she were as warm and moist as the southwest wind that blew northward up the Oregon coast.

Grey sure as hell aimed to find out.

Rachel Thomas stood upon the raised platform just inside the saloon. Dressed again as Chinook, she

14

scanned the hazy interior, looking for tonight's client. Catching her blurry image in the mirror behind the bar, she almost laughed aloud. No one would believe that the woman reflected in the silvery surface was not at all what she seemed.

A bevy of men filled the dusky, close quarters of the drinking establishment. Everyone here represented some aspect of commerce in the Astoria port— shipowners, sailors, landholders, loggers, financiers, and cannery workers. In the dim light and without her glasses, they appeared as no more than bodies with blurred features. Most had come to drink, to unwind after work. Others had come to buy the company of a soft, yielding woman.

The nature of the business that transpired in this flesh market never failed to shock her. She'd studied the reproductive process extensively in medical school. She knew clinically what passed between a man and a woman. She also knew that a male's libidinous nature was twice as strong in this type of environment. This greatest of all weaknesses would allow Rachel to carry out her plan. This same weakness had served her purpose well. Two men, thus far, had paid for their sins against her and her family. And, after tonight, only one more would remain.

Her knowledge as a doctor, coupled with her nearsightedness, had helped her play her role to perfection. By avoiding direct eye contact, she had thus far managed to thwart the attentive urges of most of the patrons, receiving instead only curious stares at what had to be the most ridiculous wig she herself had ever seen. And without her spectacles most faces were no more than hazy silhouettes. Since Rachel trifled only with

15

her chosen victims, she felt quite safe in her guise as a "sportin' gal."

She propped her hands upon the rail and leaned forward, assuming her most wanton and practiced pose. Soon Opal would be along to point out their night's prey. Until then, Rachel would be required to look and act like one of the girls and hope she would not be bothered by the customers.

Tonight she was Chinook.

Squinting, she sought her fuzzy reflection again in the mirror behind the bar.

Something old, something new;
Something borrowed, something blue.

The flitting thought of the bride's bequest caught her temporarily off guard. Though she was bedecked to catch the eye of the man she sought, the incongruity of pristine white bridal dress and her "bride of the night" costume was laughable. Her boots were indeed her own, *old* and worn. As were the chamois drawers that she'd found in a secondhand store when she'd been in medical school in Michigan. Worn over soft lamb's wool drawers, the supple leather had defended her body against the biting cold of the midwestern winters.

Glancing down at her exposed cleavage, displayed daringly in the decolletage of her borrowed dress, Rachel fought the impulse to pull up the peacock-green satin. On loan from one of Opal's girls whose build was similar to Rachel's own, the gown fit her like a glove but for one exception. The other girl hadn't been nearly so well endowed. Pulling at the skunk boa around her neck, she allowed it to settle more modestly across her breasts.

The concealed waist suspenders holding up her silk

stockings were blue. Her jewelry was new. Payment for medical services rendered—when she'd stitched a Madagascan sailor's ear back to his head after it had been bitten nearly off in a barroom brawl.

He'd touted the jewelry's value when he'd given her the large teardrop brooch and matching earrings. But when Rachel had taken the stones to have them appraised, she'd learned they were as worthless as the crafty seaman's hide. Far less valuable than look-alike sapphires with six gleaming rays, the diopsides possessed only four. Nevertheless, they still had a certain appeal. All in all, for Rachel's purpose, Chinook's disguise was acceptable.

Standing tall, she settled the boa back across her shoulder. At least her last piece of borrowed finery helped conceal her exposed breasts from too many probing eyes.

"Well, sugar, I see our fish has arrived."

Having slipped through the back door leading from the adjacent welcome house, Opal paused beside Rachel, suggesting with her eyes the location of their next catch.

Rachel followed Opal's gaze across the room and saw the blurred figure of a man leaning against the bar.

"My guess," Opal remarked, barely moving her mouth, "the way he's eyeing you through that mirror, he's already interested in nibbling."

Both women laughed conspiratorially.

"He surely is a looker . . . our new harbormaster." Opal smiled a dreamy approval.

Rachel wished she had her spectacles so she could get a better look at the man. But she didn't. So she'd just have to wait until she was close enough to him to form her own opinion. She also wished Opal hadn't added her own comments. She didn't need to be hearing any compliments about a man she considered to be a criminal. And that's what he was, she reminded herself. A criminal. Nothing more.

She looked again toward the bar and the shadowy figure. "Is everything ready?"

"You just get him to the room, and we'll be right behind you."

Rachel laughed. "I'll just twitch my tail, and like the others before him, I'm sure he'll take the bait."

"No doubt, sugar. He'll nibble. But you, sweetie, are going to miss the pleasure of the catch." Opal's throaty laughter filled the space between them.

"Believe me, friend, I'll get my reward."

On these words, Rachel descended the stairs. Swaying her hips as she'd often practiced in front of her looking glass, Chinook walked across the room toward the bar and her next quarry.

"Buy me a drink, mister?"

With aroused pleasure, Grey's eyes drifted from the top of the woman's spun sugar hair to the skunk boa draped across her hidden delights. Even in her preposterous garb she was a belle for sure. And surprisingly, this woman lacked the scent of the cheap cologne of her working sisters. In direct contrast, this woman radiated a fragrance all her own—a sweet, earthy scent, as though she'd been dancing among the woodland firs. His eyes slowly returned from their journey down her body and halted on her face. Raw desire jolted through

18

him when she repaid his heated look with one of her own.

Although he knew her name, he wanted to hear it pronounced from her own voluptuous mouth. His eyes never left her lips. "And to whose company do I owe this pleasure?"

She didn't disappoint him. The way she formed the name "Chinook" made him imagine those same full lips performing another equally pleasurable task.

"And you, honey. Do you have a name?" She traced a finger slowly up his sleeve.

Grey watched her trail a path along his arm and briefly wondered about the absence of paint on her nails. Every dove he'd ever known, his mother included, wore paint on her fingernails. But her sherry-colored eyes forced his observation out of his mind.

"Grey Devlin," he croaked, sounding like a boy on his first date. He downed his drink, attempting to wash away the hoarse rasp, as the pink and green confection pressed herself against his side.

"I like your name," Chinook replied, smiling up at him. "In fact, Mr. Grey Devlin, I think I like you very much." She batted her long lashes like a practiced courtesan.

"I like you, too," Grey replied, encircling her with his arm and pulling her up against him. The boa remained in place between them, but Grey had no doubt of the charms that lay hidden beneath it. Her breasts, crushed against his chest, felt full, firm, and ripe.

Rachel wasn't prepared for her own response to the ruggedly handsome harbormaster. Opal had been right

19

when she'd said he was a looker. Up close, he took her breath away.

A tawny lock sprigged over his forehead, and from her position, clamped against his wide chest, she could see that his hair was neatly clipped. Blond strands curled slightly at his nape, dusting the top of his white collar. He had an arresting face, and she found herself captivated by the dimple that slashed a deep crevice in his left cheek when he smiled. Which at the moment he seemed to be doing a lot.

She forced her attention from the dimple that flirted outrageously with her good judgment to the man's eyes. But she found no relief from her dilemma there. Expecting the same cold, calculating response of others before him, she found instead a strange warmth that grew with the same intensity as his smile. The color of the polar sea, clear and unyielding, his eyes met her gaze with a searing clarity that found its way to her very soul. And while she wondered what icy dangers lay hidden beneath the surface, she felt her insides melting.

Grey studied the woman he held in his arms. What he saw behind the riotous pink curls was a beauty. Eyes the color of fine sherry reflected the lanterns' flames in their warm depths.

Near the corner of her right eye she had a small beauty mark. Grey fought the sudden urge to press his tongue to the spot . . . to lick it away if it were fake. But somehow he knew it wouldn't be a velvet patch. He imagined God had seen the perfection of His creation, and so stamped it with this small approval.

"Do you want to go to my room?" she whispered, her warm breath teasing the pulse beneath his ear.

Although Grey didn't usually pay for a woman's services, Chinook intrigued him. He was so aroused by the prospect of bedding her that he would have paid a month's salary to buy her for one night.

"Lead the way, my little sweetmeat."

Grabbing his hand, the tantalizing wench pulled him behind her through the crowd to the platform where he had first seen her. As they moved, Grey concentrated on the provocative sway of her hips, captivated by the way the green satin dress cupped her buttocks, shimmering and caressing her with every step.

Although Grey had never visited the sporting house next door, he knew the door they approached exited into an open breezeway between the two buildings. Opal's territory, Baldy had informed him. It was common knowledge what transpired there.

His fantasy of what would occur when he and Chinook finally reached their destination made him grow hard with need. Very soon he'd bury himself in the warm moistness between her legs. Very soon he'd be in paradise.

A biting cold wind trespassed on his thoughts when the door to the saloon banged shut behind him. Except for a lone red lantern that hung beside another door several yards away, it was pitch dark in the narrow passageway.

Instantly alert, Grey checked his surroundings. Kidnapping men to become sailors was a profitable business in the port, and Grey had no intention of being shanghaied himself. If things went as planned, Astoria's crimps would soon enough be moving to other ports to collect their victims for sea duty. There would be no business for them here.

When they reached the door beside the red lantern, Chinook paused and edged closer to him. Wrapping her arms around his neck, she trailed kisses up his exposed throat. Again Grey luxuriated in the softness and the scent of the woman. His irregular breathing and hers, joined with the soft lapping of the tide against the pilings, cautioned him to prod her into movement.

"Don't you think we should continue this inside?" he whispered, between blowy kisses on her ear. "I'm not hankering to be shanghaied, honey. Loving you in this dark passage is mighty appealing, but it's not exactly safe. Besides, it's too cold to dangle, if you know what I mean."

He felt her stiffen in his arms, but then immediately turn soft and pliable again.

"Scared?" she asked, straightening his collar as though he were a small boy instead of a man about to explode his britches. "I shouldn't think a big, strong man like yourself would be afraid of anything." She patted his chest.

She was delighting in tormenting him. And with the red lantern backlighting her pink hair, she could have passed for a devil from hell.

"Come on, then," she quipped, seeming to sense his reluctance to tarry outside. Moving away, Chinook pushed open the door and he followed obediently behind her.

Once inside the hall, the familiar cloying smell of mixed cheap perfumes hit him and he had to stop himself from pivoting on his heel. If it weren't for the beguiling allure of the woman with him, he would have.

Looking around, he realized they'd entered through the back entrance. Somewhere up front would be a parlor. Every whorehouse had one—at least every one his mother had worked in. Drifting from the front came the tinny sounds of a piano and voices joined in merriment.

Chinook paused beside a door at the end of the hall. Grey watched her fingers curl around the glass doorknob. A series of sensations ran through his body as he imagined her doing the same thing to his enlarged sex.

His hand found the door above her head, helping her to push it open. Once inside, he heard it click shut behind them and pulled her into his arms.

"Not so fast, mister . . . Grey." The little teaser wiggled free of his embrace and moved to a bureau beside the bed. "I want my money up front." Chinook tapped a spot on top of the chest with her finger. "I don't spread my legs for any man . . . for no man till I see the green." Seeming to check her speech, she stood a little taller. He grinned at her efforts. Trying to be a proper lady, was she?

Grey crossed the room and stopped a few feet away from her. "Greedy little thing, aren't you?"

"In all things," she answered, sliding her tongue slowly across her upper lip. Her gaze lingered on the bulge in his trousers and he thought he'd pop before he could unbutton his pants.

"Just how much is this little romp going to cost me?"

"Twenty dollars."

"*Twenty dollars?* Honey, you must be good."

"Put your money right here and I'll show you how

23

good I am.'' Again she tapped her unpainted finger on top of the chest of drawers.

Instead of walking out, which he wondered why he hadn't yet done, Grey found himself fishing inside his pocket for the outrageous sum. With his background he usually had an aversion to whores. But this woman seemed different, not the usual type found in the flesh shops he'd lived in. This one seemed refined, both in speech and manner. Perhaps circumstances had brought her here—a lost husband, lost money, no skills. In wilderness like this she wouldn't be the first. Something in his gut, however, led him to believe something else was going on. As if she were playacting.

He tossed the money toward her and she snatched it from the air. Her quick movement sent the boa skimming across her shoulder, revealing her bosom. In that moment, Grey knew she'd be worth every penny he had to pay. His eyes feasted upon the creamy silkiness of her nearly exposed breasts. The tops of her nipples peeked over the green satin fabric like two dusky-colored half moons.

With a sharp intake of breath, he stared. Chinook's gaze followed his and she defensively crossed her arms over her chest. When she looked up into his eyes, her face grew as pink as her hair.

Not the actions of a sporting girl, Grey thought, stepping closer. As though she sensed her error, she immediately dropped her arms, bracing herself against the furniture, only causing her breasts to jut farther forward.

Below the shadowed valley at her bosom, Grey saw the jiggling motion of the black teardrop brooch that adorned her gown. Preoccupied with its movement, he watched it until it had stilled. Then he reached for the free end of the boa and slowly pulled the woman toward him. Their lower bodies met and his arms encircled her.

"Now, Pinky, I expect to see if you're worth my twenty dollars."

Trying to steady her erratic pulse, Rachel rested her arms on the harbormaster's chest and dropped her head backward, watching him from behind her half-lowered lids. "Oh, I'm worth it," she promised, her fingers moving to unbutton his shirt.

In studying medicine she'd encountered many naked bodies, men and women both. But all her years of schooling hadn't prepared her for the devilishly attractive man who stood so brazenly before her, watching her every movement. He smiled down at her, his dimple a deep crater in his cheek, while she slipped the shirt away from his wide, muscular shoulders.

Opal had schooled her in the craft of seduction. But until the harbormaster, Rachel had plied her newly learned skills with the same professional detachment that she showed her patients. In the attempt to divorce herself from her calculated moves with Grey Devlin, however, she found she couldn't. He clouded her very thoughts with his presence.

By the time she'd freed Grey from his shirt, Rachel's face felt feverish. His body smelled clean, like sunshine and sea.

Fiery tremors shot through her when he jerked her against his chest. Her low-cut neckline allowed her to feel his heated skin against her own. Never before had Rachel felt this strange hunger for a man's touch. Never before had she experienced desire. Her nipples tingled with a life of their own, ordering her to free them from their restraints. She wanted to throw all caution to the wind.

He pressed hot kisses to her neck, her earlobe, then his tongue dipped inside her ear. Overcome with sensations, Rachel clung to him, her mouth opening greedily to allow his tongue's exploration. Their mouths mated. Her heart hammered so forcefully in her chest she almost didn't hear the signals from behind the adjoining wall.

Thump, thump, thump. At last, the sound penetrated Rachel's overheated brain. She pushed free of Devlin's arms. She had to return the signal or Opal would think their plans had gone awry. Grey reached for her, trying to pull her back into his embrace.

"Not so fast, sugar," she replied, gently pushing him away. "I like a slow ride, and right now I've worked up a powerful thirst."

Rachel walked to the far wall where a decanter sat on a small table. With clumsy aptness, she rammed the table hard against the wall, knowing that Opal would recognize the signal for what it was. Pouring two drinks, she stirred the white powder that had earlier been placed in one glass and spun around to face Grey.

Her breath locked in her throat. While her back had been turned, Grey had removed his trousers. Now he stood beside the bed like a proud stallion waiting for his mare. Her eyes went immediately to his erection, protruding large and bold from a nest of golden hair. Although Rachel had studied the male anatomy extensively in school, nothing had prepared her for the sight of the glorious male before her. She nearly dropped both glasses.

Not certain of her next move, she stood speechless. Never with her other victims had she allowed their confrontation to progress this far. Usually, she'd given them the drink immediately upon entering the room and they'd passed out soon after. This time her own body had betrayed her and she condemned herself for surrendering to Grey's attractiveness.

He stood there, smiling at her, anticipating her attention. When she hesitated, he curled his finger, motioning her to him.

"We do have all night, honey, but I'm planning on getting my money's worth."

Not knowing what else to do but play his game, Rachel donned her Chinook pose and walked toward him. "Well, let's drink a toast to this evening," she replied, handing him his glass, "and then get on with it."

"Oh, I plan for you to get on it, sugar. Just as soon as I finish my drink." He clinked her glass with his. "Cheers." Then he tilted his head back and downed the contents.

"Now you just lie down," Rachel ordered over the rim of her glass, "and I'll be with you as soon as I get out of these clothes." She watched him, waiting for the sleeping powder to take effect.

When he lowered himself to the bed, Grey felt his knees tremble. Gripped by an attack of lightheadedness, he questioned if the last few days of miserable weather had prompted a case of the ague. Of all times to be seized with sickness. Just when he was about to bed an angel.

He glanced across the room, seeking out his pleasure. She still stood in the same position. Why hadn't she removed her clothes and joined him on the bed? He watched her image blur into a smudge of red and green. The tingling of his stomach turned to nausea and he thought if he could relieve himself of the drink he'd downed, he'd feel much better. But he'd only embarrass himself by throwing his insides up all over the floor.

The way the room was spinning he felt as though he'd ingested a drug. The drink. The damned, whoring female had slipped something into his drink!

Grey tried to stand. Fresh air. He needed fresh air to clear his brain. But his strength ebbed from his body like a receding tide. Falling back onto the lumpy mattress, he grabbed the edge of the blanket draped across the end of the bed and barely managed to cover his nakedness. His last conscious thought before darkness consumed him was . . . *why?*

Despondent, Rachel stood frozen, staring at the harbormaster's prone form. From the very beginning she hadn't felt so sure of this one. For reasons she didn't understand, she'd been drawn to his easy charm.

And his name had not been among those on her father's list.

She knew, however, that he'd allowed a shipment of opium into port, supposedly destined for the Chinese population, the same opium that had killed a prostitute—a defenseless woman just trying to keep food in her mouth.

No, she reasoned. Grey Devlin had to go. He was as guilty as the rest of the criminals who ran the waterfront and probably in cahoots with them as well. No, she'd done the right thing.

The door opened and Opal and two of her girls entered. Closing it behind them, Janie and Lou followed their employer toward the bed where Grey lay like a stiff,

28

waiting to be laid out for burial. One look at his state of undress and Opal's questioning gaze snapped to Rachel.

"He didn't?" she asked, her eyes wide with wonder.

Rachel shook her head, but continued to stare at the sleeping man.

Lou bent and lifted one corner of the blanket. "Sakes alive, would you look at that. His lizard done gone and died on him." She and Janie burst into giggles.

Rachel slapped the blanket from Lou's hand. At her reaction Opal eyed the girls to silence with her stony expression.

"You all right, sugar?" she asked. When Rachel didn't answer, she touched her on the arm. "The boat is waiting."

This snapped Rachel out of her reverie. Taking charge again, she helped the women wrap Grey's body in the blanket, open the trap door beside the bed, and lower him into the waiting dinghy below. The unknown seaman reached up with a banknote, then set his oars into the water. Steering from beneath the bawdy house, he slipped into the darkness where a ship waited for its cargo.

Lou closed the trap door and stood, dusting her hands together in a show of finality. "Good riddance to bad rubbish," she chirped, handing the fifty dollar banknote they'd received over to Opal. The three women covered the door with a rug to conceal its location.

Rachel scooped up Grey's discarded clothes. "I guess we should have sent these with him."

"He'll be in uniform soon enough," Janie added. "He won't be needing them duds."

For an instant Rachel thought of her father and wondered what kind of clothes he had been forced to wear.

Not enough to keep him warm against the blustery sea winds, she was sure. She pushed the image from her mind.

"In Tahiti they don't wear clothes," Lou added, and the two girls giggled again before Opal shooed them from the room.

Alone together, Rachel pointed out to Opal the twenty dollars she'd received from Grey. "Add that to our fund," she ordered.

Opal took the money and stuck it in her pocket. "Seventy dollars. Pretty good for a night's work, wouldn't you say? This money will help our women friends in the camps."

Rachel nodded, still holding on to Grey's clothes.

"Well, I'd better get back to Baldy's. Don't want to be away so long I might be missed and cause someone to get suspicious."

Opal walked to the door, then turned to face Rachel. "You all right, Doc?" she asked again.

"I'm fine," Rachel answered, "just tired. I'll change my clothes and leave through the side door."

"You do that, sugar, but you be careful walking the streets at night. See you tomorrow." Opal closed the door behind her.

Standing in the middle of the room, Rachel buried her face in Grey's clothes. The scent of sunshine and sea marsh floated up from the depths of the bundle and for a moment she was transported back to Grey's arms . . . but only for a moment.

A short time later, Doctor Rachel Thomas slipped through the side door of the bawdy house and headed toward her own home on Franklin Street.

30

Chapter 2

Tightly wrapped in the swaddling cocoon, Grey awoke to an uncontrollable chattering of his teeth. Freeing one arm from the confining wool, he pulled the corner of the blanket up around his head and tried to twist himself into a more comfortable position. His bones felt chilled through to the marrow.

He searched the inky blackness that enveloped him. Dampness hung in the air, and for an instant Grey thought he was back in the tiny dank cell that had claimed two years of his life. Those lost two years that had brought him to Astoria and to the man who had put him there.

At the slight movement of his head, a sharp pain vibrated throughout his skull. He tried to sit up, but the effort proved too much. Giving in to his weakness, Grey released his hold on the present and fell again into the deep well of sleep.

His dreams were troubled by the presence of a pink-haired witch. She lay stretched out beside him on the soft bed, teasing him with her nearness while refusing him the warmth his body craved. A fiendish smile formed upon her red lips. He reached for the bodice of her dress, intent on seeing the rosy moons that threatened to spill over the top, but she disappeared before he could lower the fabric.

The bed began to tilt and Grey felt as though he were floating on a long continuous wave. Bracing his feet against the footboard, he tried to steel himself against the rolling movement of the bedstead. Beneath his shivering body the ribbed mattress cut into his bones.

The witch had returned. She hung suspended above him shouting, "Twenty dollars, twenty dollars." With her unpainted fingers, she snatched the green bills from his hand, stuffing them into the valley between her breasts, behind the twinkling black brooch. "I'm worth it . . . I'm worth it," she taunted him. Then, laughing, she disappeared, swallowed by the night.

Grey forced his eyes open. He lay on his side, soundless, waiting for the fog to lift from his brain. With each controlled breath he took, his mind fought its way back to lucidity.

Beneath his ear he heard what sounded like the constant slapping of water against wood. He lay motionless, taking in the rhythmic splash of oars and the alternating sweep and drag of a small boat being pulled through the tide. Above him, someone rowed the small craft over the water's gentle swells.

Alert now, Grey knew where he was and where he was bound. Trapped on the floor of the bateau, Grey Devlin was headed out to sea.

The pink-haired whore had shanghaied him. And if he didn't act fast, he'd soon be loaded upon some ship and sent halfway around the world.

Imitating a drugged moan, Grey rolled to his back. He shifted the blanket enough to seek a better look at his captor.

It was so damned dark, he could hardly see. But slowly his eyes adjusted until he could make out his abductor's silhouette against the night sky.

Grey lay stretched in front of the sailor, his feet toward the stern. His vulnerable head lay a foot or so away from the seaman's boots. He knew immediately why he'd been placed in this position. To keep him from escaping. One swift kick of the brute's foot and Grey would be lucky to see daylight again.

Escape would not be easy, for sure. Damn. If he'd faced the other direction, he could have kicked the son-of-a-bitch in the chest.

The minutes ticked away, while he pondered his dismal prospects. Grey had heard stories about the fates of shanghaied sailors and the ruthless captains under whom they sailed. He could lie here and accept his destiny or he could fight. At this point, anything he tried would be better than the alternative—even drowning—if he were lucky enough to make it into the water. Even that would be better than being imprisoned again.

Within the folds of the blanket he pulled his legs toward his chest and found he'd been left unbound. For that he gave thanks, for otherwise escape would have been impossible. He watched the man poised above him on the narrow seat. If he could manage to knock the man overboard, he'd borrow his boat for the return trip to shore. Judging from the man's stature, his task wouldn't be an easy one. Surprise would be his only defense.

With effort he sprang toward the unaware rower, butting his head into the man's stomach.

"What the hell . . . ?"

A whoosh of breath escaped the seaman's throat as he doubled over from the surprise impact. Enraged, he lunged at his hostage. With one meaty fist he grabbed the blanket still wound around Grey's chest and aimed his other at Grey's face.

Like a child's seesaw the boat teetered, taking on water as first one side, then the other, skimmed the surface. Kicking free of the blanket, Grey dodged his opponent's thrust. The blow intended for his face missed, but the side of his face caught the grazing imprint of the man's ring. The rough stone left a searing furrow from his cheekbone to his ear.

In prison Grey had learned to fight. He'd had no choice in order to survive. Now he drew upon every dirty trick he'd ever mastered to overcome his enemy.

He found his nakedness worked to his advantage. When his assailant grabbed for him, Grey's mist-dampened skin prevented him from gaining a tight grip.

The seaman hunched down and reached into his boot. "I'll cut ye pecker off afore we finish." Again he lunged. Barely able to make out the man's shadowy form, Grey felt sure he now wielded a knife.

With lightning speed he grabbed his opponent's wrist and squeezed with all his might. The sailor's grip loosened and the knife fell from his grasp. Grey heard it splash into the water. In the next moment, Grey brought his knee up and into the fellow's groin.

The man doubled over from the pain. "Ye whoring bastard!" He slumped against Grey's chest.

34

Grey tried to sidestep his captor's body but failed. Feeling his footing slip, he thrashed the air to keep himself upright. But the boat was too narrow to allow him room to regain his balance. Grey shot toward the water.

When the icy sea made contact with his bare skin, it nearly took his breath away. He surfaced quickly, searching the darkness for the small craft. Without it he was as good as dead.

Behind him he heard the splashing of oars. He turned and swam toward the sound.

As he neared the dingy, Grey saw the sailor. The man stood in the middle of the boat, one oar poised above his head. "Take that, ye bugger!" he shouted, bringing the paddle down perilously close to Grey's head. If the man couldn't keep his bounty, it was clear he intended to knock his brains out.

Grey propelled himself backward only to escape the flailing paddle by inches. "Can't we talk, mate?" Grey called, hoping he could convince the man to take him back to shore. "I'll make it worth your while."

"Ye'll be shark bait afore long," the seaman taunted him.

Again the paddle came down, forcing Grey to dive beneath the water. He surfaced several feet away, safe but freezing.

"I'll strike no bargain with the likes of ye!" the sailor shouted. His wild laughter echoed across the darkness.

Each dip of the oars carried the little boat farther away. Grey followed it for a distance, then decided his pursuit was useless. The man wouldn't help him. He'd been left to drown. He was alone in the frigid black water.

Approximately a mile downwind of the scuffle, Eland Taithleach sat in his small fishing boat listening. Sounds of the struggle in the unlighted craft carried across the open water as though they were only yards away from where he drifted.

Tully, the name everyone knew him by, had extinguished his lantern when he'd first heard the commotion—not that he didn't believe in helping his fellow men, because he did. But the waters around Astoria were noted for the reckless crimps who shanghaied for profit, and Tully didn't fancy himself spending the last days of his retirement on some ship bound for the Orient.

And it wasn't fear for his own hide that kept him from barging in on the small party. Those who knew him in his youth were well aware that he possessed much more than the guts of a butterfly. As a younger seaman he'd mustered for many a good fight, throwing punches first and asking questions later. And most of the time he'd come away the victor.

But age had brought stiffness to his joints and wisdom to his brain. Tully knew better than to test the limits of his physical endurance. He wouldn't be of much help to anyone in a scrimmage, but being a good fisherman he had the patience of Job. And so he'd decided to wait, to remain anonymous until the circumstances demanded he do something different.

Listening to the drifts of conversation from the other dingy, Tully decided he'd been right about the small boat's cargo. Apparently the stiff had awakened from his drugged stupor earlier than anticipated and had fought his captor for freedom.

He'd heard someone go into the bay. And as cold as this water was, the poor bastard was headed nowhere but to Davy Jones's locker unless Tully could get to him first.

He manipulated his small boat in the direction of the other craft, basking in the thrill of the rescue. With the wind and tide—and a little luck—he hoped he could find the man.

Tully couldn't call out to the swimmer. His voice might alert the man in the boat and solicit his return. Instead, he hoisted his small canvas sail and lighted the lantern on his skiff. Hopefully the beam would draw the attention of the man in trouble. In the fog no wind caught in his sail, so the old seaman pulled his oars through the inky blackness toward the voices.

To Grey it felt like hours since he'd been in the water, although in reality he knew it couldn't have been more than ten or fifteen minutes since the shanghaier had abandoned him. He cautioned himself to keep moving, to stimulate the warm flow of blood through his veins. Treading water, he tried to get his bearings, knowing that soon enough his strength would ebb away like an outgoing tide.

As harbormaster, Grey's job was to execute the regulations respecting the use of Astoria's harbor. It was also his responsibility to know the waters as well as the pilots who guided the ships over the treacherous Columbia River bar. In a prayer of desperation he hoped this knowledge would help save his life.

Because of the fog that blanketed most of the area, Grey could barely make out the lights of the wharf.

Only the distant toll of a fog bell helped him to identify Smith's Point and the lower end of the Astoria peninsula. A hell of a long way to swim, he thought, especially with the current drawing him toward the ocean. The sailor who had left him for shark bait was probably assigned to a ship that lay at anchor just beyond the channel opening.

His only chance of survival would be to head toward the Fort Smith peninsula. He was a strong swimmer and with any luck might make it to shore. On a clear night he might have been rescued by a fisherman, but that possibility seemed remote at best. This was not a good night for fishing.

With deliberate strokes Grey swam toward what he hoped to be the shore. In the enveloping darkness it was hard to tell. He thought he saw blinking lights, but then his eyes could be playing tricks on him. With the sky's heavy cloud cover, the dense fog, and the miles of water surrounding him, a star's twinkle could be easily mistaken for a light.

And for all his struggle, he knew he probably had as much chance of reaching the distant shore as he did a distant star. But Grey wouldn't be defeated—not yet. He'd try until he couldn't try anymore.

He swam on, but the cold water and the constant pull of the tide threatened his every effort. His strokes were ineffective. He was getting weaker.

The ever-changing currents of the river toyed with him as though he were no more than a piece of flotsam to be tossed about at will. The abysmal darkness of water and sky held him suspended in a purgatory of their own making.

"Help!" he yelled, but against the void of the night

he knew the sound of his cry was no more than a weak whisper. I won't give up, he willed himself. I will not drown.

A vision of the pink-haired harlot flashed before his eyes. Curse the witch who had brought him to this. He would survive. And when he did, he'd find the whore and make her pay. With renewed vigor Grey pulled his body through the water, more determined than ever to make it to shore.

The wind whipped up white caps that ruffled the swells, making his progress more difficult. With every forward stroke the tide's force sucked him back again until the world around him became an amorphous void.

Swallowed by the water, he rolled beneath its surface like a human shell, tumbling at the current's will. His lungs felt as if they would explode from the pressure of the water holding him down.

Air. He needed air. With every ounce of remaining strength, Grey fought the tumbling force.

And then as quickly as he'd been seized by the angry torrent, it released him. Like a cork he popped free of the water's grasp. Surfacing, he gulped in great swigs of air.

He scanned the dark expanse for anything recognizable. Unable to see his hand in front of his face, Grey was still the river's prisoner. His feet probed for the bottom, but his search proved fruitless.

He treaded water, trying to measure his location. When he'd been tumbled by the unexpected currents, Grey had hoped he'd been near a shallow bar. But if he had, he'd just as suddenly been tossed free of it. And the direction to swim in order to find it was lost to him as well.

Astoria's lights were no longer visible. His location in the great body of water was more uncertain now. Had he been pushing himself not, as he had hoped, toward land and life but straight into the arms of the open sea?

Fear threatened to overwhelm him. *Maybe I passed through the channel that opens into the ocean. That would explain the turbulent water I encountered.* No, he reasoned, it wasn't possible. He hadn't been in the water long enough to have reached the channel, and he would have seen the Point Adams lighthouse.

"Don't panic," Grey warned himself, seeking the calm of his own voice. "You're still alive, and for now that's all that matters."

While he swam, he continued to talk. "I'll reach land soon. I've survived this long. I'm going to make it. . . ."

But suddenly, the swift current grabbed him again, pulling him beneath the surface and tumbling him like a piece of driftwood. Grey opened his mouth to protest but realized too late his mistake. Water rushed into his throat, choking him. His nose filled with the fiery liquid, burning him, blocking out his breath.

He slammed against something hard and unyielding. A thousand claws tore at his naked flesh. Now Grey knew he was going to die. His strength sapped, he gave in to the water's will and quit struggling.

Grey awakened to the scent of pipe tobacco and fresh coffee. Sun streamed through a small window above the bed where he lay. He couldn't believe he was alive. His last coherent thought before the water exercised its

40

power over him had been one of acceptance. He'd fought a good fight, but the ocean had been his master and had won. And now he'd been spared.

Lying on his stomach, he lifted his head and looked around at the familiar cabin, still questioning that he was alive. But when he tried to roll over onto his back, there was no doubt in Grey's mind. He was alive.

But the gut-wrenching pain that shot through his body made him wish that he were dead. His backside felt as if he'd received twenty lashes for bad behavior— as if the very skin had been ripped from his muscles. Moaning, he slumped back upon his belly.

"Alive, are you?"

Grey turned his head toward the voice. "Just barely." His old friend, Tully, sat at a planked table where he worked on cleaning his clay meerschaum pipe. He looked up from scraping the bowl with his pen knife. "Seems, son, I'm always savin' yer no-good hide."

"For once I'll have to agree with you," Grey answered. "My hide, to which you so fondly refer, doesn't feel as if it's much use to anyone at the moment."

"Don't look much better neither." The whiskered old man pushed back from the table, stood up, and approached Grey's bed. "If you want my honest opinion, it don't look like there's enough left to hold yer bones together."

"I'd appreciate it if you'd keep your opinions to yourself," Grey grumbled. Wearily, he dropped his head back into the cradle of his arms.

"My doctorin' skill is what's kept you alive for the last two days," Tully informed him. "I'd advise you to be a bit more appreciative."

41

Grey jerked his head up, wincing from the sudden movement. "Two days? I've been here for two days?"

"Could say that. Out more'n in. And most of that time you kept me awake, mumblin' about some pink-haired whore."

"Chinook," Grey muttered. She'd been with him even in his delirium.

"This here Chinook wouldn't have anythin' to do with your bein' in that boat on the way to Chin'ee, would she?"

"How'd you know that?" Grey asked, his interest piqued.

"I didn't. But with all yer blubberin' the last two nights, and with where I found you, it weren't hard to guess."

With the memory of his fateful encounter with the whore, Grey felt an inner rage surface again. Oddly enough, this time he directed it more to himself for having succumbed to a sweet, clean-smelling woman while knowing full well what she was. He should have known better—certainly he'd had enough lessons from the crib—his fantasy to bury himself in her softness had only buried his brain in his crotch.

"I might as well tell you," he proceeded, "since you've already heard pieces of this miserable tale from my own lips. But . . ." He looked at his old friend squarely, his lips pursed in warning, ". . . one smirk out of you and I'll have you keelhauled."

Tully planted himself in a nearby chair and took a puff of a freshly packed pipe. "I'm listenin'."

Grey's experience flooded back to haunt him—how he'd been drugged, his waking up in the boat, his fight with the sailor, and the seeming hours he'd spent in the water. Even now, he couldn't say how he'd survived, or how he'd gotten to Tully's cabin.

"I swear I never knew what they were up to," Grey finished, recalling the tart in conversation with the gal who called the shots at Baldy's. "But I do know one thing. Our mutual friend doesn't quite have the corner of the stolen sailor trade in this port." He kicked at his cover sheet in contempt.

"But, by damn it, a wild-arsed floozie and her gang?" Tully ran his hand over his mouth as much to hide his reaction as in thought. "Don't be so hard on yourself," he consoled. "Fact is, coulda happened to anybody. What say we keep this little adventure under our hats for the time bein'?"

"What say you'd *better* keep this under your hat. I'm not finished with that little teasing female yet, not by a long shot." Grey winked at Tully. "Seriously, friend, the quieter we keep this little incident, the more we may be able to learn. Hell, they could all be in this together."

Curious, he asked, "How'd you find me anyway?" He pinned Tully with a stare, waiting for an answer.

"Lucky for you, I happened to be checkin' my fishin' lines. I heard the scuffle between you and the other fellow, but I didn't know it was you, at least not till I found you on the sandbar." Tully scratched his white head.

Grey had been right about the wave action that had nearly drowned him. It had been a sandbar that caused it. He motioned with his head toward his backside. "What did I hit that did that?" He did not dare twist around to see for fear of the consequences of such a move.

"You tangled with barnacles. From this angle, looks like a whole crop of 'em. Good fishing around that old piling . . . on a calm day, mind you."

43

Tully stood and bent over to examine Grey's bare buttocks. "Your backside looks like a piece of uncooked salmon." He added, bending lower over Grey's behind to get a better look, "Don't look like my *tobacki's* workin'."

"Tobacco?" Grey whipped his head around. "What the devil—?"

"Best thing in the world for wounds. Draws out the infection."

"No wonder my ass is as sore as a boil . . . you've probably poisoned me."

"Now is that any way to say 'thank you?' " Tully protested, swelling up like a blowfish from Grey's insult. "I never claimed to be no doctor. But you know as well as I do, at sea I seen it cure many wounds that might o' otherwise been fatal."

Tully's fingers pressed against the injured skin. Grey nearly vaulted from the bed. "Confound it, man, if you wanted to kill me, why didn't you just leave me to the sharks?"

"Now just you hold still. I'm only checkin'. Still got some mean lookin' places back here. From the looks of these cuts, I think you need a real doctor."

"Oh, no," Grey insisted. "I don't need no sawbones poking around on my private parts." His skin throbbed where Tully had poked him. "Give me my clothes and let me get out of here. Ballard will have my head for not showing up for work for two days."

"Took care of that already. He just thinks you're laid up."

"I'm laid up, all right. With a crazy man whose trying to kill me with his barbaric treatment."

Tully ignored Grey's caustic remark and kept on

talking. "Doc Wilson's out of town. Won't be back for a week. After I fished you out of the water and brought you here, I asked into his whereabouts."

"I told you, I don't need a doctor. Just bring me my clothes." Grey tried to push himself to his knees, but the movement made his flesh feel as though it were being peeled from his bones. Frustrated, he flopped back upon the bed.

"You'll be needin' the town undertaker if I don't fetch a doctor soon. These scrapes are all pink and festered-looking. Some of 'em are starting to ooze pus."

"Spare me the particulars, please," Grey ordered, "and since the good doctor happens to be out of town, what do you suggest we do in his absence?"

"I know you're new to our fine city, but we do have more'n one doctor." Tully waited for a reaction.

None was forthcoming. Apparently Grey hadn't learned that the only other resident doctor in town was a woman. Knowing his friend as well as he did, he knew Grey wouldn't take kindly to having a female, *in the role of a doctor,* inspecting his private parts.

Disheartened, and angry at himself for being in such a position, Grey only half-listened to Tully's words. "Come to think of it, I didn't know there was more than one doc. Only met Wilson in passing . . . whose the other fellow?"

"Ol' Doc Thomas," Tully tested the waters, waiting for an explosion from Grey. Still none was forthcoming. "Family's been here for years. Mighty fine doctor, too. Removed a fishhook from my finger a while back."

Grey didn't trust doctors. Most of the ones he'd encountered hadn't known any more about doctoring than Tully did. But the way his rear was throbbing, he

45

knew he needed something more for his wounds than the old man's tobacco cure.

Reluctantly, he ventured, "Will he come here? I sure as hell can't walk to him, wherever that is."

"Oh, I think I can convince her to make a house call."

"Well fetch him then, and let's see what he can do." Grey dropped his chin back onto his arms. "I sure can't spend the rest of my life in this position."

Tully could have bitten off his tongue for his blunder. He shuffled to the door as if the hounds of hell were after him. "I'll be right back," he said, slipping his arms into his coat. He donned his cap, intent on escaping the cabin before his friend recalled his slip of the tongue. If Grey knew he was going after a woman, he'd raise a conniption. Better to wait till Doc Thomas walked through the door. She'd know how to handle him. She was good with difficult patients.

Grey heard the door close behind Tully. Suddenly, like a bell going off inside his head, he recalled the man's words. *Oh, I think I can convince her to make a house call.*

"Tully!" he shouted. "You old mangy sea dog! You get back here!"

But Tully, waiting on the opposite side of the door with his ear pressed against its frame, never said a word. He just turned and hightailed it up the street to the doctor's house.

"Damnation," Grey cursed aloud.

That old fool had bamboozled him into being examined by a female doctor. *A female, for chrissake.*

And all Grey could do was lie here like a goose waiting to be trussed up for Christmas dinner.

Chapter 3

Rachel poked and prodded the soil that nourished her cherished herbs. Through her kitchen window buttercup sunshine spilled onto her precious potted garden. Like her father before her, Rachel believed in the use of plants for healing. Not only did she use them in treatments she prepared for her patients, but as an additive to her own foods as well.

Rachel adjusted her spectacles with her wrist and pinched a fading blossom from a marigold. "Thank goodness the rain has ended," she chatted with the plant as though it were a child, "but then you probably haven't noticed." Rachel examined the bloom's fluted petals, enjoying its simple beauty. "Your color always emulates the sun," she added.

Setting the blossom aside, she pressed her nose into the feathery leaves of a sweet cicely plant. Immediately, she was rewarded with its myrrh scent, making her wish for summer days. Once the weather turned mild, Rachel would be able to wander the woodlands around Astoria once again, in the search of wild herbs to add to her collection.

But today was not a day to be frowned upon. When she'd peered out her window earlier, she'd been greeted by an azure sky. It was a welcome reprieve from the rain and cold of the past two days. The sun was out in force, drying up the town's muddy streets, and Rachel hoped her lethargic mood as well.

She had slogged through the last couple of days, performing her daily tasks as usual. But since sending the new harbormaster out to sea, she'd been unable to dispel Grey Devlin from her mind. Or her misgivings.

True, he'd allowed the opium shipment to slip into the port unnoticed. His responsibility as regulator of the port, *if he were honest,* would have been to confiscate the illegal drug and turn it over to the government. So why, she worried, hadn't he done it?

Poor Maggie had been a victim of his neglect; because of him she'd died of an overdose slipped into her drink. The sailor who'd killed her was today a free man, having sailed away on the morning tide. But in Rachel's mind, the guilt rode on Grey Devlin's shoulders. If he'd been doing his job, the drug would never have made it into port and Maggie might still be alive.

But then, Rachel asked herself, who was she to administer her own style of justice? Strange, this thought had not even entered her head when she had meted out the same fate to two of Astoria's most notorious crimps. Their names had been on her father's list, responsible for his death and the misfortunes of many others by their illegal activities.

The harbormaster, however, did not fall into the same category. Rachel had obtained cold, hard proof of the thugs' guilt, but only hearsay about Devlin. Since the moment she and the women had abducted him, she'd questioned her own principles, especially as a doctor. Was she no better than the others?

But it was more than this that bothered her. Grey Devlin had left his mark in a way no other man had. Even now the memories of that night swarmed inside her head, sending shivers of pleasure up her spine.

In all her twenty-five years she had never experienced passion, nor the power of carnal love. But for the past two days she'd thought of nothing else. Grey Devlin had made her burn with a fire she never knew she possessed. After sampling his kisses, it was as though Rachel had swallowed some magical potion that had sent her off into a realm of physical delights.

"Look at me," she scolded herself, "I'm doing it again." She stood frozen in her tasks, thinking of the man and the moments of passion they'd shared. Then she recalled Lou's words after they'd rolled the man's body down the chute, *"Good riddance to bad rubbish."* Rachel's sentiments, in tune with Lou's, spurred her into action. Yes, she decided, it was best that the new harbormaster no longer resided in Astoria.

Rachel gathered up the softwood cuttings that she'd taken from several of her parent plants. In a separate pot she rooted them and set them aside. Gathering up the mustard seeds she'd harvested earlier, she walked to the pine tavern table in the center of the kitchen. She'd just poured the dried brown seeds into a mortar when she heard a knock at the front door.

Rachel walked through the hallway, wiping her hands on her apron. Through the door pane she recognized a friendly face.

"Why, Tully," she announced, opening the door, "how nice to see you." She looked him over from head to foot in her best doctoring fashion. "I hope your finger's not bothering you." Her gaze lingered on the weathered thumb where weeks earlier she'd removed a large fishhook.

"No, Doc, finger's fine. But I have come seekin' your assistance."

"Do come in."

Rachel steered Tully into the small surgery in the front of the house, the same room her father had used for his own medical practice. She motioned Tully toward a chair. "Now what can I do for you?"

"Ain't me, Doc, it's my friend." Tully removed his seaman's cap and fingered it nervously in his hands, refusing the offered chair.

Since he had agreed to keep Grey's attempted shang-haiing a secret, Tully groped for a plausible explana-tion. "We got a little carried away the other night checkin' our fishin' lines. Temperature was cold enough to freeze the whiskers off a sea lion."

Rachel waited for him to continue and after a moment when he didn't, she prodded him. "And?"

"Well, Doc, things got a little out of hand. We decided we'd warm our insides with a little taste of whiskey and before I knew it, we were both plum boozy. And warm," he added as an afterthought. "My friend, he fell out of the boat. When I hauled him back in, he got cut up on the barnacles."

Rachel turned her back on Tully, trying to shield a smile. He was such a principled man. For him to admit such a story to a *mere woman,* even though she was a doctor, took a lot of courage.

In control again, she turned toward him and scolded,

50

"You both could have drowned out there, and who'd have been the wiser?"

"Yes ma'am, I know, but it was so danged cold. And if it'd been later into the warm season, I'd a had them barnacles scraped off my boat, and he'd a never gotten cut."

"Well, I guess those things happen." Rachel tried to ease the older man's guilt. "But I'm certainly sorry for your friend. Those lacerations can be very painful."

"Oh . . . he's in pain all right. So much so, he couldn't even walk here. That's why I came to fetch you. He's waitin' in my cabin."

"I'd best gather up my things. Tell me how bad his wounds are." Rachel walked to the small apothecary chest and retrieved her doctor's bag. "I'll need an idea of what I'm up against so I won't have to return here for something I don't have with me."

"He's cut up pretty bad. Looks like a skinned mackerel," Tully volunteered. "No fever yet, though. I guess that's a good sign."

"How long ago did this happen?"

"Near two days. He's been sleepin' most of the time."

Rachel checked her bag to make sure she had plenty of clean bandages, castile soap, witch hazel, and petroleum jelly. Pulling out several of the small drawers in the chest, she searched her stores for oils and tinctures. From the locked side of the cabinet she removed a small flask with the word "chloroform" clearly labeled on its side. Once the items had been stored in her bag, she removed her apron and allowed the seaman to help her on with her cloak.

She picked up her doctor's bag. "I believe that's

51

everything.'' With that, she locked the front door and followed Tully down the steps.

The streets were teeming with activity as the two walked back toward the wharf where Tully's small cabin was located. A bracing breeze blew off the ocean, bringing with it the briny smell of the sea.

Glad she hadn't worn her straw hat, Rachel inhaled the salty air, enjoying the warmth of the sun bearing down on her shoulders and bare head. With the morning's rising temperature and the brisk walk, she wished she'd left her cloak behind as well.

Across the bay, Rachel could see the distant hills where a forest of fir trees marched up their slopes. She inhaled deeply, relishing their fragrance in the thin air. Rachel loved Astoria. All the time she'd been in school in the Midwest she had missed it terribly. And although her father had warned her not to come back, Rachel couldn't have done anything else. She'd been born here. She was as much a part of this town as were the firs that grew from seedlings to maturity.

They came upon a paper hawker, and Tully stopped to buy a copy of *The Astorian*. They continued on, the old man scanning the headlines and Rachel trying to read them over his extended arm. From what she could see, there had been no news of the missing harbormaster.

It had been two days since Rachel and her friends had shanghaied him. Surely by now he would have been missed . . . by someone. She'd even frequented the post office more often than usual, hoping to hear word of his disappearance. But she'd heard nothing.

Moving down the planked roadway, Rachel nodded to several of the merchants who stood outside their small mercantile stores, enjoying the day. Although the respectable women of the town went out of their way to ignore Rachel, the men usually acknowledged her with a polite enough greeting.

Her father had been right. Being a woman in a man's profession was not easy. A woman doctor was frowned upon by most. But Rachel intended to change their collective opinion. She'd been given the talent and had learned the skills. And eventually she would win their confidence by proving herself a capable physician.

At least she had some patients. Thus far she'd treated several sailors with minor injuries and illnesses. And although the society ladies still preferred Doctor Wilson's services over her own, the women in the logging camps were always glad to see her. And the women who worked the saloons accepted her for the confident doctor she knew herself to be. And now Tully had sought out her help for his friend. She smiled to herself. Her practice was definitely expanding.

Nearing the small clapboard house that Tully called home, Rachel detained him with her hand upon his arm. ''Your friend's name—you forgot to tell me who I'd be treating.''

Tully hesitated before answering, ''Well, Doc, I better warn you, he ain't too excited about bein' treated by a woman doctor.'' Tully tucked the folded newspaper beneath his arm and scratched his head. ''But I convinced him, you're a better doctor than that old addlepated Wilson.''

''And of course, Doctor Wilson happens to be out of town,'' she reminded him.

They walked to the front door stoop.

"I'm certain if he's in as much pain as you suggest, it won't take him but a moment to adjust to my gender. Now what did you say his name was?"

Tully turned away from her and knocked softly on the door. "It's Grey Devlin, our new harbormaster. Let me have a moment with him before you go inside."

Grey Devlin, the harbormaster. Rachel felt as though she'd been dealt a solid blow to the chest. How can that be? she worried. We sent him to sea.

Tully pushed open the door and paused on the threshold. "I've brought the doctor," he announced.

"You conniving, sneaky, back-stabbing old pirate. Why didn't you tell me you were going to fetch a lady doctor?"

"Because I knew you'd react just like you are," Tully countered. "She's here, she's a good doctor, and I expect you to treat her with respect." Tully closed the door and all Rachel could hear were their muted voices while the argument continued.

Her face burned as hot as if she stood too close to a blazing fire. All she wanted to do was run as far from her waiting patient as her wobbly legs would carry her.

What if he recognized her? Trying to pace her breathing, she reasoned the chances of that happening were impossible. She looked nothing like the prostitute Chinook. Rachel waited, trying to combat her uneasiness, knowing the next few moments would undoubtedly be the most difficult she'd ever have to face.

She recognized Devlin's smooth, whiskey-sounding voice. Even standing on the opposite side of the logged wall, its deep, husky tone sent goose bumps popping out on her arms.

54

Too soon, Tully opened the door and stepped back outside.

"His bark's worse'n his bite," he allowed, but he looked as worried over Grey's reaction as she felt about her own. "I'll just wait outside 'til you're finished."

"Thank you, Tully, this shouldn't take long." The doctor in Rachel took over when she walked inside.

"I don't need any doctor," Grey Devlin barked when she stepped inside the door and closed it.

"What you really mean, sir, is that you don't want a woman doctor." Rachel took a deep breath to still her own nervousness.

The harbormaster lay upon a small cot near the wall, his upper body bare, his lower body covered with a sheet. He looked just as he had the last time she'd seen him, but now, instead of sprawling on his back, he lay upon his stomach. And now he had a reddened gouge across his right cheek that disappeared beyond his hairline.

"You got that right, lady. I don't want any woman doctor gawking at my private parts."

"Gawking? Mr. Devlin, I promise you I didn't come here to gawk. I've seen many 'private parts' of both men and woman, and I assure you, you have nothing I haven't seen before." Rachel walked across the room toward her patient, realizing for a moment just how true her statement was.

Grey watched her approach. She was even worse looking than he'd imagined a woman doctor would be. Dull and plain—that's how he'd describe her. Her hair was a pleasant enough color, but she'd twisted it so

55

tight on top of her head it pulled her eyebrows into winged arches above the rimmed spectacles she wore. Her eyes, peering at him through the thick lenses, reminded him of a fish he'd kept in a jar as a child.

"Shall we have a look?" Rachel asked, stopping only inches away from the bed. She wasn't at all certain if she were up to looking at what lay hidden beneath the sheet, and it wasn't his injury that bothered her.

"I told you, I don't need a doctor," Grey grumbled.

"Your friend seems to think differently, Mr. Devlin."

"My ex-friend, you mean." He pulled the sheet higher over his backside, wincing from the friction.

Rachel placed her bag upon the table and began to remove some of the jars she'd brought with her.

"Tully tells me you were injured when you fell out of his boat. Is that how your face got scraped as well?" The only answer she received was a quick touch of Grey's fingers to his cheek as though he'd forgotten about that injury. With a little antiseptic it would heal clean. She wasn't so sure about the lesions concealed beneath the sheet. "You know barnacle wounds can easily get infected if they aren't properly cleansed."

Grey still refused to relinquish his cover. "I guess he also told you that he tried to poison me by packing them with pipe tobacco."

"No, he didn't mention that. But under certain circumstances it would probably be an acceptable treatment."

"Not acceptable to me."

"What is acceptable to you?" Rachel was losing her patience with the man's attitude. "Tully was only trying to help you. He did his best. Now, won't you let me do mine?''

Grey had unclothed in front of numerous members of the opposite sex, but he'd always had the advantage. Now he didn't, and the prudish-looking female who eyed him as if he were some insect to be dissected made him feel very uncomfortable.

"I'm waiting, Mr. Devlin," Rachel prompted. "I really want to look at you."

"I'm, sure you do, *Miss* Thomas. Is that how lady doctors get their amusement? By looking at their male patients?"

"Don't be crass, Mr. Devlin. I assure you, I have better things to do than ogle male patients."

Anger at his impertinence rushed through Rachel. Although the man was sick, his behavior was unacceptable and she would not tolerate it.

"I studied for many years to become a physician and I assure you I am a good one, in spite of my sex. But, if you choose to die of an infection that might possibly have been prevented, then who am I to stop you?"

Rachel whirled around on her heels. Regardless of her oath to protect life, at the moment she wished the irritating man on the cot would drop dead. She tossed the items she'd removed earlier back into her medical bag and stomped toward the door.

"Wait!" he shouted.

She paused with her hand on the knob and looked up at him.

Grey motioned to her. "All right. I'm sorry if I offended you. Give me another chance. As much as I'm against this examination, it appears you're all I have. I'll try to be agreeable."

"From what I've witnessed since entering this cabin, that will be quite a task for one with such a churlish attitude." Rachel turned and leaned against the door.

A spunky thing for a prudish woman, warped tongue and all, Grey thought as he once again scrutinized the woman doctor.

"Truce," he half-whispered, showering her with a disarming smile.

His dimple creviced his left cheek. Until that moment, Rachel had forgotten what a handsome specimen he was, even with his scarred face. Flustered, she walked back across the room and stopped at the table. Her palms felt sweaty when she released the handle of her medical bag.

"Then I suggest we get on with it," she said, trying to regain her composure.

"Or off with it." Grey flung the sheet from his backside, then rested his chin upon his folded arms. He stared straight ahead.

Rachel again removed her medications from the bag. Crossing to the bed, she tried to soothe her patient . . . and herself. "Think of me as your mother," she said calmly, "doctoring some childhood scratch."

Grey would have laughed at the comparison of his voluptuous mother to the modest doctor, but at that moment she chose to poke his wounds. He gritted his teeth to keep from yelling while his backside burned like the fires of hell.

"I'm sorry, Mr. Devlin," she apologized. "But we need to clean these cuts or they are going to get infected. In fact, I'm concerned with a few of the areas already."

Rachel pondered her next move. She was concerned

about how sensitive his skin was. The abrasions would heal on their own, but some of the deeper wounds were beginning to form scabs and she didn't want to scrape away the healing tissue. From Grey's reaction to her touch, he'd never allow it. What she really wanted him to do was to soak in a warm antiseptic bath.

She searched the cabin for the items she needed. In one corner she saw Tully's bathtub, but Grey would never be able to sit in that unaided. Rachel needed something that would allow him to sit in the water, but not directly on his sensitive backside.

And then she saw it. Hanging upon the opposite wall of the cabin was a large lifesaving ring. She walked across the room to examine its size. Rachel stifled a giggle when she read the name of the ship inscribed on its canvas wrap, *USS Assburne*. She had the tools for her treatment, but how would she ever get this proud man to consent to sit inside the ring in Tully's tub? Walking back to her patient, she pondered the best way to proceed.

"Mr. Devlin, I want you to take a bath."

"A bath?!" he shouted. His reaction was exactly what Rachel had expected.

"My God, madam, in case you haven't noticed, I can't even sit on my—" Grey caught himself before he finished his sentence, but his meaning came out loud and clear.

"I realize that," Rachel interjected, "but I believe I have a solution to your problem."

Grey eyed her skeptically when she explained the procedure to him. "I assure you, sir, you will feel so much better after a good soaking."

He weighed her suggestion, looking from the life ring

hanging on the wall to Tully's bathtub. There was some logic in what the doctor suggested, and he could already feel the soothing rewards of a good hot soak.

After a few seconds he looked back at her. "I'll agree to this nimble-brained scheme of yours on one condition only."

"And that is . . . ?" Rachel waited for his response.

"That you swear an oath of secrecy that you'll never tell a living soul what transpired here today."

"Not even Tully?"

"Least of all Tully. I'll handle him myself."

"If it will make you feel better, as a doctor I'm not allowed to divulge that information to anyone."

While water boiled on the cast iron stove, Rachel pulled the bathtub closer to the bed. Then, climbing upon a chair, she lifted the ring from its place on the wall. After the tub's water reached the required depth, Rachel measured out tincture of calendula and other medicinal oils into the liquid. She stirred the water with her hand, then placed the ring inside and stood back to admire her handiwork. A perfect fit. Stealing a glance at Grey's bare bottom, she only hoped he'd fit into the ring as easily.

From the cot where he lay, Grey watched Rachel work. Earlier when he'd waited for Tully's return, he'd felt like a goose. Now watching the doctor stirring up her caldron—testing it for warmth—he knew he would soon be in the stew.

At last Rachel had everything ready. The hardest part would be to get Grey into the tub without injuring his male ego.

"Are you ready?" she asked him.

"Think I'll fit in that ring?" His voice sounded doubtful.

"It looks like a perfect fit to me," she replied, and blushed when he raised one golden brow.

No matter how much she tried, Rachel couldn't think of the harbormaster as just another patient. Grey Devlin disturbed her in ways she'd never been troubled with before. His nakedness brought to mind, all too vividly, their last encounter. She pushed away those disturbing thoughts and moved to the bed to help him rise.

"How blind are you?"

Temporarily taken aback by his question, she replied, "Without these glasses the world is a blur."

"Then remove them," her patient ordered, daring her to refuse.

"Excuse me? You can't be serious."

"Dead serious. If you remove them, you won't be able to watch me make a fool of myself when I try to sit in that circle."

"And dead you might be when I lead us both into a tumble because I've tripped over something."

Handing him a clean towel to cover his front, Rachel tried to reassure him. "I promise I won't think of you as foolish. I'll think of you only as my patient who needs my assistance. I suggest we get you into that tub before the water gets cold."

With her instructions and help, Grey managed to slide from the bed. His feet firmly planted on the floor, he pushed himself upright. The skin on his backside stretched taut. Pain shot through his buttocks. He hobbled toward the tub, one arm over Rachel's shoulder and the other holding the towel over his exposed loins.

If Rachel lived to be a hundred years old, she would never understand the male animal. Only nights ago Grey had been like the stallion, proud of his prowess, and ready to mount the mare. But today he'd become more like a newborn foal, thrust into an alien world, unsure of his maleness.

Grey paused beside the tub and looked down at the floating ring. "You must be kidding . . . *Assburne?*"

"It's appropriate, is it not?" Rachel couldn't hold back her smile.

Unable to contain his laughter, he responded, "It's appropriate as hell."

Together they managed to settle Grey into the steamy solution while he continued to hold the towel across his front as if it were a lifeline.

Water sloshed over the tub's rim, wetting Rachel's dress and the surrounding floor. She steadied him, allowing the lifesaver to gain its buoyancy. Soon Grey floated in the tub like a cork on the water.

"Ah," he sighed, relaxing as the curative waters caressed his raw backside.

"Feels good, doesn't it?"

Grey nodded his head in confirmation and closed his eyes.

On her knees and with her arms resting on the tub's rim, Rachel felt glad that she'd eased Grey's discomfort—because inwardly she held herself responsible for his injuries. Doctors were to heal pain, not inflict it. Again her demons surfaced and she questioned her earlier attempt to rid Astoria of its harbormaster.

Wagons and carriages rolled by the little cottage, their wheels making dull thuds across the uneven planks. A whistle sounded as a ship departed the harbor, and the steady ticking of a ship's clock filled the silence of the little cabin.

Grey opened his eyes to find the doctor on her knees beside him, her arms propped upon the rim of the tub, her own eyes closed in quiet repose. The steamy water had caused her hair to sprig in wispy ringlets around her face, softening the severity of her hairdo. Her face was flushed pink from the heat, and he saw that the lenses of her glasses were clouded. Grey reached up and lifted the wire spectacles from her face.

Rachel's eyes popped open. "What are you doing?" she demanded.

"These aren't much good all steamed up." Grey wiped the lenses with a corner of the towel that covered him.

"I'll do that," Rachel insisted, reaching across him for the glasses—an action she soon regretted when she found herself sprawled across Grey's floating lap, her chest mere inches above his hidden crotch.

Rachel grabbed for the opposite side of the tub to brace herself. Her sudden movement sent the water sloshing about. Grey, in his floating ring, bobbed up and down, his sodden lap connecting with her equally sodden bosom.

Thoroughly shaken, Rachel struggled to right herself without sending Grey's tender backside slamming into the bottom of the tub.

"Are you *Wynken* or *Blynken?*" Grey asked, a teasing note in his voice.

She stole a look at his face over her right shoulder. "What?"

Then she remembered the nursery rhyme. The insufferable man was thoroughly enjoying her discomfort. He grinned at her, his dimple forming another deep crater in his cheek, his wintery eyes sparkling with mischief.

"I'm *Nod* too eager to be sailing in your wooden shoe," Rachel replied, shoving herself upward.

Grey's iron grip halted her ascent. Rachel searched his face. His eyes were no longer glowing, but had darkened to a chilly blue. With dripping wet fingers, he grabbed her chin and turned her face away from him. Rachel felt his icy stare rake across her profile.

"What's the matter with you?" she demanded. "Let me up this minute." But her order fell upon deaf ears.

It can't be, Grey thought, studying the black mark near Rachel's right eye. Then his reasoning powers calmed him.

Impossible, he decided. This drab little sparrow couldn't possibly be the colorful Chinook. Coincidence, he concluded, when he finally released her and set her back upon her knees. Nothing more.

"My glasses," Rachel ordered.

"But of course." Grey started to slip her forgotten spectacles back upon her face, but she grabbed them from his hand and replaced them herself. Again, the lady doctor reminded him of his fish from long ago.

There was no way that this woman could be the same fish he'd tangled with two nights ago. There was no way that this woman could be Chinook.

Chapter 4

"He's returned," Rachel announced, pouring tea into a Staffordshire cup.

She handed the cup to Opal, poured one for herself, then took her own seat at the small garden table. Early shoots, not quite ready to open, popped their heads out beneath the old maple in Rachel's backyard. With a warming breeze off the harbor, the women basked in the out-of-doors, enjoying the pleasant afternoon, along with the tea and sandwiches Rachel had prepared for them.

"Who's returned?" Opal asked. She raised the dark blue porcelain cup to her lips and sipped the warm liquid.

"The harbormaster."

Opal spewed the tea from her mouth as though she'd ingested arsenic instead. She plopped the delicate cup back into its saucer and dabbed at her mouth with a white linen napkin.

"He's alive?" she asked, her eyes as large as the china plate that held a pyramid of tiny tea sandwiches.

"Of course he's alive," Rachel answered. "I'm a

doctor, not the town's undertaker.'' She picked up the plate of sandwiches and passed them to Opal.

"I'm sorry, sugar.'' Opal splayed her fingers in refusal. "After that news, I won't be able to eat a thing.''

"Eat," Rachel commanded her. "You'll need your strength to help me decide what we should do with the man, now that he's back.''

Eyeing Rachel skeptically, Opal obeyed, helping herself to several pieces of the wafer-thin bread spread with Rachel's homemade jellies and fresh butter.

"Before I die of curiosity, when and how did he get back?''

"The when and how is a mystery. All I know is that Tully fetched me yesterday to tend to his wounds.''

"Wounds? You mean he was shot?'' Opal pressed her fingers against her breastbone as though she were having trouble digesting the bite of food she'd just swallowed.

"No. He was cut up, though.''

"Knifed?'' Opal leaned across the table, her hand moving from her chest to her throat.

"You might say that.'' Rachel smiled devilishly. "It seems those barnacles he came up against had some pretty sharp edges.''

"Barnacles . . . oh, my.''

The two women exchanged knowing glances, well aware of Grey Devlin's nakedness when they'd sent him down the chute.

Opal's brown brows arched mischievously. "Cut up pretty bad, huh?''

"Let's just say he won't be sitting too easily for a few days.''

Unable to restrain themselves, the two women burst into conspiratorial laughter.

When Opal had regained her composure, she asked, "Nothing else of *value* injured?"

"Nothing you need concern yourself with," Rachel answered. Too late, she felt the full impact of Opal's worldly stare and realized her response had been sharper than intended. Merciful heavens, Rachel thought, I'm jealous of Opal.

Attempting to correct her error, she added, "I mean a doctor is not free to divulge such information." In the warm afternoon, her face felt suddenly hot.

But Opal continued to study Rachel openly. "Of course, sugar. Who am I to question the man's condition, or your position as his doctor?"

"Oh, Opal, I didn't mean to sound abrupt—I guess I'm just nervous. Who knows what Grey Devlin will do now? I'm sure he'll take it upon himself to find out who shanghaied him. Why, he could even be in cahoots with the crimps working the waterfront. And if he is, he won't rest until he finds out who double-crossed him. He'll come to you to find out about Chinook."

"So let him come." Opal shrugged her shoulders. "I know what to tell him."

"But I'm worried," Rachel replied. "If something happened to you or the other girls, I'd never forgive myself."

"Sugar, we girls know how to deal with men. We do it all the time."

"But it's not fair that you should have to take the brunt of Devlin's investigation while I stay hidden behind my starched aprons."

"Look, Doc, when we entered into this scheme, the plan was to get rid of the men who beat up on whores, the same animals who left families without providers. We knew there would be risks." Opal's lips tightened for an instant before she again lifted her cup. "Believe me, sugar, I've handled men a lot worse than Grey Devlin. And in spite of what happened with the shipment, he appears to be a gentleman."

Gentleman, hah! Rachel thought, recalling the terrible things he'd said about a woman doctor looking at naked male patients. The rogue was anything but. "I know," she answered instead, "but I never expected to see him again."

"But, Doc, you must admit, he's a real looker." Opal's face sparkled with mischief. "A sight for these eyes to be sure. And for sure a cut above most of the men who hang around the saloon."

"So he's nice looking," Rachel replied, feeling her face flush to crimson. "But he knows it, and in my book that makes him unattractive."

"Not so, sugar. In my business, 'Pretty is, as pretty *is.*' It's a lot easier to bed a handsome man than one with no teeth who smells like day-old fish."

Rachel couldn't hold back the laughter in her voice. "I suppose you're right. I've treated a few patients who smelled as though they hadn't bathed in a year, and who hadn't brushed the few teeth they still had."

Both women giggled.

Rachel studied the woman who sat across from her. Dressed in her fashionable peacock blue dress—shipped from New York City, she'd said—Opal could have easily passed for one of the respectable ladies up on the hill. The blue velvet hat covering her brown curls boasted a tropical bird nesting on a bed of brilliant feathers. In Rachel's opinion Opal looked chic.

None of the ladies up the hill, however, would have dreamed of entertaining a woman like Opal in their homes. She simply wasn't acceptable. But then none of them had suffered the hardships that this logger's widow had endured. Since becoming Opal's friend, Rachel had learned that people did what they must in order to survive—as Opal had.

Opal knew well the disasters caused by the abominable men who stole a woman's innocent husband by night. As a new bride, several years earlier, she and her groom had arrived in Astoria, bringing with them dreams of dairy farming. To save enough money to buy a piece of land in the valley, her husband had taken a job in the logging camps. But within months Opal's husband had been shanghaied, leaving her without her man in a hostile land.

A woman with no skills, and no family back East, Opal had tried to find employment in the town. But like so many other women who found themselves in her same situation, she learned there were not enough decent jobs to be had. The canneries took on women workers, but the work was seasonal and the jobs all taken. So Opal had turned to selling her body for a profit.

Being resourceful, she had saved every penny she earned until she'd accumulated enough money to purchase the small house next door to Baldy's Saloon. From the day she moved in, she'd never bedded another man for money. She focused instead on being a good businesswoman and running a clean enterprise.

Hers became the haven for many women who like

herself had been left penniless, until they could decide what they should do. Some stayed on with her. Some went back to their families. But no matter what course they chose, Opal made sure the choice was theirs for the making.

It was when one of Opal's girls was nearly beaten to death by a drunken sailor that Rachel was called in to tend to her injuries. A rare friendship began to form with the house madam. As much as they lacked in common, they shared a bond not easily understood by outsiders. Their lives had been drastically altered by shanghaiing. They had both lost those they loved.

Their friendship became an alliance. With nothing to lose, they decided to fight back. They declared clandestine warfare on the slave traders and created a fund for the destitute women whose husbands had been shanghaied.

"What now, Doc?" Opal asked her, folding her napkin and placing it on the table.

"I suggest we lie low for a while. The shanghaiing in this town is much too organized. People disappear and no one in authority asks questions. It's almost as though the officials were afraid to address the issue. The *Astorian* covers what it knows, but those reporters are newspaper people, not law enforcers. And they know not to ask the wrong questions. They might not be around long enough to report the answers.

"I tell you, Opal, someone big is running this operation. Those two crimps we nabbed were too influenced by greed to see beyond their noses. But Grey Devlin is another matter. He's the only one who's reappeared, and the only one who's encountered Chinook. We'll wait to see his reaction. If he approaches you or the others with questions, I want to know.''

''And what will you do? Keep him as a patient? That may be dangerous.''

''I'll be fine. This way I can keep tabs on him, insisting that his wounds need to be watched until they are completely healed. In the meantime, maybe we can learn what he is doing to find the hooker.''

''Do you think he'll recognize you?''

''Are you joking?'' Rachel dropped her hands to her side. ''Do I look anything like Chinook?''

''The curves are the same, and I don't believe our man would forget a curve.''

''Believe me, Opal,'' Rachel responded, shaking her head in dismay, ''the harbormaster is not interested in this dowdy little wren.''

The bawdy house owner stood to take her leave. She popped open her lace parasol and the two women walked on the ballast stone walkway toward the front of the house.

They'd only rounded the house to the small front yard when they encountered two society women strolling past the gate.

Spying them, Opal winked at Rachel and said, ''I'll take that medicine you prescribed, and I'll see you again in a few days.'' The women turned up their pert noses and crossed to the other side of the street.

''You'd think I had the plague,'' Opal responded, watching the ladies hurry away without a greeting.

''Not you, Opal . . . me. I went to school with those women. My father doctored their families. They can't comprehend why a woman would wish to practice medicine. To them my reasons must be dark and sinister, not to mention unladylike. So they react in the only way they know how—by pretending I don't exist.''

''Well, they should be ashamed of themselves. You're a wonderful doctor.''

''And you're a wonderful friend.''

Rachel hugged Opal and sent her on her way, lingering at the white picket fence. What a shame, she thought. It didn't matter that she'd grown up in Astoria and that her father had been well placed in the small community. After she'd come home and hung up her own shingle, none of her old friends had come calling.

Only Doctor Wilson had come, but more to gloat and to inform her of the error of her undertaking. Rachel suspected he feared his own practice would suffer by her presence, but to date his predictions had been right. No one came requiring her services.

Doctor Wilson was a society doctor and most of the time he didn't trouble himself with patients unless he knew he'd be paid for his services. So Rachel made do, attending the less fortunate. Another reason, she imagined, that no one farther up the hill would request her services.

But for the moment Rachel was satisfied. Her patients had little, but what they owned they shared. Payment for services included anything from coins to trinkets to fresh produce. At least she wouldn't starve.

And since she'd come home, Rachel had made it a part of her routine to visit the logging camps in the area, administering to the women and children. Most could not come to her, so she went to them.

Rachel believed ''what one can't cure, one must

endure," and for the moment she had enough. She turned and walked back to her garden to clear away the remains of their lunch.

Grey Devlin pushed open the front door to Rachel's house and entered the hallway. When he closed the door, a bell jangled, announcing his arrival. He glanced at several chairs placed along one wall in the long hallway, supposedly for patients. All the chairs were empty.

He knocked loudly on the door frame and waited, but no one answered his summons.

It had been two days since Tully had brought Doctor Thomas to his cabin to attend Grey's injuries. Rachel's doctoring appeared to have helped him. He was still alive and not in the throes of delirium brought on by infection.

But Tully was about to drive him to madness. He had assumed the position of Grey's nurse, helping him with the hot soaks and applying the medicinal salve to his wounds afterwards. For two days, Grey had endured Tully's worrying over him like an old maid aunt, giving him orders, and making certain he did everything the doctor had prescribed. But enough was enough. Today, after this visit, Grey would return to his own room at the boarding house. He simply wasn't the type to take to coddling.

He had spent the last two days either standing up or lying on his belly. And although the older man had never mentioned it, on more than one occasion during the last two days Tully must have found the location of the injury amusing. The man's smart-ass grin was much too broad and much too frequent.

Grey's skin wasn't yet completely healed but at least he'd managed to make it this far on foot. His sensitive backside made all other modes of transportation impossible. If he could only sit on one of those chairs.

"Doc, you in here?" he called out. When there was no answer, Grey took a few steps deeper inside the hallway. "No wonder she doesn't have any patients," he grumbled to himself. He shifted restlessly on his feet, listening to the creak of the floorboards beneath him.

A room on his left stood open. As he inspected the interior, Grey decided it must be Rachel's surgery.

The room's two windows allowed for plenty of outside light. A yellow rectangle of sunshine checkered the polished wooden floor.

Stepping through the doorway, Grey studied the small clean room. He'd never been attended by a woman physician before now, and his curiosity was piqued. What kind of woman would choose such an unorthodox profession?

Except for a portrait in a lacy metal frame, the spotlessly clean room held no personal touches. Looking more closely at the tintype, he saw the images of three people. Family, he supposed. The picture sat on a desk in the corner between windows. Near it several medical books were piled in a neat stack. Two chairs were placed beside the desk, one for the doctor and one for the patient.

Focusing on the padded leather examining table that took up the center of the room, Grey considered fleeing the doctor's house. He envisioned himself spread out over its sterile surface, his backside as bare as the day he was born, with the spartan lady doctor looking on. He calmed himself. She was a doctor, nothing more.

Where was she, anyway? True, he'd arrived earlier than his appointment time, but had it been that much earlier?

The remainder of the room seemed to contain the essentials needed for a physician's practice—an apothecary chest filled with bottles held towels on top, probably covering the instruments of her trade, a small table on wheels, and in the corner a bentwood clothes rack. And hanging from a peg on the wall, a human skeleton.

Intrigued, Grey stepped into the surgery to get a better look at the chalky-looking fellow. Bones as clean as this, wired together to replicate the human design, he'd seen only in books. So captivated was he by the body's basic structural support, he didn't hear Rachel approach until she tapped him on the shoulder.

He jumped as though he'd been shot, slamming against the skeleton. The bones clattered like pellets in a rattle. He instinctively reached out to support the remains that threatened to crash to the floor. Encircling its bony ribs with both arms, he felt a listless arm drape across his shoulder. Together they looked as if they were about to begin a macabre dance.

From behind him came Rachel's deep throaty laughter. He swung around, sending the skeleton's legs swinging wide before they clacked into immobile silence.

"I suppose you think this is funny," Grey scolded, staring at the bespectacled woman in her oiled white silk apron. The heat of embarrassment burned his face.

"I see you've met Cal," Rachel quipped.

75

Grey's heart pounded from the havoc he'd nearly wrought. "Cal?" He transferred his gaze from the fish-eyed doctor to that of the grinning skull.

"Yes. My father named him," she explained. "Most skeletons are called Bones. But my father christened him Calcium—Cal for short. I've danced with him myself, just as you. Of course," she needled, "That was when I was a young lady and interested in such things."

Rachel walked over to Grey, removed Cal from his embrace, and hung him back onto his wall hook. "Cal hasn't danced in a number of years. I'm surprised he still knows how."

My stars, Grey thought, not only was the doctor as homely as sin, she was cuckoo as well. Dancing with skeletons . . . and calling them by name. Doctor Rachel Thomas was the oddest female he'd ever encountered, and the sooner he could get out of her house, the better off he would be.

Rachel peered at him from beneath her thick spectacles. "How are you today, Mr. Devlin?" she asked, assuming a professional composure.

Having been reduced to floating in a bathtub in a life-saving ring, Grey's dignity now felt trampled at having been caught dancing with her skeleton. How many other embarrassing incidents would he suffer before he would finally be free of this woman? For the moment Grey gritted his teeth and replied as graciously as he could, "Much better, thank you."

"And your buttocks?"

Hoping to escape further examination, he added, "So much so that I don't believe I require your services any longer."

76

"I believe, Mr. Devlin, I should be the judge of that."

The doctor promptly thrust a white sheet into his hands. The smell of sunshine drifted from its pristine folds. "I'll step outside while you slip out of your clothes. Once you're settled on the table, call me." Pulling the door shut behind her, Rachel left him alone in the room.

"Get out of your clothes, get settled on the table", he mimicked. Grey hated masterful women.

He'd undressed enough in front of the opposite sex that it shouldn't bother him by now. But the fish-eyed doctor made him feel uncomfortable, as though he'd been caught playing with himself. The moments passed and Grey stood rooted to the same spot, still fully clothed.

"Are you ready, Mr. Devlin?" Rachel called from the other side of the closed door.

He looked at the sheet in his arms, then toward the door.

"Hell and damnation," he mumbled, "I might as well get this over with."

"Did you say you need assistance?" she asked.

Grey didn't answer. When he dropped his trousers, he could hear Rachel moving on the opposite side of the wall. Again the floorboards creaked and he imagined her peeking through the key hole, watching him.

This thought unnerved him more. With warm insolence, he replied, "You anxious for me, honey?"

Grey thought he'd settled his inhibitions concerning the woman doctor, but apparently he hadn't. After their encounter in Tully's cabin with the floating ring, he thought he could handle anything the good doctor

77

decreed. But here again, he found himself feeling as jittery as a virgin in a bordello.

"Nervous, are you?" she called, from the other side of the door.

Nervous as hell, he thought, peeling off his shirt and dropping it on the clothes rack over his trousers.

"I shouldn't think a big strong man like yourself would be afraid of anything."

Her words held a familiar ring. The phrasing, the diction tugged at Grey's mind. He'd heard that voice, those exact words from someone else, but for the life of him, he couldn't remember where. Strictly her bedside manner, he decided, dismissing his orphaned thought.

Naked except for the sheet tucked beneath his armpits, Grey crawled up onto the leather table and settled on his stomach. Pressed against the cold tabletop, his manhood would probably turn to ice.

Spreading the sheet over his backside as best as he could, Grey called to Rachel, "The lamb is ready for the slaughter."

Soft laughter floated from behind the door. Grey buried his head in the crook of his arms, questioning how such a prudish-looking woman could have such a warm and sensual laugh. Was there more to the lady doctor than was apparent?

"Mr. Devlin, you must relax. I'm only your physician," she consoled him.

"Ah yes, like my mother, you said. . . ."

Rachel walked over to the apothecary chest and uncovered her instruments which lay on top of a clean Turkish towel. From her chest she withdrew a smoky glass jar of oil and from another jar, cotton bandaging.

78

Gathering her supplies onto the small table, she wheeled it over to her patient.

"Now let's have a look, shall we?"

As Rachel leaned over him, Grey felt the heat of her body through her oiled silk apron. If the leather table hadn't felt like a slab of winter ice, he probably wouldn't have noticed her warmth. Suddenly he knew why a moth was drawn to a flame.

Although Doctor Rachel Thomas didn't look much like a woman, she certainly smelled like one. Her perfume floated around him, swaddling him with her earthy myrrhlike scent. He envisioned moss and woodlands and again was bothered by the nettling thought that he'd encountered that same fresh fragrance on another woman.

Her gentle fingers prodded his backside. She oohed, aahed, and uh-huhed before asking him outright, "Does this hurt?"

"No," he replied, determined not to flinch when she touched an overly sensitive spot.

With his head still nesting in his arms, Grey watched Rachel moving about the table as she reached for more supplies.

Beneath the covering of her dull gray dress her breasts appeared full and round. The sparkling white apron she wore only emphasized the projecting curves of her bosom. And when Rachel leaned over his bare back, and her breasts accidentally pressed against his naked skin, Grey responded, not to the doctor but to the woman. He held his breath, feeling that his hidden parts might poke a hole in her fine leather examining table.

At that moment, Grey decided he'd do or say anything that would bring this office visit to an end, short of agreeing to another visit to the woman doctor.

"I believe, Mr. Devlin," she said, "you're on the mend. There doesn't seem to be any infection. The abrasions are healing nicely and the deeper cuts are forming crusts. It is a critical time, though. We don't want to do anything that will cause those wounds to seep."

"You mean like sitting, or squirming around on my backside?"

"Exactly. Can you manage that?"

Rachel walked back to the apothecary chest, slipped a key into the lock, and opened the door. He watched her remove several bottles of medicine, all labeled "chloroform." Setting these aside, she dug deeper into the shadowy cabinet, and finally found what she sought.

"You'll need this for when you start to itch," she said, placing a tin of Petro-carbo salve beside him on the table.

"Itch?"

"Yes, and try not to scratch because it will only delay the healing process. I'll see you when you're dressed." Rachel turned and left the room.

Grey threw on his clothes as quickly as possible. When he'd finished he walked to the front window and waited for Rachel's return. Thank heaven this ordeal was almost over.

After a few moments, Rachel appeared, smiling. "I do hope I'll be seeing you again."

"Again? I think not," Grey replied. Her assumption made him feel testy.

Now that she'd released him, it would be a cold day in hell before he came seeking her medical services again. He'd rather have the barbaric ministrations of Tully over the intimidating ones of the female doctor.

"But I don't understand . . . " Nonplussed, Rachel stared at him from beneath her wire-rimmed spectacles.

"Now who in their right mind would come here when Doc Wilson is in town?" he asked, not intending to bruise her ego, but speaking frankly.

"But, surely, you can see I'm a capable doctor."

He thought he saw her eyes narrow in anger behind her glasses, but she quickly looked away.

"After all," he ventured, trying for a reasonable explanation, "you are a woman—" Grey wanted to say he felt more comfortable seeing a man, but Rachel didn't give him time to finish. Instead, she bristled like a porcupine.

"Twenty dollars please," she ordered, her hand extended.

Taken aback by the exorbitant fee, Grey gasped. "Twenty dollars! That's highway robbery. I'm sure Doc Wilson wouldn't charge me more than five."

"Twenty dollars and not a penny less." She pinned him with her eyes. "One house call and one office visit."

Damnation, Grey grumbled, what was it about the women of Astoria? Twenty dollars, this—twenty dollars, that. After all, he wasn't made of money. But he reached inside his pocket, pulled out a clip and peeled off the required amount of bills. Irritated beyond belief, he marched to the front door.

"No woman is worth that much money," he added, opening the door and stepping outside. Without even a farewell, he slammed it shut behind him.

"Arrogant beast," Rachel muttered to herself. She rushed to steady a framed sampler threatening to jump off the wall with the force of Grey's departure.

Rachel had thought her skills as a doctor would win Grey Devlin's respect. Whether he was a fiend or not, somehow it mattered that her efforts meet with his approval. Heaven knew she'd tried hard enough. But this man was no different from all the rest of the people of Astoria. Because she was a woman, he doubted her abilities.

No woman is worth twenty dollars.

Grey's words echoed in Rachel's mind. She knew of one woman that the harbormaster had thought was worthy of such an exorbitant fee. But that woman was good for spreading her legs, not for spreading ointment on his wounds. There simply was no justice in the world. Rachel turned and walked back into her empty surgery.

Outside Baldy's Saloon, Grey stood propped against a post. He reached inside his back pocket and pulled out the cheroot Baldy had given him earlier in the evening. Striking a match, Grey placed it against the end of the cigar and took several quick puffs. The tip fired to life, glowing ember red in the darkness. The scent of tobacco filled the air around him, for the moment stalling his discontent. Since leaving the doctor's house earlier in the day nothing had gone well.

He'd returned to Tully's cabin, announcing his plans to move home. When he'd complained about the doctor's exorbitant fee, Tully had immediately given him a dressing down. Words led to other words, and soon

Grey had spilled his guts about his parting encounter with Rachel. He could still hear Tully's reaction, accusing him of being pigheaded, opinionated, and downright disreputable. Grey knew he was all these things and more, but he didn't appreciate his best friend reminding him of his shortcomings.

After checking in with his landlady, Grey had enjoyed a decent meal. The first he'd had in three days, although he'd been forced to eat it standing up. Afterwards he'd changed his clothes and gone in search of the siren who'd sent him to sea.

All of his questions remained unanswered. No one—not Baldy, not the other girls who worked the saloon, not even Opal—knew the whereabouts of the pink-haired whore.

Baldy had been glad to see him—had said he'd missed his visits, things weren't the same without him. Although Grey never came out and said he'd been shanghaied, he could tell by the man's greeting that his friend was innocent. He trusted the man. But Opal, he wasn't so sure about. After all, his own mother had been a whore and he could never trust her.

To Grey's questions, the madam claimed that Chinook never hung her corset anywhere for very long. According to Opal, Chinook was somewhat of a gypsy, working the saloons up and down the coast. Grey wondered at the similarity of a gypsy whore to a gypsy moth. The only difference he could see was that a whore sucked the sap from a man's body, whereas the moth sucked the sap from the forest and shade trees.

He hadn't let on to Opal why he was interested in finding Chinook, other than that he'd enjoyed her services. Until Grey did some more investigating, or found out who wanted him out of Astoria, he would remain silent about his shanghaiing. All anyone knew about his absence of the last few days was that he'd been feeling poorly.

Taking another drag on his cigar, Grey pushed away from the pole and ambled down the road. His thoughts focused on Rachel Thomas. No matter how much he wished to banish the lady doctor from his mind, he couldn't. After Tully had reminded him of his arrogance, Grey had felt lower than a snake's belly.

He hadn't meant to make the doc angry, or even to insult her. But he'd done both. Everything he'd said had come out wrong, just as everything had been wrong since the first day he'd met her in Tully's cabin.

No matter how much he tried to convince himself that she was a good doctor, Grey didn't feel comfortable with a woman in that role. However, he did owe her an apology. And he'd make it a point to recommend her medical service to others. He owed the lady that much.

A breeze blew off the bay, bringing with it the ripe smell of decomposing fish and decaying vegetable matter. A frog's chorus tuned up for its nightly performance and the constant clanging of a buoy bell could be heard in the distance—all the familiar sounds of the wharf that made Astoria feel like home. But from now on the bell's hollow toll would always be a reminder to Grey of his narrow escape from death.

Pausing at the corner of an alley, Grey listened. Someone or something struggled within its depths. Instantly alert, he waited, straining to hear the muffled sounds. A whimper sliced through the darkness and was hushed by more scuffling sounds.

Was it only a stray animal rummaging through some garbage, or was it another crimp at work? After Grey's recent experience, he could easily identify with any poor soul who might find himself in the clutches of shanghaiers. Grey threw down his cigar, stomped it into blackness, and vaulted down the alley.

Once he'd been swallowed up by the dark, his night vision kicked in. Several windows from the upper story of one of the buildings splashed a muted glow in the dark passageway. Grey paused behind a mountain of stacked crates—waiting, listening.

He heard it again—the whimper of a trapped animal. Something was definitely amiss. Reaching inside his jacket, Grey withdrew his pocketknife and switched open its blade. He waited for the right moment to attack.

Two shadows appeared on the dead-end wall. Muted images with soft edges struggled together in an ugly waltz. Red hot anger slashed through Grey when he recognized one of the shadows was a woman. He sprang into action.

Grabbing the attacker from behind, he jerked the man off the woman. Like a sail that had lost its wind, she crumpled to the ground. Grey spun the surprised man around, smashing his fist into the fellow's jaw and poised the knife for action. But with a quick knee thrust in the stomach the man flopped, lifeless, to the alley floor.

Grey dashed to the woman's side and scooped her up in his arms. She felt as limp as a rag doll as he carried her. When at last they reached the lamplit street, he looked down at her listless face.

It was a perfect oval, her bones delicately carved.

Her lips were parted slightly, showing only a trace of pearl white teeth. Her thick dark hair, pulled from pins still caught in the tangles, hung in heavy waves over Grey's arm, and he wondered why he'd never noticed this fascinating creature before. Her skin was flushed from the struggle, but in the light of the nearby street lamp, its smooth glow could have passed for alabaster.

Slowly, the woman's eyes blinked open and she squinted up at him. He smiled and her own lips formed the trace of a smile. Grey's heartbeat quickened and for a moment he never wanted to relinquish his hold.

"Are you all right?" he asked.

"Mr. Devlin?" She seemed to recognize his voice. "Is that you?" She stiffened in his arms.

And then he saw it, the small identifying black mark close to her right eye.

Acute disappointment flooded through Grey when he realized the woman he held in his arms was none other than the lady doctor. Then shock replaced disillusionment. Without her glasses—with her magnificent hair flowing halfway down her back—Rachel Thomas was a beauty.

He reluctantly released her legs and helped her to stand. "What are you doing down here alone this time of night?" He could hear the snap in his voice.

"I had a patient. A man got in a brawl at one of the saloons and needed stitches. I was on my way home when that drunk attacked me." She pointed toward the alley.

"Do you realize what might have happened to you if I hadn't come along when I did?"

"But I—Oh, my heavens, my bag. My medical bag is missing." Rachel fingered her nose and searched the immediate area. "Oh, no, my glasses are gone." She gave Grey a look of desperation.

"Is this where the man attacked you?" he said, thinking what a pity she should ever have to cover such beautiful eyes again.

"Yes, it is. He was sitting, leaning against the building when I passed. In the next moment he was wrestling me into the alley."

"Well, you're pretty damned lucky that wrestling is all he did."

Rachel dashed toward the alley, frantically searching the ground. "I must have dropped my bag in the struggle."

"Look, Doc, it's as black as pitch in there." He reached her, detaining her with his hand upon her shoulder. "I suggest I see you home. Then I'll come back with a light, find your bag, and return it to you tomorrow."

"But what if someone stumbles upon it and steals my instruments?"

"No one is going to stumble upon it in the next thirty minutes."

"But the man down there, what about him?"

"It's my guess he won't be stumbling anywhere for the rest of the night. Last I saw of him, he was out cold."

"But he could need my assistance."

Grey felt powerless against her determination. "Doc, the man attacked you. I can't believe you would entertain the idea of doctoring him after that."

"Mr. Devlin, I am a doctor and—"

"You're duty-bound to attend him. I know." Grey finished for her. "You wait right here. I'll walk back there and check on him. If I find he requires your help, I'll tell you. If he's fine, I'll walk you home.''

"Under the circumstances, I guess that will have to be acceptable.''

Grey disappeared into the darkness. Minutes later he was back. "He's out like a melted-down candle and probably won't wake up until tomorrow.''

"You think?" Rachel asked, her face filled with concern.

"I do. Besides what could you do for the man without your glasses and your doctoring bag?''

Ten minutes later, they stood in front of Rachel's house.

"About this afternoon,'' Grey started, "I want to apologize for my behavior. You're a very good doctor, and I do appreciate what you did for me. It's my own prejudices that make me feel uncomfortable with a woman doctor. It's not your fault.''

"Then you believe I'm a capable physician?''

"I believe you're a very good physician. And to show you how much confidence I have in your abilities, I'd be happy to refer patients to you, if there is a need.''

"Why, Mr. Devlin, that's very honorable of you. Thank you.'' She showered him with a heart-stopping smile.

They walked up onto the porch and Rachel pushed open the front door.

"Well, thank you again. Good night.'' She started inside.

But Grey didn't move to leave. "Doc,'' he asked, delaying her retreat, "would you please do me a favor and not be walking around Swilltown all hours of the night? It's not a safe place for a lady alone.''

Rachel stopped and looked to Grey. ''Mr. Devlin, what happened tonight is most unusual. I feel very safe down there. Most men see me coming and going at all hours, and they never bother me.''

But Grey knew with a certainty they'd never seen her the way she looked tonight.

''I'm a doctor, Mr. Devlin. I take risks every day, attending people who require my help. You might say, I'm like the ladies of the night. I provide a service, just as they do.''

Grey knew it was fruitless to argue, and he didn't really wish to argue with the woman who stood beside him. Tonight something had happened to him when he held the woman doctor in his arms. Until tonight, Grey had neither recognized her beauty nor seen her as vulnerable. He had an unexplainable urge to protect her, but he knew she'd never appreciate his thoughts.

''I'd better go in, but thank you again for your help.''

''I'll bring your things by in the morning.'' He turned and bounded down the stairs.

As Grey later walked back toward the alley with his lantern, he questioned Rachel Thomas's logic about the ladies of the night. As far as he was concerned, there was absolutely no comparison between the tainted whores of Swilltown and the chaste lady doctor.

Chapter 5

Martha Purdy settled herself into the Windsor chair in Rachel's parlor. Even with her beaver coat and head shawl, the woman was still shivering. And the rest of the town had stored away their winter fur wraps weeks ago.

Rachel handed her visitor a cup of lemon-laced tea. "Here, ma'am, won't you drink this while we talk? Perhaps it will warm you up a bit."

"I'm afraid it won't help," the older woman answered between convulsive shudders. "I can't seem to get warm, no matter how much covering I have, or how much tea I drink." She took a sip of the hot brew. "I'm just so glad you're all right. I heard the shocking news about your attack last night, and I just had to see for myself that you had suffered no harm."

Rachel pulled another chair alongside and sat. "That's most kind of you. But as you can see, I'm perfectly all right. Thanks to our new harbormaster," she added, still not believing that he had appeared out of nowhere when she had needed him most. She drew a deep breath. "How did you come to hear the news? It only happened last evening."

"Why, Mr. Devlin lives at Purdy House. And God bless him, after he arrived home last night he was issuing strict orders that I was not to be out and about after dark in the future." The older woman shook her head in disbelief. "Imagine that. Telling me what to do and what not to do. Me, old enough to be his mother, mind you." Forsaking her tea, the woman grew more animated with every word. "And when I says to him, 'And who's to walk my dog before bedtime?' he answers, 'I will. I need the exercise.'"

Miss Purdy chuckled, bringing on a fit of coughing into her handkerchief. When the spasms had ended, she continued to sing the praises of her boarder. "Why, if a man had spoken to me like that years ago, looking out for my concern the way he did, I'd have grandchildren on my lap today." Again the coughing started.

"How long have you had this cough?"

"Oh, it's hung on for about a week now," the landlady calculated. "But it doesn't seem to be getting any better. My throat's a little raw, too."

Rachel studied the woman's face. Hers were not the twinkling, vibrant eyes Rachel had come to recognize in the woman over the years. Rather, they looked glassy and dull. "You could have fever," she suggested. "You do look a little flushed."

Knowing that the proper town ladies had continued to patronize Doctor Wilson, even after Rachel had returned home to practice, and knowing that her colleague was in town, she worded her next question carefully. "Is there something I can do for you?"

Martha Purdy looked at her hostess sheepishly.

91

"This is not a social visit . . . though it should be." She shifted in her chair nervously. "I've been remiss in welcoming you back home. Your parents were such lovely people." She reached out her hand to Rachel. "And I miss your father's doctoring." Leaning closer, she whispered, "Not to be making any comparisons, but he was the best doctor this town ever had. I'm so sorry he's gone."

"I, too," Rachel agreed. It was difficult, even today, talking about her father without feeling guilty that she had not been around when she might have been able to help him in some way. "But since he's not here," she said with a smile, "how can I help?"

"Fact is, Mr. Devlin sent me down."

Curious, Rachel pursued the woman's explanation. "He did?"

"Said you were a fine doctor—that he'd seen you do your best work."

The scene in Tully's bathtub came floating back, teasing Rachel's senses. She couldn't suppress a smile at remembering. "I suppose he did at that." Helping Martha Purdy out of her chair, she said, "Well, then, let's step across the hall so I can have a look at that throat."

Thirty minutes later, the landlady was armed with powders for her fever, syrups for her throat and, in spite of a protest, a prescription for two days of rest in bed.

"I know no one oversees things as well as you do," Rachel admonished her, "but I remember your cook and cleaning lady. They can do quite nicely without you for two days."

"I wouldn't worry so much if it were the two of them doing the work."

Rachel narrowed her eyes. "What do you mean?"

"I mean that before I could put on my apron this morning, Mr. Devlin had me ushered to the davenport in the parlor. Before I could complain, he had prepared breakfast himself . . . for everyone."

Rachel listened to the woman's words. What an enigmatic man, this Grey Devlin. A man who would walk a dog for another, cook breakfast for a household, refer a new patient to a struggling *female* physician. Could this possibly be the same man who had allowed a shipment of opium into port? The same man who at her own hands had almost died at sea?

"Oh, before I forget," Martha Purdy reminded herself aloud, "the Women's Aid Society is holding a box social Saturday night over at Grace Episcopal. I'd be very pleased to have you attend with me."

This was the first Rachel had heard of the church function. Though she made it a point to attend services, this past Sunday had found her handling an emergency down at the pier.

"That's sweet of you, Miss Purdy. But Saturday nights can be very busy for a waterfront doctor. Besides, I think the church members are still a little uneasy around me."

The landlady bristled. "Nonsense. Why, most of these members you grew up with. There's not a one among them who doesn't know your name."

"That's what would make it all the harder to attend. Miss Purdy, you know very well that none of them understand why I followed in my father's footsteps.

93

And with the types of patients that I have, many have attached a certain perceived reputation to my name.''

''Rachel, my dear. It matters not what those 'holier than thou's' might think. Besides, this gathering is for a worthy cause.''

Rachel laughed at the woman's enthusiasm. ''Father Huntley sees that all the church functions are for worthy causes. I must admit, though, I do miss the fellowship my family enjoyed among the congregation.'' She fingered her apron with regret. ''Thank you, anyway, but I really must decline.''

''More's the pity,'' the older woman said. ''I was hoping to make amends to you and at the same time allow for one more donation to the logging families upriver as far as Camp Ross.''

''Camp Ross? Why, I have patients up there. Oh, Miss Purdy, indeed that is a worthy cause. Those families have so little as it is.''

In that moment Rachel changed her mind. It was one thing to socialize, quite another to contribute to a fund-raising drive. Besides, with the help of her herbs, not only could she cook up the tastiest foods this town had ever seen, she had money to contribute. She and her waterfront ladies had, to date, collected over four hundred dollars. Suddenly, she couldn't wait to see the surprised faces when she presented her contribution to Father Huntley.

''On second thought, Miss Purdy,'' Rachel responded, ''perhaps it is time I made myself a little more available to the community. Perhaps much of my isolation has been my own fault. However,'' she pointed out, ''Saturday's only four days away. I want you resting until then. And I'll meet you at the church. I never know when I might receive an emergency call.''

Miss Purdy clasped her hands. ''Wonderful. But try to be early. The entire town is invited.'' She winked. ''Even Mr. Devlin.''

''I'll try, ma'am, I'll try.''

A tumult of emotions swept through Rachel as she thought about the following Saturday evening. She'd prepare the best basket she could and hope it would draw someone to bid on it. At the same time she wondered how she could possibly share a meal with some poor unsuspecting soul who might reap the disapproval of the community. And lastly, she considered her own motivations. Would her presence and her contribution change anyone's notions about her?

Banners strung high above the street snapped in the late afternoon breeze, underscoring their written invitation to the fund-raising social. The vacant lot adjacent to Grace Episcopal Church had been transformed into a garden, festooned with sashaying streamers and fancy signs announcing ''Come one, come all.''

Rachel hardly recognized it as she approached. As a young child she'd explored and played in this very lot and many others about town with her friends. It had seemed almost like playing in the woods, though not so far away from home as to be considered dangerous.

Someone had hung Chinese lanterns from the lower branches of the large willow tree that grew in the center of the lot. Three generations of children had played around its trunk—herself included—swinging and climbing upon its many boughs. This afternoon it served as a natural covering for the festivities, its new spring growth forming a canopy like a giant green umbrella.

Apprehension tingled along Rachel's spine. She'd worked in her kitchen all morning, preparing food for her supper box that would be auctioned off with the others. Then she'd spent the early afternoon preparing herself for the social as well. Her food she knew would be palatable, but she felt less sure about her appearance.

Her pleated garnet serge skirt with the matching oatmeal and garnet-striped Basque belonged to her other life—the one she'd left behind in Michigan. The person she'd been while attending medical school and social functions in the Midwest no longer existed. But as Rachel glimpsed the tiny silver buttons that filed down the front of her military-styled jacket, something of her buried past emerged.

A breeze unfurled the shorter ends of the hair she'd secured earlier with a *grosgrain* ribbon at her nape. Once the sun set, bringing with it the damper temperatures of evening, Rachel knew her hair, without the benefit of a tightly wound chignon, would corkscrew into a thousand waves.

But today, in hopes of again being gathered into the folds of the town, Rachel had set aside her austere hairdo and with it her unyielding resolve. Miss Purdy's visit had been the benchmark of a renewed determination to lure more Astorian females to her practice. And deep inside herself, Rachel knew Grey Devlin's confidence in her skills had been the catalyst.

Right away Rachel sighted Martha Purdy waving, motioning to join her at a long table covered with a snow-white cloth. Several people milled around the parklike area, conversing in small groups as Rachel approached.

"Here, dear, give me that box," Miss Purdy demanded, nearly grabbing it from Rachel's hands. She placed her nose to its covering and sniffed. "I don't know what's hidden beneath this plain covering, but it certainly smells ravishing."

Watching Martha Purdy place it on the table beside other, beautifully decorated containers, Rachel suddenly felt the urge to snatch it back. She looked at the brown paper wrapping on her box supper and knew no one would bid on its ugliness. How pathetic her sprig of fading marigold blossoms—tied with a gingham ribbon—looked beside the lace and satin concoctions belonging to the other women. She'd been so careful in her food preparation that the outside wrapping had seemed superfluous. Now all she wanted to do was leave before she was further embarrassed.

"There you are," Miss Purdy interjected, looking past Rachel and smiling as though the president himself had graced her with his presence. "I see you've brought that crusty old fisherman with you after all."

Rachel whirled on her heel. Her heart almost vaulted from her chest when she saw Grey Devlin and Tully strolling toward them.

She hadn't seen the harbormaster since he'd returned her medical bag two mornings earlier, shortly before Martha Purdy had called on her, and she was dumbstruck by the handsome man dressed in his Sunday best. Beside him, Tully, too, had dressed for the occasion, looking more like a refined old gentleman than the salty dog everyone knew him to be.

"I needed a hook, line, and sinker to get him dressed," Grey addressed his landlady, "but he took the bait when I touted the possibility of a decent meal." Grey's eyes met Rachel's and he winked at her.

Tully gave his young friend a look of disdain. "You know I only came because I believe in helpin' folks less fortunate than the likes of you." His welcoming gaze dusted Rachel before coming to rest on the older woman. "But I must confess, a good home-cooked meal is right hard to pass up."

"Why, Tully," Miss Purdy reminded him, "I've been trying for years to get you to take meals at my house. But you're always too wrapped up in your fishing lines to be lured away." She sashayed like a fluffed-up pigeon for Tully's inspection.

Why, Rachel thought, Martha Purdy's enamored with Tully. The idea tilted her lips into a smile. Stealing a look at the seaman, Rachel could understand her interest. With his snow-white whiskers and thick head of hair, Tully was quite the dignified-looking man. A little too portly for his own good health, perhaps, but it fit his seafaring image—especially with the calabash pipe secured in his teeth.

Throughout the repartee Rachel felt Grey's eyes on her. "And how are you, Doc?" he asked. His dimple caved in the side of his cheek when he smiled at her. The red streak across his right cheek had all but disappeared, leaving only an additional faint character line to an already attractive face.

"I'm fine, thank you, Mr. Devlin. And you?"

"Much better, thanks to you." He looked her up and down then added, "You look mighty pretty today, all gussied up for the occasion."

Rachel could feel the heat from her blush and chided herself for reacting in such a simple-minded way. But secretly she was glad she'd taken the extra pains with her appearance, realizing now she'd done it to seek Grey's approval.

More and more people kept arriving. A festive air hung over the small lot, filling the warm spring afternoon with friendly sounds. Several women acknowledged Rachel's presence with friendly smiles. But Rachel was certain that courtesy was due to nothing more than Miss Purdy's attendance at her side.

Rachel noticed something else while she stood with the landlady and the two men. Grey Devlin drew the female populace of Astoria to their little group the way a flower drew a bee to its pollen. In dresses of silk and serge, they floated around him like brightly colored butterflies darting about on a summer breeze. And the handsome harbormaster seemed to be in his element, bandying heart-stopping quips with the best of them. Curious glances were passed Rachel's way, but quickly set aside when the women undoubtedly decided she'd be no competition.

Martha Purdy stepped away to busy herself at the table, leaving Rachel and the two men in conversation. At that moment a petite woman hurried across the yard and threw her arms around Rachel, nearly knocking her off her feet. "Rachel, is it really you?" she asked. "I hardly recognized you."

Taken aback, Rachel gave her spectacles a self-conscious nudge and stared at the young woman. Then she recognized her.

"Why, Sarah Collins, I heard you'd married and moved away from Astoria." Rachel hugged her friend again. "You're the last person I expected to see here today."

Sarah paused, looking anxiously over her shoulder, as though searching the crowd for someone. Then she turned back to Rachel with what looked like an expression of relief.

"I did marry and move away for a short while," Sarah explained. "But we came home after father's death. We're living in my parents' home up on the hill." She grasped Rachel's hands.

Rachel recalled with clarity the big house on the hill. When she was a youngster, Sarah's house had been the most elaborate and well-appointed home in Astoria. It had belonged to her grandfather. One of the earliest settlers in the area, he'd made his fortune in shipping. His only daughter had married a young minister from back East, and they'd taken up residence in the family mansion after Sarah was born.

The woman who now stood before Rachel looked nothing like the Sarah Collins she remembered. Sarah had been the envy of all the other girls who'd called her their friend. She had always reminded Rachel of a Pierre Jumeau bisque fashion doll, sparkling and delicate with her blond hair and china complexion. Not only had she been beautiful, but vivacious as well, and overflowing with mischief. She was also one of the most gracious individuals that Rachel had ever known.

"I wanted to come see you." Sarah glanced away from Rachel, then added, "But I haven't been well."

Rachel's trained eye had already decided that. Her old friend looked haggard, her eyes dull, her skin sallow. Her beautiful thick blond curls looked thin and frowzy. And her lightweight cape failed to hide the fact that she was well into pregnancy.

"I am a doctor," Rachel bent to whisper in the other woman's ear. "Maybe I could call on you."

"No!" Sarah abruptly replied. Then as though realizing how her answer must have sounded, she added, "I'm fine now . . . I'm with child." She squeezed Rachel's hands.

"Then congratulations are in order. I'm so happy for you." Rachel started to introduce Grey and Tully and would have said more but for an interruption by an elegantly dressed gentleman who'd strolled up behind Sarah.

"Well, my dear," he said, ignoring the fact that Sarah still stood with Rachel's hands in her own, "I see you've found our new harbormaster." The man placed his bony fingers on Sarah's shoulders, and Rachel watched her shift uneasily beneath his touch. "You have exercised your manners by introducing yourself, I hope." His lordly tone chilled the air.

"She certainly has, Ballard. You should have told me you had such a lovely and charming wife."

Both women looked at Grey in surprise. Throughout their intense conversation, he had stood quietly by without calling attention to his presence.

"That's my Sarah—always the lady."

The man smiled but Rachel saw no warmth in his eyes. He took his wife's arm. "Now come along, dear." Ignoring Rachel, he turned to the harbormaster. "Grey, I have some people I wish you to meet. . . ."

Grey hesitated. "I believe you've met Doctor

Thomas," he added, refusing to tolerate Ballard's bad manners.

"Ah, yes," Ballard replied, facing Rachel. "The woman doctor." His acknowledgement seemed a mere afterthought, but he pinned her with his cold eyes.

Instinctively, Rachel disliked the man. Life in the logging camps was harsh enough with the constant dangers that faced the woodsmen. But she'd heard from her women friends about Ballard's camp—the deplorable working conditions, the unnecessary safety hazards to beat the competition to market, and the escalated costs of goods sold in the company store at Camp Ross. The purpose of this fundraiser was to help ease the burden on the families in the camps. It seemed ironic—strictly for show—that Ballard would be attending this gathering today.

"Come, Grey, I insist you meet these people." With no more than a polite nod to Rachel, he slipped his other arm around Grey's shoulder and steered both him and Sarah away.

As she watched the threesome disappear into the crowd, Rachel recalled the letter she'd received from her mother about Sarah's wedding.

It had been the social event of the year. But rumors had flown about town that the Reverend Collins had not been too pleased with his only child's choice of a husband. Soon after their marriage, the couple had left Astoria to set up housekeeping in San Francisco. Rachel's mother had mentioned that Reverend Collins's health appeared to deteriorate after the wedding and he died soon after. In later letters from her mother, Sarah Collins Ballard was never mentioned again.

If Rachel was as good a doctor as she believed herself

to be, she knew Sarah was definitely unwell. Her friend looked like a walking corpse, and here she was, expecting a child in a matter of weeks. Rachel would have to find a way to help Sarah, or soon two more lives would be lost.

Children ran to and fro, chasing one another beneath the tree's leafy arms and crawling up into the same branches Rachel had climbed herself as a youngster. Sighing, she recalled those times when life had been simple, when she'd had no worries, and she'd been surrounded by her parents' love. Now she stood alone beneath the same tree, in her same hometown, feeling as lost as a baby bird when tumbled from its nest.

She looked around hopelessly. Martha Purdy had captured Tully and they, too, had disappeared. Rachel wished she'd never agreed to come to this social. It had been a bad idea. These people would never accept her as an equal—not until she gave up her medical practice. And that she would never do. If it weren't for the bidding that would soon begin for the decorated suppers, Rachel would have sneaked away.

"My absence certainly would go unnoticed," she mumbled to herself, knowing all too well that her modestly dressed box would also go unnoticed when put up against the others.

"Fifty cents . . . I hear fifty cents," the auctioneer called from atop a crate beside the covered table. He nodded, smiled and sniffed as he held up a beautifully decorated basket to his nose. His hand was practically hidden in the tangle of rainbow ribbons that hung from its handle.

As the bidding began, the spectators formed a horseshoe around the table. Standing alone in the crowd, Rachel hoped she didn't look as conspicuous as she felt. She'd long since lost sight of Grey. By now he'd probably found more interesting female company to spend his time with.

"Gotta another purty box for bid." The auctioneer held up a container covered with delicate lace. Its creator had woven clusters of red silk roses among its webbed covering.

"Who'll open the bidding?" he called to the admiring crowd.

"Seventy-five cents," a voice shouted.

"I've a bid for seventy-five cents from the back." Then, recognizing the man, he added, "Our new harbormaster has just bid seventy-five cents. Does anyone wish to top his bid? It's a beautiful box, just like the young lady who made it."

Rachel looked across the space and saw that Grey had worked his way through the back of the crowd to stand on the edge of the half-circle. A young woman Rachel didn't recognize hung onto his arm. She wore, pinned to her pink dress, a cluster of the same silk roses that adorned the lace on the box. With a twinge of unexplainable sadness, Rachel tried to tear her gaze away.

"I bid three dollars."

Someone else had entered the bidding. Rachel searched the crowd, envying the young woman's popularity. How nice it would be to have two fellows interested in sharing your box supper, she thought.

The young woman looked up at Grey with soulful eyes, waiting for him to raise his bid. When none was forthcoming, the auctioneer continued with his chore.

"Going once, going twice . . ." Another young man broke through the crowd and pushed forward. ". . . sold to Mr. Chester for three dollars. A good price, sir. Don't you agree?" The proud bidder shuffled through the crowd—his face the color of pickled beets—to claim his prize. Appearing none too happy with the outcome, the young woman reluctantly released Grey's arm while glaring at the young man who had displeased her. "Oh come on, Hector," she grumbled, leading him away from the circle of grinning onlookers.

"Mary Jane, you knew I wouldn't let no one outbid me." The young man's voice floated through the crowd that had split to allow them to pass.

At that precise moment, Rachel's gaze locked with Grey's. He smiled at her and winked, causing her heart to whack against her rib cage.

"Now, ladies and gentlemen, what am I bid for this?"

Rachel saw the auctioneer pick up her own carton. Looking at the brown paper wrap, all she could think of was the fish market and the way it had smelled when the merchant parceled up her salmon. She mentally chastised herself for her choice of coverings and her lack of creativity.

"Purrrty marigolds on its front." The man sniffed at the corner of the box. "And something in here smells good enough to eat." Everyone laughed at the auctioneer's antics.

"Fifty cents," came a bid from the back of the crowd.

Rachel's face grew hot. She didn't dare look toward the bidder, but whoever he was, she felt thankful for his participation. After all, fifty cents was better than nothing.

"One dollar fifty," came another bid. Rachel stared straight ahead to the table. She didn't need to look to know who'd placed the bid. She'd recognize Grey's whiskey-sounding voice anywhere.

But from another point in the assemblage, someone shouted out his price. "Two dollars."

Curiosity overwhelmed Rachel. Could three people be interested in her homely little box?

"*Twooooo* dollars, gentlemen. Anyone wish to top this bid?"

"Three dollars."

Rachel's gaze slid toward Grey where he stood with his arms crossed over his chest, rocking back on his heels. Tall as he was, he seemed to stretch, craning his neck, searching for a sign of his competition.

Warmth spiraled through Rachel. It made her feel good that Grey wanted to buy her supper, in spite of its meager wrap. From all the praises sung about him recently, he was probably showing his support for someone whose unsightly box he felt would never have otherwise been taken. Without a doubt he couldn't know it belonged to the lady doctor. It was one thing to have made amends for his insults, it was quite another to have to spend his social evening in her company. Of that Rachel was certain.

Again a commotion sizzled in the audience and from another spot outside the crowd came a higher bid. "Four dollars," the mystery voice offered.

Now everyone was curious. Whispers rumbled

throughout the crowd as they sought out the bidder. This was more than any box had drawn yet. And this one certainly couldn't compare with those still left on the table.

"Five dollars!" Grey shouted, not willing to be out-bid by the others.

"Do I hear five-fifty?" the excited auctioneer asked.

Everyone waited, listening, searching the crowd. Five dollars was a small fortune to pay for a supper box. Rachel couldn't believe her good fortune. It pleased her to know that the Women's Aid Society would be receiving so much for her plain creation. But anxiety welled deep in her heart. She worried that someone else would outbid Grey.

"Sold to the new harbormaster for five dollars. Will the young woman who prepared this please come forward?"

Embarrassed, Rachel stepped from the ranks and walked toward the table. Mumbles filtered through the crowd when they recognized the lady doctor.

"Doc," the auctioneer yelled above the crowd, "what'd you put in here . . . pills?"

The crowd laughed good-naturedly. After all, this was a charity function.

Grey joined Rachel at the table, not looking at all surprised that the meal belonged to her. He placed the five dollars in the auctioneer's hand and took the box in exchange. Cheers and congratulations on his generous donation flooded the group. Other men patted Grey on the back as he led Rachel to the outskirts of the crowd.

* * *

Tully stood beside Martha Purdy, smiling like the cat that just swallowed the supper fish. He'd been busy, running from one side of the crowd to the other, placing bids and making everyone think several parties had been interested in Doctor Thomas's box.

Tully didn't really care what everyone else thought, but he'd accomplished what he'd set out to do. Although his young friend wasn't aware of it, Grey had just proven what Tully had already begun to suspect.

Grey had known the carton belonged to Rachel. They'd both overheard the landlady when they'd arrived. If asked, he would have made some excuse about not wanting the doctor to feel bad because no one offered for her box.

But Tully hadn't been born yesterday. He remembered Grey's outburst over his argument with Rachel Thomas and the revealing spark of interest in his friend's eyes whenever he mentioned her name. What Grey's lips couldn't say, his eyes had given away.

There was a lot more to the lady doctor than what appeared on the outside. After all, he'd just paid five dollars for the plainest-looking box on the table.

And to Tully that said it all.

Chapter 6

Grey led Rachel toward a section of fallen tree trunk and removed his jacket. Spreading it across the natural seat, he ordered Rachel to sit. Then he plopped down beside her in the bed of wild clover that come summer would be in full bloom. With his long, muscular legs spread out in front of him, he leaned against the log and placed Rachel's box on his lap.

"Doesn't smell much like pills," Grey teased her. Lifting the box to his nose, he took a deep whiff, then resettled it on his thighs.

"You don't think I'd waste my good pills on the likes of you," Rachel countered. Here she sat with the man she'd dared to hope would purchase her supper and she could barely manage her tongue to form intelligent words. She felt so nervous she wasn't sure she'd be able to eat a bite of anything she'd packed.

In the fading afternoon sun his hair resembled corn silk. A playful breeze lifted several strands, routing the scent of soap, sun, and sea her way. No man, she mused, should be so handsome or smell so heavenly—or sit so close.

"What secrets lie behind this plain wrapping?" he asked, playfully glancing over his shoulder at her. His tanned fingers trifled with the gingham knot that secured the wilting marigolds.

"I like plain," Rachel lied. She recalled how she'd chastised herself for the box's simplicity. But Grey Devlin had paid five dollars for it. Maybe he liked plain as well. Feeling more confident, she added, "Didn't your mother ever teach you that it's what is on the inside that counts?"

"Not exactly her philosophy," Grey mumbled into his lap. "But shall we test your wisdom?" He slipped the ribbon from around the box and peeled back the lid.

With bated breath, Rachel waited for his response. She knew the feast would earn her praise because she prided herself on being as good a cook as she was a doctor.

Tucked inside the box were two smaller flat wicker baskets. Rachel had lined each one with an embroidered "tidie." Each depicted her much loved spice plants—soapwort and lavender. But Grey seemed more interested in the feast she'd prepared than in her fancywork.

"I'm so hungry my backbone is about to gnaw on my stomach." Grey looked up at her, showering her with his beautiful smile. One long finger delved through the goodies.

"All my favorite things," he added. "Cold roast beef, pastry biscuits, yellow cheese, jam puffs, stewed fruit. . . . Why Doc, you're just full of surprises."

Twisting around to face her, Grey thrust one of the baskets into her lap, then settled at her feet, Indian

110

style. He continued to praise Rachel's culinary skills while shifting his gaze from the basket's contents to Rachel. "And for dessert, cold plum pudding. Gosh, I can't wait to eat."

Rachel studied the grown man who sat before her. He looked like a kid at Christmas time. His exuberance over her feast made Rachel's heart sing. She was glad she'd spent so much time preparing it.

"You didn't tell me you knew how to cook as well as you fix people up." He chewed a biscuit with relish.

Rachel picked up a wedge of cheese and plopped it into her mouth. Chewing and talking at the same time, she replied, "And you, sir, didn't tell me what a fine cook you are."

Puzzled, Grey looked at her, then comprehension dawned. "Ah, I see that Miss Purdy's been flapping her gums."

"I do believe the woman is enamored of you." Rachel gave him a teasing smile. "You'd best be careful, or you might find the noose of matrimony slipped around your neck."

Grey hooted. "I don't believe I have anything to fear from that quarter . . ." He paused, looking over his shoulder as though searching for eavesdroppers. "Actually, I believe my old friend Tully holds the lady's heart."

Amused, Rachel asked, "Tully? Why, she'll never land that one."

"I don't know. Bigger fish than he have been caught and fried." Grey held her gaze, his blue eyes sparkling with mischief.

Unaccustomed to a man's company other than on a professional basis, Rachel suddenly felt flustered and

111

far too warm. Some long-buried instinct told her Grey was flirting with her. And as someone who had never flirted, except in the disguise of Chinook, Rachel questioned how a lady should respond to his easy banter.

His perfectly shaped mouth lifted at the corners into a teasing smile. Rachel's heart quickened and she found herself studying the deep dimpled hollow in his cheek. Swallowing the remains of her jam puff too fast, she almost choked on the flaky pastry. Grey slipped a bottle of ginger beer into her hand, his expression all too knowing.

"Drink," he ordered. "I'd hate to lose the cook before I get to know her better."

This sent another bout of warmth to Rachel's cheeks. Unable to think of a witty reply, she sat in silence, focusing her attention on the sun as it dipped into the sea.

From where they sat they had a perfect view of the bay. The clouds on the horizon looked like pink and gold pillows, the water a satin counterpane. Down on the wharf, lights blinked into life, announcing the ongoing activities of Swilltown.

Farther up the hill where the larger houses sat, servants would be lighting lamps in the ornate parlors. In the deepening shadows of dusk, beneath the dignified old willow, Rachel watched the Chinese lanterns sway in the soft breeze, their golden orbs filling the twilight with a fairylike aura.

"Miss Thomas, I give you my most professional diagnosis."

Rachel looked at him wide-eyed. "What do you mean?"

"That you are, indeed, as good a cook as you are a doctor."

His compliment brought Rachel back to the present. "Why, thank you, sir." While the man couldn't possibly know the extent of her medical skills, he had, nevertheless, handed her the supreme compliment.

He dusted the few crumbs that had landed in his lap with her embroidered "tidie", then lifted the napkin for inspection. "I like your fancywork." He dipped his nose into the folds. "Smells good, too."

Rachel was touched by his actions. She knew her face mirrored the setting sun and welcomed the encroaching darkness that hid its glow. Although she felt awkward with Grey's unexpected flattery, his praise made her heart soar.

"You are full of surprises." His eyes locked on her, daring her to look away.

Not knowing what else to do, and unable to handle his nearness a moment longer, Rachel jumped up from her log seat.

"I suggest we join the others," she said. "It looks as though Father Huntley is about to make an announcement." Fidgeting, she waited for Grey to rise.

"Well, we certainly mustn't miss the Father's announcement," he added. The intimate moment had passed.

Grey uncoiled his legs and stood up. Using the tree trunk to balance the supper box, he bent and repacked it. When he'd finished, he turned toward Rachel, the ribbon and marigolds in his hand.

Bowing from the waist, he presented her with the small nosegay. "My lady."

"You keep them," she countered. "You paid for them."

The gallant display made her feel sillier still, but Rachel wasn't certain what bothered her more—his deed, or his reference to "my."

Seizing the upper hand, Grey responded with an exaggerated smile. "Very well, I will."

He then tucked the pitiful-looking bouquet into a buttonhole on his shirtfront and winked. Then with the supper box placed firmly beneath one arm, Grey offered Rachel his free one and led her back toward the gathering. Rachel's fingers, resting in the crook of Grey's elbow, burned from the contact.

They located Tully and Miss Purdy, and the foursome stood together exchanging pleasantries while waiting for the priest to begin his speech. But Rachel paid little attention to the chitchat around her. All she could think of was how handsome the harbormaster looked with her weakened marigolds resting a few inches below his strong chin.

"Ladies and gentlemen, may I have your attention, please." Father Huntley's voice lifted above the noisy conversation.

He stood upon the same crate the auctioneer had used earlier. A hush fell over the crowd. "My good friends, we just tallied up our money, and we've raised eighty-three dollars this evening."

Cheers rumbled throughout the group. With over fifty boxes put up for bid, the fundraiser had been a success. Suddenly Rachel remembered her real reason for attending this function tonight. She had another donation to add to the fund.

"Oh, my, I completely forgot," she mumbled. She

114

reached inside her *grosgrain* bag and withdrew her small roll of bills.

Miss Purdy, Tully, and Grey looked at the money she clasped in her hand.

Rachel looked over at them. "I have a donation . . . from some of my patients."

"Patients?" Miss Purdy's eyes became sharp and assessing. Tully and Grey stood mutely, studying what looked like a small fortune in Rachel's palm.

Everyone attending the fundraiser tonight knew the kinds of patients Doctor Rachel Thomas treated. And although this was a charitable function, most present would be far from impressed to hear that her patients had contributed to the fund.

Just as Rachel started forward to present her gift, Miss Purdy's hand restrained her. "Child, do you think it wise that you stand up before this crowd of lions and announce your benefactors?"

"But . . . I don't see what difference it makes," Rachel answered.

The older woman still restricted Rachel's movement. "Why don't you let me handle this for you?" she encouraged her.

Rachel hesitated, searching Miss Purdy's face. The money she intended to donate didn't come from her patients per se, but from the ladies of Swilltown. Were their contributions to be considered tainted because of who they were . . . victims of a society's prejudice?

She realized the wisdom of the older woman's words, but in Rachel's eyes, everyone was created equal. And as she'd learned from Opal, some people did what they had to do in order to survive. Just because these narrow-minded folk didn't approve of her clientele, the money the "brides" had donated would buy the same amount of food and supplies that theirs would.

Tully and Grey looked anxiously between the two women, their own expressions now doubting the prudence of Rachel's avowal before everyone present today.

"Girl, it might not be wise," Tully offered.

"Please, Rachel," Miss Purdy implored, "let me handle this."

Rachel shifted nervously on her feet, her gaze drifting from one to another. She knew her donors expected no recognition for their generosity, but only wished to help those who needed help. Her decision made, she pressed the bills into Martha Purdy's hand.

"Bless you, child," the older woman whispered.

Miss Purdy elbowed her way through the onlookers. With her hand waving above her head and her voice carrying above the noise, she called, "Father, wait, please. I need to speak with you."

The babble abated while everyone stood waiting to learn what Miss Purdy wanted that was important enough to interrupt the proceedings. Several minutes passed as Miss Purdy and the cleric conferred. Everyone strained to hear what was being said. Then Father Huntley again stood tall above his listeners.

"Ladies and gentlemen, it has been brought to my attention that a very generous donation has been made to our cause." More rumblings rolled throughout the interested crowd. "It seems that Doctor Rachel Thomas has taken it upon herself to donate one hundred fifty dollars to the Women's Aid Society." Several titters floated across the lot, but Father Huntley was not one to be deterred by rudeness. He quieted them with a scolding look.

"She wishes to do this in memory of her late father, Doctor Theodore Thomas, whom we all knew and respected. To remind us all of her father's dedication to the people of this town and his unwavering concern for all people, especially those less fortunate than ourselves."

Soft mumbling spread across the crowd. Several people searched out Rachel where she waited between Grey and Tully. Rachel stood tall, her expression never wavering. Some of the attendees looked toward her with compassion and understanding, while others were noncommittal.

Then, from the back of the group someone started clapping. Everyone was drawn to the hollow sound. The crowd parted, revealing her old friend, Sarah Ballard. The young woman stood beside her husband applauding, in spite of the severe looks he rained down upon her. Briefly, Rachel and Sarah's eyes met and understanding coursed between them. And Rachel knew at that moment that Sarah Ballard would become her patient.

Others in the crowd, seeing one of their own showing support for the lady doctor, took up the applause. Father Huntley's mood became exuberant. From his pedestal, he motioned for Rachel to approach him. "Come, child . . . come, come. Everyone here appreciates your charity."

Rachel came forward, her steps feeling lighter than they had since she'd been back in Astoria. When she reached the cleric's side, he placed one hand upon her shoulder and raised the other in supplication.

"Let us bow our heads in prayer," his rich baritone voice intoned.

Silence fell upon the group. While they prayed, Rachel bowed her head, allowing the peace of Father Huntley's prayer to calm the raging conflicts inside her. By coming here tonight, she felt a small door open to her. And although she wasn't certain of the outcome, Rachel knew she'd taken a step in the right direction.

With the prayer finished, Father Huntley continued. "Miss Purdy tells me that Doctor Rachel makes a trip to the logging camps once a month to see those in need of medical attention. I propose, therefore, we send our contributions with her. Who knows better than she the best way to put the money to use?"

Everyone acknowledged his suggestion with another round of applause.

"I'm going Monday," Rachel said, caught up in the crowd's enthusiasm. "I'll be happy to take the contributions with me. There are so many who will benefit from your generosity."

In the following moments, Rachel shook so many hands she thought her arm might fall off.

Someone had tuned up a fiddle and the sound of a stringed waltz floated throughout the square. Men and women chose partners to take a turn across the grass. Brothers and sisters, playmates and enemies, grandmas and grandpas all joined in the dancing.

Rachel removed her spectacles and placed them in her purse. Nothing more would be expected of her tonight besides chatting with those who approached, and for the first time since she'd returned home she found herself acutely conscious of wanting to look her best.

From where she stood on the sidelines beside Father

Huntley, she saw Tully and Miss Purdy glide by, then Sarah Ballard slowly following the lead of her ramrod-stiff husband. She searched the makeshift dance floor for Grey, but he was nowhere to be seen.

"May I have this dance?"

Warm fingers encircled her arm from behind. Recognizing his low, gravelly voice, Rachel turned to face Grey.

"I don't dance," she replied, uncertain if he could hear her declining over the knocking of her knees.

"Why, Doctor Thomas, you told me just yesterday that you and Cal often danced together." Amusement flickered in his eyes.

"When I was a young girl and cared about such things," she reminded him.

"Would you consider being that young girl again . . . for me?"

"I don't see that well, especially in low light." Without her glasses, Rachel feared embarrassing them both with what might end up a bungling attempt at dancing. But as she looked at Grey's face, his damnable dimple caved in his left cheek, crumbling any further arguments.

Grey steered her toward the others. "It will be easy, I promise. I'll lead. All you'll have to do is follow." He whispered in his thick, husky voice, "Close your eyes and pretend I'm Cal." He beamed down at her.

"You have the same smile," she countered. He aptly whirled her around the floor.

"But, I still have all my teeth," he reminded her.

This brought a barrage of laughter from Rachel, and with it her fears tumbled away on the wind. And his advice worked. Rachel tried closing her eyes. To her

119

amazement she found her dance partner quite easy to follow. He was tall and commanding enough to guide her every step. His protective arm kept her balanced, and with each beat of the music her confidence grew.

Pretty is as, pretty is as. . . . Opal's words beat in rhythm with the waltz as they circled the floor with the others. But when Rachel opened her eyes and saw the animated expression on Grey's face, she felt Opal's philosophy didn't set true with the harbormaster.

In the last few days, Rachel had seen glimpses of the inner man that she never expected existed—his kindness when he rescued her from the drunk, his recommendation of her medical prowess to his landlady, and lastly, his insistence that he take over the walking of Miss Purdy's dog so the older woman wouldn't be out alone at night.

And although Rachel wasn't ready to trust Grey Devlin completely, she sensed that if his perfect outer shell were peeled away, what lay beneath might blind her with its beauty.

Pretty is as, pretty is as. . . . Rachel found that dancing with Grey was not as hard as she had suspected it would be. He was an accomplished dancer.

"If you'd allow me, I'd like to go along with you when you go to the camps," Grey announced.

Rachel nearly missed a step. "Why ever for?" she asked, her usual frankness rising.

"Because a harbormaster needs to learn as much as he can about the cargo that affects his jurisdiction. This would give me a good excuse to see logging from the source, to know what to expect when it comes down-river for shipment."

Was this the same man who'd allow an opium shipment to slip into port unnoticed?

Rachel worried over the comparison. A man who claimed to take such an interest in his job wouldn't have allowed such an error.

"With you acting as my guide," Grey continued, "it would certainly make my job easier. I've never been into any of the camps, but I've toyed with the idea of a visit for some time now. Since you know many of the loggers, maybe you could introduce me to the camp bosses, open up doors that might otherwise be closed to a stranger."

The music ceased and Grey led Rachel to the sidelines. She wasn't certain that she wished to spend a whole day alone in the company of Grey Devlin. Besides, he could have an ulterior motive for wanting to accompany her to the camps.

Rachel dug for an excuse to refuse him. "But as harbormaster, doors would automatically be open to you, with or without my presence."

"I'm still considered an outsider in these parts."

Earlier this evening Grey had seen how uncomfortable Rachel felt with him. Throughout dinner, she'd avoided eye contact and held herself aloof when he'd tried flirting with her. But when it came to her profession, she was a very independent woman. She would not take kindly to his expressing concern for her safety.

Grey liked the lady doctor, even more than he cared to admit. Since her attack the other night in Swilltown, he found himself worrying about her. After all, beneath her starch and vinegar, she was only a woman and shouldn't be tracking about all hours of the day unescorted. He pinned her with his stare, waiting for an answer.

But Rachel still wasn't ready to agree. "My canoe is very small, and what about your backside?"

"Let me worry about my backside," Grey grumbled beneath his breath. He still had trouble accepting her as a doctor, and her knowing about the injury to his private parts. But not wishing to lose his argument, Grey quickly sought another means of persuasion.

"You might need a second party along. Especially since you'll be carrying such a large sum of money with you. I'm not saying anything is going to happen, but wouldn't you hate to have someone steal all that money? Then what would happen to those poor destitute families?"

"Why, I never thought of that," Rachel replied honestly. "But no one has ever bothered me before. Why should they now?"

"I'm sure all these people here are honest folk, but you know how news travels in a wild port town." Grey felt as though he'd scored a victory, so he pushed forward. "Could be someone out there might feel they need that money more than someone else."

Rachel appeared to be weakening. He could almost see the wheels inside her head spinning as she weighed his words. Finally she responded.

"Very well, Mr. Devlin. Under the circumstances, I'll agree for you to come along. But I leave here before sunup and return well after sundown. Are you up to such a schedule?"

"I'll be there with bells on," he replied, glad that he'd convinced her of the wisdom of his argument.

If anything unforeseen happened to Rachel, Grey would be around to help. But at one of the camps he had other things to attend to. Escorting Rachel Thomas would also give him the excuse to seek out his own answers about Frank Ballard's activities.

"Mr. Devlin, it's getting late and I have an early day tomorrow if I'm to leave Monday. If you'll excuse me, I'll see Father Huntley, then be on my way."

"Then I'd be honored to see you home. We can talk more about our excursion."

"That won't be necessary," Rachel replied. "And this excursion you speak of so lightly will certainly not be an enjoyable outing for either of us."

Grey pretended to be humbled with his choice of words. "Strictly a charitable mission," he confirmed. "But I would like to talk with you further about it."

"Oh, very well," Rachel agreed. She looked at him peculiarly but didn't argue with his request to escort her home. Stating their brief goodbyes, they started down the street to Rachel's house.

Purple, salmon, and gold tinted the early morning as the two lone travelers in a small canoe made their way up the Columbia River. Daylight spilled from the brightening sky, weaving its gilded rays through the tall firs that lined the riverbanks and hilltops like sentinels standing at attention.

A crisp, cool breeze whispered off the distant mountains, perfuming the morning air with a scent that smelled more like Christmas than early April. The tattoo of a woodpecker's beak echoed throughout the forest and a meadowlark's gurgling joined in the early morning muster.

Grey dipped the paddle into the glassy water, moving their small craft up the waterway. A scowling Rachel sat facing him from the bow of the canoe, having reluctantly relinquished her place in the stern, along with the paddle, to Grey.

There was no way in hell he was going to allow a woman to row him up the river like some highborn river king. Even though he'd invited himself to come along on this trip—a fact which Rachel had repeatedly reminded him of—there were some things that a man just didn't do. And having a woman row him up the river was one of them.

Only his constant badgering about the money's safety had kept Rachel from setting off on her own. They'd reached a stand-off, neither one of them willing to give in to the other. After thirty minutes of arguing, and with Grey consenting to take turns at the paddle after they'd cleared the wharf, Rachel had finally agreed.

"Nice morning," he offered, hoping to break the strained silence between them.

Rachel sat ramrod straight on the seat in front of him. And for all the attention she'd given to his overture of peace, he might as well have been a ledge on one of the surrounding mountains. But Grey was not one to be thwarted, so he plunged on.

"It's been a while since I rode in a canoe," he offered.

"Another reason why you should have let me take charge."

He dipped his face toward his lap, not wanting Rachel to see the smile he was having difficulty holding back. At least they were making some headway. She no longer brooded in silence.

"How do you think it would have looked for the

harbormaster to be paddled away form the wharf by a woman?'' he asked her.

"Frankly, I couldn't care less how it would look,'' Rachel was quick to respond. "It seems you've forgotten this is my craft, my supplies, and my patients we are going to see.''

Rachel paused to catch her breath. "And, need I remind you, I've made this trip many times without your company. In truth, I rather enjoy my solitary wanderings.''

"Are you always this cheerful in the morning?'' Grey asked, dipping the paddle on the left side of the boat to steer them closer to the bank. He didn't want to be so far out in midstream that they risked the chance of being caught in a logjam.

When they'd met at the pier, her appearance had reminded him of her plain-wrapped supper box of Saturday night. She looked functional but dull as gully dirt in her brown split skirt and matching jacket. Her wool cloak was of the same drab color. Her glorious hair was tucked beneath a straw hat that looked as though part of it had been a goat's supper. It was difficult to imagine the woman as the same beauty he'd rescued from the drunk, or the same one he'd held in his arms at the box social.

"Did anyone ever tell you you're as contrary as a set-down jackass?'' he asked her.

Grey thought he noticed the beginnings of a smile on Rachel's lips before she lowered her head. He bent lower, trying to see beneath the floppy hat brim that concealed her face. Then he heard it. That deep, warm, rich laugh that made his insides turn to jelly. And his outside—one place in particular—turn hard.

"Only my father, and I've never heard that expression used by anyone but him." Her resentment vanished and she laughed as though she were really amused. "And the funny thing is, I know it's the truth."

"Take pride in it, do you?" Grey asked, glad that they were talking again.

"Maybe just a little."

Rachel's throaty laughter carried in the light breeze and joined with the caw of a crow perched in a nearby tree.

"Are we friends again?" Grey asked.

"I suppose so, since we're stuck together for the duration of this trip."

"Good. Then, friend, help yourself to an apple in my knapsack and hand me one. I've already worked up an awful hunger." Inwardly he couldn't hide the admiration for a woman who would undertake such an arduous journey on her own. Hers couldn't be an easy life.

Rachel took advantage of one last jab. "Well, if you hadn't decided to work so hard . . . " She reached into Grey's bag and pulled out red apples. She laid one on the seat beside him. "I see you brought yesterday's newspaper . . . ", she opened the sack wider, ". . . and books. I didn't know you liked to read." She sounded surprised.

Grey gave an extra pull on the paddle and locked onto her questioning gaze. "There's a lot you don't know about me." He passed her an easy grin. "The books are only for the moments when you don't need me. I certainly don't want to get in your way." His teasing wink brought on another smile and he couldn't take his eyes from Rachel's face.

"You should smile more often, Doc," he said,

thinking what a pretty face lay beneath her easy scowl. At his words, Rachel shifted in her seat and looked out over the water, obviously uncomfortable with his compliment. Noting her reaction, he added offhandedly, "Takes years off a body."

She did have a pretty smile now that her earlier smugness had disappeared. It lit up her entire face and creased the corners of her eyes into laugh lines that made him want to smile back. Even with her spectacles. As homely as he had first thought them, it surprised him that he hadn't noticed her glasses before now. He decided then that he had picked them for his target of disdain when all the time it had been the woman's haughty treatment of him.

When he saw her like this, relaxed and with a teasing ring in her voice, Grey knew there was more to the doctor than she cared to reveal.

"Now tell me about the camps we're going to visit."

She deliberated for a moment. "Only one today but, in my opinion, the worst. You remember Mr. Ballard? He owns it."

Rachel remembered that Ballard had spurred Grey away to introduce him to some of his associates. Just how friendly the two were she didn't know, but she'd find out soon enough. When it came to human suffering, Rachel believed in speaking the truth.

"He runs Camp Ross, the worst in the district. He pays the poorest wages, and his company store's goods are so expensive that most of the wages earned by his employees go right back into Mr. Ballard's pocket. You have to understand that the families that live in the camps buy most of their staples from the camp stores. Getting to town is too difficult for them."

She paused, searching Grey's face for a response, but it was unreadable. So she continued.

"Most of the camps supply a fund to families whose husbands are injured, until they can return to work. But not so in Ballard's camp. When the men are injured, Chinese laborers are brought in to replace them. If a man can't work, he loses his home and his credit. And if a woman's husband disappears—not uncommon in Astoria—she is put out of her home, or charged such an exorbitant rent for her shack that she can't stay there. The sad part is that most of these women have no skills, and some have families to feed."

"Hence the fundraising."

"Yes, and the money also helps others in other ways. Some of these families are very large with many young ones. It takes more to feed the children than their husbands make."

Having a baby every year not only strained the family income but wore out the overworked women as well. Rachel didn't mention that educating women of child-bearing age was as much of her practice as caring for expectant mothers.

As the canoe made its way upriver, the woods came alive with the sounds of industry. Chopping, sawing, shouting, and the thundering crash of the giant firs smashing into the ground echoed throughout the forests. Flumes, chutes, and holding dams were visible along the banks, clear signs of logging activity in the area.

"We're almost there," Rachel said. "Soon you will see the dock where we'll tie up." She pointed to a small inlet, then directed Grey's attention across the span of water to where dozens of trees lay in a log dump, waiting to be floated down the river.

"I'd hate to meet them on a dark night!" Grey shouted above the increasing din of activity.

Rachel smiled an acknowledgment. "The only thing good about Ballard's camp is his cook. At least, he does one thing right. He's smart enough to know that a cook can make or break a camp. These men work hard, long hours and require a lot of nutrition. If the food isn't good, those not trapped in debt to the company store will move to a camp where it is."

Grey's stomach rumbled at the thought of food. His early morning breakfast had long since left him, and the apple had whetted his appetite. Four hours of paddling had made him very hungry. "You think he'll feed me?"

"I'm sure she will, if you tell her you're with the doctor."

"She? You mean the cook is a woman?"

The boat thudded to a stop against the pilings. Rachel hurried to secure the front end of the canoe. Then she carefully stepped onto the low dock and waited for Grey to tie up the other end. He handed her her medical bag along with a container of supplies and other provisions she'd brought.

"I'll be busy most of the day with my patients," she said. She bent to gather up her belongings. "When I'm finished I'll meet you at the cook house, probably around five o'clock."

"Don't you want some help?" He pointed to the bundle in her arms. "Or maybe want to eat first, or introduce me to the cook?"

"I'm not hungry now, and I have much to do. When Blossom gets one look at you, that's all the introduction you'll need. See you." Rachel turned and started up

129

the hill, then turned back to face him. "That big building over there is the cook house."

"You mean the one with the sign that says 'Cook House'?"

Rachel nodded her head, smiling, then hurried up the path.

Well, Grey thought, this is just great. Deserted in the middle of a Clatsop County timber camp. He hadn't expected to be abandoned the minute they set foot on shore. He slung his pack over his shoulder and looked around, taking in the layout of the camp.

It didn't look like much. Crude wooden bunkhouses lined the perimeter on one side. Dilapidated cottages, not much more than shacks, lined the other, cresting the hill before him, probably meeting the path Rachel had taken. A similar sign to the one over the cook house labeled another building "Camp Store." Beside the camp store, under a lean-to, four men sharpened blades on huge grinding wheels. From the next building came the constant "tink, tink" of a smithy's hammer. Behind one of the shacks, three small children played near a woman hanging out her wash.

Grey was surprised to see so little activity. But where people were few, sounds were many, echoing from the surrounding mountains. Axes thwacked, saws rasped, and trees cracked and crashed in their fall to earth. He knew as soon as the whistle blew the place would be filled with starving lumberjacks.

The smell of coffee and other aromas floated across the clearing, making Grey's mouth water. As hungry as he was, the cook house was as good a place as any to begin his investigation. He went in search of the cook named Blossom.

Chapter 7

Grey entered the cook house door and closed the door lightly behind him. Before him three rows of wooden tables, covered in black oilcloth, took up the length of a large mess hall. Place settings were lined up along the tables—cups, bowls, and plates, each inverted upon the other. Wooden benches stood beside the tables, with enough room to seat perhaps fifty men. Sunshine spilled in through glassed windows on both sides of the room, giving it a bright, airy feeling.

Through a door in the back of the room came the clatter of pans and a commanding voice that carried the finesse of a field marshal. "Libby, throw that slab of bacon in the pot. I'll get to it in a minute. Greta, those beans ready yet?"

The door swung open and a burly woman came barging through, carrying the largest coffee pot Grey had ever seen. Her salt-and-pepper hair was pulled into a thick braid which hung down her back. Her heavy face hinted at years of sampling her own cooking. And her once-white apron, now faded to a dull gray, wore food stains like a badge of honor.

She stopped when she saw Grey. "Well, what we got here? A new sign-on?" She laid the pot down on a sideboard and glanced at the watch pinned to her shirt. "Mister, you got less than one hour to get checked in, learn what your job is, find an empty bunk, wash up, and get back here. That whistle goes off at twelve sharp, and if you ain't here on time, you'll be workin' on an empty stomach."

She started back to the kitchen. "We got three rules around here—wash your hands, no talking at meal-time, and don't be late."

Grey stood, transfixed, as the woman made her point. Obviously, he had found Blossom. "I'm not here to work—"

"Hah!" the woman roared, interrupting any further explanation. "Well, if you ain't come to the wrong place." She lowered her voice to a harumph. "Unless you're one of them night shift fellas, in which case you got all afternoon to do nothin'." Her tone, if it could have been taken for warm, now cooled significantly. "But unless you're bound for a bunk and a pillow, you gotta feed your face, too." She drove her message home, clarifying that in this place she was in charge. "Just be back here when that whistle goes off."

"But, I'm—"

"What?" She looked him over as though he were a simpleton. "You tongue-tied or somethin'? You got somethin' to say, just spit it out. I ain't got all day."

Grey rushed out his words before the woman could disappear back into her kitchen. "I'm with the doctor. The name's Devlin."

The cook's face took on a bright Sunday school expression. "Well, glory be, man, why didn't you say so in the first place?'' She wiped her hands on her apron and pranced down a row of tables toward him. ''Any friend of Doc Thomas's is a friend of mine.'' She pumped his hand hard in genuine welcome.

He returned her hearty greeting. ''You must be Blossom. Doc Thomas speaks highly of you and I can see why. This place smells like somebody's grandmother's house on Thanksgiving.''

''Oh, go on with you.'' Blossom swatted the air with her fleshy hand. ''You wouldn't be tryin' to charm me, now would you?''

Grey gave her his most engaging smile. ''I was hoping I might be able to get a bite. The doc and I set out pretty early this morning.''

''Well, set yourself down and have some coffee.'' She yelled back to the kitchen. ''Libby, bring our friend here some fresh brew. And pile up a plate of stew and baked beans.'' She gave Grey an assessing look. ''And see if the cornbread's done. This man needs some meat on his bones.''

''That's mighty nice of you,'' Grey said, settling on one of the benches. ''I don't want to impose.''

''Impose? Try scrubbin' all them up after dinner every day . . .'' She pointed to large cooking pots hanging from a ceiling rack at the end of the room. ''And then havin' to start over at nine in the evening to feed a third shift when everyone else is done his chores.'' She shook her head. ''Now that's what I call imposin'. But I guess it's worth it.''

A tall, thin woman appeared with a plate piled so high with food that Grey knew he'd never finish it all. She set it down before him, then returned with a steaming cup of coffee. The woman accepted Grey's

133

thanks with a courteous nod and light smile, but said nothing. In a moment she was gone, back to the preparations for the noon meal.

"Now you eat," Blossom ordered, "and when you're finished you can take a plate to the doc."

Grey picked up his fork and tackled a potato. "Thanks, but she seemed eager to get to work. Said she wasn't hungry just yet. Mind if I wander around when I'm finished? Then when the men have eaten, I'll come pick up a plate and take it to her."

"You do that." Blossom stood against the open kitchen door. "And if anybody gets nosy and wants to know what yer doin' around here, just tell 'em I sent you." She mumbled just loud enough for Grey to hear. "Ain't none of those bosses' business anyway." She pointed a warning finger. "Just stay out of the way of where they're fellin'. No need in you bein' one of Doc Thomas's patients, too." With that she disappeared into the kitchen, the door swinging shut behind her.

Grey chuckled at the robust woman and her statement. And the recent picture of himself floating naked in a life ring at the doc's own doing.

The shriek of the lunchtime whistle called a halt to work. Grey made his way along the road toward the timber that was being harvested for market, passing men covered in shavings and mud, dressed in pants that didn't quite hit their ankles. Though he'd never before entered a logging camp, he had prepared for this day by reading everything he could get his hands on about logging—at first because he was curious about Ballard's latest enterprise, then because of the sense of adventure that went with the job. Everything up here had a purpose. Even the little-boy look of the men's trousers—to prevent snagging on tree roots and low branches.

These men took every precaution they could to keep injury at bay. From their conversations in the saloon he'd learned they had enough trouble just looking out for the "widow makers," high branches that often gave way when a tree fell, or from "kickbacks" when a tree bucked on its own stump and toppled in the wrong direction. These men were lean and wiry, all sweat and sinew—not a fat one among them—and from the energy they burned, Grey could see why.

He followed the rutted tracks through the giant Douglas firs until he came upon a clearing. Standing on the outskirts, he marveled at the mighty labor that the lumberjacks had already accomplished. Here, for every fifty trees still standing lay one fallen soldier, as if Paul Bunyan himself had stepped through the woods, downing trees under his massive boots. Some of the logs had been chained and now rested upon a long skidroad—greased cross logs imbedded into the ground. Eight bull oxen, yoked by twos, waited patiently to pull the next load to the river.

Whipsaws, ten feet long, sat balanced in trees eight or so feet above the ground, ready to sever the lifeblood from their existence. Grey had heard tales of severe injuries just from men carrying these saws to their worksite, balancing the great lengths while the saws jumped around on their shoulders at the slightest movement. At the same height, three-foot long spring-boards stood wedged into the trees, waiting for the jacks to climb upon them to complete their amputation.

From what Grey could determine, Ballard's logging company probably hired upwards to eighty men at a time, working from first light to last. But Grey could not shake Blossom's mention of a night crew. Without bright lights strung throughout the forest, no one could see his hand in front of his face to do anything productive after dark.

Rachel had told him these people were hard workers and low-wage earners, and most of them honest. From what Grey knew about Frank Ballard, he couldn't imagine the man running a camp just for the usual profits generated by the other companies. It wasn't Ballard's style. That man was up to something.

Grey had learned the hard way that Frank Ballard would do anything to earn a goldpiece and save his own hide. He'd made that clear enough. To this day Grey still felt a catch in his stomach at his own naiveté when the former ship owner, in covering his own bungled smuggling attempt, had pointed the finger at his young captain. If it took Grey the rest of his life, he would bring down the scoundrel and everything he stood for. And right now he aimed to find out why Frank Ballard had turned to logging.

Making his way along the skidroad, Grey came to the river. Several giant logs, stripped of their branches and bark, lay tied together against the shore. Before the day was over, others would follow. And by first light tomorrow, the entire boom would be headed downstream. In looking at this process of harvesting and shipping, Grey still couldn't forget Blossom's words. What good was a night crew in this type of operation?

Grey looked at his watch. The forest was coming alive

again with the sounds of industry. It was time to make his way back to the cook house and pick up Rachel's lunch plate. She was bound to be hungry by now.

When he arrived, Blossom was waiting for him at the open door with a cup of coffee in her hand. "Saved the doc a big helpin' of stew," she announced. "But first, come on in and have a piece of pie. And I want to hear what's new in town."

Grey accepted her offer and they both sat at a cleared-off table, Blossom asking one question after another. "Don't get to chat with the people from town much. And by the time we get a newspaper up here, it's old news."

"Maybe not so old this time," Grey responded. He reached into his knapsack and pulled out the *Astorian* from the day before. "Here," he said. To thank you for your hospitality."

Blossom looked at the paper as though she'd been handed a birthday gift. "Well, thank you." Then she laid it aside to resume her visit. "Did you learn anything while you were out wandering?"

"From the size of those trees I can well imagine how hard these men work. They have my sincerest admiration."

"Yep," Blossom answered, "and mine. They work from six in the morning till they can't see at night. From 'can to can't,' we call it. And they do it without a lot o' complainin'." She gave a hearty laugh. "At least I don't hear the complaints. Not about the food anyway." She leaned closer. "That's why I don't let

137

'em talk in the cook house. If they can't talk, they can't complain.''

Grey joined in the woman's laughter. He wrapped his hands around his cup and leaned closer. "Mind if I ask you a couple of questions?''

"Shoot. What you want to know?''

"Well, for one thing, I saw some children behind one of the cottages. Are there many up here?''

Blossom counted on her fingers. "Eleven, counting the newborn down at the Olsons'.'' She gestured toward the row of shacks.

Grey shook his head. "I wouldn't have guessed the men would have their families up here.''

"Most of 'em don't. A lot of the families live around Rainwater, near the sawmill. Little more civilized down there. But for what you get, you gotta give. These men are in the woods for weeks at a time. That means they don't see their kin but a few times a year, unless they move on. Four of the men chose to bring their wives and younguns with 'em.''

She nodded her head in resignation. "Not much up here for the little ones, but they manage. Sometimes I let the older ones help slop my pigs or set the tables.''

"Do they get any schooling?''

"Not what their mamas don't teach 'em. They'd have to quit anyway by the time they hit fourteen. That's when the bosses put the boys on the line.''

Grey couldn't believe his ears. "Fourteen? But that's men's work out there. They could get hurt.''

Blossom acknowledged his comment with a curt nod. "They can and they do. But their wages bring in a little more for each family, and that helps pay toward the company store debt.''

Grey knew his disbelief had not been lost on the cook. "Think of it this way," she said. "If Papa gets hurt, at least the family's still got income. Could be worse."

"I suppose," Grey answered, still enraged that a young boy, hardly out of short pants, should be required to put his life on the line for Frank Ballard's profits, or anyone else's if this was common practice.

"You said you got a few questions," Blossom pursued. "What's the next?"

Grey was glad to change the subject. "You said you have a night crew. It's got to be pitch black out there after dark. What kind of work can be done without light?"

Blossom finished off her cup of coffee and poured herself and Grey more from an enamel pot. "You'd be surprised" was the woman's answer. "Now there's a group of how-do-you-do's for you. There's only a few, but between you and me they get paid top dollar. And they're the uppitiest bunch of scrappers around. Got their own bunkhouse and bath shed. You'd think they was royalty. Don't much care for 'em myself, but there's where the boss has one-upped the competition. Did you see the logs ready to be sent down the flume?"

"I did. I figured they'd go at early light tomorrow."

"Not so. That's when the other companies will be sending theirs down. Ours will be headed down tonight."

"After dark?"

"Sure. They're locked together tight as a tick and it only takes a few men with lanterns and their sharp-pointed peaveys to guide them along. By morning, when the others are jamming the river trying to get

139

their logs downstream, ours are already at the sawmill or sittin' in the harbor, waiting to be shipped out.'' She clapped her hands together, smug that Camp Ross had thus far outwitted the competition.

By the time Grey found Rachel she had gathered a following. Children from the various households had accompanied her along the way, carrying her supplies and eagerly awaiting their rewards of bright red stick candy. They now stood in front of one of the last bunkhouses, shushing one another and preaching that the injured men inside needed to have peace and quiet.

Grey stepped past the children with Rachel's dinner plate. When he opened the bunkhouse door, the stench of sweat and tobacco juice mingled with the musty odor of work clothes. Bunks stacked two-high and mattressed with cedar boughs, lined the walls and filled the center of the floor, leaving little room for their occupants to crawl in and out.

At the ends of the beds, wooden-legged deacon benches were placed, affording the only seating in the bunkhouse. Canvas pants—some smeared with grease, others with tar—stood in the corners of the room. The same pants, the same bunks, the same odors that Grey recognized from many a ship he'd sailed on. Life and men were much the same everywhere.

Six men lay upon their bunks and Rachel her shirtsleeves rolled to her elbows, stood at a table, pouring water from a large metal pitcher into a basin. Her medical bag lay on a towel beside her. She looked up when Grey entered the room.

"Hi, Doc," he greeted her. "I brought you some

food. Thought you might be hungry.'' He set the plate down on a bench.

Rachel was now bareheaded and the shorter ends of her hair had escaped their confining braid. In the low light her coloring was soft and subdued and Grey caught himself staring at her. She'd put in long hours already without stopping and still somehow looked as fresh as morning dew. He marveled at this woman who gave so much and asked so little in return.

''That's very kind of you, Mr. Devlin. I'd forgotten how hungry I was.''

Rachel introduced Grey to the men in the cabin. They were friendly enough, but he could tell a couple of them were in a fair amount of pain. One man's leg was wrapped in bandages from his foot to his knee.

''What happened to you, friend?'' Grey asked.

''Confounded whipsaw tried to take my leg off on Friday.'' He looked over at his bunk mate. ''I told ole Simpkins to never start working in a new area on a Friday. Somethin' always happens when you do, you can count on it. 'Monday,' I told him. 'That's when you start new pickin's.' He oughta know that by now.''

Rachel gave Grey a light wink. ''Some people might call this superstition.'' She smiled at the bandaged man. ''But Charlie could be right. After all, look what happened.''

A man in the next bunk chimed in with his own complaint. ''If the danged saw had been sharper, it might not o' taken such a chunk outa yer leg.'' He pointed to his own bandaged thigh. ''Dadgummed dull axe attacked me.'' He took a puff from a fresh-rolled cigarette. ''If they'd keep this equipment sharpened, half of this stuff wouldn't happen.''

141

Grey spoke up. "Gentlemen, when I walked up, I saw grinders busy at work."

"Yeh, right," the one man replied. "Only four, I'll bet. In a camp that should have at least a dozen. And you get one grindstone tiltin' wrong, no man's gonna touch it. Bad luck." He snickered. "I tell you, I'm sick o' the bosses cuttin' corners where they shouldn't be cut—won't fix the grindstones. Won't hire enough men. I get back on my feet and I'm gone." The man ground out his frustration.

Rachel began unwrapping the first man's bandages while addressing the second. "Sam, I'm glad you brought that up. Maybe it's high time I spoke my piece to Mr. Ballard. When I get back to town, I'll see if I can have a word with him. It could be he doesn't realize himself some of the problems you've got up here."

"Well," Charlie offered, "you can try. But he don't listen to the men up here. He sure won't be listenin' to the likes of a lady like yerself, no insult intended."

"None taken," Rachel assured him. "But it wouldn't hurt to try, now would it?" She went back to her work, cleaning the man's wounded leg.

Just hearing Rachel express her intent to confront the camp owner sent cold chills through Grey. Braver folk than she had learned long ago not to face Frank Ballard. He was the type who stood for no questioning of his methods. He could make men suffer, even disappear—or land in prison as Grey had. After what Grey himself had suffered at Ballard's hands, his own life would be endangered if the rogue even suspected his motives for being here today. And he had no intention, regardless of her noble purpose, of allowing Ra-

142

chel Thomas to walk into a situation she couldn't control.

"Doc," he offered, trying to divert her attention, "can I give you a hand while you eat?"

Rachel reached for a wet rag. "No, thank you. But I do appreciate your thoughtfulness. I'll get to it shortly. However, you could do me a favor."

"Anything."

"The children so look forward to my visits, but they're still children and they're still noisy." She pointed to a sack inside a carton lying on the floor. "Could you please pass out another round of sour sticks and ask them to play somewhere else?"

Grey nodded. "A favor asked is a favor done." He grabbed his own bag and headed toward the door.

"I'll still see you about five."

"Anytime you're ready, Doc. I'll be waiting."

Two hours later Rachel packed up the last of her medical supplies and wished her bunkhouse patients farewell, handing each a few dollars to cover bed and board until they were again able to return to work. "This is only repayment," she told them when they threatened to balk. "If it weren't for your labor, these communities would never be constructed. You're the ones building our towns, plank by plank. We owe you."

At five o'clock she thought her back might break. Today she'd treated fourteen patients—men, women, and children—and called on nine more. Now they had more than scrip with which to buy their supplies at the company store. Several, if they wished, could settle

143

their debts today and move on. On her next trip up-river, Rachel would distribute more funds in other camps. For now the Women's Aid Society would be pleased to hear she'd accomplished this much this soon with their money.

Rachel closed the bunkhouse door behind her and retrieved her hat and cloak from an outside peg. She removed her glasses, wiped them off with her cotton handkerchief, then replaced them. Starting down the path toward the cook house, she spotted the group of children, not scampering around as they had earlier, but resting around a tree near the blacksmith shop. In their midst, leaning against the trunk, sat her traveling companion, his ankles crossed in front of him. His hair was mussed, as if he'd been running. The children stared at him in rapt attention while Grey read from a book in his lap. All of them, including the grown man, were sucking on sour sticks.

She strolled up and caught Grey's eye as he finished the last page. "Why, Mr. Devlin, you are just full of surprises. I've never seen the children this attentive. What are you reading?"

Grey held up the book for her perusal. *"The Celebrated Jumping Frog of Calaveras County.* I've never met a person yet who didn't like the story." He stood up and brushed off the seat of his pants. "Well, little ones, it's been my pleasure. I hope you enjoyed the book."

The children jumped around and clapped their hands in unison. "Thanks, Mr. Devlin, thanks." They gathered around Rachel. "Can he come again, Doctor Thomas? Can he . . . please?"

Rachel, watching the enthusiastic children, hungry for learning, couldn't keep the smile from her face.

"We'll see, children, we'll see. I'm glad you enjoyed the story. Now hurry home before you all miss dinner."

The children scampered away and Grey slipped his book back into his sack. Taking one of Rachel's parcels, he repeated the children's plea. "Can I, Doc? Can I come again? Please?"

She looked up at him from beneath the broad-brimmed hat. "Oh, Mr. Devlin, you are quite the charmer."

They walked along in silence, Rachel looking up from time to time to watch the breeze playing with Grey's ruffled hair. She wondered just what he and the children had been doing before finally settling down to read.

"I'm surprised you thought to bring a child's book with you."

Grey frowned at her, feeling displeasure at her assumption. "I'll have you know, not that many years ago it started out as the hottest newspaper article up and down the coast of California." He pressed a gentle rejoinder. "And it was *not* because of young readers. You may know a lot about doctoring, but it seems you still have something to learn about Mark Twain."

Rachel gave him a look of remorse for her effontery. "Then my apologies to you and Mr. Twain."

"Accepted."

At the dock the sun was setting low over the water and the wind had kicked up. Rachel reached to untie the canoe from its mooring when a sudden gust sent her hat whipping across the dock and into the water.

The wind unleashed more hair from her confining braid.

Grey dropped the bag he was carrying and plunged to his knees. "I'll get it," he said, stretching his lean body out over the surface. He caught the hat before it had a chance to float out of reach.

Rising, Grey slung the water from the hat and looked at Rachel. "Thank you," she said, reaching out to take it from his hand. Instead, he just stared, his eyes as brilliant as a summer sea, and raised his arms over her head. Rachel blinked to break contact and stayed her hand.

He stepped closer and lowered the hat slowly, adjusting the brim over her mass of escaped curls. But instead of releasing it, he lightly pulled the hat toward him, bringing Rachel with it. "No," he said. "Thank you."

Mere inches from his face, Rachel searched his Viking blue eyes for his meaning and felt her breath catch in her throat. "For what?" she asked.

"For this," he whispered, his lips slowly descending to meet hers. Grey pulled Rachel closer, caressing her mouth with his own.

Rachel felt her eyes close and her body go limp, caught up in the sweet smell of seagrass and the pull of his touch, so new and wonderful. His mouth lingered on hers, his kiss commanding, yet surprisingly gentle.

Just as slowly he backed away. "And for this."

She forced her eyes open, trying to comprehend what he had said. "For what?"

"For bringing me here. For showing me the real you."

Rachel didn't know what to say. No man before him had ever touched her like this, had made her want to be kissed again. She felt the flush of heat streak up her neck.

Grey seemed to grasp her discomfort. His next words became a light tease. "Can I come back, Doc? Please, please?"

Rachel dipped her head to hide her embarrassment. "We'll see, Mr. Devlin. We'll see."

Strolling down Franklin Street, Grey gave the white Chihuahua its lead. He didn't particularly like Miss Purdy's dog, which he thought looked more like a rat than a canine, but walking her pet each evening suited Grey's purpose. It allowed him to pass Rachel's house without looking as though he were spying on her. Which in truth, he was.

After their visit to the lumber camp three nights ago, Grey had been unable to think of anything but the lady doctor. Perhaps if they'd never shared that kiss, he could have wiped her from his mind and concentrated instead on the information he'd learned about Ballard's logging operations. But the memory of their sweet embrace lingered in his thoughts.

At the end of his leash, Tootles yipped at something at the edge of the road before darting back to Grey's side. Shivering nervously at Grey's feet, the dog sought his protection.

"It's okay, boy," Grey consoled him. After a few minutes, the animal ventured on ahead, christening every object he encountered.

Grey would never understand what his landlady saw

in the pint-sized dog. Personally, he preferred a larger breed, one that would be more of a companion, or at least protection for its owner. But Miss Purdy considered this dog family.

As Grey neared the doctor's house on Franklin Street, he saw that light beamed from every window in the house. He paused across the street, permitting Tootles to explore the area, while he searched for a glimpse of Rachel.

When the dog became bored with his sniffing, Grey allowed him to lead him farther down the street, not wishing to appear obvious in his surveillance. But his thoughts lingered at Rachel's house, imagining her inside, possibly tending a patient, or doing whatever lady doctors did in their free time.

Rachel had just stepped to the side of the house to pick a few tulips when she saw Grey walking his landlady's dog down her street. Slipping into the lengthening shadows of darkness, she watched him.

Lately, every time she'd encountered the harbormaster, her body temperature seemed to climb, making her feel flushed and warm all over. This evening in the cooling dusk, her reaction was no different.

He cut a handsome figure in his tan trousers, white shirt, and brown sweater. Even from this distance her eyes were drawn to his muscled thighs, trim waist, and broad shoulders. Rachel had only to close her eyes to recall his own, as blue as the Pacific, and that glorious dimple on his cheek.

Watching the twosome, she wanted to laugh at the picture they rendered—such a big man with such a wee dog. One faulty step from Grey's foot would undoubtedly turn the landlady's pet into a smudge.

But it was this contrast between man and beast that won Rachel's approval. That such a hulking man could show such charity toward the delicate little dog, or be so concerned for Miss Purdy's safety that he'd taken it upon himself to walk her dog nightly. This, along with the memory of him sitting beneath a tree surrounded by children and the kiss the two of them had shared, had turned Rachel's world upside down.

Since that afternoon, Rachel had been unable to think about anything else. At night her dreams were haunted by the memory. By day she'd find herself staring vacantly into space, feeling a whisper of desire pulse through her body. Then she would berate herself for her maidenly display of infatuation.

When she'd dressed as Chinook, hadn't she witnessed first hand Grey's skill with women? His attempt at seducing her had nearly succeeded, and Rachel shuddered when she considered what might have happened if Opal hadn't knocked on the wall when she had. Even then she'd been enamored of the man.

Rachel watched Grey and the dog move down the street without a glance in her direction, convinced that he performed this nightly ritual only because he was concerned for the older woman's safety. The route he took by her house each evening had nothing to do with the kiss they'd shared. Of that she was certain. Their quick peck had surely meant nothing to an experienced and handsome man like Grey Devlin. With this thought reinforced in her mind, Rachel finished her cutting and returned to the security of her house.

* * *

Darkness had completely enveloped the town when Grey and Tootles made their return trip up the street toward Miss Purdy's Boarding House. Grey crossed Franklin Street, his pace slowing as he neared the boundaries of Rachel's yard.

Bending over, he picked up the Chihuahua and stuffed the dog inside his sweater. Tootles settled himself close to Grey's warmth, obviously content to be riding instead of walking.

On prior evenings when Grey had headed back up the street, all the lights on the front of Rachel's house had been extinguished. Tonight her shades had been lowered, but soft light reflected behind the eggshell paper. Her windows glowed like a dance hall. He stiffened, wondering if perhaps she had encountered an unexpected caller.

After confirming that no one watched him, Grey stepped over the low picket fence into Rachel's yard. Her closest neighbors were several vacant lots away, and few people strolled the streets of Astoria after sundown.

Giving the bundle in his sweater a soothing pat, Grey slipped past the porch, then the surgery's front window, and rounded the corner of the house. Here he found large rhododendrons edging the foundation, relieved that he could blend in with their leafy silhouettes. If caught, his reasons for being there would be hard to explain.

Hiding in the huge bushes, Grey examined his motives for trespassing onto Rachel's property. Just what were his reasons for snooping around the doctor's house like a thief in the night? His volunteering to walk Miss Purdy's dog gave Grey the excuse he needed to check on Rachel's safety, but it didn't give him permission to peek in her windows.

His unorthodox behavior, he reasoned, came from his mistrust of Frank Ballard. Not only had Rachel criticized the conditions of Ballard's camp, but she seemed intent since their visit to take it upon herself to challenge those conditions publicly. Tully and he had both agreed that after what had happened to Rachel's father, Rachel herself was at risk. Ballard wouldn't allow her to stir up a hornet's nest, especially if she dared to implicate him in some way.

At the back of the dwelling, Grey paused before a lighted window. It had been raised several inches to allow for the flow of fresh air. From inside, the sounds of a music box stole past the small opening. Grey listened to the mechanical pings as a melody floated outward on the escaping air. Curious, he bent toward the window's crack and peered inside.

By the time his mind registered what his eyes were seeing, he realized he was staring at a lady's boudoir. Rachel's bedroom. Grey jerked upright.

A startled Tootles fidgeted nervously inside Grey's sweater and Grey waited for an accompanying bark. Trying to still his own erratic heartbeat, he whispered reassurances to the dog—visualizing a picture of himself being hauled away to jail and later being labeled the town's Peeping Tom.

A wiser man would have fled, but Grey felt compelled to stay. Glued to his spot in the tangle of rhododendron branches, he summoned the courage to look beneath the window again. This time he caught movement in the room.

Never, if Grey Devlin lived to be a hundred, would he forget the sight that awaited him. It was a scene of sterling clarity that would remain forever etched in his mind, as real as the moment it happened.

As the music box tune blended with her deep, throaty hum, Rachel, her glorious dark hair hanging in wavy disarray down her back, waltzed around the small room with her arms around the bleached bones of Cal. Together they moved in perfect rhythm as though they'd performed this same dance countless times before.

Her voluminous gauzy nightrail swished around her bare feet that looked small and pink against the dark wood floor. Stunned by the vision before him, Grey envied the skeleton's place in Rachel's arms and the warmth of her full bosom pressing against Cal's frigid bones. Rachel's glasses were missing, but her familiarity with the room left no barriers to the dancers. They swirled and dipped like ethereal beings—Rachel's gown resembling a film of cobwebs floating in the flaming light.

Beguiled, Grey watched, wishing himself her dancing partner. Then his thoughts turned on him, slamming against his chest like a smithy's hammer. At that moment Grey knew he could never have the woman behind the windowed wall. Just the sight of the bleached bones in Rachel's arms was a cold reminder of the differences in their backgrounds, differences that could never be surmounted. The educated lady physician would be repelled by the self-taught man who'd been born a bastard to a whore. He turned away.

Grey belonged in the saloons in Swilltown, courting

152

the girls who worked the bawdy houses. The lady doctor in the plain wrapping, who danced with skeletons, belonged in a world Grey Devlin could never be part of.

With the dog nestled beneath his sweater, Grey slipped from his hiding place among the leafy branches and hurried up the road to Miss Purdy's Boarding House.

The crystal table lamps formed a muted glow against the walls of the Ballard front parlor. Sarah Ballard sat in the corner of the velvet Chesterfield, her slippered feet propped on a footstool. She sat in silence, across from her husband, concentrating on the needlepoint in her hand. But in her husband's presence she felt far from relaxed.

For the third time in as many days, Frank Ballard rebuked her support of Rachel at the box social. "I hope, my dear, you are proud of yourself for your unseemly behavior. The only excuse I could find for it was that you aren't yourself these days."

Sarah yanked the needle upward through the heavy linen so fast, she missed the next stitch. "If you didn't want me acting unseemly, Mr. Ballard, you shouldn't have taken me out."

"You know perfectly well why I went and I wasn't about to leave you at home, even though you are as big as a cow."

Sarah refused to let her husband's words pierce her skin. Most women in her condition became teary at the oddest moments. She had vowed to keep her tears at bay almost from the day she and Frank Ballard had married.

During their courtship he had plied her with sweet words and promises. After the marriage he had changed overnight. He turned cold and his words cruel. More than once she had thought he would strike her upon the least provocation. So she had learned to keep her distance and to keep her feelings and opinions to herself. Until Saturday night.

Sarah had been so proud of Rachel. She had loved her dearly during their school years and had missed her terribly after Rachel had gone away to study medicine. Regardless of what her husband thought of her actions, it had felt wonderful standing up for her old friend and hearing others join in.

"I'm going to see her," Sarah said, a touch of nonchalance in her voice.

Frank Ballard looked up from his reading. "Who?"

"Rachel."

"What on earth for?"

"So she can check me over and make sure the baby is all right."

Ballard slammed shut the book he was reading. "You most certainly will not. You have a doctor . . . a good one."

Sarah continued to study her needlepoint. She could think better this way, without having to lift her head and confront her husband's look of censure. "And after tomorrow I'll have a better one."

She could hear his temper rise with his voice, but she was determined to remain calm. She had practiced this conversation over and over for two days. "I'm telling you, husband, that from now on I shall be seen by Doctor Rachel Thomas, whom I respect and admire . . . whether you like it or not. And quite frankly, I don't understand why you would object anyway."

"Because she's a wharf rat just like her father before her. I'll not have my wife in the company of the likes of her. Why, you'll ruin both our reputations."

Sarah felt more exasperated by the minute. "Why, Mr. Ballard, how kind you are with your manners. Until Saturday night, others may have shared your estimable convictions. But not anymore. I'm afraid, husband, that you stand alone." She rethreaded her needle. "And since you mention Rachel's father, I've been meaning to ask you about him. I remember his coming to visit you the afternoon before he disappeared. I'm sure you were the last of us to see him. I don't suppose you'd care to shed any light on that call, would you?"

Ballard gave his wife a warning glance. "Strictly business, my dear, nothing more. But about his daughter, I say this only once more—you stay away from her or I'll—"

"You'll what, Frank? Lock me in my bedroom? Tell the world that I'm not myself? Don't even think it."

Ballard's face had taken on the color of the large ruby ring he wore on his finger. The ring that had belonged to Sarah's grandfather. "That sounds very much like a threat."

"No threat, dear. Just a simple statement." She continued sewing. "The fact of the matter is that I intend for Rachel Thomas to be my physician. If you object, I do not care. If you forbid it, I shall leave you. And I don't think you would dare to risk that."

Sarah could hardly believe what she had just said. But for far too long she had kept her words to herself.

"You think I cannot get along by myself, woman? You married me. That makes you mine, my property, as much as this house and your inheritance. Don't forget that for a moment."

Sarah gave her husband a condescending smile. "Oh, I don't. But I have one thing that will never be yours without me. You're so busy mingling and mixing with all the people who really matter in this town. Do you for one minute think they would even look your way if I were not with you?" She paused to let her words sink in. "No. I didn't think so."

Frank Ballard looked at his wife for the first time tonight. Not through her as he usually could, as though she were a mere speck of dust. The words she had flung at him enraged him like a red cape waved before a bull. She had, in her calm, mousy voice, made him feel impotent.

He had known what he was doing the day he proposed to Sarah Collins. His plan was set. From seaman to shipbuilder to shipowner, he had climbed up and over anyone who got in his way. He had long since formed his goals. Politics was his next step, and he intended to pocket anyone he could on the way to the capitol.

But to accomplish this he needed this millstone around his neck, and the realization made his stomach boil. As a Collins, his wife represented old family, old respectability. She was the key that opened doors to him. And the hammer that could crush him in a single blow.

As much as it riled him to see his wife taking up with Theodore Thomas's daughter, he could see no way of fighting her on this matter. He would humor her . . . for now.

156

Chapter 8

At ten o'clock the next morning, Grey stood in front of his office window, looking out over the harbor. Sloops, schooners, brigs, and barks floated lazily on the glassy water. A medley of masts and rigging cross-hatched reflections on the mirrored surface. Usually this scene calmed his troubled thoughts, but not so this morning.

Grey had managed to get little sleep the night before. When he finally did drift off, his dreams had been invaded by the vision of Rachel dancing, her rich brown hair swirling around her shoulders like a mink mantle.

As the early sun appeared over the eastern mountains, lighting his room with obtuse shadows, Grey had suddenly been overwhelmed with loneliness. He liked Rachel and had wanted to know her better. But after their trip to the camp, the kiss they'd shared, and the feelings she'd stirred deep inside him, Grey knew to entertain such an idea was folly.

Rachel was an educated woman, could probably name every bone in the miserable skeleton she owned.

He, in comparison, learned only from what he saw or read. Moreover, a respectable woman like Rachel Thomas would have little use for a man of his background.

So with a determination he didn't feel, Grey had forced his brain into action and his limbs into motion. He'd learned long ago the best way to forget his problems was to bury himself in his work. And he'd come to the docks this morning to do just that.

He couldn't change who he was or what had happened to him, but he could change Frank Ballard's plans to manipulate people for his own gain. Regardless of how long it took, Grey intended to bring down the man who'd sent him to prison. The same man who'd ruined his chances of ever captaining another ship.

And when his goals were accomplished, he'd leave Astoria and the lady doctor behind.

Stepping outside, Grey closed the door and glanced about. A damp mist hung over the tops of the towering evergreens, and until the sun burned it off, the air would remain cool. Grey nestled deeper into the warmth of his jacket and walked toward the loading area farther down the wharf.

Timber rigging and trestles, waiting to load the next vessel, rose high above the canneries that dotted the piers. The last of the small fishing boats were pulling away—one by one—from the cannery docks. Sea gulls screamed overhead, soaring on a briny current of air that blew landward, others hovering over the outgoing boats. Pausing, Grey watched them for a few moments before continuing on his way.

His thoughts kept reverting to the cook's enthusiasm

over Ballard's competitive brilliance. But a night operation was a puzzle. If it were possible for a crew to work on the murky waterway without mishap, then why didn't the other lumber bosses do the same thing? Most lumbermen shied away from shipping logs by night because of the high risk. But Grey knew Frank Ballard would never put a man's safety above his own greed.

As far as he knew, only log pirates worked under cover of darkness. It allowed them to sneak in and steal from booms that had been roped together waiting to be sent downriver. These stolen logs were then sold to bootleg sawmills or outgoing ships that never questioned where the timber had come from. Was that what Ballard's men were doing?

When Grey neared the landing and scanned the water, he believed without a doubt that Frank Ballard was indeed into log pirating. Timber covered the harbor, much more than would have been cut by now in Ballard's camp.

A rough estimate would put the amount of Douglas fir at more than five thousand board feet, waiting to be loaded onto anchored ships. There was no way in hell the boom Grey had seen in Ballard's camp could have yielded a lot this size. Unless he had a cold deck waiting somewhere else. A pile of logs waiting for transportation was always a possibility. But knowing Ballard, he doubted that. The man would sell everything as fast as it was cut.

Grey squatted beside the mass of floating logs, looking for the identifying mark of their owners. Several that hovered near the dock did have Ballard's brand imprinted on their ends. But it would take more than a few to convince Grey that the others floating farther out in the boom would be the same.

Later that night, Grey stood propped against the bar in Baldy's Saloon, nursing a beer. Tully stood beside him, relating his fish tale to the young man on his opposite side.

"Grandpappy salmon," he heard Tully tell his enraptured audience of one. Grey had heard the fish story so many times, he could have recited it himself. "Biggest dang fish ever caught by a man. He was so large, he pulled me little skiff like an unbroken donkey pulls a cart. His runnin' and buckin' almost made shark bait out of me, I tell you . . ."

Tully's yarn faded into the distance while Grey mulled over his discovery. He had been right about the logs. He'd walked across the floating wood about to be loaded upon the waiting schooners, checking for branding as he went. The brands of two other camps mingled with those of Camp Ross.

He could have easily halted the loading then and there. But Grey couldn't be sure the other timber hadn't come down the flume with their owners' permission. If it had, he'd be responsible for holding up loading and the payment each camp awaited. If, on the other hand, the logs had been pirated, then Grey would be unwise to tackle the problem on his own.

Knowing the mayor to be more puppet than leader, he dared not approach the man with his suspicions. Too much crime ruled the harbor as it was to believe Astoria's mayor had any interest in interfering in Frank Ballad's organization. The man would run to the scoundrel with Grey's complaint, his loyalty insuring him another term in office. Grey not only would ruin his chances of catching Ballard in a criminal act, he would also be risking his own life.

Not that Grey's life was all that precious. He simply wanted to vindicate himself, to prove to himself he was more than the offspring of a whore. Until he had more information on Ballard's operations, it was best not to say anything.

He thumped his empty mug back upon the bar. "How about another round?"

"How many's that?" Tully asked, pinning Grey with his eyes. His captive audience had strolled away in search of more interesting company.

Surprised at his friend's question, Grey shrugged his shoulders. "I don't know—maybe three or four. When the hell did you start monitoring how many drinks I have?"

Tully responded with a harrumph. "Something bothering you? You've been as remote as India ever since you came in here tonight."

Grey watched Baldy refill his glass. "Got a lot on my mind." He stood staring into its golden depths.

"Wouldn't be in the shape of the doctor lady, now would it?"

Grey jerked his head up, surprised by Tully's insight. He forced a laugh. "Hate to disappoint you, old man, but why would I be thinking about the doctor?"

"Only a hunch, mind you. But I ain't wearing blinders. I saw how you outbid them other fellers for her box supper . . . and then that little boat ride you two took up the river. I just thought she might be softening up your hard heart."

"The doctor? You can't be serious." Grey laughed, but it sounded false, even to his own ears. Picking up the mug, he took a big swig of beer. "Rachel Thomas is not my type," he added without so much as a glance at his inquisitor.

"Looked like your type when you waltzed her around the meadow floor the other night." Tully allowed his words to sink in then added, "Wasn't that you I saw accompanying her home later? Or was that some other gent?"

Exasperated, Grey emptied his mug and caught Baldy's eye for a refill. He turned around, propped his elbows on the bar and looked at his longtime friend.

"You'll be the *last* to know, if and when I do get interested in a female. And rest assured, when I do find one that interests me, she won't be as homely as the female doctor."

"Well, good," Tully replied. "I'm certainly glad we got that settled. I feared you were about to tie the knot."

"Tie the knot?" Grey shook his head in disbelief. "Tully, my life is not like one of your fish tales. You can't direct it however you please. I told you long ago I don't believe in the happily ever after."

The unbeckoned image of Rachel with her hair flowing down her back surfaced in Grey's mind. Reaffirming his earlier resolve, Grey eclipsed the picture and added, "Especially with a homely woman doctor."

"I've seen worse," Tully retorted, acting none too pleased with Grey's lack of respect for his fishing adventures. "Besides, didn't think looks mattered much to you when you paid five dollars for her *plain* old dinner box."

"I felt sorry for the woman, nothing more. Now would you leave it alone?"

"Whatever you say." Tully raised his hand to ward off any further arguments. "Only wanted to clarify the situation in my own mind."

It always amazed Grey how the older man could read him. He'd been doing it since their first meeting when Grey was nothing more than a twelve-year-old urchin. He'd run away from the whorehouse where he'd pretty much raised himself and stowed away on the *Galatea* docked at Seattle. Tully had been first mate. When the seaman found him trying to steal food from the galley, he'd taken the frightened boy under his wing, going so far as to convince the captain to make Grey a cabin boy. From that day on, Tully taught Grey everything he knew about ships. He'd also taught him to read in order to "make something" of himself when he was grown.

During long months at sea Grey proved to be a voracious reader, poring over books that the sailor had stashed in his cabin—books engraved with the name Eland Taithleach. But after catching Grey reading his name aloud, Tully had given him such a scowl that Grey assumed few knew him by other than his nickname and he preferred it that way.

Tully became the father Grey never knew, and Grey imagined himself to be the son that the weathered, rugged first mate had forgone in his early years. It had been Tully who had kept him going during the two long years he'd spent in prison. And it had been Tully who'd been waiting for him when he'd been released.

Now the two men stood shoulder to shoulder in the silence that followed their friendly bickering. In the bar's dim light, Grey glanced down at Tully's whiskered face. Beneath his old friend's mustache, he thought he detected a smile playing at the corners of his mouth.

The outside door flew open and a wiry little man skittered inside. Spying Grey and Tully beside the bar, he rushed toward them. Man or element, Grey couldn't determine which had caused the flames of the many candles stuck in beer bottles throughout the room to flicker.

"Evenin', Abner. Whose fire you going to?" Tully's question solicited laughter from Grey and Baldy.

Not pausing to catch his breath, the little man blurted out his next words. "They just tried to shanghai Reverend Bailey."

"Hold on a minute . . . slow down." Grey managed to check him. "They?"

"From his own church. Crimps threw an overcoat over his head and tried to tie his arms to his sides."

Abner's voice, wrought with distress, commanded the attention of the others in the room. All eyes and ears were tuned to Abner's tale.

"Thought they had the janitor. See, the preacher hired him to ring the church bell. Understand he was a former sailor who'd been sick and stayed in port. From what I learned, tonight the janitor was out of town, so the reverend goes up in the tower to ring the bell for the evening's services. When he was halfway down the steeple stairs, they set upon him."

Murmurs rumbled throughout the bar while the others listened to Abner's account.

A stranger shouted from the group. "Pretty bad

when a minister is abducted from the house of the Lord.''

Abner continued, a smile lighting up his face as he recalled the incident. ''Rumor has it that the reverend was a former prizefighter and tonight it seems he showed his stuff. After the three of them had rolled down the stairs, the minister got up, threw one of the crimps backward, and used his boxing skills on the other. That's when they realized they were fighting the wrong man and ran off.''

''And how'd you come by this story, Abner?'' Grey asked him.

''Taking my wife to church for evening services. Saw with my own eyes the reverend's torn clothes and bleeding hands.'' As an afterthought, he added, ''Got a brand new overcoat, though.''

''A man's not safe anywhere,'' someone in the crowd mumbled. ''We're like sittin' ducks. The law can't protect us.''

''Or won't,'' another answered. ''Maybe we should all take up prize-fighting.'' Again, laughter blared from the crowd.

''An eye for an eye . . .''

Abner soon forgotten, the other men left him standing beside Grey and returned to the card games they'd interrupted when he'd entered the saloon.

The three men turned their backs on the room and faced Baldy behind the bar. ''Maybe,'' Tully suggested, ''we should form a community watch. Even if we can't do anything about the shanghaiin', if the crimps believe that a group has banded together armin' ourselves, maybe some of this here craziness will stop.''

''Won't work and you know it,'' Baldy said. ''You

can't fight those crooks. Too many of 'em. And once they learn who we are, guess who'll be floating face down in the Columbia River?''

But Tully wasn't to be deterred by Baldy's opinion. "Tonight the reverend's experience proved that if we fight back, maybe these men will think twice before jumpin' the next feller. If they believe they'll be met with force, they won't be as apt to jump you.''

"Hold on, hold on." Grey held up his hand, recalling his own recent experience with shanghaiing. "Sounds like a good plan, but I'm not sure about putting it into practice. Most of their victims are either drugged or so drunked up they aren't even aware of their circumstances until they wake up at sea.''

"But what about the ones who ain't?" Tully asked. "Like the preacher man.''

"You know men aren't going to give up drinking, whoring, or whatever, even if it means saving their own hides,'' Grey reminded him.

"True." Tully nodded in agreement. "But if we start spreadin' rumors around the waterfront that a vigilante committee is bein' formed to protect citizens, I guarantee it will put the crimps on the defensive. No one, crimp or not, wants to have his head blowed away.''

"I don't know." Abner shook his head. "My wife and children couldn't survive if anything happened to me. You know as well as I do that the ringleaders of these crimps won't like us making waves.''

"What are you?" Tully bullied him. "Some danged lily-livered coward?''

"Of course not, but I ain't no fool neither." Abner's face turned a bright red. "All you got to worry about is yourself. And who'd want an old blowhard like you anyway? Ain't fit for nothing but fishing."

"Seems to me, you do a bit of fishin' your own self, with this same old blowhard you're speakin' so highly of."

"Boys, really," Grey interrupted them.

Although the two men had been friends for years, had grown up together in Astoria, they bristled like porcupines at one another.

"But Tully may be on to something." Grey focused his attention on the others. "Even if this vigilante committee never gets formed, the possibility that the crimps might meet with opposition could well make them think twice before jumping an unsuspecting man. If the four of us try spreading a rumor around Swilltown that a group is being started, we just might get their attention."

"That's what I'm afraid of," Abner added remorsefully.

Slapping the bar in excitement, Tully looked from one to another. "Good, it's all settled. And since I ain't fit for nothing but fishin' . . ." Tully eyed his childhood friend. "I'll be more than happy to spread some stories around town. Always did enjoy baitin' hooks and watchin' them worms squirm."

"Mark my words, you'll be *feeding* the worms before it's all over," Abner replied. His face had taken on a green cast. "All of us will."

From the stairs across the room, Opal watched the four men at the bar. They'd been so intent on their conversation, they hadn't even noticed her when she'd approached them earlier.

She'd started to interrupt their conversation, anxious to see how the harbormaster was faring after his ordeal at sea. But when she'd caught the drift of their conversation, she'd remained quiet, inconspicuous, listening to them.

Grey hadn't been back in Baldy's since the night he'd asked questions about the whereabouts of Chinook. And though the harbormaster might have decided to shy away from the place where he was nearly recruited for sea duty, Opal imagined his absence had more to do with his interest in the doctor. And she further suspected that his interest was reciprocated. Doctor Rachel could say what she wanted about the weaknesses of the man, but her voice always became softer whenever Grey Devlin's name was mentioned in conversation. It struck Opal as funny that he had no idea the doctor and Chinook were one and the same.

Opal had eavesdropped only long enough to catch the word "vigilantes." It was good that the girls had called a halt to their activities. The last thing they needed was to come up against men who planned to take the law into their own hands.

But then, maybe it wasn't such a bad idea after all—this vigilante force. The police chief didn't seem too interested in arresting the crimps, and Mayor Gates himself showed no appetite for changing the status quo. Opal had decided long ago that the whole town, mayor included, were either too afraid or too highly paid to take a stand on shanghaiing.

Tomorrow Opal would give Rachel this latest piece of news. She wondered what her friend's reaction would be to the harbormaster's position. Opal was no fool. Men and women were her business. Although the doc would never admit it, Opal knew Rachel felt more for Grey Devlin than a desire for revenge.

"They're planning to shanghai Tully!" Lou exclaimed to the three women. "Tonight!"

The women sat in Opal's back parlor, absorbing this latest bit of gossip. Admission to the parlor, off limits to the other working ladies, was by invitation only.

"Tully? But why him?" Janie asked. "He's an old man, ain't good for much more than conversation."

"You speaking first hand?" Lou teased her.

"Ain't none of your affair what goes on between me and my customers."

All three women looked at Janie. "Well," she added, rather sheepishly, "Tully is my friend, but I'm sure, if I tried, I could make him rise to the occasion."

She and Lou giggled at the innuendo.

"Girls, please. We have important things to discuss here, and it isn't your prowess in bed." Opal looked at Rachel, rolling her eyes heavenward.

Rachel had become so accustomed to the girls' coarse prattle that it no longer made her blush. In fact, she found herself enjoying the women's company. Not many, she concluded, could boast such a frankness about their situation and still keep their humor.

Opal had sent word for her to join the others this afternoon, indicating the urgency of a meeting. She'd come right away. It had been more than a week since her friend had delivered the news about the vigilante committee, along with Grey's part in it.

169

This piece of information about the harbormaster only made Rachel puzzle more over an already complicated situation. There were so many contradictions about the man, Rachel felt she'd never know all the intricate parts that composed the whole. Since their trip to the timber camp, she'd been downright bewildered by his actions.

Only half-listening to the chitchat around her, Rachel sank into the sofa cushion and into her thoughts. Any mention of the harbormaster brought back with absolute clarity the sensations that had bombarded Rachel on the pier, when his lips had touched hers. Why had Grey Devlin kissed her? Even now, days later, she could recall that kiss in vivid detail, the memory making her insides feel as pliable as soft clay.

Rachel had never had the time for a man in her life, never expected to. Long ago she'd dedicated herself to her work, it being the only partner she needed. But from their first meeting, Grey Devlin had worked havoc on the careful plan she'd laid out for herself.

She knew he'd been ignoring her. And Rachel ached from his slight. He still walked Miss Purdy's dog nightly. She'd watched him from her refuge behind her lowered shades. But they hadn't spoken since their camp visit, and the one time she'd encountered him on the street, he'd acted as though she had the pox.

Maybe, she decided, after he'd sampled the merchandise, he hadn't been impressed with the quality. Unlike herself. She blushed at the very idea, but she wanted to sample more.

Rachel wanted to question Opal about Grey's strange behavior, but to do so would only make her appear naive or like some flustered old maid. But she was both—a twenty-five-year-old woman with no experience with the opposite sex. In the end, Rachel had elected to remain silent.

"So, Doc, what are we going to do about Tully?" Lou's question brought her back to the present.

"Do?" After a moment of deliberation, Rachel answered, "We stop them."

"How do we do that?" the three women asked simultaneously.

"We won't. But Chinook will."

"Chinook?"

"It's perfect." Suddenly Rachel was caught up in her own excitement. "No one can identify Chinook, but they can identify the rest of you." She looked from Opal to Janie to Lou. "As Chinook, I can distract them."

"You forgot the harbormaster," Opal volunteered, worry stamped on her face.

"He won't be around to identify me," Rachel assured her. "Now, Lou, tell me everything you learned."

Settling herself more comfortably in her wicker chair, Lou began. "One of my regulars, who works for Rooster Crowe, visited me last evening. He'd already had more than his share of whiskey when he showed up, and when he drinks too much his tongue wags like a dog's tail."

"I'm sure that ain't all he wags," Janie offered.

"True, but not as much as usual. He needs more help when he's under the influence." Lou laughed and so did Janie.

"Please, Lou," Opal chided her employee, "spare us the theatrics and get on with the story."

"Sorry, Doc," Lou apologized, beginning again where she'd left off. "Well, after I'd taken him to heights unknown by mortal man . . ."

Janie snickered. "You wish."

". . . He was so grateful for the experience he tried to impress me by bragging about his successes. Told me he knew some very important people in this town, powerful people who are above the law. And Rooster, disgusting man that he is, according to my friend, is the front man for this highly important person."

"Sounds like Rooster Crowe needs to take a long voyage, if you ask me."

Rachel recognized the name from her father's list—the last name they'd never gotten around to.

"No one asked you, Janie. Now will you please let Lou finish?" Opal quieted the girl with a stern look.

"Well, it seems the crimps aren't too happy with the vigilantes. Got some of the men lying low, fearing retaliation. Apparently, two crimps were beaten up by someone posing as a church minister."

Rachel had heard the story of Reverend Bailey's near shanghaiing. She also knew it wasn't someone posing as the church minister, but the preacher himself who had done the good deed.

"Why have they singled out Tully as the organizer?" Opal asked her.

"Because he's the one visiting around the saloons and spreading the rumors about taking up arms. There's a ship that sails for China on the morning tide, and Tully is supposed to be on it."

"Maybe we better tell him what you learned so he can warn the others."

"No time," Lou confirmed. "They're going to take him tonight, when he comes in from fishing."

Opal turned to Rachel. "We can tell the harbormaster. He's Tully's friend. He'll know what to do."

Rachel shook her head in disbelief. "Have you forgotten not too long ago we tried to rid Astoria of its harbormaster?"

"But I thought seeing how you seem to be enamored with the man, that you didn't believe him to be guilty."

"Enamored? Why, Opal, whatever gave you that idea?" Rachel felt the heat of a blush spread all the way to the roots of her hair. "True, he did happen to purchase my box supper, and he did go with me to the logging camp. But I promise you it was nothing more than to make certain no one tried to steal all that money I carried."

Rachel settled her round spectacles on her face. She'd flushed so from nervousness over Opal's accusation that the dampness had sent them sliding down the bridge of her nose. "I assure you our relationship was strictly a business arrangement."

She knew before the words were out that she was trying to convince herself as well as the others. "And we still don't know if we can trust the man. Maybe he's the important someone this Rooster Crowe reports to."

Everyone mulled over Rachel's statement, agreeing that what she said could be true.

"All right, Doc," Opal finally said. "We'll let you be Chinook and distract them, but we'll be hiding in the darkness. We won't allow you to take undue risk." The others agreed with their employer.

"Now this is what we'll do . . ."

Chapter 9

Tully's house sat at the hindmost part of the street, away from the other dwellings that lined the wharf. Behind the structure, a thin covering of firs grew upon the gentle, swelling hills that served as a backdrop for the thriving town. To the cabin's left the land slid downward into a small, shallow cove.

Chinook, with Opal, Lou, and Janie in tow, hastened down the planked roadway leading to Tully's cabin. They approached the house with caution, hoping not to draw attention to their visit. But if they were detected, the women had invented a story about their destination: a group of well-paying sailors had invited the girls to attend a bonfire party. It was to be held on the stretch of deserted beach that lay beyond the town.

When they reached Tully's little house, the interior was suffused in darkness. From all appearances, he had not yet returned from his nightly fishing trip.

According to Lou's garnered information, the crimps planned to jump Tully on the beach when he moored his small fishing boat. Crowe's men had been very thorough with their investigation, fully aware of Tully's routine. The drunken braggart had gone so far as to tell Lou the exact time they planned to steal Tully away.

It was ten o'clock by Opal's watch when the "brides" reached the well worn path that passed through the copse of trees that led to the water's edge. They'd worked out their plan to the last detail. Tully should be back within the hour.

"Remember, Doc," Opal whispered, "once you get the men's attention, you must keep their backs to the wooded path."

"I know, I know." But darkness couldn't conceal the worried expression on Opal's face. "I'll be fine," Rachel assured her, giving Opal's hand a reassuring squeeze at the edge of the sandy beach. "Once I have their attention, all you'll have to do is wave those hankies beneath their noses and they'll drop like flies."

"Let's hope they drop before they have time to drop their trousers and jump on you," Opal warned her.

"Don't be such a worry wart," Lou consoled. "Chinook will be just fine, and we'll be close enough to help her if she needs us."

"Believe me, the chloroform will work," Rachel promised. "You just have to keep the soaked rags over their noses and mouths for a moment."

Rachel was counting on the drug's effectiveness to pull off their plan. If it didn't work, she'd have to be ready with another defense. Whatever that would be.

"Please be careful," Opal begged, signaling the others to follow her back into the shadows of the trees.

Rachel watched them until they were out of sight. Then she looked out toward the water. Lights on the distant ships glittered like the stars overhead. One of them could be Tully's own boat heading home. Feeling a need to conceal her exposed position, Rachel hurried down the beach to hide behind a cropping of rocks near the water's edge.

Dressed again as Chinook, she leaned back against the tall rocks to wait. Her pink hair hung in flyaway curls halfway down her back, and the skunk boa felt warm around her almost bare shoulders. Clad only in her green bodice, chamois drawers, silk stockings and boots, she'd left the skirt and long train of her costume back at Opal's. If she needed to defend herself, she'd be better able without the added weight of the heavy material.

Rachel found a smaller rock and sat, fingering the black teardrop brooch pinned in its customary place at the deep vee of her neckline. She tugged on the exposing bodice, trying to stuff herself farther in, but soon gave up. It was no use; she was too buxom for the skimpy front.

Minutes ticked by. The rock's cold surface soon penetrated the warmth of Rachel's leather drawers. Seized by a sudden chill, she rubbed her bare arms. She wanted the night to end and for Tully to be left in peace. It galled her to think that other men took it upon themselves to change one's destiny for pieces of silver. Or worse yet that someone would order Tully's shanghaiing because he'd spoken out against the crimps. She pushed both unsettling thoughts to the back of her mind when she heard two men coming down the beach toward her.

Oh my God, she thought, what if they picked the same rocks she hid behind to wait for Tully's landing?

Rachel jumped up, easing deeper into the fissure

176

formed by two man-sized boulders. It was a dark night with no moon, and she prayed the intruders wouldn't see her in the shadows. Water soaked through the bottom of her boots and Rachel realized she was now standing in the edge of the bay.

The men's voices carried on the wind. "Bloody ol' man won't be no trouble. We'll have 'im drugged and sent on his way before 'e knows what hit 'im. Show the old coot how we deal with vigilantes."

"Rooster says we better not bungle this one. He's still riled because we messed up with the church janitor."

"Shush . . . I hear a boat gliding across the water."

The two men didn't speak again but squatted a short distance from where Rachel hid. Their silhouettes blended in with the jutting formations of bedrock.

Rachel dared not breathe for fear of alerting the men to her presence. Her knees were banging together so badly they sounded like cymbals to her own ears, and she feared the noise would give her away. Paralyzed, she waited in the rock's damp crack. The success of their scheme depended upon her taking the crimps by surprise.

A catchy tune floated across the water. Although she'd never heard Tully sing before tonight, Rachel recognized his voice. It was raised in a hearty solo.

"T'was on a Black Baller I first served my time.
To my yeo, ho! Blow the man down!
And on that Black Baller I wasted my prime,
Oh, give me some time to blow the man down!"

The song stopped as the little skiff's bow hit the edge of the sand with a loud skidding crunch and the anchor splashed into the water. Tully's lantern cast an amber circle of light around the small boat, and molten gold beams quivered on the cove's black surface. After retrieving his gear from inside the boat, Tully picked up the lantern, stepped into the water, and waded toward shore.

The two men in front of Rachel sprang into action.

"What in tarnation?" Tully thundered, raising the lantern higher, when the crimps bolted toward him. Realizing he was under attack, he swung the string of fish he carried at one attacker's head. A wet thump echoed across the darkness.

Rachel's first reaction was to help her friend. But caution warned her that she must wait a few minutes before she made her appearance known. She prayed silently that Tully would escape without too many injuries.

Tully swung the lantern at his offenders, but they were younger and quicker and the lantern missed them by inches before thudding to the ground. It rolled a few feet before stopping, washing the pale sand with a circle of yellow light.

Helpless, Rachel watched the tussle. The crimp who'd been walloped by the string of fish lunged at Tully while the other man held the old man's arms behind his back. Old Fishhead delivered a cutting blow to Tully's eye, then a solid punch to his stomach. No longer a match for two crimps, Tully sagged to the ground.

It was time for Rachel to move. Slipping from her hiding place, she sashayed toward the men.

"Why, sugars, what kind of party is this?" Her voice carried across the darkness. The surprised crimps spun around to face her. When Rachel reached the circle of light, she stopped, thrusting one leather-wrapped hip provocatively in front of her. "Why, I'm not even here yet, and you boys are already fighting over me." She faked a laugh then added, "I was invited to a *wienie* roast."

The crimps snickered over her choice of words, sizing her up from her head to her toes. Then Fishhead ordered, "Get out of here, bitch. This ain't no place for you."

"I'm sorry," she retorted, "but Chinook goes nowhere till she gets her money."

"Money?" They both gawked at her.

Rachel snatched the skunk boa from around her neck, waving its free end in the crimps' direction. Even in the dimly lit circle, she could see their eyes snap to her low-cut bodice. She moved deftly around so that she stood between the water and the men.

"Go on and git," the other man warned.

Spreading her legs apart, Rachel placed her hands upon her hips and threw back her shoulders. "I agreed to bring the buns for them wienies, and I'm as anxious as you to start cooking. Wanna dawdle before that old geezer comes to?"

All eyes focused on Tully's prone form. He lay on his side motionlessly.

"What you say, Zeke? We got plenty of time." Fishhead's eyes darted between Rachel and his cronie. "Might as well show the lady a good time. Boat won't be here for another hour."

Zeke hesitated.

Rachel had to convince them. She ran both her hands down the side of her body. "What you say,

Zeke? I'd show you both a good time." She picked up her heavy pink hair and let it fall behind her shoulders.

Fishhead was eager but he still had to convince his friend. "I'll go first. You watch the stiff, and whatever else you want to watch." He leered at Rachel. "Then you can have a go at 'er."

Old Fishhead licked his thick lips as he took in Rachel's full length—from the tips of her soggy boots to the top of her head.

Still hesitating, his partner smacked his mouth while running his eyes up and down Rachel. "Okay, but don't take all night. And don't use her all up. I want my fair share."

Rachel jumped up and down, clapping her hands in glee, appearing as eager about their coupling as they were. "There's plenty for the both of you," she added, and watched Fishhead slither toward her, looking as dangerous as a desert rattler.

"Right here good enough?" Rachel asked, flopping down upon the beach. She patted the dried seaweed that had been washed in earlier by the tide and now covered the sand like a thick mat.

"Any place is good for me." Fishhead now knelt beside her on the ground. "Where'd you get them fancy drawers, gal? I ain't never seen any like them before." He ran his grubby hand up the inside of her thigh, while his eyes raked down her front.

"They ain't leather, they're chamois. All the way from Europe," Rachel boasted.

"You from Europe, too? I ain't seen you around Swilltown before."

"I'm from everywhere and nowhere," Rachel answered, feeling as though she might regurgitate what

180

little supper she'd had. The man's fingers poked at her intimate parts.

Rachel kept reminding herself that in order to save Tully from the same fate as her father, she had no choice but to allow the repulsive man access to her body. The sooner the crimp lay on top of her, the more interest the other would have in watching the show, and the sooner her ordeal would be finished.

"Quit jawing and get on with it," Zeke insisted, "or you come over here and I'll go first."

His jibe prompted his pal into action. It was clear to Rachel that her greedy foe wasn't about to relinquish his advantage. Forcing her thighs apart, he leapt between her legs. She watched as he fumbled with the buttons on the front of his britches until his extended red organ popped free of the confining material. Quickly, he worked his trousers down over his hips.

"Them fancy drawers snap open?" he asked, his black eyes never leaving Rachel's.

They did but Rachel prayed he wouldn't find out for a few more minutes.

"Don't you like to play?" she asked, pulling the man atop her. He buried his face in her cleavage and claimed the tops of her breasts with his tongue.

"You're real sweet, honey," he managed between breathless licks. "You and me, we're gonna be friends for a long time."

Rachel knew the man was excited. His lower body ground into the apex of her thighs. His forceful movement skidded her over the cutting seaweed. He nipped and pinched at her breasts with his teeth, then moved higher to kiss her mouth. His breath reeked of sardines, and Rachel jerked her head away in disgust.

When she did, she saw the girls sneaking up behind his buddy. The man sat beside Tully's head fondling himself, totally unaware, while he watched the show in front of him. Thank heavens it would soon be over.

Knowing her next move depended upon getting the man back to a kneeling position before the others could successfully slip the cloth over his nose and mouth, Rachel waited for just the right moment. She moved with him, as though she, too, were in the throes of passion. Out of the corner of her eye, Rachel watched as Opal, Lou, and Janie lowered the chloroformed crimp to the sand. It was time.

"Now, sugar. I need you now," Rachel crooned, thrashing her head back and forth. She acted as eager as her partner for the final act.

"Ol' Pete's ready for you. I'll fill you up real good." He slipped back upon his haunches while his shaky fingers searched for the opening in Rachel's drawers that would grant him the entrance to paradise.

When he did, Opal, Lou, and Janie grabbed him, placing the chloroform-soaked rags over his mouth and nose.

"Take that, you bastard," Opal vocalized her loathing.

Rachel watched the man's shocked expression before his eyes rolled back into his head and his lids snapped shut. He toppled like a felled tree across her chest.

Almost hysterical, Rachel cried, "Get this leech off me."

The three women managed to roll the man's dead weight off Rachel and when they did, Rachel crawled away. No longer able to contain her retching stomach, she emptied it in the sand.

"You all right?" Opal asked, tears brimming in her eyes.

"I'm fine now but, Opal, I was scared senseless."

"You did just fine."

"But how can you stand—"

Opal quieted her with a hug. "We do what we have to. Just as you did tonight."

Rachel sought the other women's eyes. Soon all four of them knelt in the sand, hugging one another and crying.

Tully's soft moans alerted them into action. They broke apart, stood, then walked to the half-conscious man.

"Go quickly, before Tully wakes up enough to recognize you," Rachel cautioned them. "I'll see him back to his cabin and tend to his wounds. We'll talk tomorrow."

"But what about them?" Lou asked, nudging one drugged crimp with the toe of her shoe.

Rachel smiled, feeling like her old self again. "We'll leave them. If we're lucky, the boat that was to take Tully will take them instead."

Cheered by the idea that the two fellows might suffer the same fate they'd planned for Tully, the three women disappeared into the night.

It was unlike Tully to be late for an appointment. Checking his watch for the second time in the last half-hour, Grey noted it was well past midnight. At eleven-thirty the newly formed vigilante committee of four had planned to meet at Baldy's Saloon. They'd agreed on the late hour because most of the saloon crowds would

183

have thinned out by then, and it also gave Tully the opportunity to check on his fish lines, as he did religiously each night.

Abner broke the silence by voicing everyone's thoughts aloud. "I told you this would happen when we started making trouble for the crimps."

Grey looked at him. "I'm sure there's a good reason for the old coot being late. If he doesn't show up soon, I'll mosey by his house and check on him."

"Mark my word, they've killed him, or worse yet, shanghaied him."

"Gee whiz, Abner. Being dead is worse than being shanghaied," Baldy interjected.

"Ain't what I'm told," Abner grumbled. "Heard tell, you wish you were dead and then you jump ship and the sharks get you."

"I'm leaving," Grey responded, rolling his eyes heavenward. "I can't handle your logic, Abner." He tossed several coins onto the bar to cover the cost of his drinks and turned to leave. "If I don't meet up with him, I'll get back to you."

"Heard from everyone in Swilltown that Tully's been making the rounds, gloating about the vigilantes. . . ."

Abner's words drifted into nothingness as Grey crossed the room and stepped outside. He paused, looking up and down the street for a sign of the old man, hoping what Abner had inferred hadn't come to pass. But it wasn't like Tully to not show up for an appointment.

Not many people out tonight, Grey thought, glancing in the direction of Tully's cabin. Three ladies of the evening were coming down the street toward Baldy's Saloon, laughing and chattering like magpies. Grey watched them until they stopped to enter the house next door.

Recognizing one of them to be Opal, Grey called out, "Evening, ladies."

"How's the harbormaster this evening?" Opal returned his greeting.

"Fine, thank you. Nice night for a stroll." Grey wondered if they'd encountered his friend on their outing.

"You know Tully?" he asked them.

Lou and Janie giggled like two school girls before Opal shooed them inside.

"Everyone knows Tully," she replied.

"Seen him tonight?"

"Can't say I have."

"He was supposed to meet me here. Unlike him to miss an appointment."

"Maybe he got tied up in his fish lines," Opal added for lightness then, noting Grey didn't seem amused, added, "I'm sure he'll show up soon."

"Yeah, maybe. Well, thanks anyway."

"G'night, Mr. Devlin." Opal waved and slipped inside the front door of her house.

Stepping down onto the planked road, Grey ambled in the direction of Tully's cabin. The crimps of Astoria were known for their ruthlessness and if they'd taken a notion to rid Oregon of the old boy's presence, they would succeed. As well-intended as the vigilantes' plan was, Grey was suddenly struck with the real possibility of his friend coming to harm. It was time to curb his rumor-spreading. He hoped the stubborn old fool would listen to him. If he found him.

The cabin, sitting at the end of the street, glowed like a beacon. Grey relaxed, taking the lights to mean that Tully was at home. He hoped his friend hadn't taken ill. Earlier in the day he'd seemed fine. But it was still a puzzle why his friend hadn't shown up for their meeting.

Stepping onto the front door stoop, his hand raised to knock, Grey stopped dead still. From the other side of the door he heard what sounded like a woman's laughter.

Why, that old rascal, Grey thought. No wonder Tully hadn't met them. It sounded as though he had more important things to attend to. Could Miss Purdy have finally cornered his friend, after all?

"Easy, honey, I'm an old man," the familiar voice pleaded, his voice carrying to Grey from behind the wall.

"Now, that's not what you said earlier," the female purred.

"Ouch . . . ahh . . . ohh."

Again the woman laughed. "Just a little bit more and I promise you'll feel like a new man."

"Be gentle, girl, gentle . . . whoa!"

Miss Purdy? No, it couldn't be. But some female was in there with the old guy. Had Tully hired a lady for the night?

Grey's curiosity was aroused. This was a side of the old salt that Grey thought hadn't been of concern for a number of years. Often enough, Tully had proclaimed that women just complicated a man's life, that they weren't worth the effort it took to bed them. But from the sounds coming from behind the wall, Grey

186

was convinced that other things besides fishing were on his mind.

Tully let out a moan. "Ah . . . that's much better."

Grey grinned, imagining the scene taking place on the other side of the door. Mentally commending the older man's prowess, he backed off to leave.

Again the mysterious female laughed, a warm, sultry verbal caress. "I wouldn't think a big, strong man like yourself would be afraid of anything," the husky voice taunted him.

Grey froze. Those same words, phrased the same way, by a voice that sounded remarkably like the one that had haunted him on occasion, floated beneath the partially open window. Grey was determined to find out whom Tully was entertaining.

Stealing toward the front window, he tried to peek around the croaker sack curtains. A slight breeze billowing the hems allowed a limited view of the interior.

Grey strained to locate Tully's cot, the same cot he'd recuperated on only weeks before. With another draft of air that swirled the woven fabric inward, Grey saw her.

Her pink hair tumbled down her back in glorious disarray. She stood before Tully, between his spread knees. Her arms were bare and looked like porcelain in the soft golden light. His friend sat shirtless, enjoying whatever it was that she seemed to be doing to him.

The wind died and with it Grey's view. But he knew without a doubt that the pink-haired whore in leather britches could be none other than Chinook. And his old friend, Tully, was almost in bed with her.

Red hot anger shot through Grey. Anger at the woman for what she'd done to him, and anger at his friend for using Grey's woman. And that wasn't all that shot through Grey's body. He felt a raw, primitive desire for the trollop, even now.

"Damnation," he mumbled, jumping back from the window. What was the matter with him? A woman like Chinook belonged to no man but walked her own path alone—just as his mother had.

He'd told Tully about Chinook, not sparing any detail of the brief night they'd spent together. Now Grey felt betrayed by his old friend. And appalled at himself. *Jealous* he was, of an old man forty years his senior.

Maybe, he reasoned, she'd been hired to get rid of Tully the same way she'd tried to get rid of him. But knowing Grey's story, why would Tully fall for her charms?

No matter what, Grey decided, he'd spend the night here, outside the cabin, waiting for the prostitute to leave. And if her intent was to shanghai the old guy, Grey would be damned sure she didn't succeed. If she were simply plying her trade, Grey would wait until she left and follow her. Then he'd get back his twenty dollars.

Grey slipped into the shadows to wait.

Not long after, he heard the front door creak open, then thud shut. He crept toward the corner of the house and waited, listening, before finally peeking beyond the wall.

Backlighted by the window's muted glow, Chinook paused for a moment on the stoop. She raised her arms over her head and stretched like a lazy kitten, revealing every lush curve she possessed.

Her breasts, full and round, jutted forward and Grey imagined he saw her nipples bud against the satin fabric of her bodice. She dropped her hands to her waist, pinched and rubbed the area, then moved lower to give her backside a quick massage.

Old Tully must have given her a real workout, Grey thought as he watched the woman from the darkness. Worn her out but good.

Chinook uttered a deep, contented sigh, then stepped off the stoop and headed toward the center of town.

Grey waited beside the house long enough to allow for a safe distance between them. When he felt confident that he wouldn't be noticed, he followed.

Indifferent and in no particular hurry, Chinook strolled down the sleepy street. While Grey dogged her footsteps, a myriad of images ran through his mind, one in the form and shape of Rachel Thomas. Here I am, he thought, in the middle of the night trailing a damned soiled dove, and one of the first things that comes to mind is the lady doctor. Damn, but I must be crazy.

He recalled the night of Rachel's attack by the drunk and her statement later about being able to prowl the streets after dark without fear. "I'm like the ladies of the night. I provide a service for men, just as they do." But Grey knew even the experienced woman ahead of him would be no match for any man who wanted her favors. Tentatively, he wondered if he were that man.

He watched her diminutive shape, noting the gentle sway of her hips in the leather britches and the swing of the pink hair that brushed the top of her well-proportioned behind. He listened to the soft clicking of her boots on the wooden planks as she made her way up the street. Each click, click, click reminded him of a fast-ticking clock, bringing him closer to the woman

189

he followed. Even now, knowing what he did about her, she still possessed the power to excite him in the same way she had the first night he'd met her. Click, click, click. Soon he'd extract his revenge from her pretty little hide.

She neared Opal's house, but instead of stopping as Grey had expected her to do, Chinook headed away from the wharf. He continued to track her, wondering if by chance she suspected his presence and intended to mislead him.

When she turned onto Franklin Street and walked the same path he himself took each night with Miss Purdy's dog, uneasiness gripped him.

He concentrated his full attention on the woman ahead of him. Where would Chinook be going at this time of night, in this section of town? Although this wasn't the hill, it certainly was a middle class neighborhood with residents and churches scattered throughout. Not a place for a roundheel like Chinook.

Stopping at a corner beneath a gas lamp, the woman looked around her as though checking to see if she were alone. Satisfied that she was, she crossed the street and headed directly toward Rachel's house.

Did Chinook require a doctor's care? Grey had heard from several people on the wharf that Rachel sometimes treated the ladies of the evening. But from what he had heard tonight at Tully's, and then upon following her, he couldn't believe Chinook was in need of a doctor.

Rachel's gate squeaked open and Chinook disappeared into the shadowed overhang of the porch. Grey knew he had to act fast if he wanted to reach the trollop before she knocked on the doctor's door. He darted across the street, practically jumped over the picket fence, and stormed up the steps before she had time to react.

Skidding to a stop, he slammed into Chinook while she wrestled with inserting a key into the lock. He pulled her back against him, catching her sharp intake of breath. The hot underside of her breasts rested upon his arm where it encircled her, and he fought the layers of pink flyaway hair that threatened to blind him. She felt hot and dewy pressed against him. Her earlier activities had obviously made her smell like a woman and Grey cursed his body for reacting to her scent. Other whores never had this effect on him. Why the hell should he feel aroused by the sight and smell of this one? And why did this woman have a key to Rachel's house?

The front door slowly swung open and Grey expected to see Rachel appear in her long frothy nightrail, looking as virginal as she did the night he'd watched her dance with Cal. But all that greeted them was the long, dimly lit hallway.

"Remember me?" Pressed against the prostitute's behind, Grey ground out the words against her ear. "What the devil are you doing here in the middle of the night?" he demanded. "And how did you get hold of the doctor's key? Are you a thief as well as a prostitute and shanghaier?" With each question Grey flung at her, he jerked her up hard against him. "Not so sure of yourself now, are you?"

As she tried to move away, his hand tightened around her torso, grazing her breast. It felt full and round, and beneath the thin bodice her nipple puckered to his touch. Where the devil was the doctor? If

Rachel didn't show up soon, he might take Chinook on the floor in the hallway.

"Answer me," he demanded again in a low growl, "what are you doing here?"

Entangled in his arms, Rachel recognized Grey's voice. He thought he had Chinook, the tramp who'd intended him harm, and he was hellbent on revenge. She started to speak but the words would not come. How could she respond without giving away her real identity? Without having him hate her all the more?

Frightened now by her own body's response to Grey's caress, Rachel knew she had to make herself known before they both did something that would embarrass them later. Grey was aroused. She could feel his erection poking into her seat. And he was angry—a dangerous situation to say the least.

"Tell me," he ordered her again. This time he picked her up and carried her deeper into the hallway, kicking the door shut behind them.

"I live here," Rachel blurted out.

The seconds that followed reminded Rachel of the still silence before a killer gale. Grey still held her in a viselike grip, but she sensed the turmoil going on inside his head.

"Let me go, please," she begged him. "I can explain."

"Explain," he raged.

Gripping her by the arm, he hauled her into the surgery.

"Light the lamp." His fingers dug into the soft flesh of her arm.

"How do you expect me to do that, use my teeth?" Rachel demanded, tired of his condescending attitude.

ENJOY ALL THE PASSION AND ROMANCE OF...

Heartfire

Heartfire Romance

ROMANCES from ZEBRA

After you have read HEART-FIRE ROMANCES, we're sure you'll agree that HEARTFIRE sets new standards of excellence for historical romantic fiction. Each Zebra HEARTFIRE novel is the ultimate blend of intimate romance and grand adventure and each takes place in the kinds of historical settings you want most...the American Revolution, the Old West, Civil War and more.

SUBSCRIBERS $AVE, $AVE, $AVE!!!

As a HEARTFIRE Home Subscriber, you'll save with your HEARTFIRE Subscription. You'll receive 4 brand new Heartfire Romances to preview Free for 10 days each month. If you decide to keep them you'll pay only $3.50 each; a total of $14.00 and you'll save $3.00 each month off the cover price.

Plus, we'll send you these novels as soon as they are published each month. There is never any shipping, handling or other hidden charges; home delivery is always FREE! And there is no obligation to buy even a single book. You may return any of the books within 10 days for full credit and you can cancel your subscription at any time. No questions asked.

Zebra's HEARTFIRE ROMANCES Are The Ultimate In Historical Romantic Fiction.
Start Enjoying Romance As You Have Never Enjoyed It Before...
With 4 FREE Books From HEARTFIRE

TO GET YOUR
4 FREE BOOKS
MAIL THE COUPON BELOW.

FREE BOOK CERTIFICATE

Heartfire Romance

GET 4 FREE BOOKS

Yes! I want to subscribe to Zebra's HEARTFIRE HOME SUBSCRIPTION SERVICE. Please send me my 4 FREE books. Then each month I'll receive the four newest Heartfire Romances as soon as they are published to preview Free for ten days. If I decide to keep them I'll pay the special discounted price of just $3.50 each; a total of $14.00. This is a savings of $3.00 off the regular publishers price. There are no shipping, handling or other hidden charges. There is no minimum number of books to buy and I may cancel this subscription at any time. In any case the 4 FREE Books are mine to keep regardless.

NAME

ADDRESS

CITY   STATE   ZIP

TELEPHONE

SIGNATURE

(If under 18 parent or guardian must sign)
Terms and prices subject to change.
Orders subject to acceptance.

ZH0294

GET 4 FREE BOOKS

HEARTFIRE HOME SUBSCRIPTION
SERVICE
120 BRIGHTON ROAD
P.O. BOX 5214
CLIFTON, NEW JERSEY 07015

"Just light it, damn it." He practically shoved her toward the desk.

Rachel found the matches and struck one. Soon the wick spurted to life, filling the dark room with a halo of light. With shaking hands she placed the globe back upon the lamp base, then turned to face him.

Disbelief hit Grey as he took in the sight of her. She stood straight and tall, her shoulders thrown back in the same proud way Rachel always carried herself. But tonight, in her harlot's dress, she looked different—no longer the starch and vinegar doctor, but Chinook in her womanly softness. And it was to this woman that Grey responded. It was this woman he intended to have.

"Well, my sweet, I suggest we get on with it."

"Get on with it?" Rachel asked, not certain she understood his meaning.

He stalked her then, and Rachel tried to sidestep his grasp. But she wasn't fast enough. He grabbed her, pulling her up hard against him. His lips crushed her own.

Rachel fought him. This was a side of Grey she'd never seen before. He'd always been so tender with her. But now he was angry, defiant—and it was all her fault.

Her heart pounded viciously against her ribcage. "Why are you doing this, Grey?" she pleaded, trying to push him away.

"Why, my sweet, did you try to shanghai me? I paid you well. Twenty dollars is a sizable sum for a tumble."

He fingered the teardrop brooch on her low neckline. His fingers lingered against her bared skin, then pressed her bosom in a way that made Rachel feel breathless.

"I'll return the money to you. Please, just let me go and I'll explain. Can't we discuss this like two reasonable adults?"

"Not until you tell me the truth." Grey backed her against the leather examining table, nuzzling her neck. He lifted her onto the table and wedged himself between her legs, encircling her body in his arms.

"Because of the opium shipment," Rachel blurted out. In her precarious position, with Grey's chest pressed against her intimate parts, she knew she had to do something to stop his craziness.

"The opium shipment?" Grey straightened, pinning her with his eyes.

"Yes. Because you allowed the shipment in port, one of the girls died of an overdose that some john slipped into her drink."

Grey's eyes bored into hers. "In other words, you blame me for the woman's death when we both know the opium could have come from somewhere else."

"I thought so at first, but now I don't know. . . ."

"Why, Rachel, I thought you to be a woman of conviction. Once you decided to do something, or formed an opinion, I didn't expect to see you waver."

Grey was becoming angrier by the moment. Angry at the woman who had set his world akilter from the first moment they'd met. Angry that he'd been suckered in by Chinook, and angrier still that he had allowed a young woman to die so that he could achieve his own ends—if in truth, it were the shipment he'd allowed in port that killed her.

"Hell, Rachel, it does my heart good to see you hold

me in such high esteem. Since I'm such a no-good, awful fellow, I might as well finish what I started with you the first night we met.''

"What's that?" she asked, uncertain she liked what Grey intimated.

"You owe me twenty dollars, and tonight I intend to collect it."

Rachel struggled to free herself from his grip, but before she knew it, she was lying on her back on her examining table with Grey's weight pinning her down. "Please," she begged.

"Good. I like my women to beg."

Grey's lips claimed hers and Rachel's world spun out of control.

Chapter 10

Grey's heart pumped so loudly inside his head he felt disoriented. What woman belonged to the soft, yielding body beneath his that drove him to near madness with desire? Was she nothing more than a scheming, wicked Jezebel? Or was she the virginal doctor who'd dedicated her life to healing, and who in the last month had won his respect as a caring and qualified physician? Was this the same woman who had found him guilty without a defense, perhaps condemning him to an early death? Or the one who stirred life into his quiescent heart?

An inner voice whispered caution, warning Grey to stop his reckless plunder. But Rachel's duplicity burned fresh in his mind. He wanted revenge. How could he have believed himself unworthy of her?

His heart ached with the realization that Rachel had lied to him, deceived him. He'd learned long ago, from his own mother, that women could not be trusted. But he'd believed Rachel to be different. Now his disappointment blinded him to all reason and he could not stop the heated, hateful words.

"So, did you service the old man?" he asked, intent upon freeing the brooch from its place on Rachel's bodice.

She stiffened at his words as though she'd been slapped. "How dare you question my professionalism!" she charged.

How dare she act insulted? She'd brought this on herself. "Depends on which profession we're talking about," he countered, barely able to see through his own pain of betrayal.

The brooch unfastened, Grey slung it to the floor, still holding her prisoner beneath him. His fingers pulled on the material of her bodice, exposing her breasts. His eyes roamed freely over Rachel's nakedness. She tried to cover her chest with her arms, but he restrained her.

In the soft light the vixen's skin looked lush and opulent. Grey's breath whistled through his teeth, every inch of him responding to her rich beauty.

"Just like your supper box," he mocked.

Bending his head toward her, he trailed kisses across the satin fullness of her breasts, stopping at one nipple. He blew his humid breath against its tip, then drew back to watch it bud.

"Stop, please," Rachel begged him.

But Grey had no intention of stopping. He wanted her, and for the moment it didn't matter if she were saint or sinner. His body responded to the shapely woman beneath him. And she didn't need a name.

He rubbed his finger over the extended tip of her nipple, crooning, "Plain on the outside, but so fine beneath." He dropped his mouth to one crested peak and gently suckled. His hand moved lower to find the opening in the crotch of her drawers. Delving his fingers into her liquid warmth, he felt her body weep against his palm.

"Let me up this minute," Rachel demanded, groping to check her own bounding emotions. "You have no right—"

"I have every right." Grey pulled himself higher upon her. Holding her face between his hands, he looked into her eyes. "I have paid for this right. And I know how to pleasure whores."

His cruel words stabbed at Rachel's heart. What did she expect? For him to woo her as the lady doctor? The very thought was now ludicrous. She'd deceived him, and because of that deceit, he believed the worst of her. No argument would convince him that she was an innocent when it came to the ways of love. He would believe what he wanted—what she had led him to believe. Her heart thudded wildly. She nuzzled his face with her own, powerless to resist his moist, tender touch.

Grey trailed kisses over her collarbone, pausing at the hollow of her throat. Beneath his lips he felt the rapid beat of Rachel's pulse and smiled to himself. Once a whore, always a whore. Less than an hour before, she had spread her legs for Tully, and now her whore's body screamed for more.

Satisfied by her response, he moved up the cord of her neck to nibble her ear. His breath swirled the pink hair that shielded it from his kiss. Brushing aside the wispy ringlets, he dipped his seeking tongue inside. His heartbeat quickened when he felt Rachel quiver against him.

She tried to shield her ear from another assault by turning her head aside. "I can explain—"

But Grey wanted no more of her lies. He pulled her mouth to his and ravished it, devouring what he could take. He wanted her, all of her.

Rachel could not begin to understand the feelings that pulsed through her at his touch. His kiss was punishing and angry, its intensity frightening as she hung suspended in a world of sensations. But, surprisingly, a piece of him brushed her with a tenderness totally unexpected. Waves of ecstasy throbbed through her, and she could no more stop her response than she could a rising tide.

Leaving her lips, he slid back to her breasts. Her skin felt dewy soft. Pulling the swollen tips into his mouth, he caressed each with tiny nipping bites. Satisfied, he crushed her against his chest and reclaimed her lips.

Between forceful kisses he asked, "Who are you tonight, my sweet? Certainly no respectable lady doctor would dress in the garb of a whore."

No longer certain who she was, Rachel answered him honestly. "Whoever you wish me to be."

Emotions Rachel never knew she possessed were released in a torrent by Grey's caresses. Her sane self encouraged her to fight his advances. But the part of her who'd dreamed of Grey Devlin nightly since their kiss at the timber camp wanted him to pleasure her body in every way he knew.

Each stroke from his calloused fingers sent shivers up and down her spine. His touch brought back memories of their steamy encounter in Opal's house when, dressed as Chinook, she had lured him there. Even now it was Chinook's body Grey craved and Rachel ached from the realization. A man like the harbormaster would never be attracted to the plain lady doctor.

Blood pounded in her brain. She wanted Grey to want her for herself. But knowing that to be impossible, Rachel made up her mind. She returned his kisses in the way she believed Chinook would respond to a man.

Rachel's timidness abruptly disappeared. Her lips became warm and sweet as she trailed kisses across his ear and down his neck, ending with her lush mouth open upon his. Her attempt at seduction, while hot and willing, was pure—virginal—not that of an experienced courtesan, and the sudden knowledge struck Grey like a bucket of icy spring water. A wave of shock pulsed through his entire being, cooling his passion. Instantly he felt ashamed of his actions.

Sliding backward, he straddled her leather-clad hips. His manhood throbbed against her womanly mound, and even in his moment of rationality, he longed to bury himself inside her. But not like this, not by forced entry. No matter what Rachel had done, no woman deserved to be raped.

But for the ragged rise and fall of her breasts she lay unmoving—proof that she was as aroused as he. His eyes found hers, and he thought he saw crystal tears in their warm, amber depths. With shaky fingers he pulled the bodice up together over her breasts.

"Rachel, I'm sorry, I should never—" His words caught in his throat.

She grabbed his hand and settled it over her pounding heart, her tears now flowing in earnest.

Grey pulled her up against him and cradled her in

200

his arms, his emotions raw. "I was so damn angry," he confessed, "but that's no excuse for my actions."

"It's all right, I'm as much to blame as you." Rachel wrapped her arms around his waist, attempting to comfort him against his own self-derision. "When you dress like a harlot, you have to be prepared to act like one. Opal taught me that."

"Ah, yes, the 'gypsy whore,' " Grey mumbled more to himself than to Rachel. "But why?" He searched her face. "I listened outside Tully's cabin. Rachel, he's old enough to be your father."

His lips thinned with contempt. He still believes the worst of me, Rachel thought, even after his apology.

With a quick tug of his hand, Grey pulled the awful pink wig from her head and dropped it to the floor. Rachel's own glorious hair tumbled loose from its pins and furled around her shoulders like spun silk. It looked the way he'd remembered it the night he'd rescued her from the drunk.

"I must go."

He shifted backward but Rachel restrained him. "Please stay," she whispered. She stilled him by dropping her hands to his thighs. "I need to explain."

Conflicting emotions raged throughout Grey. He wanted to stay, to hear her out. But he wanted more than anything to believe Rachel to be an innocent. If he were to learn she was not, the admission would destroy them both.

"Tully is my friend. And tonight, as a doctor, I tended to some injuries he received."

"Injuries?" Grey reared back to stare at her. "What happened to him?"

In vivid detail, he recalled the scene in Tully's

201

cabin—the old man sitting shirtless upon his cot, with Rachel between his spread knees. Bits and pieces of their conversation tugged at his memory. He felt his chest lighten at the obvious conclusion. And all this time he had thought Rachel was about to bed his friend.

"But why the disguise? You don't normally attend your patients dressed this way."

"Only Tully can answer that," she whispered.

"Why Tully? Why not you?"

"Because as a doctor, I can't divulge that information to anyone."

"Well then, I suppose I'd better pay my friend a visit."

He'd stated his intent but he didn't move. Still straddling Rachel's legs, he lingered, refusing to relinquish her nearness.

Rachel didn't move either. Each only stared at the other across the distance, the silence building around them like the eye of a storm.

"I'd better go," he announced again. He smiled at her and started to leave.

"Don't please," she whispered. "I'd like you to stay."

Her words were like a balm to Grey's soul, but he knew they'd been said only to heal the breech between them.

"Rachel, if I stay, we both know what will happen."

Her answer came matter-of-factly. "I want it to happen."

Grey's breath caught. "I want it, too, more than you know." He ran his fingers through his rumpled hair. "But not like this. My God, woman, I could have hurt you. How would you feel later?'' He grabbed her shoulders and held her steady.

His question hung between them for several charged seconds.

''I'll feel wonderful.''

He couldn't believe his ears. Nevertheless, her frankness pleased him, reminding Grey again of the woman who'd won his admiration in the past few weeks. She was a doctor. She knew more about the body's anatomy than he could ever hope to know. But that was in the clinical sense. And now that he knew her to be a virgin, how could he take her most precious gift when he had nothing of value to offer in return?

Rachel must have sensed his thoughts. ''I've never been with a man before tonight, not in the carnal sense. But in medical school I studied the mating procedure.'' She took a deep breath before continuing. ''I want you to show me how it's done. . . . '' The request was calmly delivered, the words of an apprentice to an artisan. Her voice trailed off, but she held his gaze.

''In other words, this will be strictly a clinical experience?'' Grey worked his mouth, trying to hide a smile.

''Well . . . yes, something like that.'' But Rachel pricked at the thought that he might very well consider her nothing more than a scientific experiment. Even that, however, was better than nothing at all.

''Then it will be my pleasure to show you.''

Slipping from the table with his back to her, Grey began removing his clothing. Rachel would never know how her open invitation had affected him. Nothing he could think of would pleasure him more than to have her willingly beneath him. Her—Rachel—the beautiful

203

lady doctor. The woman who had teased and lectured, smiled and argued with him these past weeks, the woman who had played with his sensibilities since the moment she had presented herself to him in Tully's cabin. Even now he couldn't get his clothes off fast enough. He feared she'd change her mind and he'd miss his chance to do what he'd dreamed of doing so often in the last few weeks.

Grey heard the whooshing give of the leather table-top when Rachel slipped down to remove her own garments. He gave her a few moments, then turned to see her standing, securely wrapped in a white sheet, her shoulders and arms bare.

"You're cheating, Doc," he teased, slowly advancing toward her.

Rachel gripped the end of the sheet against her bosom. "Now I know how ridiculous you felt when you had to disrobe in front of me."

"Yeah, under the circumstances it was tough."

"But now it's not?" She eyed the naked man who stood unashamed before her.

"Now I'm in control," he replied, his dimple slicing his cheek when he smiled. "Shall we begin our examination?" He moved his golden brows in comical exaggeration while setting her back upon the table, then leaned against her covered knees. "I promise this won't hurt."

They both knew it would.

"I'm a little nervous," Rachel replied.

"It will be over in no time. And if we're lucky, you might even enjoy it."

"And you?"

"I'll probably die of pleasure."

As she sat on the edge of the table, Grey slowly peeled the sheet away, then stood back to admire her. To him Rachel would never look more beautiful. Except, perhaps, for the night when he'd watched her dance with Cal. Her skin was flushed—perhaps from their earlier encounter, perhaps from her own candor. Grey knew only that her beauty took his breath away.

He dropped the sheet behind her, then lifted her to lay her gently upon the table surface. Once again he settled himself above her. He braced his arms against the table, feeling the muscles in his arms quiver from sheer nervousness. Slowly, he lowered himself to her.

Rachel felt Grey's warm, naked length pressed against her own. It was wonderful, she decided, being so intimately close to a man.

And what a man he was—big, strong, and capable of doing whatever he wanted to her. But Rachel was not the least intimidated by this knowledge. She had seen him at his worst—in the throes of an angry rage, and even then he had been gentle with her. In his own way he was now as defenseless as she. Like all women since Eve, Rachel felt the heady power she wielded over this man. His need made them equals.

With complete trust Rachel abandoned herself to the world of passion. She allowed Grey full reign of her body and in turn discovered things about a man she'd never learned in her textbooks.

When Grey's fingers found the hot dampness between her thighs, she groaned with pleasure, then at his coaxing gently steered him to the entrance of her being, exalting in the power she held in her hands.

"Oh, Rach, I can't wait much longer." His husky whisper blew against her ear like the summer wind.

"Then don't," she barely whispered as she wrapped her legs around his thighs.

Rachel tried to think like a doctor, to remember what she'd read about arousal and the pain she'd feel from his entry. But her woman's mind washed away all textbook images. Her pulse throbbed with insatiable need, her soul craved for him to become one with her.

By her consent, Grey entered her with one swift thrust. Breaking through the barrier that held all her womanly secrets, he buried himself in her liquid warmth. She didn't cry out, but smiled up at him through her rich brown lashes.

"If I hurt you I'm sorry," he apologized.

"I should die such a painless death."

"There's more," he promised, encouraged by her response.

"I'm eager to learn," she replied, instinctively gathering his length deeper inside her.

He bent to kiss her ear, her nose, her mouth. Then he propped on his hands, his eyes gliding slowly over her as soft as a caress.

Rachel's gaze sought the place where their bodies were joined and felt an uncontrollable desire to cry, not with regret, but because she was so moved by the experience.

"You're beautiful, you know," he whispered.

She blushed rosy with pleasure. "So are you."

Grey felt her muscles tighten around him and pressed himself deeper within her silken grasp. Together they began to move in perfect rhythm in the ancient dance of fulfillment while Grey tried to hold back his need. Some moments later he felt her climax and in that instant poured himself into her womb. Spent, their bodies shiny and slick from their heated efforts, they lay joined in the aftermath of love.

Their passion receded in slow degrees, like the endless revolutions formed by a water drop on a still pond. They lay entwined, both lost in their personal thoughts.

It was Grey who moved first, but only because he feared he might crush the woman beneath him.

When he withdrew from Rachel's body, she frowned, hating the cool emptiness when their naked flesh separated.

"You're an apt student," he whispered, nuzzling her ear while balancing himself on the narrow table beside her.

Rachel sighed. "It was better than I ever imagined it to be." She rolled to face him.

"But next time I suggest we try a bed." He placed a light kiss upon her nose.

Grey's suggestion of a next time sent Rachel's spirits soaring. She drank in the comfort of his nearness, basking in the feeling that she was desirable.

"You don't like my table," she teased him.

"I love your table. It's our audience I'm concerned with."

Rachel stiffened in surprise. "Our audience?" She followed the direction of Grey's stare.

From the other side of the room where a trace of early light brightened the dark corner, Cal grinned at them from his hook on the wall.

"Right nosy fellow, I'd say."

Rachel laughed—that deep throaty laugh that made Grey's insides melt. "Another curious pupil," she answered, smiling.

Grey planted playful kisses in the hollow of her throat. "Shall we show him more?"

Lavender daybreak colored the world outside the surgery windows. Somewhere in the distance a cock crowed, reminding Rachel that morning was fast approaching.

"Oh my goodness." She pushed up on her elbow, nearly sending Grey flying off the table. Only his agility saved him from being thrown onto the floor. He slipped down and pulled the sheet around Rachel's shoulders. No longer locked in the warmth of Rachel's embrace, the room felt chilled. Quickly, he gathered his clothes and began to dress.

"Aren't you afraid I'll see your private parts?" Rachel teased, watching his every move from where she still sat on the examining table.

"After last night I don't own anything private." His answer had the desired effect. Rachel blushed crimson. But dauntlessly she replied, "I've never had such a cheeky patient."

"Patient?" Grey's eyes widened with surprise. "You treat all your patients with such tender love and care?"

"I told you I'm a good doctor."

"Too damn good." Grabbing her, Grey lifted Rachel from the table and slid her down his length until her feet rested upon the floor.

Taking her in his arms, he kissed her—a kiss that snatched Rachel's breath away and started the blood thrumming through her veins. It took all her resolve to break away from his embrace.

"I have a patient coming this morning," she replied breathlessly.

"Anyone I know?" he whispered between kisses.

Stilling her hands against his chest, she added. "Not this morning, but this afternoon I do."

"Who?"

"My friend, Sarah Ballard."

"Ah, yes, Frank Ballard's wife."

Grey recalled the woman who had championed Rachel's contribution to the loggers' fund. He'd admired the lady's pluck, standing up to her overbearing husband in front of the whole town. But Ballard's displeasure regarding his wife's actions had not gone unnoticed. He wondered what Mrs. Ballard had suffered later, in the privacy of their own home.

"She's expecting a child," Rachel offered, "and she wants me to be her physician."

"Do you think it wise to encourage her patronage?"

Grey wasn't certain whose welfare he feared for more, Rachel's or Ballard's young wife. Sarah Ballard had been frail-looking. Sickly was an even more apt description.

Rachel considered Grey's misgivings. Given how Ballard had so rudely snatched Grey from her company to introduce him to his colleagues at the supper, it had appeared that the two men were acquainted. The only logic for his statement, therefore, would surely be because she'd been upset over the conditions of Ballard's camp. And her threat to take him to task. But caring for Sarah was another matter entirely.

After much thought, she answered, "Of course it's wise. Sarah sent a note yesterday saying she'd come by this afternoon, and, quite frankly, I'm thrilled."

"All I can say, Rachel, is don't be meddling in affairs that don't concern you." Grey tucked his shirt-tails into his pants.

"Meddle? I'm a doctor, and Sarah has expressed a desire for me to attend her during her pregnancy. I don't call that meddling."

From the look on Rachel's face, Grey could see a storm brewing. After what they had just shared, an altercation was the last thing he wanted. "Maybe 'meddle' wasn't the right word," he added, hoping to soften his statement.

"I believe meddling would be more aptly described as what I intend to do when I see Sarah's husband again. The deplorable conditions in his logging camp should be brought to his attention and rectified. If he doesn't see fit to make some changes, I'll have everyone in this town questioning the man's business practices."

"That, my love, is the last thing you need to do."

Rachel stood facing Grey, the sheet she'd pulled around her earlier temporarily forgotten in her attempt to defend her position. One side had slipped down, revealing one dark aureole. Grey lifted the errant sheet to cover the inviting distraction. He cupped his fingers around her arms and pulled her close.

"Listen to me, Rachel," he pleaded, "you must not confront Frank Ballard with your accusations. He is not a man who will deal lightly with your interference."

"But, Grey, he should not be allowed to hold those poor families in bondage just because he's richer than they are."

"You're making more of this than is needed—"

"I'm not," she insisted and tried to pull away.

"Rachel, listen to me." He shook her. "There are things you don't know about Ballard. Things I can't explain to you at this time, but I'm ordering you not to confront him.''

Rachel pulled back from him. ''And what right do you have to order me?'' Her temper flared out of control. ''Because you bedded me? Does that automatically give you the right to govern my opinions? Any man with half a brain and any schooling at all would not feel the need to order a lady about!''

Grey flinched as though she'd struck him. As soon as the hateful words had escaped her lips, Rachel wished she could reclaim them. Instead, she softened beneath the weight of his withering stare. ''I'm sorry.''

Defeated, Grey dropped his hands to his side and turned to leave. Rachel ran to him and threw her arms around his waist, searching his eyes for understanding. ''I shouldn't have said that. I lost my temper.''

For what seemed an eternity he neither moved nor spoke. His arms hung limply at his side. Where fire had burned earlier in the depths of his blue eyes, now there was only ice.

''Please,'' she begged, ''don't leave this way.''

Unable to deny his own longings a moment longer, Grey took Rachel into his arms. He lifted her chin with his finger.

''There are things I can't explain to you now. Things about myself. I need you to trust me in this.''

''But what things?'' she asked. He didn't answer but continued as though she'd not spoken. ''Promise me you'll stay away from Ballard's house.''

''I can't do that, Grey. Sarah is going to be my patient. She's very near her delivery time. I'll have to make house calls.''

"Then promise me you won't confront Ballard with your complaints."

Rachel hesitated. She wanted to tell Ballard how she felt about him. She wanted to alert the world to his wrongdoings. But because Grey had asked her to trust him, she knew she must. For the time being anyway. She'd concern herself only with Sarah's welfare.

"I promise."

"That's my girl."

Grey gave her one last kiss before he left her.

Rachel watched from the window as Grey exited through her front gate. When he'd disappeared around the corner of the house, a heavy emptiness settled over her. Weeks before, if anyone had told her that she'd be standing in her own surgery watching her lover disappear, she would have laughed at the absurdity.

Long ago, Rachel had given up any girlhood dreams of settling down with a man, contenting herself instead with her medical practice. But now, as his scent clung to her hair and skin, she realized that loving Grey Devlin was as easy as drawing a fresh breath. Maybe, she thought, recalling the scene in Opal's house so long ago, she'd loved him from their first encounter.

She no longer worried over his guilt or his neglect of allowing the opium shipment into port. He'd asked her to trust him, and for now that was all she could do. She turned from the window to prepare herself for her first patient of the day.

Chapter 11

Rachel stared at the wan face of her old friend and wanted to cry. The lively, sparkling poise of the Sarah Collins she had known all her life had changed to one of solemn frailty. The sweetness was still there, written in the depths of her eyes when she spoke, but her vivacity was gone, replaced by a wariness—a guarded one—as if the woman stood braced for some emotional attack.

Most women took on a radiance when they were with child. Their cheeks became rosy, their nails grew thick and strong, their hair glistened like the rays of the morning sun. Sarah's face had the same pallor Rachel had noticed the last time she'd seen her. Her nails appeared dry and brittle, and her corkscrew ringlets, gathered into a severe chignon, had turned dull and lifeless.

The first act of a physician in assessing a patient was to look, to take note of any signs out of the ordinary. And Sarah Ballard, standing in the doorway of the surgery with her hand in Rachel's, looked far from an ordinarily healthy woman in her last stages of pregnancy.

"Come in and let's see how you are." Rachel took her friend's wrap and seated her beside the large desk. She took her own seat before expressing her welcome. "I'm so glad you came."

Sarah smiled for the first time since she had greeted Rachel at the front door. "I, too. I should have come long before now."

From her desk drawer Rachel retrieved a sheet of paper and a pen. "We have much to catch up on, but you must be eager to know how your baby is faring." She scribbled on the paper, remembering her own sense of fulfillment in having finally known a man in the biblical sense, and how complete he had made her feel. Looking at Sarah Ballard, Rachel pictured herself full with Grey's child, then blinked against the intrusive thought. "We'll talk as we go along."

"I'd like that," Sarah replied, her hands clasped tightly over her stomach. "I probably shouldn't dawdle too long, though. Frank—my husband—doesn't like me to be gone from the house."

Rachel laid down the pen and studied her friend with a curious intensity. Sarah seemed like a distraught child, ready to bolt from the room. "My dear," she said, trying to calm the woman, "you have taken the first step toward really caring for yourself and your baby." Her next words were a gentle inquiry. "I must ask this, for your answer affects how we'll see you through the next few weeks. How do you feel about this baby?"

Sarah reared back in her chair. She seemed astonished by the question. "Why Rachel, what a thing to ask. Of course, I'm thrilled about the baby. He—or she—is the one thing I have that I feel close to, that I can call my very own.''

At her explanation Sarah's eyes lit up for the first time, and Rachel could see in their depths a glimmer of hope for the future. She had seen this look many times, the revealing message that no closer bond existed than that between mother and unborn child as she neared her time of delivery. And now that Grey had shown her the deep intensity of love-making, Rachel suddenly ached to feel her own baby move beneath her heart.

But what her patient didn't say was equally clear. It confirmed for Rachel what she had already suspected—that life with Frank Ballard wasn't ideal. "In that case, dear friend, you and I have a lot of work to do.''

Sarah responded with a raised brow. "Work? But Doctor Wilson said I needed rest, though I don't sleep well at night.''

"And Doctor Wilson was right . . . to a point.'' Sarah made more notes on her paper, then touched on a more sensitive area. "Sarah, this may seem like prying, but you made a choice to have me for your physician. Now it is my responsibility to give you the very best care I am capable of rendering. You remember how my father used to poke and prod when you were sick with the fever? And how he wouldn't let you rest until you had confessed to him that you had taken your grandfather's medicine just to see how it tasted?''

Sarah gave Rachel a smile then, a real honest-to-goodness look of mischievous delight. "I remember,'' she said.

"Well, today you're going to get more of the same,

except those were childhood questions. The questions I ask today will require grown-up replies. And they may not be so easy to answer."

Sarah sat staring at Rachel, nervously wringing her hands. "Rachel," she finally said, "I know we were very close when we were in school . . . and I'd like nothing better than to renew that friendship. But the fact is I've been under the care of Doctor Wilson for several months now, and he never put me on edge by delving into my personal life." She stopped for a moment. "That is what you're about to do, isn't it?"

Rachel reached over and placed her hand on her friend's. "It may seem that way, and it may seem totally unnecessary. But I want you to know that anything you tell me—anything at all—in our patient–physician relationship remains strictly between us. No one—not your husband, not any relative or acquaintance—will know what we discuss. It will all remain confidential, like a private secret. No one else will know unless you tell them."

She patted her new patient's hand affectionately. "And you know how good we were at keeping secrets." That elicited a laugh from Sarah and suddenly she seemed at ease for the first time. "All right," she said, "you can ask your questions. But if I feel you're prying, I'll tell you so."

"Fair enough. And if you tell me so, then we'll discuss why I asked you in the first place."

Sarah suddenly reached up with a handkerchief to dab at her eye. "I just can't believe you've come so far. A doctor. A real doctor. When you went off to school, I remember dreaming about you and trying to reach out to you, but I never could. Now that you're

216

back, I fear I've lost my best friend to a higher calling.''

''Nonsense. I'm not going anywhere.'' Rachel picked up her stethoscope from her desk. ''Now let's take a listen to your heart. You do still have one, don't you?'' Sarah chuckled at the quip and Rachel thought she heard, somewhere deep inside, her old school chum coming back to life.

After Rachel had completed her examination, she had determined that Sarah could expect her baby to appear in about three weeks. But since firstborns were notoriously late, she warned her that another four to five weeks wouldn't be that unheard of.

''And here is the schedule I've worked up for you.''

''This is the work you warned me of?'' Sarah gave her new doctor a look of reproach.

''Indeed. It lists the foods you must eat, including red meat and dark green vegetables, lots of milk, and your outdoor activities.''

''Activities? But my baby is almost due.''

''You can handle this. If your garden is as beautiful as I remember, it should be a pleasure to be out in it. I want you walking around, drinking in the sunshine. When you don't feel like walking, sit outdoors with your feet up. With activity and plenty of fresh air during the day, you'll sleep better at night.'' Rachel handed Sarah her list and another paper with instructions for an expectant mother.

''I don't understand,'' Sarah added. ''Why didn't Doctor Wilson give me all these instructions?''

Rachel had no intention of warring with the illustrious society physician on the hill. So she let the question pass with, "Let's just say, as a new doctor I've learned some new methods."

As Sarah donned her wrap to leave, Rachel took her by the shoulders. "There's one more thing I'm prescribing. You'll find it on the paper, but of everything written on it, this is the most important—you are to have absolutely no stress." She looked deeply into her friend's eyes so as not to be misunderstood. "I mean it, Sarah, no stress from any quarter. It's not good for you and it's most assuredly not good for your baby."

When Sarah lowered her eyes, Rachel knew she'd gotten the point across. "I promise," she murmured.

"Fine, that's all I ask. And from the strength of the little fellow's heartbeat, he's going to thank you for taking such good care of him."

"Him?" Sarah seemed curious that Rachel could tell the gender of her baby.

"Or her."

The sun was setting as Sarah Ballard left. Rachel stood on her front porch a moment longer after her new patient's buggy had pulled away, straining to see some sign of Grey Devlin and his landlady's dog coming up the street. But it was still early and Grey was probably at the pier finishing up his day. Besides, she scolded herself, why should it matter so much whether he passed her house tonight or not?

As she turned to go back in, Rachel caught a glimpse of a man on the other side of the street, sitting in a doorway reading the paper. She wouldn't have thought anything unusual about him had he not made an effort to keep his paper spread in front of his face as though he didn't wish to be seen.

For an instant Rachel relived the nightmarish ordeal on the beach and wondered if one of the same men was spotting her for yet another attack. The way the man sat, with his elbows propped on his widespread knees, his newspaper not six inches from his face, sent a cold chill up her spine. This was not a man leisurely recapping the day's events. This was a man keeping an eye on her.

Trying not to appear that she had noticed him, Rachel stepped back into her house and locked her door. Then she watched through the windowpane to see what the person would do next. She didn't have long to wait.

Bending down a corner of his paper, the man stole a glance toward her house, then seeing that she had gone inside, folded his newspaper, stood and tucked it under his arm. He shifted his yachting cap on his head and removed his pipe from his lips before starting down the street toward the water.

Rachel breathed a sigh of relief, then immediately questioned the man's motives. Why on earth was Tully watching her house? There was only one way to find out. Rachel whipped the door open.

"Tully!" she called. The old sailor checked his stride before turning her way. "Could you spare me a moment?"

A look of surprise crossed his face, as if he'd just been caught with his fingers in the candy jar. He hesitated, then hunched his shoulders and started across the street in her direction.

Tully opened the garden gate and ambled to the porch. "Evenin', Doc," the old man said, looking up

219

at Rachel. He seemed slightly abashed at having been caught watching her house. "I was just passin' by on my way down from Miss Purdy's and thought I'd rest a spell on that there stoop." He turned to point to where he'd just been. "Funny, I didn't realize I was right in front of your place until you hollered at me."

Rachel looked down on the sailor, his puffy eye having taken on a deep purplish cast. Although it must still be tender, it did add a touch of character to his kindly but weathered face. All in all, he looked none the worse for wear, and for that Rachel was grateful. But she still didn't know why he'd been spying on her house.

"Come now, Tully," she scolded in her most tolerant voice. "You're telling me you've been visiting Martha Purdy and that you just happened by? Why, I know she's sweet on you. Just wait until I see that dear lady and tell her how glad I am that you came to call."

"Now hold on, Doc." Tully cleared his throat. "Maybe you don't really want to do that . . . bein's it might embarrass Miss Purdy an' all."

"And why would it do that, do you suppose?" Rachel raised her brow at the old sailor, his flimsy excuse for being in her neighborhood about to backfire on him.

"Well, maybe . . ."

Rachel figured head-on confrontation was the best tactic. "You didn't really just come from the boarding house, now did you?"

Tully stared at the ground and shifted his newspaper under his arm. "Well, I guess not." He amended himself. "Not just now, that is."

"Well, what was it you were doing, just now?" Rachel prompted.

"Okay, Doc, you caught me. I can't lie to you. You see through me anyway." He grinned at her. "Yep, I was watchin' you."

"But, why? If you needed to see me, why didn't you just come on in?"

"You don't understand, miss. I didn't need to see you. I just needed to watch you. There's a difference."

"Won't you come in? I think you need to explain."

Tully looked around to see the street deserted. "No ma'am," he said. "I need to be on my way. Got things to do." He paused as if to find the right words. "I just thought I owed you. Those fellers who attacked me on the beach ain't been caught yet. I been nervous ever since you walked me into my house and told me who you were."

He shook his head in disbelief. "Why, when I come around on the beach and I'm starin' at this here party girl in leather britches, I thought I'd gone to my reward." He laughed at that. "Always wondered if when I died I'd get me a *fallen* angel."

His expression turned serious. "But then I heard yer voice and thought I was dreamin'. Doc, I still can't figure out what happened or why you were there in the first place." He looked her up and down. "And you bein' no more'n pint-sized. How in the world could you have outwitted them two devils?"

In a low voice she answered, "Chloroform."

"Chloroform?" He looked incredulous. "The knock-out drug?"

"The very same." She gestured toward her surgery. "Being a physician does have its advantages."

"B-but—" he stammered. "It makes no sense. There was two o' them and only one o' you."

"Let's just say I had the help of the angels." She smiled then, thinking he hadn't been so far off in his appraisal of the situation. "The important thing is that you're safe."

"For the moment. How'd you find out I was in trouble anyway? And why didn't you git some help?"

"It was late," she lied. "I was treating a sailor who had overheard the plan at Baldy's. He said he didn't know who else to tell. Said he didn't know whom he could trust. Seems you've got friends in this town."

"Who?" Tully removed his cap and scratched his head. "And did he go down there with you?"

Rachel found her way out of further explanation. "Tully, you're asking questions I can't answer now. You know doctors can't talk about their patients. Why, then they'd have no privacy at all. Everybody'd know their business and their ailments. Let's just be grateful he told me."

Tully screwed up his face at her reasoning. "I just wanted to thank him."

"It's as good as done. Your friend now knows you're safe and life can get back to normal for a while."

"Not while them two jackasses is out there somewhere. Uh, sorry, Doc," he apologized. "And you're not safe either. Not if'n they saw you."

"Oh, but they didn't. That is, they didn't see Doctor Rachel Thomas. What they saw is exactly what you saw: a prostitute dressed up in all her finery. And believe me, it's all safely packed away. It served its purpose. I don't plan to be using it again."

"But where'd you get such an outfit?" He stopped for a moment. Turning his head to the side, he seemed to be searching for something buried in his memory.

"I've seen you before. I mean," he amended, "I've seen you dressed like that before. No one could forget that long, fluffy pink hair."

His eyes crinkled in thought and Rachel knew he was about to recall more. Tully was Grey's close friend. And after being fished from the cold bay and being nursed for days, Grey was bound to have furnished him with a full description of the harlot who had lured him to sea.

Rachel felt her pulse begin to race. "All right, Tully. This time you've caught me. I borrowed the outfit from one of the girls at Opal's."

"Borrowed? Whatever for?"

"Think about it for a moment. In a town like this, who's the safest woman to walk the streets at night?"

It took no more than a second to respond. "A whore."

"Precisely. Before the other night when I was pulled into a dark alley by some drunk, I never stopped to worry about walking on the wharf at night if I had to tend to a patient. Nobody had ever bothered me before. But since then I've been thinking it might be safer to blend in with the women who normally walk there."

"Bejeezus, woman," Tully roared. "Doc, this whole town knows what happened to your father. That poor man would roll over in his grave if anything happened to you. You gotta promise me you won't ever do nothin' so stupid again. So what if the crimps do get me? I ain't nothin' worth riskin' your own neck fer. I done lived my life. You got a full one ahead o' you—a husband, babies . . ." His voice trailed off into thin air. He captured her gaze with his own tormented one. "You promise me, *right now,* you won't try none of this

223

foolishness again. I won't rest easy thinkin' you're about town lookin' fer trouble.''

Rachel stared at Tully. She had never seen him so worked up. And his words—husband, babies—with them came the image that had haunted her throughout Sarah's visit, that of Grey Devlin and the thought of some day carrying his children. Her blood turned warm at the very idea.

The old man looked ready to explode, scolding her as if she were his child, and a reckless one at that. Under other circumstances she would simply shoo him away, placating him with her shallow assurances.

But Tully looked genuinely alarmed, and no frivolous treatment of his concern was called for. ''I'm sorry if I gave you cause to worry,'' she said. ''I really do promise to be careful from now on. I don't wish to relive the other night any more than you do. But, Tully, you must promise to be careful, too.'' She tried to lighten the moment. ''After all, my practice is growing with all the patients you keep recommending to me. I can't lose that now, can I?''

Tully looked downright smug as he squared his shoulders and started to back off down the front walk. ''You're right, Doc. Just don't be fergettin' that fact.'' With that, he opened the gate.

Rachel reached for her doorknob, then looked back. ''And, Tully,'' she added, ''It's very thoughtful of you to want to watch over me. But it's really not necessary, truly.''

The old man faced her, the lines on his face set. ''I'll be the judge of that.'' With that, he started down the street, leaving Rachel staring after him.

* * *

With rain drumming outside, the crackling fire took the chill off Tully's cabin and added a warm glow to the walls filled with memorabilia from the old man's years at sea. Grey took another sip of hot coffee from an enamel cup and watched his friend across from him, puffing on his white clay pipe.

The strong, sweet scent of tobacco permeated the room, and Tully, though still bruised from his ordeal on the beach, nevertheless seemed content with the world. Against his snow-white hair and beard and ruddy complexion, his swollen left eye had taken on an ugly, deep purplish cast. But at least he could open the eye and it would improve . . . thanks to Rachel.

". . . Then she tells me 'chloroform,'" Tully was saying. "That's how she knocked 'em out. Said she had the help of the angels." The old man shook his head, snickering. "I tell you, there's more to this story than she's lettin' on."

"I'm sure there is." Thinking back to the moment when she stood facing him in her home, Grey still couldn't believe what Rachel had accomplished, or that she had dared to try. Just as he couldn't believe his reaction to her the moment he'd realized her identity. Not some prostitute who could harden a man's shaft with the right practiced look or stroke, but a beautiful woman who had touched his very soul.

He willed his mind back to the present. "I passed Opal's on the way here after your attack. She and two of her girls were returning home from this direction, huddling and giggling until they saw me. Then they hushed as if they'd been sharing some big secret. I'll

225

bet you a week's worth of whiskey they had something to do with you not being on your way to Hong Kong right now."

"So that's what she meant by the angels. I knew there was no way she coulda been workin' alone. Them brutes that attacked me were sent from hell." He took a long puff on his pipe. "I swear, that's some little woman. Now you're tellin' me the doc and Chinook are one and the same and that she tried to shanghai you because she thought you were crooked. Then she risks her neck to save me, not fearin' the devil himself."

He looked over at Grey, tapping the table with his forefinger. "When she was standin' over me fixin' my face, I was in no shape to be comparin' her to the whore you had described, who nearly had you killed. Then when we were talkin', she changed the subject real quick like." He shook his head in wonderment. "Imagine, Chinook and Dr. Rachel . . . one and the same."

He worked the stem of his pipe in his mouth. "But we gotta see to it she doesn't try nothin' like this again. It scares me to think she could end up like her papa, poor man. I'm afraid she's just like him."

"What do you mean?"

"Not willin' to put up with this town goin' to rack and ruin. Or watchin' innocent folk get hurt and killed while the law does nothin' to help." He pointed the stem of his pipe toward Grey. "That was the way of her father, Dr. Theodore Thomas. A good man he was, too. I got to know him pretty well while you were in prison. Decided to come back to my hometown for a while. Guess my roots were callin' me. Anyways,

226

with you gone, somehow the sea no longer held the same appeal for me. My breathin' got bad for a while and he treated me for weeks on end.''

He looked down at his pipe. ''Even had to give this up for a time. We talked a lot. I told him about us— you and me—about how I'd known you since you were a scrawny kid, and he told me about his work and his family. That's when I learned about his daughter. Never got to see her, though, bein' she was away at school. He was so proud of her. Still would be, yessir.''

''So he was a social reformer, too?''

''You bet he was. Complained all the time about the new owner up at Camp Ross. Seems Frank Ballard practically stole the place when the old owner couldn't meet his payroll. Old Mr. Ross had his timber stolen right out from under him more than once. You don't sell your timber, you don't pay your men.''

Grey sat up, instantly alert to the turn in conversation. ''So that's how Ballard went into the logging business.''

''Yep, and right away he started cuttin' pay, cuttin' corners, and overchargin'. Workers up to their necks in company store bills couldn't leave, and morale dipped real low. And you well know, when morale drops, accidents rise.''

''And Dr. Thomas started protesting conditions.'' Grey could see the resemblance between father and daughter with every word his old friend spoke.

Tully looked over at him, nodding. ''To the point of writing articles for the *Astorian,* but nothin' was ever done. Sometimes when I'd take my meals up at Miss Purdy's, I could see Ballard's house up the street. Some real rough-looking characters came and went from there, including that scalawag, Rooster Crowe. Why that man's not behind bars I'll never know. There's a sayin' in this town that this 'rooster' crows at midnight. Seems every time he shows up, trouble starts brewin' and by midnight men start disappearin'. I got real worried about old Doc Thomas. Every time he had to see a patient down here after dark, a couple of us would tag along—until that night he disappeared."

Tully pursed his lips and shook his head. "The last time I saw him leave his house was when he went up to Ballard's one afternoon. He came away from there lookin' none too happy. Before I had a chance to talk to him again, he was gone."

"So you think Ballard had something to do with the doctor's abduction?"

"Either him or that no-good Crowe. And I don't believe old Rooster's smart enough to act on his own."

"Can you remember anything about the men who grabbed you?"

"Not a danged thing except one of 'em had an iron fist. I wouldn't be surprised if they answered to Crowe, and to that Ballard feller."

"Meaning that perhaps Frank Ballard didn't stop with abducting Rachel's father."

"Could be," Tully replied. "Could be."

Grey rose from the table and poured another round of coffee for Tully and himself before he sat back down. "You know Rachel has taken on Ballard's wife as her patient."

"I know. I saw her leave the doc's house while I was there."

Grey stared at the contents of his cup, becoming thoughtful. "Sarah's baby is due pretty soon. It's only a matter of time before Rachel starts seeing her at her own home, and I'm not at all comfortable with that arrangement."

"But she should be all right if she's there to take care of Ballard's wife. She's not a threat to the man, not like her father was."

Grey looked over at his friend. "You remember how he snubbed her at the box social. Just being introduced to her turned his face into a block of ice. You don't think he suffered a sudden attack of guilt, do you?"

"Come to think of it, he did pull you away right quick to meet his cronies."

"Well, I have no intentions of sending her up to that house alone. Not with him there."

"Won't you look just a mite suspicious escortin' the lady doctor in the middle of the day when you're supposed to be on the job?"

Grey gave his friend a sheepish grin. "Not since I learned for sure why Ballard had me hired, to ignore his log pirating. Now I have specific reasons for calling on him and giving him regular reports, and he'll love the idea that I'm playing right into his hands."

He took a swig of coffee, then planted his cup on the table. "You know, I almost believed the mayor when he told me he wanted me for harbormaster because I could read regulations and navigational charts. Almost—until he informed me that Ballard had recommended me. Then it all added up—no one of good repute would hire me after prison and this job was waiting for me. All I had to do was agree to focus on certain functions while overlooking—how did Ballard put it?—slight irregularities. And now I know what they are." He gave a groan at the audacity of the man who had sent him to prison.

"I rotted away two years of my life for something that scoundrel did, and I promised myself that some-day we would settle up." He laughed aloud. "If only Ballard knew the real reason I took this job—"

"Your life wouldn't be worth an ounce of chewin' tobaccy," Tully answered for him. "You've got to keep Ballard thinkin' he can trust you. If you tip your hand too soon and tell anyone else what you know about the log piratin', he'll know you let the word out. And you'll be shark bait for sure."

"Tully, old man," Grey responded, "right now all I want to do is keep the lady doctor away from Ballard. And the less she knows, the better off we'll all be. No need in her getting in the middle of my investigation."

"Right." Tully rubbed his beard thoughtfully. "And I don't suppose you'd be tryin' to keep her out of danger at the same time . . . merely in the name of friendship." His blue eyes, one ringed in purple creases, twinkled at his words.

Chapter 12

Grey smiled at her. From where he sat across the kitchen table, he radiated charm and sophistication. The blue stripe in his cotton shirt duplicated the exact color of his eyes. It had been three days since Rachel had seen him, and he appeared to have grown more handsome in the meantime.

"And how have you been?" he asked, pouring ruby red wine into a crystal glass. Reaching across a vase of sweet-smelling lilacs in the middle of the small table, he handed her the drink.

"Busy," she replied.

Rachel accepted the spirits and eyed the jewel-colored liquid before putting it to her lips. It felt cool to her parched mouth.

After having shared such an intimate act with Grey only days before, Rachel never dreamed she'd feel so uncomfortable in his company now. After his arrival some thirty minutes earlier, they'd exchanged the normal pleasantries about the weather and events before the silence between them had built to gargantuan proportions. He, too, seemed uncomfortable. Had she been wrong in inviting Grey here this evening?"

"How is your new patient?" he asked, after taking a bite of his salmon steak.

His question took her by surprise. In the last few days, Rachel's practice had picked up. She'd seen several new patients, including two women who'd attended the fundraiser. She stared blankly at him.

"Sarah Ballard," he reminded her.

"Oh, Sarah. She's doing very well, thank you." Not knowing what else to say on the subject, Rachel lifted her glass to her lips and took a big gulp. The wine flamed a path down to her stomach, but didn't relieve the anxiety building inside her.

Her action drew a questioning look from Grey, but he continued to chew his food with fervor—thankful, Rachel imagined, to be doing something with his mouth since small talk seemed impossible.

"You outdid yourself with this meal."

"Thank you." Rachel smiled at him, wishing the lump in her chest would dissolve so she could swallow her own dinner and verify Grey's opinion of her cooking.

She'd slaved all day preparing their meal. Priding herself on her cooking skills, Rachel enjoyed sharing her culinary creations with others. Since her return to Astoria there had been no opportunity to cook for anyone other than herself and she'd looked forward to sharing this meal with Grey. Although the town would surely frown on the idea of a young, respectable woman entertaining a man unchaperoned, Rachel had given this propriety but a moment's consideration. After all, she was not just any young woman. She was a doctor, adult and independent, quite capable of making her own decisions. But perhaps she had acted too hastily. The evening just wasn't going as she'd envisioned.

She knew the food was good—salmon steaks and boiled potatoes in a dill sauce with tiny green peas. For dessert she'd made a sponge cake and planned to top it off with her own brandied peaches. Earlier she'd rummaged through her father's supply of dinner wines stowed away in the small root cellar at the back of the house, choosing a deep red burgundy for its rich color. But no matter how good the food looked or tasted, if she and Grey could do no more than exchange a few tense pleasantries, then Rachel knew the dinner was futile.

Not only had she prepared a fine meal, she'd also worked overtime on her appearance. For the first time in Rachel's life she wanted to impress a man with her feminine graces. As the minutes now ticked away into an hour, Rachel believed herself sadly lacking in such attributes.

She'd chosen her outfit with care. A gold checkered dress made of light wool with fresh lace at her throat and wrists that a friend from school had said made her look like a true gentlewoman. She'd washed her hair with lavender soap before securing the mass of mahogany ringlets back from her face with a gold velvet ribbon. In a last-minute decision, she'd even removed her glasses.

With her mother's topaz earrings sparkling in her ears, Rachel had felt presentable when she'd opened the door and found herself rewarded with Grey's approving smile. But now, because she was sadly lacking in the graces of small talk, the whole evening was disintegrating before her eyes.

How was it possible, she wondered, that a reasonably intelligent, educated woman, couldn't make one light and amusing remark to her handsome dinner partner? All she could do was color outrageously when she caught him staring at her through the cluster of flowers. Rachel shifted nervously in her chair, wishing she could disappear into the cracks of her freshly polished floor.

Things were not going as Grey anticipated. He stared at the beautiful woman across from him, the scent of flowers and herbs strong in the small, close kitchen, trying to think of something to say that would put them both at ease. But clever conversation seemed to be as absent as the dwindling light outside.

Grey had done nothing for the last few days but dream of this woman who'd surrendered herself to him so willingly a few nights before. When he'd received Rachel's dinner invitation, he'd counted the moments until he could be in her company again. But after his arrival at the appointed time and after their first pleasant exchange of conversation, he felt as though his tongue had been tied into a knot.

He'd always prided himself on being entertaining, and had been told by other women that he was a charmer. But tonight he found himself sadly lacking in witty conversation. After much deliberation, Grey's thoughts turned morose. All the books in the world would never allow a man of his station to be on equal ground with the lady doctor.

He realized now, too late, he'd been a fool to allow things to get out of hand a few nights before. A tumble with a less than proper lady was one thing. But a woman of Rachel's social stratum, that was quite another. Regardless of what other women thought, to the one woman he wanted to impress, he knew he'd never measure up. The sooner he could eat and excuse himself, the better off they both would be.

Eyes the color of fine sherry peered at him through the stalks of lilac. He had to look a second time before he realized she had removed her glasses. He was touched that she had perhaps tried to impress him without them. He was even more touched to realize that with or without them, he would have thought her beautiful. But it was obvious that she was as nervous as she was lovely. She ate little but kept raising the wineglass again and again to her lips for something to do with her hands.

From the way she handled her glass, Grey supposed Rachel did not often indulge in spirits. For him it was equally awkward, for a seaman was much more at home with a glass of whiskey or a tankard of ale. For that matter, sitting across a flower-laden table from a beautiful, refined woman made him feel all the more out of place.

Grey looked around the small, cozy room, admiring its decor. "I like your kitchen." His voice seemed to knell through the room's silence. Rachel's garden of herbs overflowed the window containers, spilling not only greenery everywhere but filling the air with a spicy fragrance. "It smells like a summer afternoon," he added truthfully.

His compliment brought color to Rachel's already flushed cheeks. "I enjoy growing things," she answered, "not only for medicinal purposes, but also to use in my cooking."

"Medicine could never smell this good."

With a grandiose motion of his hand, Grey indicated

the whole kitchen. He felt pleased when his words brought a genuine smile to Rachel's face. The first since the evening had begun.

"You grew all of these?" When Rachel responded with such exuberance, Grey felt he'd indeed tapped a reservoir of information. But luck was not to remain on his side. With another sweep of his hand, Grey knocked over his wineglass. A wave of red liquid splashed across the front of his shirt and puddled in his lap.

Rachel jumped up from the table. Grabbing a towel, she quickly moved to his side.

"Your clothes, they'll be ruined." She blotted the deep red stain, covering both his stomach and crotch. On her knees beside him, she continued to wipe, until she suddenly realized what she'd been doing.

Her face turned the color of the blotch. "Oh my . . . I'm sorry." She tried to pull away.

Grey's hand stilled her wrist. His eyes sought hers. The air between them felt charged. And then he was kissing her.

With breathless, exciting kisses he smothered her mouth, and Rachel returned them with the same reckless abandon. Grey's earlier intentions about eating and taking his leave were forgotten in the maelstrom of emotions that swept them both away.

"You're not only good at growing herbs," he whispered huskily in her ear. He trailed kisses down her neck, relishing the feel of her beneath his lips. He spread her fingers against his enlarged organ. "Rachel, you make me senseless with desire."

She reveled over his maleness, loving the feel of his erection pressed against her palm. It was difficult for her to conceive that she wielded such power over this beautiful man who now made her own core gush with liquid fire.

Standing, Rachel pulled Grey up from his chair. "Come with me." Her voice was little more than a shaded plea.

Like a man hypnotized, Grey followed as Rachel led him away from the kitchen and into the narrow hall. Pausing outside a closed door, she pushed it open and drew him inside.

Twilight had settled around the little house. Rachel left his side and moved across the room. While Grey waited, his eyes adjusted to the diffused darkness. A myriad of shapes told him he was in a bedroom.

Rachel stood with her back to him. He heard the match make contact with the flint—smelled the tangy scent of sulphur—before an amber glow flooded the opaque dusk. The room took on a burnished glow.

Everywhere Grey looked he saw lace. White lace hung in weblike patterns throughout the room. A scarf of woven flowers covered the top of a pine chest. Lace-work spilled over the pedestal tables that flanked each side of the canopied brass bed. Rachel moved to the other table and lit the second lamp. Soon its amber glow buffed the room's whiteness.

Lace covered the bed canopy and formed a swag above the roller shade in the window. Like twin water-falls, two panels of lace spilled from the top of the window to the floor. The same window, Grey recalled, where he'd stood weeks before and watched Rachel dance with her skeleton.

Botanical prints decorated every wall. On one of the tables a white porcelain vase held sweet-smelling lilacs.

Matching floral rugs lay on the floor on both sides of the double bed.

Never in all of Grey's life had he seen a room so utterly feminine and tasteful. And one that seemed so out of character for the woman who presented such a dour side to the world.

That woman stood now in one corner, watching him, waiting for his reaction. And Grey sensed that what he said or did in the next few moments would make or break his relationship with Rachel.

His eyes focused on the bed. It, too, was covered in white with lace pillows resting on the bedcover. Grey imagined Rachel lying there nude, in the field of woven white adornments.

Releasing his breath slowly, he captured her gaze. His chest hurt with an indescribable emotion he couldn't name. Perhaps it was the realization that Rachel was sharing a part of herself with him that he knew for certain she'd never shared with another. Whatever it was, he ached to hold the woman.

"Just like your supper box," he finally managed to reply, "only better."

"You like it?" she asked shyly. The light from the lamps danced in the depths of her deep brown eyes.

"Darling, I love it."

Relieved at his declaration, Rachel flew across the room and landed in his arms. The earlier tension had flown. They were no longer awkward dinner partners. Now they were lovers, in each other's arms, where they belonged.

He lifted her up, swinging her around in a circle as they both laughed in unrestrained merriment. Grey then slid her leisurely down his length before releasing her.

"But now for the best part."

His fingers worked the small buttons of her dress, freeing each one. He peeled away the layers of Rachel's clothing until she stood nude before him. She did the same for him. Their eyes locked in loving combat while each rediscovered the other's body.

When it was no longer possible for them to stay apart, Grey lifted Rachel into his arms and strode to the bed. He dropped her on the downy cloud of softness, then joined her, reveling in the scent of freshly laundered sheets, the smoothness of cool linen against his naked skin, and the very eager and willing female beside him.

He touched every satin inch of her flesh, and she in turn repaid his favor. Soon they were tasting what their hands had explored until the fires of passion left them burning with the impatience of unfulfilled desire. At the moment Grey finally thrust into the delicious wet heat of her body, Rachel cried aloud and they both quivered with the pleasure of contentment.

Sometime later Grey finally managed to say, "Thank you."

Rachel snuggled against him and smiled. "For what?"

"For sharing all of yourself with me."

"This included?" she teased, tightening her muscles around him where they still lay attached.

"For that in particular." He groaned his satisfaction.

Soon, with Rachel's gentle coaxing, their passion boiled again. Grey felt her pleasure peak, then took her over the edge, joining her on the downward spin. The rhapsody of their blending was almost more than he could grasp.

Spent, he slipped from her sweet moistness and gathered her close. Pulling the linen bedcover over them both, they drifted into a deep, restful sleep, reserved only for satisfied lovers.

Hours later Grey awakened. Rachel no longer lay beside him, but had donned her glasses and a nightgown similar to the one she'd worn the night he'd watched her through the window.

So completely absorbed in the book she was reading, she didn't realize he was watching her. She sat at the foot of the bed with one leg tucked beneath her, the other one stretched out across the bed, revealing one thin ankle and bare foot.

Her dark hair spilled over her shoulders and down her back in a cascade of deep, thick waves. Even in the suffused light, Grey could see the lush curves of her body, barely visible through the filmy material of her gown.

"And what are you reading, my love?" he asked, propping back against the bed pillows.

She looked up and smiled. "I'm sorry, I didn't realize you were awake." She closed the book and pushed it aside.

Reaching for the discarded volume, Grey opened it to the dog-eared page. "You're just full of surprises." He raised his eyes to meet hers over the edge of the book. After reading a few lines, he responded, "All this," suggesting the interior of the room with his hands, "and poetry, too. This leads me to believe the good doctor is a romantic."

Rachel grabbed for the book, thinking he was poking

fun at her. "Because I'm trained in the sciences doesn't mean I can't enjoy the arts as well."

Ignoring Rachel's outburst, Grey thumbed through the pages until he found a verse that appealed to him.

> She was a phantom of delight
> When first she gleamed upon my sight;
> A lovely apparition, sent
> To be a moment's ornament;
> Her eyes as stars of twilight fair;
> Like twilights, too, her dusky hair;

He dropped the book to his lap and began reciting the words from memory. . . .

> But all things else about her drawn
> From May-time and the cheerful dawn;
> A dancing shape, an image gay,
> To haunt, to startle, and waylay.

He looked up to meet Rachel's eyes. "Old Wordsworth knew what he was penning when he wrote those words." His gaze raked over her appreciatively. "Could it be he had you in mind when he wrote it?"

She stared at him, surprised again at this unpredictable man. "Why, Mr. Devlin, you are just full of surprises." Joy bubbled in her chest.

Her father had loved poetry, but she never dreamed she'd meet another man who enjoyed the written word as much as he. Even now the polished beauty of verse could bring tears to her eyes.

Grey's voice pulled her back to the present.

"Aboard ship I had plenty of time to read." In prison, too, he pondered, though he didn't voice his thoughts. "I read everything I could get my hands on. Still do. You can learn a lot from books."

"Like the habits of the Celebrated Jumping Frog?"

241

"Exactly," he replied, pleased that she'd remembered the story he'd read to the children in the camp.

"My father loved poetry as well."

"Did your father also like white lace?"

Catching the drift of his meaning, Rachel laughed. "No, but he did like music."

She sailed from the bed to her dressing table and turned the key in her music box. Moments later the tinkling strains of a familiar waltz filled the room. To the strains of the melody, Rachel swayed and swirled around the room like a young girl at her first dance, beaming at Grey each time she turned to meet his eyes.

When the music finally wound itself down, Rachel stopped at the end of the bed. Her face glowed from the exercise. Winded, she asked, "Are you hungry?"

"I am that," Grey responded, his gaze delving beneath the gauzy fabric of her gown.

"For food, you lecher."

"Lecher, is it?" Grey dived for the foot of the bed, but Rachel dodged his advance.

"We never had our dessert." She skipped toward the door. "I'll be right back.,"

Minutes later she returned, carrying a tray with two plates, each filled with sponge cake and brandied peaches, and two large glasses of fresh milk. Settling the tray on the bed, she nestled against Grey, propped against the headboard.

"I thought we had dessert earlier." Stealing a sideways glance at Rachel, he took the cake and began to devour the delicious sweet.

Rachel laughed. She felt giddily happy, sitting beside him in bed. It felt right, as if they belonged together. The

242

way it should be between a man and woman. The way the dime novels she'd read suggested.

Rachel refused to dwell on the possibility that Grey didn't feel the way she did. During their lovemaking, he'd never mentioned anything about a permanent relationship, or how he felt about her, other than wanting her. He'd never said he loved her. But sometimes, Rachel decided, actions spoke louder than words. And he had called her his love. For now she would be satisfied with that.

When they'd finished their last drop of milk and eaten the last crumb from their plates, Grey moved the dish-laden tray to the floor.

"Now that you've tempted me with your scrumptious dessert, my love," he whispered, "it only makes me want more." He held her trapped beneath one sheet-wrapped, heavily muscled thigh.

"More?" she asked, not trying to get away. She felt playful—mischievous. "You mean another slice of cake, topped with peaches, dripping in brandy sauce?" She stretched lazily beneath him.

He gave a soft rumble. "I mean, I intend to make myself drunk on the whole dessert," he was quick to respond. Grey craftily removed Rachel's gown and tossed it to the floor. "From the mouthwatering cake . . ." He nibbled at her neck. "To the succulent peaches . . ." He played his tongue over her breasts, tasting first one nipple, then the other. "To the most delectable sauce of all." He continued down her body, kissing and tasting as he went. "After that, we'll let nature take its course."

And they did. Two or three more times before dawn glowed pink against the horizon.

Chapter 13

Rachel knew without a doubt that she was in love with Grey Devlin. Since the night of their dinner she'd thought of nothing else. The following day, Grey had sent word by a messenger that he'd been called to Portland on business. She missed him unconditionally and couldn't wait for his return.

In his absence, it was as though something were missing from her life. Before she'd met him Rachel had been content to fill her time with her medical practice and her gardening. Performing these routines still gave her pleasure, but they failed to excite her the way they once had. Each morning she awakened, hoping this would be the day of Grey's return.

Today she had something else to look forward to. Rachel would call on Sarah Ballard at her home, to check how her patient's pregnancy was progressing. It would be nice, she thought, to see her friend again. And to take her mind off her loneliness, if only for a while.

Because the morning had debuted warm and clear, Rachel chose to make the trip to the Ballards' home on foot. As she neared the imposing mansion, she was again reminded of her youth, when she and Sarah had played within the board and batten walls of the house Sarah's grandfather had built.

During those times, the garden had been attended by a yard man who worked fastidiously to groom the grounds to perfection. Sarah's mother had insisted that the side porch be abloom during the growing season with hanging baskets of flowers in every shade of the rainbow. As Rachel paused on the walkway leading to the front door, her eyes sought out the side porch. No profusion of flowers hung beneath the gingerbread trim. Disappointment settled over her at the discovery.

But, Rachel reminded herself, Sarah was not her mother. Except for the absence of the familiar blooms, the house still held a certain appealing grace. It had been recently painted and sparkled like a white gem against the verdant lawn.

She knocked on the massive door and surveyed the sweeping porch. While she waited to be admitted, her thoughts reverted to Grey's warning and her promise to keep her opinions to herself regarding conditions at Ballard's camp. Now weighing the evidence of wealth around her, she found that promise extremely hard to swallow. But because Grey had been so earnestly concerned with her welfare, Rachel would keep her promise and say nothing. For the time being at least.

She wondered if Frank Ballard would be at home today. If she did by chance encounter him, he could snub her again if he wished. But she intended to show her utmost professionalism. Rachel felt responsible for Sarah's health and knew her friend needed her attendance the remaining weeks of her pregnancy.

Rachel hadn't realized her dread of meeting Frank Ballard, face to face, until the large front door opened. Seized with apprehension, she fully expected to see him standing on the threshold. Instead, she was greeted by an elderly woman dressed in a charcoal grey uniform and white apron. At the sight of the maid she sighed with relief.

"I'm Doctor Thomas," she announced. "I've an appointment with Mrs. Ballard."

The dour-faced woman stepped aside to allow Rachel admittance into the large entry hall. Then she closed the heavy door, locking it with a key that hung from a ring at her waist.

"I'll announce you," the maid replied, without so much as a welcoming smile.

Rather dismal soul, Rachel thought, as she watched the woman disappear up the grand staircase. Poor Sarah. Even her housekeeper left a lot to be desired. Thank goodness she had been able to keep Agnes in her employ. But Rachel wondered at what expense Sarah had fought to retain the faithful woman who had helped raise her.

She thought it strange that the maid insisted on locking the front door after admitting her, but who was she to question the way the Ballards ran their household? The woman's strange behavior was soon forgotten as Rachel glanced around the familiar hall.

It was as though Rachel had been transported back in time. At any moment she expected Sarah's parents to step in and greet her as was their custom when any guest, no matter how insignificant, paid a visit to their home. Toward the back of the long, wide hall, she heard several doors open and shut. Perhaps Frank Ballard was closeted in the family library. If he were, she hoped he stayed there.

On many a rainy afternoon Rachel and Sarah had wiled away the hours in the cozy inglenook next to the fireplace in the front parlor. Glancing in that direction, Rachel walked in, noting the elaborate overmantels that framed the fireplace opening. Still displayed on them were the same curios and other exotica from faraway places that had always thrilled her and sparked her imagination.

First her gaze, then her fingers, traced the familiar carved words above the mantel: *Illumination, Warmth, and Purification.* Rachel had felt all this and more in this house of long ago.

"Mrs. Ballard will receive you now," the maid announced.

Rachel nearly jumped out of her skin, unaware until that moment the woman had returned to collect her. Feeling quite foolish, she apologized. "I'm sorry. I was wool-gathering."

The woman said nothing but moved up the huge staircase, indicating that Rachel should follow.

She led her to a door at the front end of the hall and knocked. When a female voice bade them to enter, the maid pushed open the door.

"Rachel, how good to see you," Sarah called from the bed where she sat propped. "That will be all, Milly. I'll ring if I need you."

As soon as Rachel stepped inside the room, she felt relief wash over her, glad at last to be free of the sour-faced woman. When the door closed behind her, she approached the side of Sarah's bed and in a low voice asked, "What rock did you overturn to find her?"

Sarah laughed, then whispered, "She belongs to my husband. Frank hires and fires all of the household servants . . . except for Agnes. She really takes care of me."

"Well, it certainly couldn't have been personality that got Milly the position," Rachel quipped.

"I have to agree, but . . ." Sarah's voice drifted into silence and she looked nervously down at her folded hands.

"And how's my favorite patient today?" Rachel asked, hoping to lift the worried expression from Sarah's face.

For the first time since entering the bedroom, Rachel sized up her patient. She was not pleased with what she saw. Her friend didn't look well. Beside the fact that her eyes were puffy and swollen, there were traces of blue circles around them. It worried Rachel that Sarah was nearing the end of her term and still appeared not to be in the best of health.

"Have you been following my advice?" She folded back the sheet from Sarah's rounded stomach to examine her better.

"Of course I have," Sarah insisted. But she seemed anxious when Rachel placed the stethoscope to her abdomen and moved it around to listen for the baby's heartbeat.

"The baby, is she all right?"

"She?" Rachel quirked her brow in good humor while she examined Sarah's ankles. She pressed them gently with her fingers, looking for puffiness or water retention. "Any headaches these days?"

"Not really. Perhaps only a slight one now and then, but nothing a cup of tea and a nap haven't helped."

"Good. How about any dizziness or blurry vision?"

"No. I just can't get comfortable in any position."

Rachel gave her friend an understanding smile. Satisfied that Sarah's blood pressure seemed to be normal, she adjusted her friend's gown and reached for Sarah's wrist to check her pulse.

"Have you been eating the foods I prescribed? Red meat, dark green vegetables?"

When Rachel pushed up the lacy cuff of Sarah's sleeve, the woman flinched. Sarah tried to smooth over her reflex by purposely helping Rachel to lift her sleeve to the elbow.

"Are your limbs sensitive, Sarah?" she asked.

"Of course not. I'm going to have a baby. Why in the world would my arms be sore?"

"Why don't you tell me?" This time Rachel pushed the sleeve higher. An ugly bruise darkened the pale skin of her upper arm. "Why don't you tell me?" she ordered again, pinning her patient with her gaze.

Sarah's eyes finally met Rachel's, but no explanation was forthcoming.

"What happened to you?" Rachel finally demanded.

Sarah looked as though she might break into tears at any moment. "Please," she whispered.

The sound was so pitiful that Rachel grabbed her friend and hugged her. "You must tell me what happened."

After several moments Sarah regained her composure enough to reply. "I fell. Yesterday, when I was walking around the yard."

"Fell. Why didn't you tell me immediately, instead of having me drag the information from you?"

"I . . . I didn't want you to be angry with me."

"Angry? Sarah, you should know better. I'm your physician. I need to know everything that happens to you in order to keep you and your baby well. We wouldn't want your baby to have suffered an injury when you fell."

"We're fine. Both of us." Her words sounded clipped, as though she were on the defensive.

"I'm the doctor. Don't you think I should be the judge of that?"

"Yes, but—"

"Have you had any pain in your abdomen? Any spotting of blood?"

"No, but do you think I hurt my baby?" The anxious look on her face told Rachel how genuinely concerned Sarah was for her unborn child.

"No, I don't. But I'll need to examine you more thoroughly.

"I'm fine, really," Sarah insisted. "Our gardener had dug some holes in the yard and I tripped in one of them. But I'm fine now. In the last few days, I've begun to feel quite clumsy."

"It's good that you think you're fine. But I'll confirm your opinion when I've looked you over a little better." Rachel settled her spectacles higher on her nose.

"Rachel Thomas, you always were a stubborn miss." With this comment, Sarah reluctantly relinquished herself to Rachel's examination.

Both of Sarah's upper arms were covered in deep reddish-purple bruises. And it didn't take a doctor to know that she hadn't acquired those bruises from any accidental fall. On the underside of each arm were four very distinct discolorations. Further examination re-vealed another identifying mark on the front of the other arm, identical to the one Rachel had first noted.

This left no doubt in her mind that someone had grabbed Sarah by the arms and squeezed her so tightly he'd left the impressions of his fingers on her delicate flesh. And Rachel had a good idea who that someone was.

If these had been the marks of a gardener who had tried—however roughly—to set his mistress back upon her feet, Sarah would have readily volunteered the in-formation. And with this explanation both women could have shared an understanding that men indeed did not know their own strength. But Sarah was not volunteering information. She was lying. Her words of protest, her shaky voice, revealed a truth that she could not bring herself to speak. That her husband had man-handled her.

"You can't believe how silly I felt when I had to have the gardener lift me back onto my feet." Sarah rattled on about her fall as though it were an everyday occurrence.

"Oh, I can well understand that. You were lucky he was there to assist you, or that you didn't break any bones."

Going along with Sarah's ruse, Rachel seethed with unleashed fury. Frank Ballard had some explaining to do. She would not rest until she'd confronted him about the bruises on his wife's arms. Sarah Ballard was not chattel, not property. She was a human being, worthy of honor and esteem. She was also fragile and defense-less and in no condition to fight off her husband's mis-treatment of her. Rachel, on the other hand, was neither fragile nor defenseless. And she would not stand by and tolerate abuse by any man upon his wife.

Lifting Sarah's gown above her waist, Rachel discovered that the delicate flesh on the side of one breast was also bruised. But in order to cause no further upset, Rachel said nothing.

"Imagine, silly old me, falling in a hole."

"Yes, dear, you need to watch where you step."

"Oh, I will from now on. You can be sure of that."

Rachel helped Sarah adjust her gown, her temper rising when the effort of dressing caused Sarah to flinch again. How could a man be so rough with a woman? Especially one in Sarah's frail condition, and carrying his child as well. Before this visit was over, Rachel intended to have a talk with Sarah's high and mighty husband. Now, more than ever, she hoped it was Frank Ballard she'd heard at the back of the house.

"Well, dear, everything seems in order. But you must promise me you'll be extra careful in the next few days. I believe your baby has changed position and his arrival could occur any day now."

"Really! Oh, Rachel, you can't believe how happy I'll be. I've dreamed of having a child to hold and love for so long now. And soon it will be a reality."

"By the way, have you been preparing the birthing supplies as we talked about?"

"Oh, yes." Sarah's face brightened. "Agnes and I have been gathering everything on the list. She's down in the kitchen now ironing sheets."

"Good."

At least Agnes was in the house. Sarah would not be left alone with only her husband and his formidable servant. Rachel bent and kissed her friend on the cheek.

"I'll show myself out. I'd like for you to remain in bed for the rest of the day. Remember, if you have any pain, send for me immediately."

With her heart hammering in her chest, Rachel closed the door behind her. The coolness of the wood, where she leaned against the door frame, felt good to her hot skin.

Advising Sarah to stay in bed gave Rachel the leverage she needed to confront Frank Ballard. And confront him she would. Bruises like the ones on Sarah's arms didn't come from falling in a hole in the yard.

Searching the upstairs landing for the dragon lady, Rachel moved toward the stairwell when she didn't see her. With each downward step she took, her temper rose. Frank Ballard was not a nice man. Every bad thing she knew about him quadrupled when she recalled the marks on Sarah's body. Rachel intended to tell him just how far she would go to protect her friend and patient from his brutality.

When she reached the foyer, Rachel marched toward the library at the back of the house. With a vengeance, she knocked, then decided a man of Ballard's character didn't deserve the courtesy. She thrust open the door and stormed inside.

"What the hell?" Frank Ballard jumped up from his chair.

He leaned across the mahogany pedestal desk that Rachel recognized as having belonged to Sarah's father and her grandfather before that. His large hands were braced on the gilt-tooled leather top, his face a mask of fury. "You have no right—"

"I have every right when it comes to the welfare of my patient," Rachel interrupted. "I saw the bruises you left on your wife's arms. Only a stinking coward would manhandle a defenseless woman, especially one who carries his own child.''

"Woman, you're out of bounds here," Frank Ballard stormed. Anger lit his cold, pale eyes. "How dare you interrupt me in my own home and accuse me of harming my own wife?''

"It wouldn't be your home if that kind and generous woman upstairs hadn't married you. And why she did I'll never know.''

"I don't have to listen to this." Ballard's face was a glowing mask of rage as he started around the desk. "I'll have you thrown in jail for trespassing . . . and for slandering my good name.''

"Slander? I think not," Rachel countered. "If indeed you weren't guilty, wouldn't your first concern have been for Sarah's welfare? After all, she is carrying your child. And if her story is true about tripping in some gardener's hole, wouldn't the safety of your unborn baby have any bearing on how you responded to my opinion?''

His expression was sardonic. "Has my dear wife filled your simple mind with these accusations?''

"My mind, Mr. Ballard, is far from simple. And, no, Sarah lied quite effectively. But it doesn't take an educated person, only one with a heart, to recognize the act of cruelty you subjected your wife to.''

"Get out of here, woman, before I lose my temper and bruise you the way you claim I bruised my Sarah. You stay away from me. And stay away from my wife. If you so much as attempt to set foot in my house again, you'll regret it. Do I make myself clear?''

"You've made yourself very clear, Mr. Ballard. Now

I'll make myself clear.'' Rachel's accusing voice stabbed the air. ''I will not stay away from your wife because she has chosen me as her physician, and I will deliver her baby. If you insist that I don't set foot in *Sarah's* house, I'll go to the newspaper with stories about the deplorable conditions of the logging camp you own.''

Frank Ballard's eyes twitched nervously when she presented him with this last piece of information, and Rachel felt a slight victory. ''I understand you have aspirations of becoming our next governor. Believe me, Mr. Ballard, if I learn that Sarah has suffered any repercussions from our private little conversation, I don't believe you'll be moving into the governor's house.''

His eyes were icy when he glared back at her. Rachel felt a slight chill creep up her spine, but she wasn't about to stop until she got her point across.

''I know things about you . . .'' Bluffing now, Rachel continued when Ballard's expression showed she'd hit a tender spot. ''Your voting public wouldn't be pleased to learn about your unsavory business dealings—''

Somewhere in the room, someone cleared his throat. Rachel forgot the rest of her thought and jerked toward that sound. For the first time since entering the library, Rachel looked at one of the two large wing chairs that faced Ballard's desk. She nearly fainted dead away when Grey Devlin, well hidden until this moment, stood and faced her. His eyes darkened with a cold fury.

Appearing to welcome the intrusion, Ballard cleared his throat and turned his head toward Grey. ''I believe you've had the misfortune of meeting our lady physician, Miss Thomas."

"We've met. Once." His eyes were cold, his voice oddly calm. And the indifference she read in his face settled over her like a shroud, wrapping her chest so tightly that she felt it hard to breathe. How could he stand here and act as though she were nothing to him?

"And what do you think of her accusations?" Ballard waited for Grey's answer.

"I think she has a mighty big mouth. But knowing her reputation among the townspeople, I doubt they'd believe any rumor she tries to spread."

Rachel couldn't believe her ears. With her eyes glued to Grey's, she kept looking for some sign of the man she'd given her body and soul to a few nights before. But that man no longer existed. In his place stood a cold and distant stranger.

"Well, what should we do with her?"

Do with her? He says that as though the two of them are working together, Rachel thought. Waiting for Grey's answer, she felt a growing uneasiness creep up her spine.

"It's best we don't draw undue attention to ourselves at this time. Maybe no one will listen to her, but someone might."

Grey continued to hold her stare, even though his voice rang with contempt. "Let her continue to attend Sarah until the baby is born, but only with the understanding that she can play doctor to your wife as long as she keeps her mouth shut." Each word he uttered slapped her as if it had been dealt with his open palm.

Ballard seemed to weigh Grey's suggestion. Rachel knew they had her over a barrel. She would never do anything to jeopardize her chances of being Sarah's physician. Having seen her friend's bruises today, Rachel knew Sarah needed her now more than ever. There was no telling what a man like Frank Ballard was capable of. He or his thugs. It was obvious that Grey Devlin fell into the latter category.

"Well, doctor, what do you say?" Ballard prodded her. He'd relaxed considerably and now sat on the edge of the huge desk, his arms crossed against his chest. "Do we deal? My wife for your silence?"

Rachel was quiet for a long time, weighing her options. Any way she looked at it, she turned out the loser. But for Sarah's welfare, she'd do anything. Besides that, perhaps she still held a winning card.

"I'm not worried about my skin," she replied, "but I am concerned about your wife. I'll agree to your terms. But if I hear that you've mentioned this conversation to Sarah, or if I find out you've hurt her in any way, either physically or mentally, I promise you, I'll ruin you."

"Or die trying," Ballard added, his face a vivid scarlet.

"If it comes to that." When she replied, her eyes locked with Grey's.

"Now that we've settled our little disagreement, I suggest you leave Mr. Devlin and me. We were in the middle of a business discussion." Ballard moved around the desk and pulled a bell cord. A few moments later Milly appeared at the door to the room. "Show the doctor out," he ordered.

Rachel turned to leave but paused on the threshold. "Don't you mean, *let* the doctor out? I noticed Milly here immediately locked the door after she admitted me. I'm no fool, Mr. Ballard. I can see she is your wife's jailor, but I intend to change all that.''

Ballard started around the desk toward Rachel, his fists clenched at his side. Grey's hand stilled him. Rachel turned and exited the room, but not before she heard Grey's reply.

''Are you going to let that dried up old maid needle you into doing something foolish?''

And Rachel's heart shattered into a thousand pieces.

Grey sat back down in the chair and with shaky fingers took the brandy Ballard offered him. *Damnation.* After he'd warned Rachel to keep her distance from Ballard, to keep her opinions to herself, the hardheaded female had done exactly what he'd warned her not to do. So much for trusting him, he thought.

''That woman could stir up a real hornet's nest if she starts accusing me in public.''

''I wouldn't worry about her. You and I both know the important people of this town want nothing to do with her. They don't approve of the lady's profession, or the clientele she treats.''

Grey took a swallow of the brandy, relishing the path it burned down his throat. What must Rachel think of him now?

''Speaking of the clientele she treats, have you ever come in contact with a prostitute that goes by the name of Chinook?''

With as much calm as he could manage, Grey looked over the rim of his glass. ''Chinook? What kind of name is that? If I had, I don't believe I'd have forgotten her. Only Chinook I know is the one that shows up on my dinner plate every now and then." He laughed at his own pun.

"Well, this Chinook has been giving some of my men trouble. I want the woman found. And when she is, I plan to deal with her myself."

Grey's mind reeled at the mention of the whore causing his men trouble. Was the man referring to Tully's near abduction? Ballard knew full well that Tully was Grey's friend. Any sailor with one leg, an eye patch, and a bad memory would know they spent time together. He could feel Ballard's eyes on him, searching for a sign of disloyalty.

Yeah, he could well imagine how Ballard would deal with the gypsy whore. The thought of the man's filthy hands touching Rachel made Grey's skin crawl. But he knew he had to continue with the ruse. "How am I to know this woman if I do meet up with her, especially if she doesn't tell me her name?"

"The whore's got pink hair, I've heard. Not many whores with pink hair. I understand she's quite a looker."

"Pink hair? Everywhere?"

Ballard hooted, nearly choking on his drink. "Well, I don't know about that. But it could be possible. Whoever finds her first can inform the other one."

They sat in silence, each lost in his own thoughts. Grey swallowed another drink of the brandy and studied the golden brown liquid in the bottom of his glass. For a moment, the color reminded him of Rachel's eyes, and he quickly pushed the image to the back of his mind.

"Don't mention the doctor's accusations. I don't

think anyone would like to hear of my wife's misfortune.''

Grey studied the older man. Was he admitting he'd beaten his wife? Sarah Ballard was big with child and not well. No woman under any circumstances deserved a man's abuse. But knowing Ballard, he realized the man was capable of anything. Probably took pleasure in beating up on his frail wife.

"I won't mention anything outside this room." He met Ballard's icy gaze. "You trust me, don't you?"

"I don't trust anyone. A man in my position can't afford to. That's why we own people and things."

The meaning of Frank Ballard's words echoed loud and clear in Grey's mind. Any other answer would have surprised him. He placed his glass on the table beside his chair. He'd had enough of his employer for one afternoon.

Ballard seemed to feel the same way. He stood, alerting Grey it was time to leave. "By the way," he asked, "how did it go in Portland? Were you able to entice any more business our way?"

"I think so. I believe I convinced several shipowners that our port fees were significantly lower to warrant unloading in Astoria. Many supplies can just as easily be transferred to smaller packets here as in Portland. And we don't have the traffic tie-ups that the captains are always complaining about there."

Grey knew that his trip should have been of interest to the mayor, to the honest businessmen of the town. But to have been sent directly by Ballard confirmed only one thing. Frank Ballard wanted his name known, his reputation as an astute businessman expanded to Portland and beyond. If things went his way, his would be a name to be reckoned with all over the state. Rachel had been right when she'd accused him of having his eye on the governor's seat. God help them all if this scoundrel got his way.

"Then I guess the trip was worthwhile after all. We'll see if it makes a difference." Ballard walked Grey to the door. "And let me know if you find out anything about the hooker. I'll have some of my other men keep an eye out, too."

After taking his leave, Grey stood outside the house, inhaling the fresh air. I'm in a fine position now, he thought. Remembering the tortured look Rachel had given him, he knew she believed the worst of him. And with her temper riled, he feared she might do or say something foolish to bring Ballard's wrath down upon herself.

Grey knew she'd never believe anything he said after this afternoon. What was he to do? All he wanted, all he'd thought about in his absence, was the reunion they'd share when he returned. Now, because of circumstances beyond his control, the whole damned situation had gone from bad to worse.

Maybe it was better this way. Grey cared more for Rachel than he wanted to admit, and that attraction in itself was doomed from the start. With this depressing thought foremost in his mind, he headed back toward the wharf.

Chapter 14

Rachel wondered that her heart still had the power to beat as she hurried frantically down the street toward her house. Grey's words had stabbed her chest as surely as if he'd struck her physically. Her tears flowed freely now while a soft wind lifted them into nothingness. Just as her dreams of a future with Grey Devlin had been heaved into nonexistence.

A few moments later, Rachel let herself into her house and locked the door securely behind her. But her little house no longer offered her the security she'd felt in the past. The rooms were too full of the present, too occupied with memories of Grey.

Her feet felt bound in heavy chains as she moved down the hall toward her bedroom. Glancing around the familiar room where she'd so recently lain with Grey, Rachel knew what she had to do. She tossed a few items of clothing into a carpetbag, then locked up the house and hurried along the street.

* * *

Grey left Ballard's house and went straight to the wharf. As much as he'd wanted to run after Rachel, to comfort her with his assurances, he knew he couldn't. All his efforts to ally himself with Ballard would have been in jeopardy. And he would lose forever the chance to bring the man to justice. Secluding himself in his office, he dived into the stack of papers that had increased in size during the two days he'd been gone.

Ballard could think that Grey had solicited business for Astoria, but in fact that was not a job for a harbormaster. He had, in fact, met with Portland's harbormaster, in an ongoing attempt to standardize regulations along the seaboard. And he had attended another meeting. The Marine Revenue Service was concerned about the illegal contraband being unloaded in ports up and down the coast.

In Grey's position as harbormaster he'd been invited. But when the mayor had insisted that Frank Ballard, a leading businessman in the community, wished to hear what had gone on at that meeting, all of Grey's suspicions were brought to light. The rogue controlled the mayor, just as he thought he controlled Grey. And to a point he did.

Grey reached across his desk and picked up his two semaphore flags, signal flags that carried daylight messages to incoming vessels, that could easily be seen as they crossed the bar. Riffling them in the slight breeze that cooled his office, he mused about his responsibility to the people of the port. Hell, Frank Ballard didn't have a clue to the real work he did. And he never would.

Grey had gone to Ballard's house with the intention of humoring the man. He'd glazed over the important things discussed at the meeting, failing to alert him to the special codes that could be sent by lights and telegraph, which would bring an immediate response from the cutters that patrolled the coast. These codes were to be used in emergencies only and in cases of suspect cargo about to be unloaded.

Ballard had seemed pleased with the report—information of no real value but enough to convince him of Grey's loyalty. Everything had gone well until Rachel had stormed into the room with her incriminating accusations.

Lord, he wished she had never been in that house. It was all Grey could do to temper his own anger when the older man had lambasted Rachel with insults. All he'd wanted was to beat the man until he became senseless. Instead, he'd remained hidden in the wings of the chair until he couldn't ignore Ballard's abusive behavior a moment longer.

He'd seen the hate and disbelief simmering in Ballard's eyes when Rachel dared to confront him. Having once suffered at the man's hand himself, Grey knew the extent of his ruthlessness. And having learned Tully's suspicions regarding the disappearance of Dr. Theodore Thomas, Grey now feared for Rachel's safety. Ballard was not a man to be trifled with and most certainly not one to be trusted.

Grey tossed the flags aside and buried his head in his hands, wishing things had been different. In the given circumstances, he had done the only thing he could, pretending no more than a casual acquaintance with the lady doctor and hating his duplicity and the cruel jibes he'd thrown at her. He could still see her staring at him, her hurt and disbelief visible in the depths of her brown eyes. That alone had almost been Grey's undoing.

He'd succeeded with his subterfuge, hoping not only to protect Rachel but to keep the cover he'd established for himself. But now, as he sat in his office, he knew Rachel needed an explanation for his actions. Grabbing his coat from a peg, he set out for Rachel's house.

A steady drizzle had come inland late in the afternoon, inviting only the adventuresome to escape out of their homes. By the time Grey leaped the picket fence surrounding Rachel's yard, he was soaked through to the skin. His apprehension mounted when he found her house locked up tighter than a tomb. He searched the front door for a note that might have given Rachel's destination and the time she was expected to return, but he found only his reflection mirrored in the shaded glass panel.

One last time, he canvassed the area around the house, checking the windows, pounding again on both doors. But Rachel had disappeared, leaving behind a growing uneasiness in the center of Grey's chest.

Where could she have gone? He knew he'd wounded her with his words, but Rachel had impressed him as being a rational woman, not one easily swayed by another's charges, even if they were hurtful.

She'd had the perfect comeback to his barbs from the first day she'd treated him, remembering how she'd set him straight when he'd tried to undermine her chosen profession. Surely, she'd seen through his ruse at

Frank Ballard's when in truth he'd uttered his insolent remarks only to protect her.

But in his heart he knew she had been hurt. Even now, he could recall the pain he'd seen in her eyes. He had to find her, to apologize.

Grey left the yard and jogged down the street toward Tully's cabin. Maybe the old man knew of Rachel's whereabouts.

Late in the afternoon it had started to rain. In one of Opal's private rooms off her back parlor, Rachel lay listening to the constant drone against the roof. Darkness had come slowly outside the windows, and with its approach activities next door had picked up. She could hear music and laughter coming from Baldy's Saloon. The revelry only made her feel more alone.

Blowing her nose in one of Opal's borrowed hankies, she tried not to think. Thinking was too painful, especially when her every thought centered around Grey Devlin. His slightest memory brought on a new rush of tears. Her eyes already felt as though they'd been sprinkled with salt granules, and her head felt stuffed with thistledown.

No, Rachel decided, to cry over something she could not change was futile. She would cease to concentrate on her sorrow. She'd think instead about her blessings. And in spite of all that had happened in recent days, she had many. And Opal was at the top of that list.

When Rachel had arrived on Opal's doorstep unannounced, her friend had immediately ushered her inside. There had been no questions, no inquisition, only an immediate, comforting hug. Then Opal had tucked her into a spare bedroom, insisting that she rest, with the promise that they'd talk later.

Now that seemed like days ago. After tossing and turning, Rachel finally fell asleep, only to have her dreams disturbed by Grey's intruding presence. When her swollen lids popped open later, his handsome face remained etched in her consciousness. Was this to be the order of her days? This deep and painful existence with no relief in sight? Rachel buried her head beneath a mountain of pillows, the blackness a comfort to her weariness.

Hours later, sometime after the break of dawn, the smell of coffee and another's presence in the room prompted Rachel to shuck her covers in curiosity. She was greeted by Opal's smiling face.

"You think you could eat something?"

Pushing herself up against the pillows, Rachel buried her swollen face in her hands. "Look at me, Opal. I'm so ashamed."

"Of what, sugar? You're not the first woman that's loved a man. And you certainly won't be the last."

The woman's response took Rachel by surprise. "How'd you know that? I never told you."

"You didn't have to tell me. Not in so many words anyway." She picked up the tray and placed it on Rachel's lap. "I'm not a doctor, but I've been around long enough to recognize the symptoms."

"If my condition was so transparent, no wonder Grey Devlin was able to make such a fool of me."

Pulling a chair closer to the bed, Opal poured herself a cup of coffee. "Eat. You'll feel better."

Rachel eyed the bowl of warm oatmeal and wondered how she could get the food past her mouth. Yesterday morning her appetite had fled, but she knew she had to eat. Her stomach suddenly rumbled in anticipation so she tried spooning down several bites. Amazingly, after everything that had happened, she was hungry.

After several more bites, she looked over at Opal. "You did send word to Sarah Ballard's house of where I could be reached, if she needed me?"

"I did, and Joseph gave the note to the gardener, who promised he'd give the message to no one but Agnes. I'm sure Mrs. Ballard is still very pregnant, because we didn't hear a word from that quarter last night."

"Blessing Number Two," Rachel mumbled more to herself than to Opal.

"I'm sorry, I don't understand."

"You don't need to. But last night, I decided to count the things I have to be thankful for, instead of dwelling on the one thing that made me so unhappy." Rachel swallowed a sip of coffee before continuing. "I appreciate your keeping my whereabouts confidential. You're sure no one else knows where I am?"

"If you mean Grey Devlin, no, he has no idea where you are." Opal sealed her words with a conspiratorial look. "If it will make you feel better, he did ask one of the girls at Baldy's last night if she knew where the lady doctor might be reached."

This bit of information sent Rachel's heart lurching to her stomach. *Maybe he does care.* But if he did, he wouldn't have flung such hurtful words at her. She quickly pushed the notion aside.

Rachel dismissed Opal's remark as if she hadn't

heard it. "You're my Blessing Number One," she stated matter-of-factly.

At her response, Opal shrugged her shoulders and left the room.

Grey had gone straight to Tully's after leaving Rachel's, but his friend had known nothing about her whereabouts. He'd dropped by Baldy's Saloon and made a few hasty inquiries about Rachel, but no one seemed to know where she had gone. That was yesterday and he'd still not located the woman.

His first thought after leaving Baldy's had left him cold with dread—that perhaps Ballard had decided to have Rachel eliminated from the town. But after he'd calmed down he forced himself to believe that even Ballard wasn't fool enough to hurt Rachel, not without first considering all of the consequences.

Rachel had been gone for two nights. Disillusioned, Grey dropped down on her front stoop like a lost puppy, imagining that at any moment she'd materialize on the street in front of him.

Her shoulders would be set in that determined way she carried herself until she saw him. Then she'd turn into the soft, giving woman he knew her to be. She'd run into his arms, showering him with kisses, glad to be with him again after their separation.

The realist in Grey knew his fantasies were an impossibility. His words at Ballard's had all but shouted that he was in cahoots with a man she detested. Words that would not easily be forgotten or forgiven by a woman like Rachel. He'd hurt her too badly to ever expect their relationship could return to the way it had been.

Gloom settled over him in a haze of dampness. The rain had stopped, but fog as dense as cotton covered the harbor, rolling inland to erase most of the town's familiar structures.

"Damnation," he mumbled. No matter how angry and hurt Rachel had been, she shouldn't have disappeared without letting someone know where she was and if she were safe.

Grey knew he deserved to be worried about her. After he and Rachel had become involved, he should have explained more to her about himself. But voicing his feelings had never been easy. He'd learned long ago the less said, the less chance that information could be used against him.

He rubbed his fingers through his damp hair. It was best, he decided, that it should end this way. Once he learned that Rachel was safe, he'd let her continue to believe the worst about him. They had no future together, and it was easier to end it now than later.

Grey stood and peered again into the gathering mist. The abominable weather matched his mood. Feeling like a beaten man, he walked toward Miss Purdy's Boarding House.

Later that evening Rachel and Opal sat in the cozy private parlor in the bawdy house, discussing Rachel's situation.

"I'm the biggest fool, Opal. I should have known a handsome man like Grey Devlin would never find me attractive. If he hadn't thought I was Chinook to begin with, he'd never have followed me home when I left Tully's."

As much as it shamed her to say it, Rachel felt a certain freedom in having exposed her vulnerability to the one woman in town she thought would truly understand how she felt.

From what Rachel said, it was evident to Opal that she missed Grey Devlin. And from what she didn't say, it was evident that she loved him.

"I never considered that I had such a libidinous nature, but Grey provoked such primitive biological urges in me, I became quite wanton. He wanted to leave, but I insisted he stay."

"And of course, he had no sexual drive." Opal was enjoying baiting her friend. "And it was only you who had an 'erection'?"

"Well, I wouldn't exactly say that."

Their eyes met, and they both burst into companionable laughter. It was good to see that Rachel could still laugh. A good sign, Opal thought to herself.

"Opal, you can't imagine how much better I feel since I've talked with you. There was a time last night when I wished I would just go ahead and die and get it over with. I honestly thought my life was over." Rachel sipped her own sherry, licking the overflow from her lips.

"Unfortunately, my dear, we don't die of a broken heart—although we wish we would, and feel we might."

Opal's eyes alighted on an old tintype. Her memories of her late husband still held the power to evoke pain. After a short pause, she continued.

"Time heals all wounds of the heart. Or at least, after a while, the pain is not so intense that it's disabling. The wound remains sensitive and acts up on days when life is not to our liking. Just as a physical wound can ache when the weather becomes burdensome. But what we must realize is that we can't allow our pain to control us. We have to control it. That's the only way I know to survive this affliction.''

"Opal, you're so wise. I count myself lucky that you're my friend.''

"I, too.'' Opal reached across and patted Rachel's knee. "Will you be all right for the rest of the evening? I need to check on the girls and put in an appearance at Baldy's.''

"Yes, I'm fine now. I'll stay here again tonight, if you don't mind, and leave early in the morning. The way my face looks—all bloated and swollen—I don't want anyone to see me.''

Opal stood to leave. Draining her last sip of sherry from the glass, she returned it to the table.

"You'll be fine now. And I wouldn't worry too much about Grey Devlin. My grandmother always said, 'If you love something set it free. If it doesn't come back to you, it wasn't meant to be yours in the first place.' ''

"I'll remember that,'' Rachel replied, squeezing Opal's hand.

Rachel's eyes filled with tears after Opal had closed the door. But they were not the same tears that had drained her soul for the last day. These were tears of understanding—and of friendship. And now because of both, Rachel would be better able to face tomorrow.

She loved Grey Devlin with all her heart. But she'd also made up her mind. If it wasn't written that he should return that love, Rachel would continue her life without him. No matter how much her heart might ache when she encountered him, she wouldn't tumble from defeat, but instead would use that pain to grow stronger.

Her decision made, Rachel looked forward to the morning when she would move back home. She climbed back into Opal's bed and soon fell into a deep and healing sleep.

Rachel had just dried her breakfast plate when she heard the banging on the front door. She set aside her dish towel and hurried down the hall to open the door. Sarah's personal maid stood on the front porch, panting for breath.

"Agnes? What's—"

"Doc, the missus, she's hurting something fierce. The baby's coming."

Rachel stepped inside and ushered the older woman into the surgery. She took off her kitchen apron and began gathering supplies for her bag, all the while questioning her. "When did the pains start?"

"They woke her up this morning."

Rachel looked up quickly to see the maid's forehead creased in worry lines. Her black eyes shimmered. "And how long ago was that?" she asked.

"About five o'clock."

Agnes stood wringing her hands, and Rachel could tell from her nervous behavior that the poor soul believed she'd somehow failed her mistress.

"Five?" Rachel's tone was little more than a quiver. "That's two hours ago. Why didn't you come for me sooner? And where's Mr. Ballard?"

She cringed at the thought of her recent encounter with Sarah's husband. In the last few days she'd thought of little else—of Frank Ballard yelling threats at her and of Grey Devlin taking his side. Now Rachel dreaded that Sarah had either been forbidden to send for her, or that she had stalled to prevent a scene between Rachel and her husband. Regardless, Sarah was not a well woman. She was taking chances she couldn't afford.

"He left a few minutes ago. Had Simpson take him to the wharf. Said he was headed upriver and wouldn't be back for a day or two. Miz Sarah said not to tell him, to wait till he was out of the house. Said she didn't need him around to bring her baby into this world." She looked at Rachel with pleading eyes. "Doc, we got to go."

Rachel's pulse quickened at the idea that her friend was up at the house, ready to deliver, with only her jailor for company. The woman had made it clear from her demeanor where her loyalties lay and Rachel could expect no help from that quarter. The only thought that soothed her was that a firstborn usually took several hours to make his entrance. "Calm down, Agnes. We should be there in plenty of time. Remember when your Nathaniel was born?"

But Agnes only fidgeted as she formed her next words. "Yes ma'am, I do. But *her* pains really started late last night."

Rachel gave the maid a piercing glance. "Last night?"

"Yes, but Miz Sarah said they were light and no need in bothering you then. She just wanted to get some sleep." Her eyes widened in distress. "So since then I've been keeping two big kettles filled with boiling water, and I took out everything you told us to get ready. But now her contractions are real close together. You got to come right away."

But Rachel was already gathering her shawl and scribbling a note for her front door for any other patients who might need her. "Come on, Agnes, we'll go back on foot. By the time I could get the buggy harnessed, we'd already be there."

Four blocks up the steep hill would be painstaking, but nothing compared to what Sarah had been going through since last evening. Rachel only prayed she was not too late. As she hurried up the street with Sarah's maid in tow, she thought about her childhood friend and how close they'd always been. And she thought about an infant, about to be delivered, whose only bond to this world would be his mother. The thought made Rachel's stomach roil. A child should be the ultimate gift from God, shared between a man and wife, the culmination of a deep and committed love.

The farther up the sidewalk she raced, the more Rachel struggled for breath. She pictured herself presenting her own newborn to her husband, someone who loved her, who loved children. The image of a tousle-haired Grey Devlin, sitting beneath a tree contentedly reading to a group of youngsters, suddenly intruded on her thoughts. Until two days ago she'd thought he would have made the perfect father for her children. But no more.

Rachel pushed the unwelcome image from her mind and focused on her friend's well-being and the hours since labor had begun. Sarah's biggest fear was something happening to her baby. Living with Frank Ballard, she had managed to maintain her sanity by knowing and loving her unborn child. By now, left alone with no one for support, she was probably scared to death. God forbid anything should happen to either of them.

Chapter 15

Rachel could hear Sarah groaning from halfway up the staircase. When she reached the master bedroom, she found her friend in her disheveled bed, up on her knees and elbows, her face in a pillow. In the midst of a contraction, she rocked her hips back and forth to relieve the pain. The drapes were still closed, and in the low light of one lamp burning on the nightstand, the place looked like a tomb.

"You're doing fine," Rachel crooned as she rubbed Sarah's back. "How far apart are the pains now?"

Through gritted teeth, Sarah only moaned.

Rachel sat with her throughout the muscle spasm, then stood and checked the room. Packages of ironed linens tied with string had been laid out on a table by the bed, just as the maid had confirmed. Wrapped in pillowcases, they had been baked in the oven "until the potato cooked with them was done," Agnes had said.

Two pans of cooling boiled water had been readied and placed on clean towels with the other supplies. On the dressing table two covered kettles sat. Rachel lifted the lids to see them filled with freshly boiled water.

Beside the bed a carved walnut cradle, the one that Sarah had slept in, was dressed in clean linen, waiting to be put to use. In the lamp's glow it gleamed with a fresh coat of wax. At the footposts of Sarah's bed were tied lengths of braided linen, noosed at the ends, long enough to reach her arms. Agnes had listened well to Rachel's directions.

Sarah didn't seem to recognize that Rachel had arrived until the contraction had subsided. Now she looked over at her while Rachel rolled her shirtsleeves to her elbows. "Rachel? Oh, God, Rachel, you're here." Sarah's hair was a mesh of golden tangles. Her white lawn nightrail was bunched up around her thighs. Her sweat-stained face was contorted with the aftermath of pain. "Help me," was all she said before she again buried her face in the pillow.

"Of course I will," Rachel assured her, trying to soothe her friend. At the same time she swallowed her own anger—anger that Frank Ballard cared so little about his wife that he felt not the least concern for her welfare. Sarah's decision not to inform him of her labor had borne that out. Labor was stressful enough with a caring husband to hold onto.

Her voice light with humor, Rachel instructed Agnes to open the drapes while she scrubbed her hands with green soap. "Let's get some light in here, shall we? So we can see how much this little one is going to look like her mama."

When the heavy drapes were pulled back, early morning sun filtered through the long lace panels onto the polished hardwood floor and across Sarah's bed.

"There now," she said, smiling approvingly, "this is a much better way to welcome your child."

Rachel walked over to the bed and called Agnes to Sarah's side. "Sarah," she said, "you can turn over now. I need to examine you. Agnes is right here. When you feel the next pain, just squeeze her hand."

Slowly Sarah rolled over and adjusted her cumbersome weight to face Rachel. When she looked up, her eyes were dull but receptive. Tears formed at the corners. "Please, Rachel, don't leave me. Help me through this."

"Don't worry," Rachel said, "I'm not going anywhere. Now, just hold Agnes's hand and squeeze tight when you need to."

The contractions continued and Sarah weakened with each one. To her relief, Rachel found the baby's heartbeat to be strong and regular.

In the middle of her examination, Rachel heard the front doorbell ring and stiffened. Surely Frank Ballard had not returned. But then he would have no reason to ring the bell to his own house. It was probably one of his business "associates."

While the ringing persisted, Rachel waited for Milly, or someone, to open the door. No one did. When she heard forceful banging, she looked over at Agnes, who stood gripping Sarah's hand, oblivious to anything but her mistress. Rachel felt a tiny prick of alarm. Surely no one would have cause to demand entry into another's home, unless . . .

"Agnes, is there anyone else here to answer the door?"

"No, ma'am, nobody but me. The housekeeper left shortly after Mr. Ballard."

"Did she know Sarah was near her time?"

"No ma'am. Not unless she questioned the pots of water on the stove. But she wouldn't have cared. Maybe that's why she left—so she wouldn't have to help."

Rachel gave a rueful smile. "I'm sure that was it."

Agnes, for all her own birthings, stood as stiff as a frozen corpse, as if the slightest movement on her part would bring harm to her mistress. She needed a job to do or she'd never make it through the delivery without fainting.

"Agnes, the bell. Would you please answer it before whoever's there decides to break the door down?"

The insistent knocking seemed to bring the servant around. "Oh, sure, ma'am." With that she released Sarah's hand from her own and started for the door.

"And, Agnes," Rachel called, "whoever it is, send him away. We don't need any extra excitement in this house right now. And please bring me up two leaves from the dining room table. That's the only thing we don't have."

The last instruction left the maid clearly shaken. "Oh, Doc, I'm sorry. But Mr. Ballard always has his breakfast on that table and he would have noticed them gone. And after Simpson left with him, I couldn't get 'em off by myself." With her words she began to cry, just as Sarah was hit with another spasm.

Rachel shooed Agnes away and reached for the makeshift ropes. She handed them to Sarah. "Here," she said. "Pull on these if it'll help, but take short breaths. I don't want you pushing yet. The baby's not quite ready to be born." At Sarah's anguished cry Rachel issued a firm demand. "Do you understand me, Sarah? No deep breaths, and no pushing."

Sarah wrenched her head up and down as a sign that she understood and gratefully pulled the lengths of cloth to her chest. Five minutes—maybe ten—remained before Sarah's contractions would begin to bring results. She had felt with her hand that the baby was deep into the birth canal, but she couldn't yet see the head. She looked at the rumpled sheets, wishing there'd been time to replace them. But Sarah was in no condition to get out of bed. What she had would have to do. Thank goodness the birth sac hadn't yet ruptured.

Rachel had just opened the first package of clean sheets and retrieved one to place over Sarah's knees.

"Where do you want these?"

Even with her back turned to the door, Rachel would have recognized Grey's whiskey-sounding voice anywhere. She turned to see him standing in the doorway—as though he'd been called—calmly awaiting orders. Dressed in his shirtsleeves, work trousers and boots, he held the two heavy leaves from the dining room table. He stared at her from the threshold, as though trying to draw a response from her.

Rachel faltered in the agonizing silence. Her pulse raced at the sight of him, her heart reacting in that welcoming way her head refused to acknowledge. For the last two days she had attempted to wipe away every possible emotion she had ever felt for him, until there'd been nothing left but a dull, numbing void. Now she felt them once more rising to the surface, threatening her equilibrium.

For whatever purpose, he must have stopped by her

house and seen her note. An enormous sense of relief washed over her.

"Thank you," she said then looked over at Sarah. She was calm for the moment, her eyes closed, her breathing even. "I need them under the mattress. I had hoped to put clean sheets on the bed, but Sarah is close to her time and much too weak to move." She looked back to Grey. "Could you please send Agnes in now? We'll get these boards under her."

But Grey was already at the bedside, staring down at Sarah. "I'm afraid the maid won't be much help. She's downstairs shaking like a dog after his bath." His voice quieted. "Can she be moved?"

"Not on her own. She's too weak."

As though Sarah Ballard weighed no more than a feather, Grey scooped her up in his arms with her still holding on to one of the cords. "Okay," he said to Rachel, "now you can make up the bed."

Rachel stared at him in wonderment, then without hesitation, began to strip the linens. Within seconds she had replaced them with fresh. With little effort she slid the table leaves under the mattress crosswise to prevent it from sagging and making the delivery more difficult.

As he held her, Grey comforted Sarah through another contraction, whispering to her as she pulled on the rope. At last her muscles again relaxed and he gently laid her on the bed. "What next?" he asked.

Rachel's heart pounded against her breast as she watched his gentle treatment of her patient. But time was running out. He had done what he could. Now she had to ask him to leave . . . for propriety's sake and for his own. Childbirth was not an easy thing to watch.

But that would leave her alone to see Sarah through her ordeal. Her mind raced to think of an alternative method for delivering the baby. She mentally flipped through the pages of her *Modern Childbirthing* text, but knew Sarah to be much too weak to assume a squatting position while clinging to the footpost.

She ran her hand over her mouth and sighed. "I can't ask you to stay," she said. "It wouldn't be proper. And it's much too messy." And to presume Sarah's permission would have been unquestionable.

Grey remained where he was, willing and unmoving. "Ask her."

Rachel reached for a rag and wet it in one of the pans, then approached the bed and began wiping it over her friend's brow. She had seen and participated in a number of births, some accompanied by husbands, others by female relatives or friends. But never had she been faced with this dilemma—a male stranger in attendance. "Sarah," she said, "Mr. Devlin is here to help us. You heard what he said about Agnes. Do you want him to remain?"

Sarah opened her eyes and looked over at Grey. As her gaze locked with his, Rachel felt a jolt from the compassionate smile that spread across the man's face. "Please stay," Sarah whispered.

He looked over at Rachel. "I guess it's settled."

Another contraction took hold and Sarah screamed. Rachel knew that time had run out. "Ever done this before?"

"No, but I'm a quick learner."

She nodded toward the two pans. "Scrub your

hands, then open the other two packages, just the out-side covers." She watched him roll his shirtsleeves without further comment, trying to dismiss the image of the virile but tender man who stood before her, this man who had turned her world upside-down. For now she must think of him only as her assistant, about to learn the skill of delivering a baby.

As if he had been around a surgery all his life, Grey followed orders, spreading out pads of ironed linen and newspapers and gathering equipment for easy reach. While Rachel continually wiped her brow with her sleeve, he seemed entirely focused on the job at hand. Then, at Rachel's instructions, he took his place at Sarah's head, holding her and her pillow in his lap.

Rachel gave him a last glance, astonished at the ease with which he had taken to his task. This rugged, worldly man, who walked with sailors and dogs, with ruffians and children, was beyond her comprehension. "Ready?" she asked.

"Ready," he answered, hugging Sarah against his chest.

"All right, Sarah," Rachel instructed her patient, "you're in good hands. Just do what we tell you and before you know it, it'll all be over. Now let's get this little one born."

Less than thirty minutes later, Sarah Ballard lay with her new baby girl in her arms. All evidence of the birthing had been removed and mother and daughter now shared the big bed, fresh-smelling with sun-dried linens. While Rachel sat beside the bed in a straight-backed chair, Grey hovered over the twosome like a protective uncle, straightening the sheets and smiling at the tiny child wrapped in a pink blanket.

"You did good work," Rachel praised her friend. She glanced up at Grey. "You, too." He only nodded and swallowed hard. His blue eyes, darkened with emotion, told her everything he felt.

What manner of man was this? she questioned, taking in his beaming face, that torturous dimple proudly etched into his cheek. His hair was again tousled and a wayward lock dangled over his forehead. His once-crisp white shirt was wrinkled and stained with sweat where Sarah had pushed and wrenched against it. With the sleeves rolled up to his elbows, he wore it like a badge of courage.

Tall and straight as a towering mast, he looked like a man more accustomed to giving orders than receiving them. But here, in this house that for so long had held no affection, he had done just that, carrying them out dutifully as if they had to be completed to perfection. He had held and crooned, rocked and whispered to make a lonely woman's distress easier to bear. And he had succeeded.

"Would you like to hold her again?" Sarah asked, smiling up at Grey.

He looked at her uncertainly. "Again? I haven't held her the first time. And I'd better not. She'd probably break."

Sarah gave him a playful wink. "She didn't the first time."

Grey looked over at Rachel, quirking his brow. "What is she saying?"

With a soft chuckle, Rachel gave him his answer. "Quite simply that when you picked Sarah up, you held her baby then. In truth, that makes you the first person to enjoy that privilege.'' Grey's eyes took on a shimmer in the sunlight that now filled the room.

"Then I'd love to, if you trust me. Come here, little one."

He gently lifted the sleeping infant into his arms and cradled her against his chest. Rachel watched him as he cooed to the child with unintelligible words. He didn't even seem embarrassed that the women were staring at him. "And do you have a name, little one?''

Sarah looked from Grey to Rachel. "I had hoped to call her Anna, after my grandmother." She paused. "But I haven't discussed it with my husband yet. What do you two think of the name?'' She, who seemed to receive so little approval these days, now sought Rachel and Grey for theirs.

"Anna," Grey said, reaching to brush the baby's head with one gentle hand. "It fits her nicely."

Rachel patted Sarah's hand. "And it's a lovely name."

Though Sarah's pallor remained, her face seemed to take on a special glow. "Then Anna it is. And Mr. Devlin . . .''

"Grey, if you please. We've been through too much together to remain polite friends now."

Sarah's lips turned up into a full smile. "I'd like that very much. . . . Grey, if I can ask just one more favor—you've done so much for me already."

"Anything."

"I would be grateful if you and Rachel would stand up as Anna's godparents." A tremor touched her lips at her own request.

Grey's expression stilled and grew serious. Rachel

watched his eyes widen with some indefinable emotion before he glanced from the infant in his arms to meet her gaze. Then he looked to Sarah, temporarily speechless. At his reaction, Rachel felt her defenses crumble, for he obviously had been touched.

Finally he answered her. "Are you sure?" The question was tenuous, as if he hadn't really believed what he'd heard.

"I'm very sure. Anna deserves the best."

Grey continued to shelter the child in his massive arms. "Then I would be honored."

Rachel felt her throat closing up. The irony of it all—two people whose bond had been severed with the swiftness of a sword now forced to form another. She and Grey would never stand before God, exchanging vows to love and cherish. They would instead stand together and promise to protect this child, to help raise her according to the wishes of the church. This was a bond that could never be broken.

As Grey moved his hand over the baby, the infant closed her tiny hand around his little finger, squeezing it as though she approved of her mother's choice. Awkwardly holding her in his oversized hands, Grey found no cries of protest, no judgment against him. Only complete trust.

Grey's head swam with doubts. This was entirely against all he'd set out to do. Taking on this role would give him ties to this place, not to mention a more permanent connection with the woman who would share his duties, the woman who considered him a lowlife. He wasn't worthy. In truth, he was scared to death.

But looking down on his enemy's child, he saw only the face of the mother, a sweet and frail woman who had probably never harmed anyone in her entire life. Grey had never been a religious man, but this was a child who would need protection against her father and his corrupt world. Determination began to set in. This was something he could take on. If as godfather, he could give little Anna no more than that before he left town, he would feel satisfied that he had done his best for her.

He felt his breath catch in his throat as he watched the child open her eyes to capture his own. What force had brought him to Rachel's door one last time this morning so that he now stood with his own plans in question? Leaving town would be so much harder, now that he and Rachel shared more than a passion he had never expected to find. They now shared a responsibility.

As Grey smiled down on his brand new goddaughter, he tried to dismiss the pain that would hit him all too soon—when his job was done and he would be gone. Behind him he would be leaving the only two women who had ever meant anything to him.

For now he held the infant close to his heart, overwhelmed at this strange new feeling of belonging.

Rachel descended the staircase with him and for the first time Grey noticed the colors in the hallway. They were bright, like this strange new awareness in his soul, the reds in the tapestries a clear crimson, the blues in the rug below the color of a summer sky.

Today he'd been handed a gift. An honor as precious to him as the most priceless gem. A woman who barely knew him had recognized in him something good, something she could trust. If only Rachel could have felt the same.

Rachel was silent as they moved toward the front door and Grey knew she was forming words and practicing them before speaking them aloud. How he wished them to be words of forgiveness, of hope. His own formed on his tongue, ready with apology.

Over and over since he'd set out to look for her, he'd memorized what he'd say to Rachel when he had the chance. But no amount of remorse would undo the hurt he had caused her. And no explanation short of the complete truth would repay her for her pain. And that for now was impossible. He would not place her in the face of danger for knowing how truly evil Frank Ballard was.

They spoke together. "Rachel . . ."

"Grey . . ."

"No, please let me explain. You need to know I didn't mean what I said in the library."

But Rachel held up her hand to stop his apology.

"No, please." She shook her head. "It doesn't matter any more. I just wanted to thank you for being here. I don't know why you came—"

"I came because I was looking for you. You had me worried sick."

"I'm sorry about that, but I really didn't wish to talk with you." She rushed on, focusing on the buttons of his shirt without meeting his gaze. "I'm just glad you were here, for Sarah's sake. You did a good job with her and for that you have my gratitude."

"Rachel, I don't want your gratitude. I—"

"My respect, then. It took a lot of courage for you to remain in that room."

She still refused to glance up.

Grey reached out and lifted her chin with his fingers. He had to make her look at him, to see him for what he was, for what he felt for her. If she could but study his face, she would know his eyes didn't lie. "Rachel, that's not why I stayed. I wanted to help. I wanted to be with you."

"Don't, please. I really don't wish to hear your reasons. They're no longer important."

"But I must explain—"

"That's just it. You can't explain. You say one thing, then act out another. And your actions were very clear. Obviously there's more to you than meets the eye. You're involved in something you're not willing to share."

She looked away, in a deliberate attempt not to face him, but he could still read the distress in her furrowed brow.

"There can be only two reasons why you'd choose not to include me. Either you don't trust me or you're ashamed. I've worked hard to earn your trust, but I can do nothing to help the other."

"Then I suppose there's nothing more I can say to redeem myself."

"The truth," she answered. "Nothing less."

The silence that ensued tore at Grey, for he knew to speak the truth would be dangerous. To do less would only incriminate him further as a liar, the likes of Frank Ballard. So he said nothing.

Eventually, Rachel opened the door and stepped back. "Grey, I've spent my life studying other people. My father used to tell me I had an innate sense about others that would help me in my work, and up until I met you I believed him. But with you it's different and sadly, I cannot trust what I do not understand. It's best we forget what has transpired between us. We're simply too different.''

She looked toward the stairs. ''I really must get back to Sarah and the baby.'' This time when her eyes swept over his, they were cloudy but her posture ramrod straight. In that moment she closed the door on their relationship. She'd convicted him without a trial, and he could do nothing about it. Now he was being dismissed.

Grey started past her, fingering his yacht cap, then turned back. ''I'm sorry, Rachel. I wish things could be different.'' His voice was husky, his tone completely sincere, but he knew she would not allow herself to hear it.

''I, too,'' she answered, then quietly added, ''I wish you well.''

The door closed behind him and Grey remained rooted on the porch for several seconds, digesting the finality of his personal relationship with Rachel Thomas. He thought of Sarah's baby, Anna, and the role he would be expected to play when he stood in the church vestibule and promised to uphold his responsibility to her when needed. He thought of the woman who would stand alongside him, promising to share that charge. And he wondered how he would ever get through the christening ceremony.

Chapter 16

"How'd it go tonight?"

Frank Ballard sat at the end of the oilcloth-covered table, working his way through a pot of Blossom's fresh-brewed coffee. At one in the morning it was well past his bedtime, but he had too much to think about to give way to sleep.

"No problem." Rooster Crowe shrugged out of his canvas jacket and grabbed an empty cup from a sideboard. Still covered in the stains and smells of riverwork, he straddled the bench across from his employer. "Rode the boom clear down past the fork. Zeke and Jones took it the rest of the way." He reached for the pot and poured himself a cup.

"Pick up any strays?"

"Nah, but by tomorrow night we'll have a few. Templeton's sluice is filling up. By then his bullpen should be ready to give way . . . ," he snickered, ". . . with a little help."

"What makes you think he won't send them down himself come daylight?"

"Heard tell the mill's got all they can handle. The

foreman asked Templeton if he'd wait to send them down the next day." He issued a shrill chuckle through the gap in his front teeth. "It'll be one fine, fat haul boarding the *Orient Queen* tomorrow."

Frank Ballard banged his fist on the table in salute to Rooster Crowe's predictions, then turned his attention to the men still riding the load of timber downriver. "I'll bet Zeke and Jones couldn't wait to get their tails back up here after their little fiasco in Astoria. By damn, I should have their heads on a platter—letting a cheap, two-bit spreadlegs hoodwink them into a trap. If it hadn't been for her, that old man would have been out of my life permanently, and the next person with some smartass idea wouldn't be so quick to start running off at the mouth."

"Yeah, you're right." Crowe sipped on his coffee. "I don't know where she came from either. Since these two been back they ain't talking much. All they keep saying is her name—Chinook—say they'd never forget a name like that—and that they want a piece of that split-tail bitch if they ever see her again. I've been checking around, but the only place anybody's seen a pink-haired whore was at Baldy's, and then only a couple of times. Seems she comes and goes and don't owe nobody nothin'."

"Well, not anymore she doesn't. She owes me. Plenty. Billups and Larsen haven't been heard from in weeks. And after hearing what this whore almost pulled off on the beach, I know she somehow got rid of them. Now they're gone and Zeke and Jones would be, too, if our own man hadn't recognized them when he rowed up to pick up that old man. You'll look long and hard before you find two more crimps who could get the job done better than they could. If this tramp has decided to take on crimping herself to supplement her income, she's going to find herself out of work in short order. I'll see to that. No two-bit trash comes in and shanghais my men right out from under my nose."

"First we got to find her."

"Oh, we'll find her all right. Or rather, you will. If that whore ever shows her face again in this town, I want her taken care of—real quietlike—before she ends up becoming some kind of goddamned legend. I can see it now . . . ," Ballard waved his hand across the imaginary headlines, ". . .'Mysterious Whore Turns Avenging Angel. Shanghais Shanghaiers, Rescues Vigilantes.' "

He pointed his finger at his employee. "Find her. And get rid of her." He stopped his gesture in midair. "No—on second thought let me know as soon as you find out who and where she is. I want the pleasure of seeing her face when she realizes what's in store for her. Little Miss Roundheels is going to find out once and for all what it means to mess with Frank Ballard."

He sat quietly in thought, sipping on his coffee as if he were alone in the room.

"Whatsa matter, Boss?" Rooster asked after several moments of awkward silence.

"I've just been thinking about troublesome bitches. Got one in my own house . . . two if you count that meddlesome midwife who calls herself a doctor. Seems I can't keep her away from my wife. If I find her in my way again, though, she'll pay hell." He shook his head as if to clear it. "Damned if she hasn't started up where her old man left off."

Ballard exchanged understanding glances with the

293

man across from him. "Must run in the family. She saw where her father got with all his accusations. You'd think she would have learned from what happened to him. Why, the way she came at me the other day, I'd swear the old buzzard had told her everything he knew about me before he shipped out."

He gave Rooster a conspiratorial wink. "But we both know he couldn't have . . ." Ballard looked over one shoulder, then the other, to satisfy himself that they were alone in their conversation. "Being she was away at that fancy school and all." At Rooster's snicker, caught somewhere between his stomach and his throat, Ballard pressed on. "Too bad he couldn't have stuck with doctoring . . . and now his little whelp is following in his footsteps. I could do without her interference, too."

He continued to nurse his coffee and looked back toward the kitchen. Behind the door he could hear Blossom whistling some off-tune melody while she worked. "Blossom," he yelled, "get your fanny out here."

The kitchen door swung open and the cook appeared in the doorway. "You called me?" She neither smiled nor cowered, just stared Ballard down in her usual barely tolerant manner. As if she had somewhere else to be, something better to do. Didn't she realize who the hell owned this place? Owned her, for chrissake?

Sweeping her ample torso with a calculating eye, Ballard felt his stomach churn at the thought of how much he paid her to keep his men well fed. More, even, than his night crew. And he had absolutely no choice. Every man for miles talked about her cooking.

She had, since she'd hired on, earned their respect

294

in her own peculiar, gruff way. Never served a compliment or a smile, just good food and lots of it. And a certain sense that she understood how hard they all worked. But she'd never attempted to include him in that number, and her quiet censure irritated the hell out of him. If he didn't need her so badly up here, he'd get rid of her, too.

"What you want?" she asked again when he didn't address her. "I gotta get back to the stove."

"When's the next time you expect that woman doctor to come up?"

Blossom thought for a moment. "Not for another two weeks anyway. Said she'd be back by the end of the month. Guess it all depends on her schedule in town." She put her hands on her hips. "Why? We got a problem I don't know about? If we have, she'd come right away."

"No, nothing. Just wondered. You can get yourself on back now." His tone clearly dismissed her—just a slight reminder of who was boss—before he turned his attention on the man across from him.

"In a pig's ass I'll wait another two weeks. I'm not putting up with that woman any longer. I want her out of my house and out of my life, for good. And I know just how to do it."

The woman lay upon a white lace coverlet, her body swollen with child. Her face was Rachel's own. Her dress of fine white linen was hiked above her hips, her legs spread to expel her painful cargo.

"Please come . . . please," she moaned, begging mercy from the temple of blue overhead, pleading for the birth of her unborn child, for strength to endure. Just when she thought she couldn't endure another contraction, a shadow blocked out the sky.

"I'm here. I've come to help you."

A man knelt beside her, smoothing her sweat-dampened hair. Grey had come at last. She smiled up into his face.

"I'm so glad you've come," she murmured, her pain somewhat lessened at the sight of him.

His fingers locked around her arms, and in the place of a comforting hug, he started to shake her. Tighter and tighter he squeezed.

"Why are you doing this?" she demanded. Her words froze upon her lips. The hurtful hands belonged not to Grey, but to Frank Ballard. He shimmered above her like a demon from hell. His cold blue gaze delved into her own.

He laughed wickedly, his teeth clamping into a sneer. "You'll never be a threat to me again," he promised. Then he started to pummel her swollen stomach. "I'll kill your Anna."

Using her fingers like talons, Rachel clawed at Ballard's eyes. His blood splattered on her white gown and the white lace coverlet. She kicked at him—swung at him—but her strength was no match for his. Soon Ballard had staked her hands and feet to the ground. He began to flail her swollen, distended belly.

"Noooooo!" Rachel screamed.
She came awake, her shriek a whisper on her lips. Her fingers gripped the bed covers, then instinctively

sought her flattened abdomen. It had been a dream, only a dream. Relieved, she pushed herself up against the headboard, her eyes grasping for light in the inky darkness.

Somewhere someone pounded. The repeated blows echoed throughout the house. The rapping persisted. Someone was summoning her to answer the door.

Quickly lighting the lamp on her bedside table, she donned her wrapper and slipped down the hallway.

"Who's there?" she called.

"Doc, you don't know me, but I've just come from Camp Ross. There's been an accident. Blossom's been hurt real bad. She needs a doctor. Sent me to fetch you."

"What happened?" Rachel asked. A picture of the healthy, robust cook spirited through her mind.

"An explosion. She needs you, Doc. I rode my horse really hard to get here. You want me to wait for you? Don't believe the nag would carry us both back."

"No, you go ahead. I'll get my things together and come right along. Tell Blossom I'm on my way."

The man waited on the other side of the door. Rachel could hear his feet fidgeting against the wooden floor.

"You sure, Doc? How will you get there?"

"I'll take my canoe," Rachel replied.

Her mind raced. It would take her a good three hours to get to the camp by water. But the roads, barely passable at best, were so rutted by recent rains it would be practically impossible by buggy—if she could wake the liveryman. And if she lost a wheel alone in the middle of nowhere, she might still be sitting there this time tomorrow. It was a clear night. With the aid of a full moon the river would be easily navigable.

"How long will it take?"

Again she heard the man's feet shuffle against the wood.

"What time is it?" she asked him.

" 'Bout midnight."

"I'll probably get there between three and four."

"You sure you're coming?" the stranger asked.

"Of course I'm coming."

"Good," the man mumbled. "Blossom said she could count on you."

His footsteps moved across the porch. He loped down the stairs, then thudded across the stone path. Rachel heard the gate slam shut.

Rushing to unlock the door, she called out, "Wait, your name?" But her night visitor was now no more than a dark shadow, retreating down the empty street. She walked back inside, taking mental note of the supplies she might need.

The night's festivities were in full swing when Grey entered Baldy's Saloon. He scanned the room for Tully, but not finding him, decided the older man was still out with his traps. These nights Tully took one or another of his cronies when he went out in his skiff, and for that Grey was thankful.

Customers milled around the bar and throughout the room. With a nod to Baldy, Grey ambled around the smoke-filled area, nursing his whiskey.

A visiting patron had taken it upon himself to provide the crowded establishment with music. He beat out a medley of songs on the out-of-tune piano as a crowd formed around him. The music lifted the haunting shadow that had surrounded Grey all afternoon and before long he found himself joining the others in song. His deep baritone voice rang out the familiar words:

Yankee Doodle, keep it up,
Yankee Doodle dandy;
Mind the music and the step,
And with the girls be handy.

When the song was over, he grinned at the woman next to him and pulled her closer into the loop of his arm. Like an old friend, she rested her head against him, and for a moment Grey imagined that her dark brown ringlets belonged to Rachel.

The woman smiled at him, her hip nudging his suggestively. Her hair was the same dark color as Rachel's, her skin the same translucent hue and for a moment she stirred his blood. But looking down on her smiling face, Grey found an emptiness in her eyes. No spark twinkled back at him, the spark that he'd come to anticipate whenever Rachel pierced him with her challenging, dark eyes. He was glad the similarity ended there. Right now he felt so damn vulnerable after Rachel's cold dismissal, he needn't be reminded of her every time he saw another woman. What he did need was the companionship of another.

"What's your name, honey?" he asked, settling the saloon girl a little closer to his side. Her womanly softness melted against him.

She elbowed him in the ribs and acted insulted. "I've told you a dozen times, it's Alice."

"Like in Wonderland?" he teased her.

She looked at him, blinking with bafflement.

"Never mind, Alice."

Tonight it wasn't a woman's brain Grey was interested in and he didn't feel up to explaining the story of *Alice's Adventures in Wonderland*. Seeing the tops of her lush breasts made him feel more inclined to make up his own Alice story. Another female might be just the medicine he needed to cure the malady he'd been suffering since his first encounter with the lady doctor.

Rachel's disappearance had made Grey sick with worry. He knew Ballard to be unscrupulous and had imagined the worst, never once considering that Rachel had gone into hiding to escape him. Thank God he'd found her this morning, after reading the note on her front door.

But then the day hadn't been all bad. It wasn't every day a man such as himself experienced the miracle of birth, or was called upon to assist in the marvel. And it would never have happened if he hadn't seen Frank Ballard boarding a barge to head upriver, or if Sarah's maid hadn't succumbed to the jitters when he'd arrived.

After encountering the distraught Agnes at the front door, and having learned that no one but the three women were in the house, Grey knew he'd made the right decision to interfere. He'd felt useful—worthy—knowing that Rachel needed him and he had been there to help. Having hurt her with his stabbing words in Ballard's library, it had been reward enough working at her side, doing her bidding to make the delivery easier.

The very thought of what he'd been about to experience had nearly stricken him with immobility. Outwardly, he'd tried to appear strong, but inwardly, his pulse had quickened and he had to force himself to breathe. But Rachel's soothing words of encouragement soon comforted him as much as they had Sarah. Rachel had been calm and professional, but her manner, her soft gaze at him from time to time, had made Grey's breathing easier, had made him feel he belonged in that room. Throughout the ordeal, he had never felt closer to her.

He had never expected more return than that—to be asked by Sarah to be the baby's godfather. The pleasing memory sent pride flooding through him. For a while he'd even thought that he had redeemed himself a little in Rachel's eyes. When he'd walked down those stairs with Rachel, preparing to leave, he'd felt like a new man, washed of his sins. Until she saw him out.

It wasn't everyday that a man gained so much and lost the only good thing that had ever happened to him as well. Birth and death, he thought, they go hand in hand. Rachel had certainly issued his death warrant with her claim to indifference.

He'd only half-heard her words—"respect," "courage," "gratitude,"—while he searched her eyes, turned deep and piercing with resolve. Grey had braced himself for what was to come.

Like a dagger to the heart, Rachel had informed him that their differences were too great to ever entertain the notion of a future together. In those few moments she'd taken him back, beyond those prison walls, to his childhood, reminding him again of who he was and where he'd come from.

Last night, he'd stayed in his room, brooding over the unfairness of the world. But he couldn't stay there forever. Whether hidden away or not, Rachel's image still haunted him. Tonight he'd come to Baldy's, looking for companionship, determined to wipe away his memories of her. After several shots of whiskey, he'd convinced himself that this was a world that he knew, one where he belonged. With the whiskey and the woman beside him warming his blood, Grey felt almost human again.

They danced together in the middle of the room, along with several other couples. As the evening grew later, the crowd thinned out and the music mellowed. Just like Grey's mood.

"Would you like to come to my room?" Alice finally whispered, pulling his head down. Her warm breath tickled his ear.

He pulled her tighter against him, hoping to ignite desire in his loins. "And then what will we do?"

"Anything that tickles your fancy," Alice replied. She traced her finger down the muscled hollow of his chest.

"I could use a good tickle," Grey replied huskily. He buried his nose and lips in the soft ringlets of her hair. They smelled nothing like Rachel's.

Giggling, Alice grabbed his hand and pulled him toward the door which led to Opal's establishment. Fresh air hit his face, reminding Grey of another night when he'd entered the alleyway with another woman. But tonight, the red lantern light did not reflect off pink hair that resembled spun sugar candy.

He gave Alice the lead and soon the entry door thudded shut behind them. The familiar hallway with its pungent perfume loomed like a tunnel in the tempered light. He followed dutifully behind her, hearing the giggles and groans of physical pleasure emanating from

302

behind closed doors. With each measured step he took, Grey realized that bedding Alice was not the answer. It would take more than a shuddering release to ease his longing for Rachel.

Stopping, he pulled the woman up against him. He needed to escape but would not cause a scene. He'd grown up in whorehouses and knew well the reactions of a scorned whore.

"Alice, I need to use the bathroom. Would you mind telling me where it is?" He faked a look of discomfort.

"The can's down there." Alice pointed to a door at the very end of the hallway. "When you've finished your business, I'll be waiting for you." She threw her arms around him, teasing him with her globular breasts against his chest.

"I'll join you shortly." Grey set her away from him, giving her rounded rump a promising tap to send her along toward her own allotted cubicle.

Relief pulsed through him when he made his way back toward the bathroom and he cursed himself for having returned here in the first place. He'd wait a few minutes before making his escape, in case Alice came looking for him.

Grey had never been one who'd dallied with sporting women, and with his head clearing, he wasn't about to start now. As a youngster he'd been taught well the ways of the flesh by his mother's circle of friends, and the experience had left him empty and disillusioned. In their attempts to give him pleasure, they had only taken. For him there had been only the momentary pleasure of release but no joy. Never any joy.

When he'd run away to sea, he'd vowed never to set foot in another pleasure palace. And until he'd met the pink-haired Chinook, he'd lived up to that promise. After having been with Rachel, snow would fall in August before he could make love to another woman—especially one who worked in houses such as this. Rachel's touch had bathed him with euphoria and contentment, alien sensations that he had come to treasure. They would not be so easily replaced, certainly not here.

Alice would probably be scalding with fury when he didn't return as promised. Women who sold their bodies for money remembered only the amount received for their services, not the man who paid them. He started down the hallway.

"Opal, we have to warn her. It might already be too late."

Grey stopped dead in his tracks and stood outside the partially open door. He couldn't see inside, but the name had caught his attention. Deciding this to be Opal's private quarters, he dared not breathe as he strained to hear the muffled conversation within.

"He said he'd sent the crazy lady doctor on a wild goose chase." The woman relating the tale sounded almost hysterical. "He said there hadn't been an accident in Ballard's camp, but there would be before the night was over."

Grey's blood raced through his body. Someone intended to harm Rachel.

Not bothering to knock, he thrust open the door and muscled his way into the room. With a collective gasp, the women gaped at his intrusion. After a moment, Opal gained control of her tongue.

"These are my private quarters, Mr. Devlin. What is the meaning of this?"

"Damnation, lady. Forget the accusations." He turned toward the woman who had first spoken and for the first time noticed a third woman in the room. "I overheard your conversation. We all know of only one crazy lady doctor in Astoria. If someone intends to harm her, I want to know about it."

The three women exchanged nervous glances. Then Opal spoke. "Tell him, Lou. If anyone can help, he can."

"But, Opal, we tried to shanghai him. We can't trust—" Lou snapped her hand across her mouth.

Opal glowered at the woman. "Tell him what the man told you."

"We can't do that," the third woman interrupted. "Rachel will kill us."

"If we don't tell him, she might not be here to kill anyone," Opal snapped at her.

The missing pieces of the puzzle slowly fell into place. Just as Grey and Tully had suspected, Rachel as Chinook hadn't worked alone. Cold, white anger flashed through him as Lou related her story.

"How long ago was he here?"

"Not long. As soon as he told me, I came right here."

"Hellfire, woman. Where is this man now?"

"He's gone." Lou began to cry. "I never seen him before tonight. He was a cruel bastard. I was glad to be rid of him."

"Don't cry, Lou, it's all right." Opal consoled the shaken woman. Then she turned to Grey.

"It appears you care more for the doctor's welfare than you've managed to convince her." The words came as some sort of ablution. "I suggest you go find her and stop bullying this poor girl. The man's gone. Can't you see she's told you everything she knows?''

Lou sobbed now and slumped against the arm of Opal's chair. Grey stood waiting for further explanation.

"You're wasting valuable time." Opal spit out the words. "Every second counts."

He swung away from the three women and barreled through the door. Opal's next words stopped him.

"And Mr. Devlin . . .''

"What?''

"Our prayers are with you."

Grey turned and ran down down the hallway, thinking of the irony of the women issuing prayers for Rachel. As if they were a conventful of nuns. He exited into the alleyway, his heart racing as fast as his feet. He marveled at the thought that these soiled doves prayed for anything and hoped with all his being that those prayers would be heard.

In her small canoe, with only a symphony of frogs for company, Rachel glided across the water's surface. Her thoughts slid through her mind as rapidly as the advancing current beneath her light craft.

The last time she'd traveled on the river had been when Grey accompanied her to the logging camp. So much had happened between them since then. Recalling the moments they'd shared, a wave of sadness washed over her. The person she'd been when they'd made that trip no longer existed.

Her shoulders ached from her efforts, but the steady dipping of the paddle into the water helped soothe her troubled spirit. Not only did her muscles ache, her heart ached as well, for the kind and gentle man she'd wounded with her declarations.

Words she'd slung at Grey played over and over in her mind. She had spoken them in desperation, fearing for the death of her heart. And they had come with such ease. But that fear seemed immaterial now that her loftiness had sunk to an all-time low. Had she allowed her pain to deafen her to Grey's explanations, to destroy the beginning of a beautiful relationship?

She had run away to hide in her misery without allowing him to speak his mind. If given another chance, would she react in the same way because of her foolish pride? As she pondered these questions, Rachel still could not be certain of her answers.

She'd been on the river for little more than two hours, having left her house as soon as she'd gathered her supplies. The river was calm tonight and conditions for traveling by canoe were favorable.

A full moon hung in the sky like a lustrous pearl, its sheen turning the watery trail to silver. The towering firs were awash in moonlight, and between their bristly limbs slivers of light brightened the forest floor.

She passed an elk drinking at the water's edge. He raised his antlered head, ready to flee, but soon realized she meant him no harm. He dipped his head back to the water and continued to drink.

Earlier she'd seen a beaver dive beneath her bow with a whittled branch clamped beneath his big teeth. Soon he'd surfaced on the opposite shore, his paddle-like tail trailing behind him like the train of a woman's dress.

Whenever Rachel made her trips up and down the

river, she always marveled at the beauty of nature—its complexities as well as its simplicities. She realized that even relationships had these same components in common.

Her thoughts turned to what she might find when she reached Camp Ross. Rachel's night visitor had been vague about the extent of Blossom's injury. She prayed she'd get to her friend in time to help her.

What kind of explosion had caused her injury? The caller had not said. In the congested camp, wouldn't an explosion have injured others as well? For all Rachel knew, several people could be waiting for her help. This thought prompted yet another one.

If innocent people were needlessly hurt because of her failure to air her complaints about the condition of Ballard's camp, Rachel would never forgive herself. Especially if she learned it was faulty equipment that had caused it. Grey had asked her to trust him, but maybe she'd been wrong in waiting to voice her opinion.

Again her thoughts turned to the darker side. If Grey worked with Ballard as he'd implied, perhaps the blame lay as much with him as with the wretched man. But it made no sense. She had watched Grey with the children in the camp, had seen his compassion for his landlady's welfare and for Sarah when he'd helped her through a difficult delivery.

How could such a man work with a blackguard who didn't possess a heart? Rachel didn't want to believe what she'd seen with her own eyes, heard with her own ears. She wished now that she'd listened to Grey when he'd tried to explain. Instead, she'd shown him the door and ushered him out of her life forever.

The mountains seemed to close in as the river narrowed into a silvery strip. Identifying her position by the terrain, Rachel reasoned she'd be at Ballard's camp within the hour.

She looked toward the shore where a strand of sugar pine once grew. It was now nothing more than a jumble of logs and splinters after a clear-cutting operation. The loggers had felled every tree in the tract before moving on to another site. In the moonlight, a vast, silent waste of stumps and snags jutted upward, like the tired old crosses of some military graveyard.

Somewhere up the mountain an owl called, repeating his two-note song at intervals. The sound echoed off the silent hills before a female hooted her reply. Nature's mating season, Rachel thought, and the memory of her own recent copulation brought an unexpected heat to her face.

Rounding the bend in the river, she steered the canoe farther out into midstream. Soon she'd pass the deserted chute left by an earlier logging operation, which marked the last hour of her trip. Like a thin scar slashed in the mountain's face, it soon appeared in the moon's luster. The peeled tree trunks that served as conduits for the logs shimmered in the silken night, quiet and desolate. Rachel removed her glasses to clean the lenses for a better view, but before she could put them on again, all hell broke loose.

First she heard the rumbling. Like crashing thunder from an angry god. Then logs shot down the deep crevice, like bullets plunging toward the water and Rachel's boat.

* * *

At the top of a small rise, Grey reined in his mount. The night was as bright as day, and the moon's reflection made the river look like a silver ribbon from where he sat astride his horse.

Remembering Lou's words, he searched about him for evidence of danger lurking in the shadows along the narrow trail. Earlier he'd passed a clear-cut strip of woods that ran down to the shoreline, and in the murky brightness the jagged stumps looked to him like tombstones. At this grim thought apprehension snaked up his spine, for it reminded him of Rachel's vulnerability and her refusal to recognize it. Why she presumed she was invincible, Grey would never know. Even under the best of circumstances, a woman traveling alone in this wilderness was a mark for all kinds of danger.

He nudged his horse forward. From the distance he'd ridden, he knew time was fast running out before she reached the logging camp. He had to catch up with Rachel before then. If he failed to get to her in time, and if she came to harm, he vowed he would personally choke the life from Frank Ballard's body.

Urging his horse to a faster pace, Grey searched the river. An owl screeched from a nearby tree and he felt his horse shy beneath him. He again reined in the nervous animal, reassuring him with soft words and a gentle touch. From the opposite bank another bird called. The air around horse and man seemed rife with tension. All other night sounds had ceased.

A sliding, yawing noise groaned through the moonlit darkness. "What the hell?" Grey snorted, his gaze snapping toward the sound.

Upstream, a hundred or so feet from where he paused, huge logs thundered down the side of the mountain toward the water. It took a moment for Grey to connect the abandoned chute Rachel had pointed out to him earlier with what he now witnessed. Timber screamed as the force of gravity sent it diving toward the river at a dizzying speed. Smoking from the friction, the logs hit the water's surface like fiery gods seeking cold, wet relief.

And then he saw her. Rachel sat unmoving in her canoe, a black silhouette against the water's silvery surface. Defenseless, she sat looking up at the mountain. She'd been as startled by the noise as he, and she sat directly in the path of the plummeting logs.

They hurtled down at her with unleashed fury, agitating the once calm surface of the river into a choppy sea. One of the pines rocketed out of the water's clutches, its end crashing against the bow of the canoe, splintering it into pieces. The blow hurled Rachel through the air and into the frothy current.

Kicking wildly, she struggled to reach the surface, barely conscious of the icy temperature. Her long skirt restricted her movements, weakening her efforts to thrust upward. Rachel clawed the water, her efforts futile.

She ripped her skirt from around her waist, kicking free of the heavy material. Then she fought her way toward the surface that shimmered like milky quartz above her head. Breaking free of her watery prison, she drank in huge gulps of air.

Her hand snaked out and made blessed contact with one of the floating logs. Never had the rough bark of a tree felt so good. Rachel rested her head against it, holding on with both hands as the gentle current pulled her back in the direction she'd just come from.

A nefarious calm hovered over the basin. Even the night creatures had stopped their chorus, as though they too sensed danger lurking in the shadows. From the top of the chute, gravel tumbled into the water, shattering the quiet.

Rachel started. This area hadn't been worked in some time. Someone was up there. Someone had sent those logs down that chute intentionally. She shifted her eyes to the summit, but without her glasses it was impossible to see. Her mind raced back to the stranger at her door, the man who had refused to give his name. Rachel knew now she'd been lured here for one purpose only. Someone wanted her dead. And Rachel knew who that someone was.

The moments dragged by while she tried to decide what to do. Her fingers cramped where she clung to the rugged bark of the tree. And now that her pulse rate had slowed, she began to shiver uncontrollably. If she didn't soon reach shore, she would surely die.

But she was afraid to move and give away her hiding place. Her only chance of survival was to remain hidden. She gave way to the current and prayed that the log would carry her away from her pursuer.

Chapter 17

"Rachel!" Grey yelled, in a moot attempt to warn her. Cold terror shot through his body as boat and woman disappeared beneath the choppy caldron of water.

Nothing had prepared Grey for the helpless feeling that rushed over him as he watched. Jumping from his horse, he ran toward the river, pausing only long enough to remove his boots. Then he dived into the whipped-up water. Like a man crazed, he swam toward the spot where he'd last seen the canoe.

Debris floated around him. He searched among the bark, the splintered wood, the flotsam that pocked the water. Rachel's straw hat swirled past him, and something butted against his head. It was Rachel's leather satchel. With as much strength as he could muster, Grey lifted her bag above his head and threw it toward a jagged outcropping of rock. If he found her, he might need the medical supplies to help save her life. Please, God, he prayed, let me find her.

Treading water, he searched frantically for a glimpse of her, then began diving, groping wildly beneath the surface, but in the murky water he saw nothing that resembled Rachel.

In those few moments the reality of his love for her washed over him like the angry, flowing current. Grey had to find her. If he lost Rachel now, his own life would end with hers. He needed her, wanted her. He would do everything in his power to set things straight between them, if God would but grant him another chance. Without Rachel his world would turn into a dark and empty void, worse than he had ever known as a child.

He surfaced again and again, spewing water. "Rachel, where are you?" But his words were no more than a croaked whisper in the night.

A flat calm once again settled upon the water. Grey looked toward the shore, hoping he'd find her there. But the only movement he saw was that of the logs, floating, like oversized alligators, downstream with the moving current.

Something caught his eye. Was his mind playing tricks? *My God, could it be?* Grey rubbed the water from his eyes. Clinging to the top of one of the logs and glazed white by the moon, he saw what appeared to be two hands. His spirits soared with hope. *Rachel.* He propelled himself toward the drifting wood.

She knew he was here. She'd heard him call out her name. Her mind reeled with doubts and fears as Rachel clung to the coasting log. Had he been up there all along? Had he been waiting for his opportunity? What had she ever done to him but love him? Had he come to finish the job? And surely he wasn't alone. No.

one man could have caused so much terror. Her mind tried to sort through the jumble of madness.

Why else would Grey Devlin be out here in the middle of the night, if he weren't responsible for the slide? Rachel had told no one about her emergency call, not even Tully. Her only concern had been for Blossom. She'd thought of nothing but getting to her friend.

Her teeth chattered from cold and fear. Oh, God, she didn't want to believe this of him. But the stark truth lay before her in the sound of his voice. Her only hope now for escape was to remain hidden. She looked around her, now cursing the moon's brightness where earlier she'd reveled in its beauty.

A peaceful quiet had settled over the river after the deafening noise from the log slide. When Rachel had first heard her name called, she'd thought she'd imagined it. But those logs had not hurled down upon her on their own. Perhaps Grey called out to her to make certain he'd achieved his goal. No matter. To Grey Devlin she was dead.

Rachel moved to the end of the log she rode for a better view of the other side of the river. And then she saw him, purposefully swimming toward her hiding place. Had he spied her? Should she swim for shore? Her heart raced so fast, it nearly took her breath away.

"Rachel, is that you?" Grey paused, treading water and calling to her again.

She wanted to cry out. To shout to this man she loved that she was alive. But her instinct to survive was greater. Too many conflicting arguments flashed through her head. Too many things had happened between them. Too many things had been said. She had too many doubts. She could never trust Grey Devlin

315

with her life. Loosening her grip on the log, Rachel sank quietly beneath the water. Then she propelled herself away from the trees and toward the bank.

She'd intended to cover as much distance as possible underwater, but swimming in the current proved to be more difficult than hanging from a floating log. Her efforts seemed futile as the drift of the river held her in its flow. She broke the surface, gasping for air.

But Grey had seen her. He was only a short distance away from where she'd surfaced.

"Rachel, wait—"

But she didn't wait. Instead, she dived again into the river's depths. This time she swam for the opposite shore, hoping to throw him off her trail.

When her lungs felt as though they might explode, Rachel swam to the surface. But luck was not to be with her. Grey had spotted her again and now edged toward her with deliberate strokes, his muscular strength pulling him through the water at much greater speed than she could summon. He would soon overtake her. She felt like a defenseless fish.

Rachel couldn't tell how long she'd been in the water, but it seemed like hours. Her strokes became stiff and slow as the current pulled at her, and the water's temperature had numbed her to the bone. She felt her strength waning. If she didn't make the shore soon, the river would claim her.

Don't panic, Rachel warned herself over and over. She had to remain calm. In medical school she'd taken swimming lessons and had become a competent swimmer. But nothing had prepared her for this. Her life had been threatened, and now the cold river tormented her, promising to swallow her up forever.

Grey was only a few feet away now. Rachel kept looking back over her shoulder, each time losing a stroke as he gained on her. But she was not yet ready to surrender, not to the river, not to Grey Devlin. She swam for all she was worth, but her efforts proved fruitless. She felt his hand clamp around her ankle. She was caught.

With every ounce of fight in her, she kicked out and clawed at him while Grey struggled to subdue her. All this time the weight of the river pushed them both toward the bottom.

Rachel tore at Grey's eyes, pulled at his hair. But the water crushed her defenses. Her sluggish movements weakened her body. And then she was fighting for air.

No longer able to breathe, she felt her lungs collapse. A thousand stars burst inside her head, splintering through the last of her rational thoughts. She'd fought a good fight, but the river and Grey had been the victors. Nothing mattered anymore.

Grey knew the second Rachel's resistance ebbed away. Her body became cold and stiff in his hold. Frantically, he clamped his arms around her and kicked toward the surface. It seemed an eternity before he broke free of the water, then gratefully he sucked in huge gulps of air, coughing and choking at the same time. But he knew he had precious few moments to waste. Rachel was dying in his arms. He had to act fast. Cradling her head above the water, in the crook of his elbow, he struck out for the shore.

When his feet finally touched the soggy bottom, Grey

stood on shaky legs. He staggered toward the bank with Rachel in his arms and lowered her to the dew-dampened grass in a hidden thicket. Whoever had sent those logs screaming down that chute might still be around, and if they tried once to kill her, they'd damned sure try again without hesitation.

He rolled her lifeless form onto her stomach and knelt beside her. He was exhausted. His arms ached with fatigue. Willing a strength he no longer possessed, he worked to pump the water from her lungs.

Soon his labors were rewarded. Heaving and retching, Rachel rid her lungs of their unwanted cargo. Then she collapsed into the grass.

A good sign, Grey decided, as he slumped beside her, flinging his weakened arm across her back. Mercifully, Rachel did not try to move away, but allowed him to warm her with his body.

"Rachel, you scared the hell out of me," he managed to croak, pulling her closer into his embrace.

But the woman beside him said nothing and soon they both fell into a fatigued sleep.

Hours later, Rachel awoke. Disoriented, she jerked upright. Every muscle in her body groaned with the sudden movement and it was several seconds before she realized she wasn't alone on the carpet of grass. When her eyes adjusted to the shady darkness, she recognized the man beside her.

"Rachel, are you all right?" he uttered softly beside her, sitting up. His hand groped for hers, but she quickly slid from his reach.

"Why didn't you just let me drown?" Her words were laced with derision.

"Let you drown? Rachel, have you taken leave of your senses?" Grey paused only long enough to run his fingers through his mussed hair. "I know we've had our disagreements, but do you think so little of me that you'd believe I want you dead?"

He moved toward her, but Rachel cowered from his advance. "Did you finally discover you had a conscience?" she asked.

"What the hell are you talking about?"

"I'm talking about you. Being here the moment after those logs slid down that deserted shoot."

"Certainly, you don't think I had anything to do with that."

Rachel heard the disbelief in Grey's voice, the indignation. Could she possibly be wrong? Had she misjudged him?

In a desperate attempt to convince her, Grey added, "To let you die . . . would be like carving out my own heart."

His declaration surprised her, but Rachel wasn't yet ready to believe him. She'd undergone a horrible shock, and even now, with the thick grass firmly beneath her, she felt as vulnerable as she had in the river.

Again he tried to move toward her, but Rachel evaded his touch. Each contemplated the other while the quiet yawned between them. Grey listened for sounds of intruders, for a horse's whinny, anything that would reveal the presence of the men who had failed in their mission. But the only sound he heard was that of the even flow of the river over jagged rocks and their own uneven breathing.

319

"Damnation, Rachel, I didn't try to kill you. That's the last thing I could ever do."

Across Grey's features Rachel saw defeat. His shoulders sagged. She wanted to believe him, but so many unanswered questions swarmed in her head. One thing she knew for certain—Grey had saved her life. In the water, when the fight had gone out of her, along with her will to live, it had been Grey who'd pulled her back from the clutches of death. If for nothing else but that, she knew she must listen to him.

"Tell me then," she added, "why were you here? And how did you know to look for me?" Her voice sounded hoarse and speaking made her throat ache.

Even in the moonlit darkness, Grey's expression looked pensive, as though a private war raged within him. Finally, he sighed.

"All right, I will tell you . . . everything you want to know. But first I've got to find my horse. I brought warm clothing and blankets with me." Concern etched his brow as though he expected her to bolt. "You need to get out of those wet clothes before you catch pneumonia. Do you trust me enough to stay here, to not run away this time?"

Rachel considered his question. Leaving her alone would give her the perfect chance to escape. But with no canoe and no horse, where would she go? Right into the arms of the men who really had tried to kill her? No, she was tired of running and besides, she needed to hear what Grey had to say, for herself as much as for him.

"I promise. I'll wait for you here."

For the first time since she'd awakened on the riverbank, Rachel saw Grey smile.

"Good," he replied, "when I return, I'll build a fire and then we can talk."

Thirty minutes later, Rachel sat in front of a blazing fire, a wool blanket wrapped around her like a cocoon. Grey had returned with his horse in tow and had immediately pulled a long flannel shirt and a pair of worn denim trousers from the saddlebags. After a heated discussion, Rachel had accepted the use of his shirt, but had insisted he don the trousers.

What was left of their wet clothing was strung over nearby bushes. Feeling warmed by the welcome heat, Rachel began to relax. In spite of her remaining misgivings about Grey, there was something wickedly exciting about sitting nearly naked beside him, with her underthings hanging in clear view. She waited quietly for him to speak.

He finally stood and walked over to his horse, his blanket flowing behind him like a regal cape. A few minutes later, he returned, plopping her doctor's bag on the ground in front of her.

Rachel felt a warm flush rush through her. "How— Where did you get it?" She looked up into his blue eyes, warmed by the fire's reflection in their depths.

"After I saw you disappear in the water, I dove in. I couldn't find you, but your hat floated by and so did the bag. I know how much this means to you, so I tossed it up on the rocks."

Amazed that he'd accomplished such a feat in the midst of the tumult, Rachel smiled her appreciation. "I never thought I'd see this again." She stroked the bag with revered fondness.

Grey noted her reaction, then added guiltily, "Truthfully, Rachel, I didn't save that damn bag because of your affection for it. I did it because I thought I might need it later. To doctor you if I found you . . . when I found you," he amended.

Rachel caught the expression in his face—part anger, part relief—reflected in his narrowed eyes. She made a weak attempt to lighten the moment. "I guess I'll make a doctor out of you yet," she replied.

Their eyes locked. Both recalled another time when Grey had assumed the role of physician. In her office, on her examining table.

"I—I mean the way you helped deliver Sarah's baby," Rachel added, embarrassed.

"Yeah, that was really something, wasn't it?" Grey shook his head slowly, as if still not quite believing the miracle.

After a moment, he poked the fire with a long branch, threw on several more chunks of wood, and inhaled deeply. He settled himself on the grass beside Rachel and joined her in staring at the blaze. Plucking a piece of sweet grass, he stuck it in his mouth.

Wood smoke saturated the air, its curly vapor lifting toward the moon-brightened sky. Under different circumstances it would have been wonderful to be here with Grey, sharing the wilderness with him. But Rachel knew that things had to be said between them. Things had to be set straight, so she, for one, could get on with her life.

"How . . . ?"

"Opal . . ."

They both spoke at the same time, then laughed nervously.

"You first," Rachel conceded.

"Opal told me where you had gone."

"Opal? How did she know? I didn't tell anyone." Suddenly, Rachel thought of her intended mission. "Oh my goodness." She started to jump up, but Grey stopped her.

"There was no accident at Ballard's camp. It was all a ploy to get you on the river alone. So someone could get rid of you and make it look like an accident. Lou found out from one of her customers."

Now that she'd had time to think about her near-drowning, Rachel had suspected as much. Grey's words reinforced her suspicions. It was probably the same man who had come to her house, then stole away into the darkness. "Then Blossom was not hurt in the explosion?"

"There was no explosion. Except for the logs fired at you from that deserted chute." Anger wrinkled his brow.

"You know who was responsible?"

"I knew nothing about those logs, Rachel." Grey held her chin and gently turned her face toward him. "When I saw you in that boat and thought you might die at Ballard's hand, I swore if God would spare your life, the first thing I'd do was tell you how I feel about you." His eyes caressed her every feature. "I love you, Rachel. With God as my witness, I love you."

Love me. Rachel's heart swelled to near-bursting. Grey loves me.

She threw herself into his arms. Burying her face in the warmth of his neck, she sobbed in jubilation and relief. Cradled in his embrace upon his crossed calves, Rachel felt her tears flow as freely as the river's current several feet away from where they sat. All her misgiv-

323

ings of the last week were swept away in the stream of emotions that poured from her soul. *Grey loved her.*

Spent at last, she relaxed against his chest.

"There's more, Rachel. I have to tell you everything."

She sealed his words with her lips, kissing him full on the mouth. "I love you," she whispered, "nothing else matters now but that."

He released a sigh that sounded more like a wounded cry but kept her in his arms. He held her so tightly Rachel felt she might suffocate.

"Listen to me first, before you commit your heart. I'm not worthy of your love, Rachel."

"Not worthy . . . don't ever say that," she insisted.

He silenced her with a kiss. "Please . . . hear me out." Then he began to speak.

"You were right when you said we were too different. You see, my mother was a whore. I'm a bastard child. I don't even know who my father was and I doubt my mother knew either."

"It doesn't matter—"

Again Grey interrupted her. "It matters, Rachel. It matters to me. Don't you understand?" He grabbed her arms and squeezed her, turning her to face him. "My mother earned her living on her back. She didn't want me. She'd tried to get rid of me, but it was too late when she finally discovered she was pregnant. Her quack physician said she'd endanger her own life and my mother valued her precious hide." He shrugged his shoulders as though the weight of the world were on them. "So she carried me full term, only to protect herself." His voice lowered to a broken whisper. "I shouldn't have been born."

The firelight illuminated Grey's pained expression and Rachel thought her heart would break. "You don't have to tell me," she crooned.

"But I do." His face was rigid, his jaw set, as if bracing for the next memory. "I was her bastard child. She called me that often, to my face. For a long time I thought that was part of my name." He laughed cynically.

Rachel watched and listened, appalled that a small boy should be shunned by his mother and then reminded so cruelly about his birth. A birth he had not caused nor could he prevent.

"I grew up in a whorehouse. I was allowed to remain underfoot only because I ran errands for the working ladies. At night they shooed me to the kitchen where I stayed until the sun came up. When I was about eight or nine, I took to roaming the streets until daylight."

"I'm sorry, I didn't know."

"There's more, Rachel. Please, let me finish." He drank in a deep swig of air, exhaling a distressing sigh. It was a moment before he continued. "As my body matured, I became a plaything for some of the sporting girls. They taught me things I'd never have learned in school."

Grey laughed softly to himself. As Rachel watched him, she saw one corner of his mouth turn up, not a smile but an unmistakable sneer of contempt. He glanced briefly in her direction as though looking for her own distaste. She met his eyes with hers, tender and compassionate. It seemed to give him courage to go on.

"And then one day I decided I'd had enough. I was

twelve years old. I'd learned where some of the women stored their money, my mother included. So I helped myself to a healthy sum and walked out the door. I went down to the wharf, hoping to stow away on a ship bound for anywhere. It didn't matter where. I only wanted it to take me so far away I'd never be able to find my way back. And that's when I met Eland Taithleach.''

Taithleach. Rachel couldn't believe she'd heard him right. ''Who'd you meet?'' she asked, never expecting him to mention that name. Shocked that Grey's Taithleach could possibly be the same man her father had referred to in his letter.

''Tully,'' Grey answered. ''He was the first mate aboard the ship I had sneaked on. He found me curled up beneath a lifeboat the second day at sea. He talked the captain out of throwing me overboard.''

Tully was Taithleach. Could he also have been her father's friend?

''Tully—he wouldn't let me call him by his given name—took me under his wing, and before long I'd earned the position of cabin boy. After that, we sailed together until he retired. On those long voyages, he became my teacher, taught me to read. After that I thirsted for knowledge. He was the best thing that ever happened to me. Tully saved my life the day he found me . . .'' He paused, remembering. ''—and many more times after that.''

So that was how they met. Rachel had suspected the friendship between Tully and Grey went far deeper than either had let on. And now that she knew Tully's real name, she wanted to question Grey about him, tell him about her father's letter, but now was not the time. Grey needed this time to unveil his own secrets.

"It was after Tully retired that I met Frank Ballard."

For a moment an abhorrent expression crossed Grey's face, but it disappeared as quickly as it had appeared. An involuntary shiver pulsed through Rachel at his expression.

"By this time I'd become an accomplished sailor, had served as first officer on several brigs and schooners. Frank Ballard approached me when I was in San Francisco. Said he wanted me to captain one of his clippers." Grey shook his head as though he couldn't believe his own naiveté.

"I checked around, learned he was quite an influential man in the shipping world. He owned several vessels that traveled back and forth across the Pacific. At the time, the man's background impressed me, as did the man himself. I'd always dreamed of captaining my own ship and Frank Ballard was handing me that dream. Hell, he was going to pay me top dollar for doing something I'd always wanted to do. A man with no past couldn't turn down an opportunity like that."

Grey paused long enough to stoke the fire. Then he settled back down, cradling Rachel in his lap.

"I sailed to the Orient several times. But on my last trip back from there, I learned that I'd been smuggling opium for the bastard. In the bowels of my cargo holds, hidden in the crates of silks and barrels of spices, I was hauling drugs between the two continents."

Rachel exhaled loudly, surprising even herself at how shrill it sounded in the quiet night. The only other noise was the sound of the fire crackling as it ate up the wood.

"There's more, my love, and I'm sure you won't enjoy it." He cleared his throat to continue.

"It doesn't matter. If you want to tell me, I'm here to listen."

"This time the Marine Revenue was waiting when we dropped anchor. It seems our owner, Frank Ballard, had gotten wind that his vessel would be searched and seized. He pleaded ignorant, blaming me, his captain. He testified in court that I'd unlawfully used his ship to smuggle contraband."

"But surely there must have been someone who could have testified in your behalf. What about Tully?" Rachel couldn't believe the injustice in the world.

"Oh, Tully tried. And several other worthy seamen I'd sailed with. But Ballard is a man of considerable influence. He brought witnesses who testified that I was solely responsible for the deed. After all, I was the bastard child of a whore. Who would believe my word against his?"

"I would, I still do—"

"Wait," he stopped her. He placed his fingers against her lips. "I lost and was convicted. And because of Frank Ballard, I went to prison for two years."

Grey stared off into the distance, remembering. He didn't like to recall those countless months he'd spent living in his own filth. But Rachel had to know everything. She had to know how right she had been. They were much too different. He could never be worthy of her love.

"When I said earlier that Tully had saved my life on numerous occasions, I meant it. If it hadn't been for him, I would have died during that time. I even contemplated taking my own life, worthless as it seemed. But then desire for revenge began to smolder. And it was that revenge that plotted the course of my actions. I served those two years and walked away a free man. But I won't be entirely free until Frank Ballard is put behind bars. He's a no-damn-good son of a bitch.''

Grey looked haggard, as though the burden he'd carried for so long was about to weigh him down. Rachel threw her arms around his neck, willing herself to absorb some of his pain. She ached for him, for the small boy he'd been, and for her own error in doubting his worth.

She'd condemned him twice since she'd known him. Once disguised as Chinook, the second time as a willful and spoiled Rachel. She loved Grey Devlin and was determined to convince him of that if it took the rest of her days trying.

''I love you,'' she whispered.

At first he didn't answer, and she thought he hadn't heard. Then he sought her eyes, as though looking for the truth in them. ''Even now? After all I've told you?''

''Especially now.''

As though seeking the gift of life, Grey grabbed Rachel's head and pulled her lips roughly to his. With desperate hunger he plundered her mouth. Toppling her back upon the grass, he held her prisoner beneath him.

''Oh my sweet, sweet Rachel. Does my past make you want to flee?'' He stroked her brow, settling her errant hair from her face.

329

"Never," she whispered. "Not in a thousand years."

"I'm a man who doesn't even know his origins. I don't even have a real name. The whores called me 'Gray.' They spelled it G-R-A-Y because it was a cold and bleak day when I was born. It seemed to fit well enough, because that whole world was drab and desolate from what I saw of it. Never any sunshine in our lives, just one house after another."

"But what about your mother's family name? Surely she would have given you that."

"I didn't know my mother's surname, didn't give a damn about it anyway. Besides, she always claimed I'd been sent from the devil. A gray devil, she'd say, fathered by a black devil. By the time I ran away, I took the names they'd always used and jumbled them up to name myself. But I wanted to forget the dismal melancholy that followed all the doves, so I changed the 'a' to 'e' and called myself Grey Devlin." He reared back and captured her gaze with his own. "Not very creative, was it?"

He gave her no chance to answer as he trailed searing kisses down Rachel's neck, then smothered her mouth, fearing what she might say, fearing her scorn. He may not have had a given name, but he knew what he was—a survivor. Now the one thing he knew he couldn't survive was Rachel's scorn.

When at last her mouth was free, he heard her breathless mumble. "It's a dashing name, Grey Devlin." She pushed him back enough to watch his reaction to her words. "And not all whores are bad. Many are, in fact, quite the opposite, simply lost souls. Some

330

of my best friends are whores. I value Opal's friendship, as well as the others'."

And the man who'd scorned whores most of his life took Rachel there on the fire-burnished grass with the moon riding low in the sky like a silver warrior. The son of a whore buried himself in the warm sweetness of the virginal woman he loved. The frustration with himself that he'd carried for years drained from his body when he poured his seed into her womb.

As his last spasm subsided, Grey reflected on the course his life had taken. Perhaps he'd been healed by this woman, the greatest of physicians.

Chapter 18

Morning came softly to the hidden grove where Rachel and Grey had spent the night. A bright and promising sun peeked over the mountaintop, sending warming rays of light slanting down its fir-covered slopes. Trees rustled with a hint of a breeze and nesting birds trilled a melody to the new day.

In her blanket cocoon, Rachel awakened to the sounds and scents of the forest and onions cooking on the nearby fire. When she lifted her head, she saw Grey no longer slept beside her, but sat on his haunches near the river's edge, diligently cleaning a large fish. For a moment she contented herself with just watching him. His every movement made her heart accelerate. He must have felt her gaze because he looked her way and smiled.

"Our breakfast." He motioned toward the pink salmon on the rock.

Getting to her feet, Rachel gathered her blanket around her and walked toward him. "But I smell onions," she replied.

"Wild ones. I found them in the streambed. They'll taste great with this salmon."

"Why, Grey Devlin, you're just full of surprises," she teased, her eyes bright with yet another discovery about this man. "You, a man of the sea, cooking fish over an open fire and flavoring it with wild onions like some trailblazer."

He grinned. "Remember, I read a lot." She watched him secure the fillets between four shaved sticks, tying them together with rawhide at each end. Gingerly he placed them beside the skewered onions that roasted above the red hot coals. "We just have to be careful the fire doesn't gobble this fish before we do."

Rachel moaned, holding her stomach. "If that happens, I might have to eat those coals. I'm that hungry."

Grey's eyes raked over Rachel with open admiration. "Me too," he replied, his look clearly stating he craved more than food. Smiling devilishly, he winked. "And how's my mermaid this morning?"

"Except for her poor, aching muscles, your mermaid is fine." His reference to "my" made her feel warm all over.

"It's so good to see you this morning," he added.

"I know," she said, fully aware of the seriousness behind his soft expression.

Their eyes locked. Each knew how very close they'd come to losing the other the night before and now this morning every second together seemed precious. Grey yawned and stretched wide.

"I don't suppose you slept all that well last night."

"No matter. As long as you did."

"You don't suppose those men are still around, do you?"

"I heard no sound of them during the night. If they'd stayed around to finish off their dirty deed, they would have struck at night, following the firelight." He looked at her, assurance written on his face. "If our fire didn't draw them out, then they're miles away by now. They probably skedaddled before they knew you were safe."

The somber moment aside, Grey plopped down onto the ground in front of the fire and patted a place beside him. Rachel accepted his invitation and sat while he served up their fare. In companionable silence they ate, topping off their meal with water from Grey's canteen.

When she had finished, Rachel fell back upon the needle-laden earth with a gratifying sigh. "Thanks for the wonderful breakfast." She stared up through the firs, watching the sun's sparkle on the gently swaying branches. With Grey here, she could have stayed in this spot forever.

He lay beside her, propped on his arm. With a long pierce of grass, he tickled her beneath her nose.

"Now, my dear," he said, "what are we to do with you to keep you safe?" He drew an imaginary line around her mouth with the grass blade, then trailed it up over the tip of her nose. "Frank Ballard is a very dangerous man. I'm worried about you. As soon as you show your face, he'll know he didn't succeed in his mission."

"I'm capable of taking care of myself," Rachel replied.

"You were lucky last night. If those logs had been a foot closer, this morning you'd be dead."

"But they weren't," she reminded him, pushing away the teasing grass with her hand.

"When Ballard finds out his henchmen failed to get rid of you, who knows what his next move might be?"

Rachel was thoughtful for a moment. "We don't even know for sure that it was Ballard who sent those logs down that chute."

Grey's face clouded. "Don't believe for a moment he wasn't behind it. Although someone else does his dirty work, Ballard instigates it."

"But he knows I'll tell everything I know about him."

"Need I remind you? Dead people can't talk."

"But surely—"

"Never underestimate that man, my dear. He could crush you as easily as this." Grey crumbled the grass in his hand and tossed it aside. After a slight hesitation he asked, "What do you know about your father's disappearance?"

The question surprised Rachel. She'd never told anyone but Opal about her father's shanghaiing, or the letter she'd received from him. But if she and Grey were to have a future together, Rachel knew she needed to tell him everything. Just as he had done the night before.

She wrapped her hands around one of his and pulled it close to her heart. His blue eyes, poised only inches away, rivaled the sky overhead—observant and probing—and Rachel paused only a moment before she recalled her nightmarish memories.

She told Grey about the letter from her father, leaving out nothing. She'd read it so many times the words flowed as though they'd been engraved in her mind. Rachel covered her mother's frail condition and subsequent death, and how she herself had been unable to stand up under the strain of losing her father.

They had been close and from the time she was old enough to tag along on his patient visits, she had learned at his hand. He had been more than a father—he had been her teacher, her mentor. She felt her eyes mist over as one wish kept assaulting her. If only she'd had the chance to say goodbye. She told Grey how, in his letter, her father had feared for her own safety, warning her not to return to Astoria.

"Why did you then?" Grey sat upright and rested his arms across his knees.

"I had to." Rachel sat up beside him. She draped her arm across his shoulders in an attempt to lighten his dark mood. "Besides, if I hadn't, I'd never have met you."

"And you might have lived to enjoy your old age," he countered.

"Don't be ridiculous," Rachel scoffed. "Can't you understand? I want those men punished for destroying my parents' lives."

"But don't you see, Rachel? You're dealing with criminals here. Ruthless men who value nothing but their own gain."

"I'm not afraid," she insisted. "No one else seems interested in stopping the shanghaiing. I can't see so many innocent people suffering because of a few heartless men. Several women I've met have had their lives ruined when their men were shipped away from them. Even Opal's husband was taken. These widows cannot find decent work and some, like Opal, end up earning their food the only way they can."

"Don't tell me about the nobility of whores, Rachel. Remember my lineage."

"Stop it, Grey. Stop feeling sorry for yourself." Rachel swallowed, trying to temper her anger. "Who knows why your mother chose the path she did? And certainly her cruelty to a small boy can't easily be forgotten. But don't lump all those women together into one category. Your bitterness will destroy you, if you let it, and I couldn't stand for that to happen."

For a long moment Grey's expression remained thunderous. Then he pulled Rachel into his arms. "I'm sure you're right, my love. I'm quick to judge those working women. It'll take some time, though, to change the feelings I've lived with all my life. Maybe, with your help, I can learn to be more tolerant."

"Oh, you can, Grey. I know you can." Tears formed in Rachel's eyes. "Opal, Lou, and Janie have been my only support since I've been back. When all my acquaintances turned their backs on me for becoming a doctor, they accepted me for myself, just as I learned to do with them. I don't know what else to call them but my friends."

"Friends, huh?" A glint of humor touched Grey's eyes. "If I remember correctly that Lou was a pretty little thing. . . ." He ducked her pretended blow. "Then tell me about your 'friends.' "

"After I'd been back in Astoria about a month, I was called to Opal's place to stitch up one of her girls. She had been beaten by a drunken sailor. Immediately a rapport sparked between Opal and myself." The memories came crowding back as though it were only yesterday.

"We'd both lost our families to shanghaiing, so we found a common bond in our grief. After that night I became their physician. Until that time they'd nursed one another as well as they could, because old Doc Wilson wouldn't dirty his hands on them. Soon afterwards, Opal told me how she'd become a madam and why."

She let out an exasperated sigh. "We found we were both angry because nothing was being done to protect innocent citizens. If the kidnapping victims weren't strong enough to fight off the crimps, their lives were worth nothing. That's when I told Opal about my father's letter and the list he'd sent me. Soon we'd organized our little group of four and started doing some shanghaiing of our own. You might say we believed in 'an eye for an eye.' "

"Was Chinook always the bait?" Grey asked.

"Yes, and for good reason, too. The other women were well known by everyone who frequented Baldy's. So I invented Chinook. She could come and go and no one would be the wiser. It worked, too . . . until you came along."

"What made me different?" Grey shifted his position, settling Rachel's head in his lap.

"Chinook was bothered by you from the moment she took you into that alleyway."

"Oh, really. Tell me more." He bent and kissed the tip of her nose.

"Never before had I allowed my little ruse to go as far as it did with you. If I hadn't been jarred into action by Opal's signal, there's no telling what might have happened that night."

"Well, I know what wouldn't have happened." Grey swelled with indignation. "I wouldn't have nearly been shark bait."

"You're still angry with me, aren't you?"

"Hell, yes, I am. I could have been killed."

"I'm so sorry. Can you ever forgive me?" Rachel pulled his face toward hers and kissed his lips. If only she could erase the painful ordeal from his mind.

Moments later Grey raised his head and found her apologetic look. "Maybe I'll forgive you."

"When you showed up at Tully's, you can't believe how shocked I was."

"No more shocked than I when Tully waltzed you into his cabin. I never had a female doctor inspecting my personal parts before."

" 'Gawking' is the word I believe you used," Rachel reminded him.

They both laughed when they recalled the scene in the cabin.

"I'd nearly forgotten," Rachel continued. "Is Tully's name really Taithleach?"

Grey nodded in confirmation. "As long as I've known him he's gone by the name of Tully. The only reason I know his first name is because he got drunk one night and told me. Said Eland sounded like a sissy's name and any person who called him that would be keelhauled." His mouth turned up at the corners.

"Taithleach was the man my father mentioned in his letter. He told me to leave our destination with him, and as soon as it was possible, he'd come to us."

"Then why in heavens name didn't you do as your father told you?" Worry and concern creased Grey's brow.

"I had nowhere else to go," Rachel admitted. "After my parents' deaths, I had to come back here. This was my home. The house on Franklin Street had been ours. No one was going to chase me out of it. Besides, this town needed a doctor who was willing to minister to everyone, regardless of who they were or where they lived." She added wistfully, "And learning what he had tried to accomplish, I could do no less." She shrugged her shoulders in resignation. "I always was accused of being just like him." She gave him a rueful smile.

"But why didn't you seek out Tully, or the Taith-leach name that you had?"

"Because I knew if I did meet him, he'd probably try to run me out of town for my safety, and he wouldn't have stopped until he succeeded. I thought it better if I didn't know who he was."

"Tully suspected you'd come back to take up where your father left off. He's always suspected Ballard had something to do with his disappearance, though he could never prove it. He told me the two of them were compiling a list of names to turn over to the government when your father disappeared."

"That would explain it."

"What?"

"Why Tully is so protective of me. But why didn't he tell me he was Papa's friend?"

"I asked him not to. I came to this town to seek my own justice against Ballard and I didn't want to draw any undue attention to you or to myself. Tully and I figured the less you knew about the past, the safer you'd be. We hoped your only interest in returning to Astoria was to practice medicine. We had no idea your father had been able to get a letter smuggled to you . . . or that you'd take up his crusade."

"In a way, I've only done as he would have." Despite the danger she'd incurred, Rachel felt pleased that she'd followed the same path her father had taken. If only he'd been here to see that she'd dared to take up his mission. He would have been horrified, but he would have been proud.

"And because of it, you nearly met your Maker last night," Grey reminded her.

"I know. I still can't believe I'm alive now. But, Grey, I cannot put my own life above the ones I'm trying to help."

"But my God, woman, you were nearly killed." Grey blinked in astonishment at her reasoning. "You should know, Ballard also is looking for Chinook. Word has it, the men who tried to shanghai Tully are hellbent to find her. They also think she might be responsible for two of Ballard's best crimps being sent out to sea."

"Good," Rachel replied, "let him think that. The 'brides' and I took care of those brutes, and if we hadn't decided to lie low after you showed up again, Rooster Crowe wouldn't still be walking the streets of Astoria either."

"Why not, I'm afraid to ask?"

"Because his was the next name on the list."

Grey roared. "That ridiculous list. What in heaven's name ever made you decide to concoct that scheme?"

"At the time it seemed so easy. In his letter my father had included names of those whom he knew to be responsible for the shanghaiing trade in this port, the ones who had taken him."

"But, Lord, Rachel, he didn't give you those names so you could act on them. He wanted you to stay away from them."

"I know, and he'd be frightfully incensed with me for changing his intentions." Her brow lifted in mischief.

"Then how did I end up being your next quarry,

ahead of Crowe?'' He glowered at her, his own mishap just below the surface of his expression.

''Because you were convenient and guilty of an equally great sin, as far as we were concerned. Anyone who would deliberately smuggle contraband into port, drugs that could kill and did, had no more business in our town than the shanghaiiers did.''

Grey became thoughtful. ''Have you ever seen Rooster Crowe?''

''No, but Opal and the girls have. They say he's a mean devil.''

''And they're right. He's got no more scruples than a mongrel, the perfect accomplice for Ballard. If you had tried to do to him what you did to me that night, he would have probably killed you then. Maybe worse . . .'' His voice drifted off.

''But we didn't and now we've got to find another way to get rid of him, before he hurts anyone else. Ballard, too.''

Grey thrust Rachel up from his lap and stood. ''Rachel, you aren't listening to me. You're an intelligent woman, more so than most, but when it comes to Ballard you're plain stupid.''

''Stupid?''

''Yes, stupid. Also dumb, hardheaded, and opinionated but, most of all, stupid.''

''But all I want to do is see that Ballard is punished. You can't blame me for that.''

''I'm not blaming you. I'm only trying to make you understand that this is not a game. Ballard wants you— and Chinook—out of his life.'' Grey ran his fingers through his hair. ''I'd hate to think what he'd do to

342

you if he ever found out Chinook and the doctor were one and the same."

"We both know he'll never find that out," Rachel replied.

"Don't count on it. Ballard owns a lot of people and he has enough money to buy all the information he can't get for free. Believe me, Rachel, it's only a matter of time before he learns your little secret."

Rachel felt a shiver of apprehension cut through her. The possibility that Ballard might learn her other identity loomed over her like a foreboding cloud. If the man found out about Chinook, then he would surely find out about Opal and the others. She'd never forgive herself if something happened to them.

"What should I do?" Suddenly Rachel felt her child self well up in her soul, unsure and afraid. She reached for Grey, wanting only for him to take her into his arms and banish her worst fears.

As though he'd read her mind, Grey held out his arms to her. "Come here," he invited, soft and soothing. He wrapped his arms around her and kissed her on her forehead, smoothing her flyaway hair back from her brow. "It'll be all right, love. But we must be careful. Our best chance is to get rid of Ballard, before he gets rid of us."

"But how will we do that? And what do you mean by us?"

"From now on *we* work together. I'll not have you pursuing that man on your own. You know where it got your father. But you have to promise, Rachel, you'll listen to me. And with that promise I must have your complete trust."

Rachel's voice was firm, final, and with but an instant's hesitation. "I promise. We'll do it your way."

"Good. Now this is what we'll do. . . ."

As Grey explained his plan to her, Rachel listened. This time, she'd trust him completely. No matter what. He'd said he loved her.

Ballard's housekeeper presented Grey a dismissive stare when she let him into the mansion. Even as he headed down the hallway he could hear her keys rattling from the chain about her waist as she relocked the door. The woman, like her employer, gave him the creeps.

The downstairs parlors sounded deserted and Grey imagined Sarah Ballard busy upstairs with baby Anna. A slight smile hit the corners of his mouth at the thought that he now had a vested responsibility for two of the people in this house. And part of that charge lay ahead of him now. He was about to confront Frank Ballard. He knocked on the library door.

"Come in," called the deep voice within. Grey opened the door.

"Well, it's about time. I sent for you two hours ago." Frank Ballard sat in the massive leather chair behind his desk, rolling his writing pen between his fingers.

"I do have a job, you know. One for which I get paid good money. I wouldn't want to let the mayor down, now would I?" It galled Grey to think Ballard expected his bidding to be done at the snap of his fingers. And though Grey would have him believe in his loyalty, his unspoken words would remind Ballard he was still his own man.

He glanced at the other men in the room. In another chair near the desk a man sat grinning up at him as though holding back some secret he was dying to share. Zeke. He didn't know the man's last name, didn't care. The man was a slimy little worm, as slippery as grease on a hot skillet, slinking around with little notice. He was definitely of use to a man like Ballard.

The other man stood staring out the French door leading out to the wide porch. He chose not to greet Grey but kept his focus somewhere outside as if avoiding having to acknowledge his presence. Crowe. Rufus T.—Rooster—Crowe. As big as an ox, as mean as a stepped-on snake. All muscle and no brain from what Grey had learned about him. Since Grey had been in town, he had deliberately avoided any contact with the man. He didn't answer to him and he certainly didn't regard him as any partner in crime.

"Well, now that I'm here you might tell me what you want."

Ballard sat back leisurely in his chair. "What I want is to know the reason you had to go and play hero upriver two nights ago."

"What are you talking about?"

"Oh, don't pretend to know nothing about the little, shall we say, incident on the water. Zeke, here, heard you yelling from the top of your lungs before you jumped in to try and save the lady doctor."

Grey brushed the little man with his cold gaze. He'd thought as much. Ballard had given the order and his men had set about to carry it out.

"You haven't answered me, Devlin. What were you doing up there?"

Grey fought to control his temper. "I'll be glad to

tell you what I was doing up there. I was over at Opal's, intent on having a little fancy fun, when I overheard this fellow laughing and spilling his guts in the next room. Those walls are paper thin, you know.' The more he spoke, the more confident he felt in his reasoning for following Rachel.

"Ever since I've been in this town that woman has been a thorn in my side. But I couldn't get out of my mind the fact that she literally took thorns, barnacle fragments, out of my back side. The last thing I ever wanted was some female sawbones touching me, but one day when I slipped off the wharf and ripped my backside open, she was there when I needed her. I figured I owed her."

He placed his hands on the edge of Ballard's desk and leaned down in his face. "I didn't know it was you trying to get rid of her. If you'd have let me in on your plan, you could have saved me the trouble of nearly getting myself drowned in the process."

Frank Ballard said nothing but looked over at Crowe, still standing at the window. Grey followed his gaze and saw the ruffian make eye contact with his boss. Something unspoken was going on here, something these men weren't prepared to share with him. Grey felt as if he'd started a book on the second chapter.

"Am I to believe you wouldn't have cared one whit whether the little woman was out of our hair once and for all?"

"Why should I care?" Grey could feel his palms sweating, but he remained cool. "It's only that I remember, right here in this very room, you agreed to let her do her job and take care of your wife. You even managed to make her buckle under with her threats against you. How was I to know you'd changed your mind?'' He stared holes into the older man. ''What's the matter, Frank? Are you telling me you don't trust me? After all I've done for you? If you don't, I want to hear it now.''

Ballard tired of fingering his pen and threw it onto his desk. ''Now, now, Devlin, don't get so agitated. Of course I trust you. It's her I don't trust. We've got a good thing going here and I don't intend for the likes of her to be messing it up. Already she's been putting ideas in my wife's head and making my life miserable. Just like her father.''

''What about her father?''

''Oh, he wouldn't stick to his doctoring, either. Got real uppity with me. Claimed I was a 'menace to society,' I think he called me. Well, I know how to deal with troublemakers.''

The door opened and another man entered, spied the others in the room, and rushed over to the desk. ''She's back, boss. I seen her.''

Ballard uttered a mirthless laugh. ''Of course she's back, Jones. We have our friend here to thank for that.'' The man named Jones swept Grey with a look of contempt. ''Why'd you go and do a thing like that? You got a itch or somethin' for her?''

If he'd had a choice, Grey would have ignored the weasel-faced man. If, however, he could divert the attention away from himself, perhaps he could delay any further plans to do away with Rachel.

''That snobbish hag in the thick glasses? Of course not. I already told the boss I was only trying to repay a debt. *If* he'd decided to let me in on his little plan, we wouldn't be having this conversation now.''

"All right," Ballard intervened, "what's done is done. We just have to go on from here."

Grey stiffened. "What do you mean?"

Ballard shrugged his indifference. "Only that we'll have to do better next time."

"There may not have to be a next time." Grey hoped he sounded convincing.

"What do you mean?" For the first time Crowe turned from the window to stare at Grey.

"Only that when I brought her back to town, she was spouting prayers of thanksgiving like some fanatic and promising she had no intention of stepping out of her own world again. Said she'd had enough of trying to right things for everybody else. She nearly drove me crazy all the way back, but I got the impression she would prefer to be doctoring and live to a ripe, old age."

Ballard made a steeple of his locked fingers and rested his chin on it. "Still, I can't help remembering what she said to me in this very room. She said, 'I know things about you.' I remember it as if it were yesterday."

Grey remembered it, too, and now that he knew she carried proof of what she knew about Sarah Ballard's husband, he shuddered to think of the consequences if he ever found it. "I'm sure she was only bluffing."

"Let's hope she was." Ballard turned to Jones. "Where did you last see Doctor Thomas?"

"Over at that old man Tully's place. I followed her there. Sounded to me like she was treatin' him for some ailment."

"Good." Ballard pulled his watch fob from his vest pocket. "It's after four-thirty. Rooster," for the first time he addressed the silent man, "I want you to

348

mosey on down to the doctor's house. Look for any evidence of what she might have that she thinks would be so interesting to the authorities. Since she's not there, she won't give you any trouble.''

Crowe nodded and started toward the door.

"If, on the other hand, she should show up sooner than we think, take a real close look at her face. I'd be interested in knowing if she has a little beauty spot on her temple.''

Dear Lord, Grey thought, the man suspects more than he's letting on. It was his last chance to prove himself. If Crowe found the letter from Rachel's father, he would probably take it out on her himself. After all, his name was on Rachel's list. If he found the costume along with it, he would want to kill her on the spot. He racked his brain, trying to remember what she'd said about it—that it would never be found. Why, he chided himself, hadn't he insisted she burn it as soon as they got back to town?

"Why don't you let me go instead?" Grey tried to keep his voice even. "I've been in there before. I sort of know the layout. And if she did come back, she wouldn't suspect anything was wrong. She'd only think I'd come to check on her.''

Frank rose from his chair and walked around the desk. "Now, now, I think you've done enough already, don't you?" He gave Grey a friendly pat on the back. "Besides, dinner will be served soon. I want you to stay and fill me in on how things are going down on the water.''

It was more than a firm invitation to dinner. It was a command not to be refused. Grey held his breath and prayed Rachel would stay away from the house until after Crowe had left.

Chapter 19

Rachel knew her appearance back in town would cause an uproar for the men who'd tried to get rid of her. But this was her home. And other than hold her head high and refuse to show her fear of Frank Ballard and his cronies, she could do nothing to deter them from trying again. She would, however, take sensible precautions. But she was determined to go about her business as usual.

Most of her morning and early afternoon had been filled with office visits, her practice having grown considerably since Miss Purdy had become her patient. And with the arrival of Sarah's baby daughter, several women from the hill no longer ignored her when they passed her on the street. She felt confident that in time they, too, would seek her out with their medical problems. For now she'd be content with what she had.

Closing her front door behind her, Rachel stepped off her porch and let herself out the gate. Tully was expecting her at two o'clock and would be worried sick if she were a minute late.

It had been late morning by the time Rachel slipped

from Grey's horse yesterday in front of Tully's cabin, and the thought still struck her that she had come so close to never seeing home again.

Tully had listened wide-eyed to their tale before the three of them began to map out a strategy of safety for Rachel. Once Ballard learned that Rachel had not perished in the bungled attempt on her life, he would be enraged. And it was abundantly clear what trouble would lie in wait for Grey once his boss learned he had been the one to save her. It would take some tall talking for Grey to explain his actions and just why he had been on the scene in the first place.

So before they left, both Rachel and Grey had agreed not to flaunt their relationship around town. The less Ballard could learn about the two of them, the safer Rachel would be and the sooner they could put this business behind them and get on with their lives. If one needed to reach the other, Tully would be their intermediary. And when Rachel and Grey left the tiny cabin, they headed in their own separate directions.

Grey's concern for her warmed Rachel's heart, but she didn't know how she'd abide passing him on the street and acting as though they were no more than polite strangers. Or how she'd be able to live without seeing him at all. It had been a little over a day and already Rachel missed him terribly.

But she'd agreed to do as Grey demanded, promising him her complete cooperation in the matter. She loved him and he loved her. And considering they were working toward a lifetime together, she convinced herself a few days were nothing.

Now that Rachel knew Tully's identity, there were so many things she wanted to ask him about her father.

With a springy bounce to her step, she walked down the street toward the old man's house, her leather bag in hand. How she looked forward to their visit this afternoon.

Tully answered her rap on the door. "And how's my patient?" she asked, lest watchful eyes be lurking nearby. On the busy wharf, teeming with sailors and stevedores, Rachel felt safer causing no undue attention to herself. It was best that folks think she was going about her medical practice as usual.

"Fine, Doc, fine, but I feel . . ." Tully's voice faded into nothingness when he closed the door behind him.

"It's good to see you, child." He winked at her and motioned her toward the table where tea awaited them. "Thought you might like a bit of refreshment after your busy day."

"How'd you know my day was busy?" Rachel asked, taking her seat. Then she stopped in mid-thought. "Let me guess. You've been reading your newspaper again."

Tully's mouth turned up and he chuckled. "One of the advantages of getting old is that no one questions why you're sittin' on the side of the road. Most of us don't have anythin' better to do."

"I can see age does have its advantages," Rachel teased him. "But you mustn't worry yourself so much for my benefit. I'll be fine, I promise. I'm being very careful."

"That's what your pappy said, too." Tully settled in the opposite chair and picked up the kettle to pour them each a steaming cup. "Hope you don't mind drinking tea from a mug," he apologized.

"Tea is tea, no matter how it's served." Rachel took

a slice of lemon and a cube of sugar, adding it to her filled cup. Picking it up, she took a sip. "Ahh, that's good," she commented, trying to remember her social graces. But the air reeled with anticipation as Rachel wanted to dive into question after question about her father's disappearance. After a moment, she asked, "How well did you know my father?"

"As well as any man knows another, I reckon. We used to play checkers together maybe once or twice a week. He was a doggone good player, too." Tully shook his head. "I miss those games."

"Checkers. I'd almost forgotten how he loved that game." Suddenly Rachel missed the quiet, intense hours she'd spent with her father over his checkerboard, remembering that he'd always been the champion. In that quarter, she'd never been a challenge.

"Who won?" she asked.

"Why, I did, of course."

She saw the teasing glint in the man's eye and figured he hadn't, but never would he have admitted it to her, or to anyone else, for that matter. Not without her father to challenge him.

"Your pappy, he was right proud of you. Missed you somethin' fierce after you left for Michigan. But he knew you had to do what you were doin'."

"I'll always think if maybe I'd been here, I could have prevented what happened."

"Girl, you mustn't blame yourself. Your pappy, he knew what he was doin'. It would have killed him to see how your mother suffered with the rumors that flew around here after he disappeared. One even had it that he'd stolen Widow Cole's jewels while she was laid up—and then hopped a ship for sunnier shores. Thunderation, if he coulda heard how the tales flew, he'd have rolled over in his grave."

"So you think he really is dead."

"Don't see how he could be otherwise. Your pappy was cut out to be a healer, not a sailor. He was made of stuff other men could only wish they had. What he didn't possess in brawn, he more than made up for in brains. Unfortunately, he wouldn't have had the strength to pull off the kind of muscle that the crews of those longhaul vessels face. Can't see how he lasted long enough to even send you that letter."

He busied himself with stuffing his pipe. "But ol' Doc did what he thought was right. If he were here today, he'd probably still be crusadin' against those crimps."

"Just like his daughter?"

"Just like his crazy daughter, I might add. Imagine, masqueradin' as a soiled dove and shippin' crimps out to sea by night. For an educated woman, you certainly weren't usin' your brains."

Rachel knew Tully meant well. He cared about her safety and she couldn't blame his tone of belligerence. Enjoying the easy camaraderie between them, she asked, "How about when I tried to rid our town of the new harbormaster?"

Tully slapped his knee in mirth. "I'll go to my grave rememberin' that boy's expression when I fetched him the lady doctor."

"He wasn't too pleased, was he?"

"No sirree, he wasn't. But after that first visit I knew there was somethin' goin' on inside that boy's head. Because of his upbringin', he never believed himself worthy of any decent woman." Tully scratched his whiskered jaw. "Funny, that Chinook turned out to be you. Makes you almost believe in fate."

"It makes you believe in something," Rachel added, recalling all that had transpired since her first meeting with Grey. "I love him so much."

"That's good, good for the both of you." He was thoughtful for a moment. "Maybe now that boy can put his self-doubts to rest."

They spent the better part of the afternoon discussing Rachel's family, Grey, and how they'd all celebrate when Ballard was finally caught at his own crooked games.

Rachel left Tully's with the promise that she'd be extra careful in the next few days. "Remember now," he said as he showed her out, "no emergency calls after dark unless someone goes with you, either me or Opal's man, Jeffrey."

"I won't," she agreed.

Walking away from the wharf, Rachel saw that Tully still watched her from his front stoop. She waved and continued on her way.

The excitement of the last few days was catching up with her. Rachel felt weary and looked forward to collapsing in bed and dreaming of Grey. She let herself in the house and locked the door behind her, then headed down the hall toward the kitchen.

Coming to a dead stop in the doorway, Rachel exclaimed, "Merciful heavens." Her precious herb plants had been uprooted from their pots and black dirt was strewn everywhere. "Who would do such a thing?" she mumbled to herself. She stepped deeper into the ransacked room, seething with rising anger.

Every drawer and cupboard had been plundered, its

contents scattered. As she made her way across the room toward the dry sink, broken pottery and glass crunched beneath her boots. The only thing that had been untouched was her apron. It still hung in its place on the nearby peg where she'd left it.

Rachel turned and, supporting herself on the sink frame, looked toward the pantry where potatoes lay spilled out across the floor. Her stock of grains had been emptied in mounds that resembled ant hills, her dried herbs scattered like heavy dust across every surface.

Why? she puzzled. All the plants she'd dried and stored were ruined. It would take years to replace them. Her mood bordered on outrage.

On the table a half-eaten jar of peaches still held the culprit's fork. This last piece of evidence sparked white hot anger. *The gall of the intruder, helping himself to my pickled peaches*.

She stood there as though her feet were fastened to the floor. Tears of frustration slid down her face. Rachel tried to comprehend the reasoning behind such a dastardly deed, but after a moment of rational thought, she knew who'd been responsible for the reprehensible act. Frank Ballard hated her—he'd made that abundantly clear. And now he must have heard she was back in town.

The sound of a waltz floated through the silent house. It took Rachel only a moment to recognize the familiar tune coming from the music box. The guilty party was still here—in her private domain, touching her personal things. Without bothering to consider the consequences, Rachel charged toward the bedroom. But at the doorway she recognized the error of her rash action.

A man sat in the middle of her bed as though he owned it. Propped against her lace pillows, his booted ankles crossed, he stared at her with a lazy sneer plastered across his face. Unmoving he sat, his meaty arms crisscrossed against his thick chest.

"Who are you?" Rachel demanded. She hoped she sounded more in control than she suddenly felt. The stranger didn't answer, but his eyes raked her body, stripping her naked.

Her thoughts only on escape, Rachel slowly inched backwards. But she stopped corpse-still when his voice roared across the room. "If you move another inch, I'll blow your head off."

For the first time since discovering the intruder on her bed, Rachel saw the silver barrel of the gun he held. It rested in the crook of his arm, its point trained on her heart. Fear writhed in her stomach. She knew by the crazed look in his eyes that he'd think nothing of pulling the trigger.

Whatever am I to do? She thought of Grey, despairing that his workday on the wharf had not yet ended. She hoped that perhaps Tully had taken a notion to follow her home. But the reality of that happening, Rachel knew, was highly unlikely. He'd followed her actions all day and would, by now, be napping. Besides, no one would suspect that Ballard's henchman would break into her home in broad daylight. And unless Tully actually came inside, he'd never know anything was amiss. All of Grey's warnings surfaced in Rachel's mind. She'd underestimated Frank Ballard after all.

But Rachel wouldn't cower under this man's attack. If he indeed intended to finish her off here and now, she would not die without a fight. In her most official-sounding voice, she demanded, "What gives you the right to pillage my home?"

"Right?" he stormed, then howled a mirthless laugh.

The man inched across the bed, his eyes never leaving Rachel. His dirty boots smeared black mud across the white linen coverlet and he grinned spitefully, revealing gapped teeth behind his cruel lips.

"Now fancy that. I went and messed up your prissy cover," he taunted.

But Rachel refused to take his bait. The man facing her obviously had no scruples. If she angered him, he'd probably beat her senseless, regardless of the fact that she was a woman. Her best chance for escape, she decided, was to say or do nothing to provoke his anger.

He stood, his eyes never leaving her, his gun never moving from its position. Then, reaching one hand under the pillows, he pulled out a bundle of gawdy clothing. Chinook's costume. The chamois drawers, the green satin bodice, and the pink-haired wig were a dead give-away.

Rachel gasped. Her throat went dry.

"You wouldn't know anything about these, now would you?" He shook the pieces of clothing, a knowing smile upon his face, then allowed them to drop in a pile upon the bed. For one hopeful moment Rachel allowed herself to think he did not know the significance of the clothes.

"Now why do you suppose these things were in the bottom of your wardrobe? You being a fancy doctor and all." He looked her up and down, his gaze delving into her own. "Wouldn't be that you enjoy dressing in the garb of a whore?"

"My patient left them," she protested.

"Your patient, hell. We both know these belong to a whore named Chinook. And I believe we both know who she is."

"I don't know what you're talking about," Rachel insisted.

"Lying bitch. My men—the ones you laid up on the beach—they described these duds perfectly. Ain't many whores in these parts with leather drawers and pink hair."

"You're mistaken," she insisted again.

Apprehension snaked up Rachel's spine. His reference to "my men" left no doubt in her mind as to whom she was speaking. Though she'd never seen him, she'd heard stories of what he did to people, just for the fun of it. Rachel had treated several women he'd used in the whorehouses. Their battered bodies were proof enough of what he considered entertaining. The protruding brow, wrinkled in malice at her, belonged to none other than Rooster Crowe.

And the man knew she and Chinook were one and the same.

"Now, my little bitch, we'll see if you're as good looking as the others have claimed." He threw Chinook's clothes at her. One of the jade buttons on the bodice stung her cheek when it snapped against her face. "Put these on," he ordered.

"Surely, you don't expect me to undress in front of you." She met his cold gaze without flinching.

"That's exactly what I expect. And if you don't want

me to help you, then I suggest you get started."
Rooster positioned himself back against the pillows on
her bed, the gun still aimed at her heart.

For a moment Rachel debated her next move. If she
didn't change soon, she knew he'd do exactly as he
threatened. By dawdling, she could invite his participation. But would she be able to distract him enough
to escape? Now that he knew what she had done to his
men on the beach, she thought better of it. Besides, the
thought of having his filthy hands on her flesh made
her stomach churn. No, she decided, she'd wait for a
better chance. Yanking the clothes from the floor where
they'd landed, she pulled herself upright and smugly
faced the wall. But even this small bit of privacy was
to be denied her.

"Turn your ass to the door. We both know whores
ain't modest."

"I'll not stand here and disrobe for your amusement."

"Oh yeah?" Rooster started from the bed.

"Pervert!" she shouted at him. When Rachel's fingers
began working the fastenings of her dress, he returned to
his perch and watched her every movement.

She slipped the garment down over her hips and allowed it to drop to the floor. Only her anger sustained
her as she stripped off the rest of her clothes. That and
the fact that her medical training allowed her to divorce
herself from her actions. Rachel had seen many nude
bodies, studied them extensively, and as long as she
blocked out the man sitting on the bed gloating at her,
she could treat her own nakedness as she would that of
another. She hurriedly donned Chinook's clothes,

wondering as she did so what Rooster had planned for her.

"Not bad, not bad at all." Lust gleamed in his eyes as they raked over her. "Come on over here and sit, so I can get a better look at you."

Rachel hesitated.

"Hear me, bitch. If I have to drag you over here, you will come."

Unable to do anything else, Rachel complied. Her heart slammed against her ribcage as she moved toward the bed and the predator nesting in the middle of it. When she neared the edge of the mattress, Rooster swung his legs to the floor and stood. Only inches separated them and Rachel felt as though she might faint with fear and repulsion.

Up close, he appeared more intimidating than he had from a distance. Earlier she'd imagined him to be a large man, but until she stood face to face with him, she'd never realized how big he was. Powerfully built, like a bull. Something in his glare reminded Rachel of a picture she'd once seen of a bull ready to charge his matador tormentor.

His free hand moved toward her face and Rachel cringed, thoroughly expecting a blow. Her reaction seemed to amuse him and he burst out laughing. Rooster taunted her then, acting as though he might hit her, enjoying watching her flinch as his hand came within inches of its mark before it stopped.

It was then that Rachel saw through his fiendish humor. She resolved, no matter what he did to her, to show no fear. Standing her ground, she glowered at him until he tired of his cruel game. Her insolence only angered him more. He snatched her glasses from her face and threw them to the floor. Picking up the pink wig that still lay on the corner of the bed, he shoved it into her hands. With shaky fingers, Rachel slipped the pink curls over her own dark hair.

"You are a mouth-watering piece of goods." His breath quickened. Small sweat bubbles dotted his brow. "Now, Queenie, don your jewels." He thrust the star diopside brooch and earrings at Rachel and watched hungrily as she fastened the pin to her low-cut bodice.

"Not bad at all," he murmured, letting out an aroused sigh. "I can halfway understand why my men were distracted."

He planted the gun barrel at the top of her bosom and dragged it slowly down, toward the teardrop brooch.

The metal burned from icy cold to fiery hot as it trailed down Rachel's skin. He's a maniac, she thought, noting his warped smile when her breathing increased. She concentrated on his smell. Even in fresh clothes he reeked of sweat and dead fish, as though bathing was low on his list of important matters. The stench made her want to ask where he had been two nights ago.

He pulled her roughly against his lower body with his free arm, clutching her hips against his aroused sex. "You want to make ol' Rooster crow?" He brushed her ear with the broken whisper, licking his lips and flicking the teardrop brooch with the gunpoint.

"I'd rather make him choke on his own warped cry," Rachel bit back.

Crowe's face turned scarlet, his pockmarked complexion blotchy. He shoved her with such force that Rachel stumbled backward against a side chair before landing in its seat. He stalked her then, coming to a halt directly in front of her.

Bending over to make eye contact, he warned, "I assure you, my little hen, I'll be riding you before this night is over." He jerked her to her feet and shoved her toward the hallway door.

"Thought you might be interested in what I found tucked inside your music box." He reached inside his vest pocket and pulled out the worn sheet of paper.

Rachel recognized it immediately—her father's letter with the incriminating list of crimps. Rooster Crowe's name was at the bottom.

"Know what this is?" he asked, shaking out the folds of the paper. "I believe that's my name." His laugh sounded cruel, malicious. He slammed the paper up against Rachel's face, and the force of his blow made her nose bleed. Red blotches spattered across the page. This, too, seemed to amuse him. He scoffed at her with frosty impudence. "Come now, Doc, a little blood don't bother you none, does it?"

The blood felt warm and sticky as it seeped down over her lips.

"Here, I'll even lend you my handkerchief." Crowe thrust it into Rachel's hand. "I wouldn't want you to ruin my new vest."

"Where are you taking me?" Rachel demanded, trying to stifle the flow of blood with the handkerchief.

"To the hen house, where else?" His hateful laughter echoed throughout the room.

The afternoon had given way to twilight by the time Rooster hustled Rachel out the back door and into the streets. She hoped someone would notice them, but she also knew it was the time of day when the neighbors would be inside their homes, gathered around their dinner tables. No one would take notice of the soiled dove and her gentleman friend leaving through the back door of Doctor Thomas's house. And if they did, they would only assume it to be two of her less-than-respectable patients.

Exiting the back gate, Rooster led Rachel toward an enclosed phaeton parked behind her house. As he forced her to step up into the vehicle, Rachel looked desperately around, hoping against hope that Grey had decided to check on her well-being. But the lane was clear. Grey was nowhere to be seen.

Crowe climbed in behind her, sending the carriage dipping and groaning beneath his weight.

Seeming unfettered by his size, he wedged his huge girth next to Rachel's. She felt the seat's hard frame dig into her delicate flesh. To add to her discomfort, he locked the gun barrel against her ribs before setting the buggy into motion.

When he turned the phaeton around and headed up the hill, Rachel knew where Rooster Crowe was taking her. She prayed that Sarah Ballard would be oblivious to her husband's plans, knowing full well if Sarah learned the costumed whore was Rachel and came to her defense, it could very easily get them both killed. Now she not only prayed for her own deliverance, but for Sarah's and little Anna's as well.

The Ballard house glowed with amber light when Rooster pulled the buggy to a stop at the back entrance. When he stepped down, his back to her, Rachel thought about escaping. She could have easily darted away into the darkness, but her fear of what might occur when Rooster discovered her kept Rachel rooted to the seat. The less commotion she drew to her arrival, the less chance Sarah would have of involving herself in this sordid affair. So instead of running she sat quietly, waiting for Ballard's henchman to help her disembark.

Crowe turned and stuffed the pistol into the waistband of his pants, then offered her his hand. But she had no intention of his touching her. But when she reached for a steady support, he grabbed her hand and yanked her forward. Rachel braced her hands against his shoulders to keep from falling flat on her face.

"You do like me, don't you, bitch?" he whispered huskily.

Clamping his arms around her waist, Rooster held her in a deathlike grip and slid her down the length of his body. Wriggling for all she was worth, Rachel managed to knee him in the groin before he dropped her feet to the ground. He grunted in pain and swayed uneasily on his feet. And although she hadn't disabled him, Rachel felt a certain amount of satisfaction in the fact that she had left her mark on him.

The back door opened and a man stepped outside. Without her glasses, she could only see him as a blur. But when he came closer, Rachel recognized him as one of the men the "brides" had chloroformed on the beach in their efforts to save Tully.

"Well, well, if it ain't the pink-headed whore."

Chortling to himself, he examined her from head to toe, and Rachel remembered all too well the sound of his voice. *Fishhead!* This was the same man who'd nearly violated her. She shuddered in disgust and looked right through him. Rooster tried to grab her arm, but she yanked it from his grasp. "I know the way," she barked and walked up the stairs toward the back entrance, as stately as a queen about to enter the court.

The newcomer fell in with Crowe as they climbed the steps behind her. "I told you she were a looker, didn't I, Boss?" Fishhead seemed pleased with his knowledge of her.

"Shut up, I'm sick of your babbling."

"Got you good with her knee, did she?"

"How can a knee to the balls be good?" he grunted miserably. "Now shut up your ugly face before I make it uglier."

Rachel listened to the two men, wishing they'd kill each other and save her the trouble. And it might very well come to that before this night was over. When they reached the door, Milly the housekeeper opened it wide, allowing them entrance.

"They're waiting in the library," she clipped, then locking the door behind them, the jailor led them toward the door that sealed the library off from the main hall. Knocking lightly, she waited.

"Open up, woman," Ballard called to her from the other side.

The matron cracked the door. Sticking her head inside, she announced, "Mr. Crowe here to see you, sir."

"About time. I'm tired of waiting for him."

Rachel caught a glimpse of the impatient man sitting behind the big desk. In his starched white shirt, his silk cravat knotted at his neck, he looked like a paragon of society. But Rachel knew it took more than fine clothes to make a man a model of excellence.

With a rude shrug he dismissed the housekeeper, saying, "You can leave for the evening, but lock the door behind you."

Ballard turned back to the papers on his desk, but then his head bobbed up, a look of triumph sliding across his face. He stood, quickly rounding his desk. "Now what do we have here?" he asked.

Crowe, again in control, grabbed Rachel's arm and shoved her forward. She nearly stumbled but managed to regain her balance before she fell. With her shoulders thrown back and her head held high, she glared at her hated enemy.

Chapter 20

Ensconced in his high-back wing chair, Grey felt his pulse nearly halt when he saw Rachel. She was dressed as Chinook, and every man in the room ogled the sweet apparition of sin who stood so gallantly before them.

If Grey dared, he would have personally gouged out the onlookers' eyes, wiping away forever any trace of the lust he read in their heated expressions. But Rachel's safety hinged upon his control. So he sat unmoving, appearing as interested as the others in this unexpected vision cast into their midst.

"That's her, Boss. That's the one." Zeke jumped up from his chair and stood gaping at Rachel.

The room was fraught with tension. Settling himself on the edge of the desk, Ballard stared at Rachel through pale blue eyes, his gaze delving beneath her skimpy garments. The moment seemed to stretch on before he announced in a voice edged with steel, "So, we meet at last . . ."

Rachel said nothing but stared back with monumental confidence. If she were frightened, she never let on. If she knew Grey were present in the room, she never acknowledged it.

He watched, growing more uneasy as Ballard appraised Rachel's body. "I'd heard you were beautiful," he said, "but I never would have believed how much so until this moment."

The man's as deadly as a cobra, Grey thought, watching Ballard's venomous gaze slither over Rachel. He knows, Grey lamented. He must have known all along. Why else would he have Rooster bring her here, dressed in a whore's garb? This had been set up even before he had reached the house this afternoon. The thought chilled him to the bone.

If he knows her identity, what else does he know? If Frank Ballard suspected his and Rachel's involvement, they were both as good as dead.

"I believe you've met these gentlemen?" Ballard inquired, treating Rachel as politely as an invited guest.

Rachel's eyes scanned the room, lighting briefly on Grey. "Some," she replied.

Grey let his breath out slowly, satisfied with Rachel's answer. She hadn't committed herself one way or the other. This was good.

But Ballard seemed not at all misled by her answer. He continued his interrogation in a taunting voice. "I understand most of us have encountered your little game at one time or another. Is that true, Miss . . . what should I call you?"

Please, Rachel, Grey's mind screamed, don't say any more.

With these last statements, Ballard's eyes sought out Grey and lingered. Fast realizing he was also a target, cold warning swept through Grey, but he kept his gaze glued on Rachel. Did Ballard know about her shang-haiing him?

Rooster stepped forward and thrust several worn sheets of paper toward his boss, his grating voice shattering the quiet. "I found these, too."

Ballard quickly scanned the pages, then passed them around for the others to see. A light grin crept along his mouth. "I guess we know now what happened to our business associates." His expression turned sober. "It seems our lady doctor is following in her father's footsteps."

Grey took the paper and felt he'd been punched in the stomach. Crowe had found the letter and the list from Rachel's father. Worse than that, he could see what looked like fresh blood splattered across the worn paper. Anger threatened to override his control. What abuse had Rachel suffered at the brute's hands before they'd arrived?

He didn't have to wait long for his answer. "She had a little nose bleed back at the house." Crowe laughed, full of himself.

"Thanks to your gentlemanly pat," Rachel replied with cold sarcasm.

Rachel had had just about enough of Ballard's grilling, and enough of being stared at like some freak in a carnival. And although she wasn't certain what recourse to take against her offenders, she felt safer just knowing Grey was present . . . and much more confident.

In one swift motion, she ripped the hateful pink wig from her head and threw it at Ballard's face. Out of the corner of her eye she saw Grey's startled movement and wondered briefly about the rashness of her actions.

When Ballard peeled the pink hair from his sweaty face, his look was lethal. He started toward her, murder in his eye.

It was obvious to Grey that Rachel's actions had unleashed Ballard's fury. "You going to let the bitch upset you again? Can't you see she's playing you like a fiddle, hoping you'll lose control and kill her on the spot?" His words split the charged air as numb terror bolted through him. Grey had to stop the crazed man before he harmed her.

"Listen to me, Frank." He jumped up from his chair. "Your wife is upstairs. She and Rachel have been friends forever, and if she hears any rough and tumble down here, she'll come running. The last thing we need is a hysterical female on our hands."

His body rigid—his fists clenched—Ballard froze. Grey's words had penetrated, but with a madman like Ballard he never knew what to expect next. After several charged moments, Ballard reined in his temper. "I can take care of my wife, Devlin, and don't you forget it." Grey suspected the added comment had been uttered for his men's benefit. "But you just may be right. A quick death would be too easy for the bitch."

Pleased with their leader's suggestion, the others turned lustful eyes toward Rachel. Grey had an idea what Ballard might have in mind for Rachel, but he had no time to dwell on his morbid thoughts. He had to act fast if he was to get her out of harm's way.

"What you gonna do with her, Boss?" Rooster asked.

After an anxious moment, Ballard retorted, "What do you think we should do with her?" His cold eyes never left Grey.

"Fuck her," Fishhead answered.

Everyone laughed at his suggestion and each man present squirmed in his britches. Grey did, too, only to go along with the ruse.

"Try it and I'll rip off your organ," Rachel snapped, surprising everyone with her remark.

Grey visibly flinched at her words. *My God, Rachel, keep your mouth shut.*

Rooster moved to Ballard's side and whispered something into his ear. The older man smiled, obviously pleased with the information he'd just received. Then he faced the others and announced, "I think ol' Rooster here has just solved my dilemma."

Ballard's remark made Rooster preen like a cock. Grey wondered what his sadistic mind had come up with. He waited with bated breath to find out, and the answer chilled him to the bone.

"It seems my old friend, Captain Jamal is in the area." A malicious smile lit up Ballard's face as he continued with his explanation. "His ship lies at anchor off our coast."

Jamal. Though the man had never sailed this far north, everyone in the room, Grey included, knew what cargo the Arab traded in—the peddling of human flesh. But unlike the other captains who waited for the crimps to supply them with crews, Jamal waited for a different type of cargo. Women.

Knowing glances passed around the room. It was rumored that Jamal paid for his quarry with precious gems. Rubies, emeralds, and diamonds as large as hens' eggs had been swapped in trade for a beautiful virgin. Poor men had become millionaires overnight for bringing Jamal the right piece of goods.

But the Arab was selective. Only the most lovely and pure were chosen to join his countrymen's households. Those who didn't pass his test were taken aboard his ship and used as a plaything for his men on the long, monotonous voyage home. If the women weren't dead when they reached his country, they died soon after.

Grey's blood slid through his veins like icicles. If he couldn't come up with an idea to save Rachel, he'd never forgive himself. He'd heard stories of how Jamal himself conducted his depraved little tests on the maidens to make sure their hymens weren't ruptured. The thought of the greasy man's fingers on Rachel was almost Grey's undoing. But an inner voice cautioned him not to lose control. Now, more than ever, he had to keep a cool head.

"So what do you think, men? Should we sell her to the jackal dogs?" He issued the question to all present, but he seemed interested only in Grey's response.

"Let me take the bitch," Grey insisted, trying to sound as though he were excited with the idea. God willing, he thought, if he were allowed to accompany her to the wharf, he could help her escape. "Surely she'll bring a good price." He looked over at Rachel and could see that she hung onto his every word. "Anyone with a body like hers is worth a king's ransom."

"Depends . . ." Ballard hesitated, ". . . if she's a virgin or not."

Grey felt an invisible noose tightening around his neck. He had to convince Ballard that she meant nothing to him. And he prayed that she would see through his cruel accusations, remembering the promise he'd extracted from her that she would trust him, no matter what.

"We both know this is the fish-eyed doctor we're

talking about. How many men would look at her and want to mount her? She's nothing but a shriveled-up old maid in whore's clothing."

Grey's words stunned Rachel. If he were acting, he'd certainly convinced her that he believed his cruel remarks. She fought back tears, remembering what they'd shared, remembering, too, that he'd said he loved her. "Trust me," he'd said, and she was trying. But the words had come so easily. Even for an actor in a play, the best lines were those spoken with conviction.

"Come on, Frank," he prodded, "let me take her. She's been nothing but a wild hair in my pants since I came here. Hell, if you'd told me you were trying to kill her the other night, I would have let her drown."

"You did screw up that scheme. If you hadn't interfered, she'd be dead now and all my worries would be over."

"But tomorrow you'll be thanking me. Think of what Jamal will pay for her. You'll be twice as rich as you are and you'll be able to buy the governorship for certain."

Rachel could see that Ballard weighed Grey's words. But she could also see he still wasn't convinced of Grey's loyalty.

I love you, Rachel. With God as my witness, I love you.

Grey's words popped into her consciousness as though he'd said them aloud. Wasn't that what love was about? Believing in each other and trusting the other in all things?

Only days before, Grey had asked her to trust him, no matter what happened. And now, in this heated adversity, Rachel's trust was wavering. She would put aside her foolish pride and do as Grey had asked. She loved him and he loved her. They were working together, and they would come through this crisis fine. Rachel didn't know who this Jamal fellow was, but if Grey wished to send her there, so be it. He would do what was best for her.

A creeping uneasiness settled in the bottom of Grey's stomach. Did the bastard know? He had to convince Ballard of his loyalty. He had to be with Rachel when they took her to the Arab. Frantic with worry, he plunged in with another argument.

"What kind of fool do you take me for? I know who butters my bread. I'm an ex-convict. If it weren't for you, Frank, I'd never have such an important job. Me, a criminal for harbormaster?" He laughed, hoping to break the tension in the room.

Ballard studied Grey for a few more moments before giving him his answer. "I believe now is not the time to discuss your loyalty. We'll talk about this tomorrow after she's gone." He nodded toward Rachel. "If you're as devoted to me as you would have me believe, one more night won't make a difference."

The hair on the back of Grey's neck stiffened. He didn't like the drift of this conversation. Ballard was definitely up to something, and Grey had the distinct feeling he wasn't included in his plans.

"And just to make you feel better," Ballard added, "I'll personally go with the lady to see her off. Perhaps, since Jamal and I are such old friends, he'll allow me the pleasure of watching him perform his little test." His expression took on a cruel scowl as he spat out his next words. "Then tomorrow, I'll be able to tell you the results firsthand."

"You bastard." Grey lunged for the older man, his fingers locking around his neck.

For a moment Rachel was too stunned to move. Then she saw Rooster ball up his big fist, ready to strike the side of Grey's head. Like a mother chick protecting her young, she sprang into action. Although no match for Crowe, she deflected his blow by hopping on his back and tearing at the flesh on his neck and face. When one of her fingers dug into his eye socket, he howled like a stuck pig.

The foray lasted only a few charged moments. Soon Ballard's thugs halted Grey's attack. One grabbed him in a rear hold while the other delivered several blows to his stomach. Then they dropped him to the floor. Rachel saw Grey slump over in pain and jumped off Crowe's back to rush to his side.

"Lock him up," Ballard ordered, his face white with rage. Standing upright, he straightened his silk tie and brushed off his shirt.

"You want me to kill him, Boss?" Zeke asked.

"Hell, no, not now anyway. I want him to have time to think about his lady friend here. Let him dwell on what fun Jamal's crew is going to have when they find out she's not a virgin."

Again Grey sprang at Ballard, but this time Rooster cuffed him upside the head. The other two men grabbed him beneath his arms and dragged him to a nearby closet. They shoved him inside, slammed the door, and locked it.

"You can't do that." Rachel lunged at Ballard, but Crowe blocked her attack.

"I can do anything I damn well please." Ballard started for the door, ordering the others as he did so,

"Bring the bitch. I'm going to enjoy this party more than I imagined."

Stunned into immobility, Grey slumped against the floor. Except for a thin crack of subdued light that slashed across the space at the bottom of the door, the inside of the tiny closet was pitch black.

His stomach fought to relieve itself, but Grey swallowed back the bile, hugging his knees to his chest. He felt light-headed, disoriented. The clumping of feet on the opposite side of the door tore at the nerves inside his head while colors exploded inside his brain. The sound and fireworks gradually vanished and Grey drifted on a muddled haze.

Lifeless, he lay where he'd been tossed, on the brink of succumbing to unconsciousness. But his mind kept fighting the invitation of delicious sleep, probing for the reason he had to stay awake. Then, like a bolt of lightning, his reason returned. Rachel. Her image hounded him, calling . . . pleading. Grey sprang toward the closed door, unleashing his fury. He had to save Rachel.

His pounding reverberated in his own ears like the sound of thunder, but no one came. He made several attempts at hurling his weight against the rigid wood, then collapsed against it, defeated. It was probably a good three inches thick. It would take a woodsman's axe to penetrate through its polished surface. Grey knew he was trapped.

Kneeling down, he tried to peek through the keyhole. Only a sliver of light reflected in the opening. Rachel's captors had apparently left the key in the lock.

If only he could find something small enough to slip inside the hole, he just might be able to jiggle it open.

Like a blind man who suddenly finds himself in alien territory, Grey lumbered around the darkened closet, barely large enough to hold two men. Its perimeter was lined with shelves filled with books and papers. Scrounging for anything that might be useful, he emptied the shelves, dumping the contents onto the floor. When his search revealed nothing that would help him escape, he stumbled back to the door. He was trapped.

Oh, God, Rachel, his heart cried. Now he would never be able to save her. Now she would suffer a fate far worse than death, far worse than anything her father could have endured.

He slid down the frame of the door and resumed his pounding. Maybe, just maybe someone would hear him.

Sarah. So soon after Anna's birth, surely she would still be at home. She had to be. Ballard's reactions to his admonishings about disturbing Sarah indicated she must be in the house. A faint hope took hold. If he were lucky, Sarah or Agnes would hear his efforts and come to his rescue. With renewed energy, Grey again battered the door.

It seemed as though hours had passed before Grey thought he heard the whisper of footsteps inside the library. Flattening himself against the floor, he peered through the lighted space. A sudden dread hit him. What if the housekeeper had heard the pounding and decided to investigate? Damnation, he had forgotten about her. There would be no help coming from that quarter. He knew where her loyalties lay. Grey waited, straining to see beneath the door.

Again he heard the soft fall of footsteps before a

shadow darkened the lamp on Ballard's desk. Someone jiggled the key in the lock and the closet door flew open.

After having been so long in the closet, the muted glow of the lamp nearly blinded Grey. Squinting, he dared a glance upward and nearly stopped breathing.

"Mr. Devlin . . . Grey! Dear Lord in heaven, is that you?"

Sarah Ballard stood in the open doorway, looking like an angel in yards of snowy white linen. Her fist closed at her lips in horror. "Your head, it's bleeding!"

Sitting upright, Grey brushed the side of his head where Rooster had clobbered him. It felt damp with sticky blood. Until Sarah had mentioned it, he'd not even realized he'd been bleeding.

"It's nothing, really." He stumbled to his feet. "I've got to get out of here. I've got to reach Tully."

"Tully? Did my husband do this to you?" she demanded.

Grey had no idea how much Sarah knew of her husband's affairs, and now was not the time to burden her with accusations. Her condition was still far too fragile, and he was fast running out of time. "No," he answered, remembering full well the big lummox who had delivered the nearly lethal blow.

The room shifted beneath his feet and he grasped the doorframe to steady himself. Sarah took his arm, supporting him while she steered him away from the closet.

"Agnes, we need your help," she called toward the hallway. "It's all right. The men shouldn't be coming back."

At her mistress's command, Agnes shuffled across the room toward them. "Oh, my, you are a scary sight."

Sarah pulled a handkerchief from her sleeve and handed it to the older woman. "Wet this with water from Mr. Ballard's pitcher. Let's see if we can clean up this wound."

"That won't be necessary," Grey insisted. He tried to move toward the door. He had to rescue Rachel. If only he could get to Tully. His knees felt like willow branches in the wind.

"Please, sir, you do owe me an explanation," Sarah entreated. "And as dizzy as you are you won't get very far. Give yourself a moment."

"How long have I been in that closet?"

"Not long. Maybe ten or fifteen minutes. We waited in the pantry until after Frank left. I heard your knocking, but I wanted to make certain no one came back before we made our presence known."

"Then you heard?"

"I saw Frank and those awful men putting Rachel into our carriage." She cleared papers from the corner of her husband's desk with no mention of Rachel's attire. "You've got to save her," she added and motioned for Grey to sit. "But you'll be no good to her the way you are." With the wet cloth she began sponging away the blood.

"All right," he said, "but only for a moment." The distress he read in Sarah's face matched his own. "How much do you know?"

"I must admit, I've been listening at doors. I heard everything. For a long time now, I've known my husband wasn't the fine, respectable citizen he would have everyone believe him to be.''

She paused only long enough to order Agnes to bring Grey a glass of whiskey. Then she began again to mop his wound.

"It wasn't until after Anna's birth and until I held that sweet miracle in my arms that I knew I couldn't stand by and allow Frank to continue with his criminal activities. My daughter deserves more than a crook for a father.''

The old woman returned with the whiskey and handed it to Grey. He downed the contents in one long gulp. Soon the hot liquid sent a tide of warmth flowing through his veins, and the room began to right itself again.

He started off the desk. "Thank you for what you did," he said. "If it hadn't been for you, I'd still be in there.''

He tried his legs for a couple of steps and reached for the high back of a chair. "You didn't happen to hear where they were headed?''

"I heard Frank shouting orders like a general when he slammed out the door. Something about a ship being anchored just beyond the Point Adams lighthouse.'' Apparently satisfied that her patient's injury looked worse than it was, Sarah stepped back to allow Grey to take his leave.

"What can I do to help?'' she asked.

"You've done more than enough. I'll handle everything from here. Besides, you shouldn't overexert yourself.''

"Pooh," she said, "all these women lying abed for weeks after the birth of a child is ridiculous. I feel better than I have in years.''

"No mind, Sarah. Rachel would never forgive herself if because of her something happened to you." He gave her one last look. "I might add, a lady like yourself deserves a better man than Frank Ballard."

"I know that." She gestured toward the door. "And if you hope to save my crazy friend, you must hurry."

"Don't worry. They won't get far now, thanks to you."

"No thanks necessary. I have to take care of Anna's godfather, now don't I?"

Happiness budded inside Grey's heart with Sarah's words. "You do at that. And now I must take care of her godmother."

It wasn't until Rachel found herself seated inside the Ballard family carriage, headed in the direction of the wharf, that she realized the total helplessness of her situation. Surrounded by her captors, escape from the moving carriage would be impossible. With Grey locked inside the closet in Ballard's house, no one remained who would come to her rescue. No one else knew she was in trouble.

With the shades lowered over the windows, the only light came from two small lamps that cast a dreary glow over the threesome. Ballard occupied one seat and she and Rooster Crowe the other. Crowe's large, meaty thigh kept rubbing against hers with the buggy's movement. She would have moved away from him, but the cramped space made distancing herself from the repulsive man an impossibility. So Rachel gritted her teeth and endured.

No longer able to abide the stilted silence, she

taunted Ballard, glowering at him in the low light. "You'll never get away with this."

He chose not to respond to her jibe but only watched her with passive indifference, as one would a caged animal. Refusing to cower beneath his cold stare, Rachel met his gaze straight ahead.

He was an impressive-looking man, to say the least, and she could well understand why Sarah had been attracted to his polished good looks. What a waste that no heart resided inside the handsome shell.

In his black cape and silk top hat, with his slightly silvered hair and pale blue eyes, he looked quite regal perched upon his seat. His long fingers, with nails buffed to satin smoothness, rested on the silver ball of a cane positioned between his legs. Even though he'd been tousled by Grey only moments earlier, his appearance remained unblemished. To the unknowing observer, he looked the part of a well turned-out gentleman, enjoying an evening about town.

But Rachel had only to look closer to see that victory gleamed within his eyes. And something else that hadn't been there earlier. Rachel recognized it immediately for what it was. Lust. She'd encountered the same expression from other men she'd met when dressed as Chinook. A shiver of apprehension tingled up her backbone when she thought of what she might have to endure at the hands of this man and others like him.

As though he'd read her thoughts, his cruel lips arched into a mocking smile. "We both know our Arab friend will not find you a virgin." He leaned toward her, his weight propped upon his cane.

Not to be deterred by his remark, Rachel retorted, "He'll not find me anything at all. I'll throw myself into the ocean and let the sharks eat me before I submit to the two-legged kind like yourself.''

Ballard burst out laughing. ''Who would have believed the prune-faced doctor would turn out to be such a beauty? And with such fire?'' Ballard shook his head in disbelief. ''I can understand Devlin's attraction now. Your passion appeals to each of our baser needs.''

''Ha.'' Rachel spat out her contempt. ''Don't compare your prowess with women to Grey Devlin's. I'm sure there'd be no contest.''

Ballard's expression turned hard and cruel. With a flick of his elegantly cuffed wrist, he snapped the cane downward between Rachel's legs, jamming the silver ball against the apex of her thighs.

Her hands pushed back the punishing instrument. ''You're an animal,'' she responded.

''With animal appetites,'' he countered. ''And if I wasn't in such a bind for cash, I'd keep your luscious body for myself instead of selling it to Jamal.'' He gave her a haughty leer. ''For your information, though you won't be here to see it, I will become governor, and I require money to do it.''

As quickly as the anger flared, it disappeared. To Rachel's relief, Ballard removed the cane from between her thighs and settled himself calmly back against the seat.

Though fear swam through her blood, Rachel couldn't stop herself from taunting him further. ''I thought this Jamal fellow didn't pay well for soiled women.''

''Ah, but for you, he'll pay a king's ransom.'' His eyes raked up and down her body. ''Let's just say, Jamal and I go back a long way. I know his own taste in women. Virgin or not, he'll pay well for you.''

Ballard's men had picked up speed and Rachel had to brace herself to keep from tumbling against Rooster. Even with the windows covered, she knew they weren't headed toward the wharf. They were traveling far too fast to still be inside the town's limits.

"Where are you taking me?" she demanded as the carriage careened in agitated motion through the countryside.

Neither man answered, but Rooster leered down at her through his injured eye. There was no doubt in Rachel's mind that if given the opportunity, he'd take his own pleasure with her here and now. The earlier display of his perverted boss had left evidence of his enjoyment clearly visible on the crotch of his pants.

Rachel refused to dwell on the smells of lust in the confining carriage. She had to keep talking to keep her fear at bay. "I'm curious," she asked, "You keep saying I'm not a virgin. How can you be sure?"

A tense moment passed before Ballard answered her.

"After the log slide, my men saw our besotted harbormaster jump into the water to rescue you. Not only did they see his heroic feat, but they hung around a while. I understand the two of you put on quite a show, tumbling in the woods."

The men hadn't seen a thing, Rachel was sure of that. She and Grey had been well hidden, and Grey had stayed awake most of the night, listening for sounds of intruders. But to hear the mockery from Ballard's lips made her face turn beet red nonetheless.

"Ahh," he crooned, "still a virgin's modesty?"

He watched her, waiting for a response. When none was forthcoming, he continued.

"Tell me, Doc, in your scientific studies, did you

ever watch a man and woman copulate? It's a shame if you didn't. It's really quite interesting, you know. Man, with his superior intelligence, reduced to the animal, rutting to sate physical needs. All in the disguise of love."

Unable to tolerate another foul word from Ballard's mouth, Rachel lunged at him, catching even Rooster temporarily offguard. Using her nails like a wildcat, she tore at Ballard's flesh. Before Rooster could restrain her, she'd clamped her teeth into the back of Ballard's hand, drawing blood. Rooster finally slammed her back against the seat, and she sat in silence, taking great pleasure in seeing the damage she'd inflicted.

Ballard's rage was an animate force. "You're lucky I need money or I'd finish you off right here." Pulling a handkerchief from his pocket, he wrapped it around his bruised and bleeding hand.

The carriage jerked to a halt and Zeke and Jones pulled the door open. "Get the bitch out of here before I kill her," Ballard ordered.

Before Rooster could push her through the opening, Rachel braced herself against the frame and turned her head toward Ballard. "In my scientific research I did learn that more people die of human bites than of animals'. I suggest you see a doctor." She wrenched her arm free of Rooster's grip and stepped regally from the carriage.

She saw they were on a rocky headland extending out into the ocean. Not far from where the carriage had stopped, she could see the pulsing beam from the Point Adams lighthouse. Though it had been years since she'd last roamed the headland, she recalled vividly coming out here as a child with her parents, before the lighthouse was erected.

She remembered how the wind would sweep through her hair, billow through her skirts, and how she would stand with her arms outstretched, feeling one with the ocean. Tonight she felt only isolation and despair. Below them she heard the surf washing against the rocks and saw the immeasurable darkness beyond.

For the moment Rooster had released her and Rachel spotted her chance. Once she got her bearings, she took off in a dead run toward the beacon. With no skirts to slow her down, she felt confident she could outrun her captors. But the terrain was rugged, and she caught the heel of her shoe in the rocks. Fishhead, with his wiry physique, had managed to catch up with her. He tackled her around the waist, bringing her to a dead halt beneath him.

"Now, Doc, you don't want to go and do that, do you?" he crooned.

Rachel felt all hope drift away on the night wind. The gravel beneath her dug into her chest. Her knees and elbows stung from the grating contact with the jagged edges of rock. She was sure she had twisted her ankle, for it throbbed within the confines of her boot.

Zeke's fingers clamped around her injured foot and Rachel saw stars. Still she fought him while he struggled to regain his own balance. But her strength was no match for his. He yanked her to her feet and led her back to the carriage.

"Tie the bitch to your wrist," Ballard ordered Rooster. "That seems to be the only way we're going to keep her from taking off."

Soon Rachel's wrists were tethered to the loathsome

man, and Crowe dragged her along like an unwanted puppy. Each time their bodies touched she recoiled, and each time she did the man stopped abruptly to bring her scantily clad chest up against his beefy forearm. Seeing through his twisted pleasure, Rachel took great care to guard her own footsteps.

Her scrapes burned and her ankle drummed with fire. But the others remained oblivious to her wounds and she swore she'd die before she mentioned her discomfort to them. A mulish thought hit her. If she were presented to the Arab marred, perhaps he'd refuse her and Ballard would never get his jewels. The idea kept her going.

They led her down a winding, narrow path that ended at the bottom of a small cove. Here the water lapped gently against the sandy beach. Moonlight slipped over the towering rocks behind them, revealing the blackened outline of a longboat. Rooster dragged her toward the moored craft.

"Gag her and tie her feet," Ballard ordered him. "I'll not have her alerting everyone within a mile's radius with her caterwauling. And if she does go overboard, I'll have the pleasure of knowing she sank like a rock."

Rachel kicked violently to no avail as the three men overpowered her. She was thrust into the longboat, her booted feet securely tied and a filthy rag jammed inside her mouth and secured by another tied around her head.

Slowly Zeke and Jones maneuvered the boat out beyond the rocks. Passing through the churning water as though they'd done it many times before, they left the entrance to the cove behind. Rachel wondered suddenly how many other women had met their fate at the hands of Frank Ballard.

Soon the ocean swelled in docile rolls and Rachel looked back at the receding landscape, thinking as she did that this might be the last time she'd ever see her beloved home. And what of Grey? He must be nearly mad, locked up in the closet with no hope of escape. With no hope of rescuing her.

Her heart ached for the man she was leaving behind. The man who had opened his battered heart and had shared all of himself with her. Rachel Thomas, the plain doctor, who'd never imagined a man could love her because of her domineering personality, her sharp tongue, and her own lofty superiority.

But Grey had looked beneath those flaws and he'd loved her in spite of herself. Now she'd never see him again. Hot tears filled her eyes, only to be lifted by the wind as they slipped down over her cheeks.

She turned to see Ballard facing her from the bow of the boat. He sat, smugly hugging his cane, watching her with a mixture of anticipation and pleasure in her distress. Rachel hoped his ill-advised confidence in his own superior strength would also be his undoing. For some reason, unknown to herself, this thought buoyed her spirits.

He leaned over and pulled down her gag. "Does the lady weaken?"

She stared at him through her tears, challenging his every move. "Never in your lifetime."

Chapter 21

It was then that she saw the ship. Even with its sails furled, it loomed up out of the darkness like some giant sea monster, the three tall masts pricking the sky like thorny spines. Rachel's heartbeat quickened as they slid through the water toward the long, sleek vessel.

"It's rumored that the figurehead has real rubies for eyes." Ballard's own lit with greedy delight as their craft turned toward the ship's bow.

"If the rumor is true, I'm surprised you haven't gouged them out."

Rachel's gaze followed his as he scanned the outline of the vessel. Mounted beneath the bowsprit, she saw the carved head and neck of a camel. In the light of the hanging lanterns on deck, the beast's fiery eyes glared down at them, like a demon from hell.

"A camel?" Rachel mumbled with a swift intake of breath. A menacing looking creature it was, too.

Hearing her response, Ballard seemed only too eager to share his knowledge.

"The Bedouins of Arabia depend on their camels for their lives. They are the ships of the desert. Jamal

390

comes from one such tribe. So when he took to the sea, he chose the camel for his talisman.''

"How charming," Rachel answered.

Someone aboard ship ordered them to halt. Although he spoke in a foreign tongue, she understood the man's intent. Ballard immediately shouted up a reply, and soon after a rope ladder was dropped over the side.

Ballard steadied the rigging, waiting for her to mount the ropes ahead of him and for a moment she thought she might enjoy such a plan, giving her the opportunity to kick his teeth down his throat. Instead, she fastened her eyes on him, biting out her words. "Certainly, you don't expect me to climb to my own execution."

"Certainly not," Ballard replied.

Another rope was hurled over the ship's side. It coiled in the bottom of their boat like a large sea snake. "We'll haul you up the same as we do the other animals."

Despite her efforts to stop them, it took only a moment for Rooster and the others to harness Rachel with the rope. Another order was issued from above and soon she swung helplessly in the air.

Her captors had made certain she wouldn't escape on the upward haul. They'd strung the rope between her legs, then encircled her chest beneath her arms. Her hands were knotted and bound behind her back. They knew what they were doing. It was obvious they'd done this many times before.

Rachel tried to wriggle free as she was slowly inched higher. At the moment she was more willing to take her chances with the sharks in the ocean than the ones waiting for her on deck. But the rope between her legs already cut into her tender flesh and any jerky movement only added to her discomfort. Soon she gave up trying to escape. A short time later she was pulled over the side and dropped to the deck like a sack of grain.

Even in her bound state, Rachel still tried to spring to her feet. But the man standing over her pressed her back against the deck with his booted foot. Her arms felt as though they would pop from their sockets as he applied pressure to her collarbone. Unable to move, and too frightened to try, Rachel stared upward into the black eyes of an Arab. The dreaded captain, Jamal. Her journey had come to an end.

Because the crew of the *Tarbish* seemed more interested in the arriving cargo than in standing watch, no one noticed the dinghy that had pulled alongside the starboard side of the anchored vessel. For that Grey thanked the heavens for he needed the distraction until the Marine Revenue cutters arrived.

Rumor had flown that the *Tarbish* had been spotted far out at sea, and Grey had doubted that it would find much of interest in a large American port. Now he saw for himself its destination.

Owned by the Sheik of Dobhara, the clipper had been purchased several years earlier from a Connecticut shipbuilder for overseas trade. Some called the sheik progressive but Grey, and others who sailed with him, had heard the stories about the cargoes of the *Tarbish*.

Jamal plied the seas, bringing with him tales of kidnapping defenseless men and women, of sweeping down on unsuspecting island ports in the name of Allah. The stories rivaled *The Arabian Nights*. But until now, Grey never thought that Jamal and his crew would venture this far north. Thank God he'd been able to get to Tully. He only hoped he'd been in time.

Tully had flown into action the moment Grey explained Rachel's dire circumstance. Manning the signal lights from the harbormaster's small office on the wharf, Tully had caught the attention of a revenue cutter just offshore.

Unable to wait a moment longer than necessary, Grey had left the old man to complete his signalled messages to the patrol boat, and he could see it turning, even as the message lights continued to flash, to head in the direction of the lighthouse.

The blackened night sky provided blessed cover as Grey now maneuvered his own skiff unseen into the shadows beside the ship. He stood and steadied himself with the rigging which laced the side of the vessel down to the waterline.

He heard the gutteral orders of the Arab captain being issued from the top deck and, though too far away to make out the words, he recognized Frank Ballard's voice in response. Hot fear coiled in his stomach for what he couldn't see, and he had to force himself to remain hidden until he could determine Rachel's condition.

Waves lapped at the sides of the skiff, rocking Grey as he stood in his hiding place. His impatience grew with every second he was forced to wait. But he could not act too soon. Not until he knew that Ballard and his men were aboard ship.

Slowly he eased his craft around the cutwater and saw that Ballard and his men had deserted their boat for the bigger ship. Thankfully Grey saw that the rope ladder, now deserted, still hung from the side. Good, he thought, I'll relieve the idiots of a means of escape. Hastily he cut loose Ballard's boat and set both his and the other craft adrift.

He mentally checked the weapons he carried—a knife in each boot, a loaded pistol with extra ammunition in his pocket, and another long-bladed knife in the waistband of his trousers. Since taking to sea in his early years, he had become fairly proficient in the use of weaponry, for he could never be less than prepared for unforeseen dangers. But the thought of using them for other than killing an attacking shark or cleaning a fish always chilled his nerves. Nevertheless, he was now prepared.

He clung to the rope ladder, waiting, listening. But in the charged darkness only the sound of muffled voices met his ears. The group had moved away from the open deck toward the ship's bow. Grey slowly inched his way upward, then paused. Words, now high-pitched and irritable—flung through the air like swordpoints. An argument was going on between Ballard and the Arab.

With his fingers gripping the bulwark, Grey lifted his head only enough to look around. So this was what a Yankee clipper, re-outfitted for the use of the Arabs, looked like. With the exception of the foreign flag and crates labelled in Arabic, the vessel looked much the way it would have before it had been purchased.

Since the vessel lay at anchor, no one stood at the helm. Except for the usual groaning and creaking noises that always accompanied a ship at sea, it was deadly quiet. Because of the hour, most of the crew had probably retired. He counted seven men standing at the bow, focused on the woman who had just been brought on board, for he saw only the backs of the assembled men.

The aft hatches remained open. Grey's first move would be to lock them to make certain no one surprised him from behind. Slowly he eased himself over the rail and dropped silently to the deck. He stole through the shadows, securing the openings as he went. This first precaution taken, he flattened himself against the helm and listened, then crept forward toward the line of men.

And then he saw her. Rachel stood beyond them. Her ramrod posture made him proud. She faced off her captors with feline cunning. If she were frightened, no one aboard knew it.

Her dark mane hung around her shoulders like a satin veil. Her voluptuous body in whore's attire was the embodiment of every man's dream, and it struck him that he must have been blind to have ever considered her plain. She was the most beautiful woman he'd ever known.

"She's worth more than that and you know it." Ballard's angry words carried across the wind to Grey's hiding place.

The Arab spat out his disgust. "You have dishonored me with your lies. You take me for a fool? If she's so chaste, why is she dressed like a whore?"

With arched brows, Ballard faced the Arab in supreme confidence. "It's a long story, Jamal. You have the time to listen?"

"I have no time and you know it. I sail with the tide." Jamal fingered his dark beard. "I know you. You would cheat me by claiming her virginal worth. It makes me wonder . . ."

Facing the turbaned Arab, Ballard bowed obsequiously. "Perform your little test if you don't believe me."

"And if I find her to be spoiled goods, I shall personally cut off your root and feed it to the sharks."

"Hellfire, Jamal. Do our years together, dealing in flesh, mean nothing? Can't you take my word?"

"Pshaw! The word of a foreign devil means nothing. After I have seen for myself that she is as you say, I shall pay you. Not before."

Ballard rocked nervously on his feet. "I need my money now. I need to—"

"You will stay," the Arab ordered. "If you have tried to cheat me, your life is mine."

Alarm charged Ballard's expression. Grey realized at that moment Ballard knew Rachel was not a virgin. He'd counted on his years of doing business with the Arab as his pledge of payment. It also meant that Ballard's men must have seen enough after Grey pulled Rachel from the river to know that they were lovers.

Damnation. He couldn't allow the filthy Arab to touch her, even though he'd very much enjoy seeing Ballard suffer the foreigner's wrath. Jamal's face had turned a high color and Grey knew that for him honor outweighed life itself. For an Arab to be shamed before his peers would mean certain death for the offender.

"He's lying. I'm not a virgin." Rachel's declaration cut through the tense air when the Arab moved toward her.

"Shut up, bitch." Ballard gulped, his growing fear evident. "Jamal, can't you see she's playing us against each other? She only wants to save her scrawny neck."

Jamal stopped, his gaze shifting first to Rachel, then back to Ballard. Then he raised his hand.

Ballard's men had barely reached instinctively for weapons they no longer carried when two rifle-toting Arabs stepped back and trained their guns on them. It was then that Grey realized Ballard and his men had been forced to surrender their arms when they'd boarded Jamal's ship. This was not to say they didn't have a few hidden beneath the folds of their clothes. Grey mulled over this last piece of information and decided rescuing Rachel might be significantly easier than he had first thought.

Reaching inside his boots, he pulled out the two small knives. With deadly precision, he flung one after the other toward his targets. The two armed Arabs toppled to the deck, blood spewing from their necks.

"Run, Rachel!" Grey shouted, bounding out of the shadows into the light. His pistol was aimed at Ballard's head.

Jamal dived for one of the fallen rifles, screaming in Arabic, but Rooster reached it first, kicking it from his reach. Within seconds Ballard's men had confiscated the Arabs' weapons. Zeke pinned Jamal to the deck with one while Rooster trained the other on Grey. In the frenzy, Jones dropped to the deck like a wounded dog, fear overcoming any desire to prove his manhood.

Frozen, Rachel could only stare at Grey. Then his order registered and she darted for cover. But her slight hesitation had given Ballard the advantage he needed. He lunged toward her and pulled her against his chest, his arms encircling her in a deathlike grip. He moved backward toward the ship's bow, dragging her with him.

"Shoot the bastard," Ballard commanded Rooster.

"I'll blow your leader away before you can get off the first shot," Grey threatened, his own gun cocked and ready to fire. Crowe's eyes flickered in defiance until he seemed to realize in this stand-off someone would definitely come up the loser. He looked back to Ballard for direction.

"Let her go," Grey ordered, his pistol never wavering from its target.

"Never, Devlin!" Ballard shouted back. Behind him the bow narrowed, but he continued his backward movement. "If you do manage to get off a shot, we'll both go over. You want your lady to splatter her pretty guts across the water?"

Ballard knew as long as he held Rachel, Grey wouldn't chance a wayward shot. And Grey sure as hell didn't want Rachel hurled into the icy, black Pacific nearly twenty feet below.

Grey moved toward him. But with every forward step he took, Ballard took one backward, dragging Rachel with him. "Let her go, Frank. This fight is between you and me. She has nothing to do with it."

But Ballard's face had taken on a mad leer. "She has more to do with this than you'll ever know, just like her father before her. I sent Old Doc Thomas to his grave, now I'll go to hell dragging his daughter to hers."

Shouts and pounding could be heard beneath the secured hatches as more and more sailors of the *Tarbish* realized their captain was in trouble. But the openings remained locked. Jamal, still lying on the deck with Zeke's rifle aimed at his heart, jerked his head toward Ballard. Grey heard him let out a string of Arabic expletives, but he had no time to question the man's re-action. All his concentration remained on his efforts to rescue Rachel.

"It's no use, Ballard. The Revenue cutters will be here at any moment now. They know all about your shady dealings. Surrender the girl and they'll go easier on you."

"You're lying," Ballard shouted back. "They have nothing on me. Only your word against mine, and what good is the word of a convict?"

"How's it goin', son?"

Without looking back, Grey recognized the welcome voice as Tully and Abner materialized from the shad-ows. They both carried weapons aimed at Rooster and Zeke.

With the appearance of the two men Grey felt the tension break. "Lord, Abner," he said in a weak at-tempt at humor, "your wife know you're carrying that thing?"

"Always did want a chance to be a hero," Abner replied. He and Tully approached Grey's side, aiming their weapons with confidence.

"I was beginning to think I'd never see you two," Grey murmured through the side of his mouth. "Ship's secured. I locked the hatches so the rest of the crew are trapped below. But Ballard here is another story. He refuses to release Rachel, and I don't dare try to down him with her clamped in front of him."

Loud horn blasts ripped through the night and sur-rounded the ship. For the first time Grey felt some hope of talking Ballard out of his insane plan.

Tully's voice broke through the still air. "They're

here, boy. Cutters surroundin' the ship. The law will be on board at any moment now.''

"Hear that, Ballard? The Revenuers are here. Tell Rooster and Zeke to drop their weapons. You don't stand a chance.''

Rachel could hear shouts and orders being issued from boats bumping against the sides of the giant hull. But as she saw it, her rescuers could be one or one hundred and Ballard would never release her. In spite of her position, she felt a strange calm overtake her, her thoughts becoming rational even as she stood captive in the brute's grip. She scanned the bow around her and realized Ballard had dragged her as far forward as they could go. Only the long, jutting bowsprit with the camel figurehead below it remained behind them.

She knew Grey would never risk a shot at Ballard as long as he held her. Nor did she relish the idea of a swim. But she would not stand here another moment like a sacrificial goat used for bait. Now was the time to take matters into her own hands. With Tully and Abner both covering Rooster and Zeke, Rachel felt her odds of escaping were as good as they would ever get.

Lifting her foot, she jammed her heel upward into Ballard's groin. The movement caught him off guard, but surprisingly he did not release her. Instead he groaned and lunged backwards, carrying her with him.

In the next instant, Rachel's feet left the deck of the ship and she was airborne. She fought to grasp rigging, rails, anything that would keep her from plunging into the black water below. From above her, she heard Grey yell out her name. In the next moment, gunfire exploded through the night.

Grey, had he been shot?

Just as Rachel's hands made contact with solid wood, she heard Ballard's scream echo through the air below her, followed by an explosive splash. Her trembling threatened to loosen her hold and only by pulling air into her lungs and talking to herself could she calm down.

After her initial shock had passed, Rachel assessed her situation. She dangled by her arms, suspended in midair, clinging to whatever had broken her fall. Carefully she swung her legs until she found an open space through which to thread her legs. Helplessly she clung to the ship's bow, like a monkey in a tree. But for the moment she was safe, though she could hardly believe it.

Above her she heard the pounding of feet and Grey's repeated agonized cry, "Rachel, Rachel!"

"I'm here," she whimpered, barely able to speak. But her thoughts were clear and her gratitude certain. Grey was alive. She held to the wood, her teeth chattering in the aftermath of fear. Her eyes held steady on the cutwater before her, for to look up was to see only canvas masting furled around the bowsprit. Below, only the inky black ocean.

She heard the whipping of waves against the hull and the firing of orders from the deck above as footsteps bounded along the ship. And then, "Rachel, my God." He'd seen her. Grey had found her. "Hang on!" he shouted. "I'll get you!"

In another time she may have given way to tears at the sound of his voice. But every fragment of her being concentrated on the tenuous grip she maintained. He was still alive, that was all that mattered. And he was coming for her. Suddenly her world seemed brighter, in spite of her precarious position.

Feeling her confidence return, she looked around more closely, curious as to what had broken her fall. As incredible as it seemed, she found herself wrapped around the figurehead of the Arab ship. How she'd managed to end up here she'd never understand, but the evil-looking camel had saved her. His snout had kept her from falling, and it had been his long neck that she'd wrapped her legs around. Her talisman, she thought, looking up into his ruby-fire eyes.

Rubies? Rachel recalled Ballard's words. Slowly she slipped her hand forward to touch the sparkling glass of the eye nearer her. It would probably be the only time she'd ever be so close to so much wealth. She splayed her hand over it, amazed to find it was the size of her palm. She moved her fingers around the edges, curious as to what held the jewel in its place. When she did, a wedge of wood slipped forward and the eyeball rolled out of its socket. Horrified, she clasped her hand around it to keep it from falling into the water below. She could hear more shouting as Grey continued to call to her. A moment later, hoisted down in a rope basket, he drew level with her.

Soon both Grey and Rachel were standing back aboard the ship. When the ropes were removed from around the two of them, Rachel nearly collapsed. Grey held her up, cradling her against him.

Law enforcement officers huddled nearby, talking to the Arab captain, while others escorted Ballard's men from the vessel. Barely conscious of the activity around him, Grey's eyes sought Rachel's, drinking in her nearness. Twice he'd come close to losing her. When he'd seen her tumble with Ballard over the bow, he'd nearly gone crazy, heedless of Rooster still holding the rifle on him. But Tully, as always, had been at his side. His shot to Crowe's shoulder had stopped the man in his tracks.

"I heard the gunshot," Rachel started, finally giving in to her tears. "I thought it was you."

Grey held her head between his hands and lowered his lips to hers. "I'm fine, my love. Ballard will never bother either of us again."

He took her into his arms and kissed her, and Rachel in turn kissed him back. Moments later they pried themselves apart, their passion rising.

"I love you," he whispered, "and I intend to spend the rest of my life proving that to you."

"I love you, Mr. Grey Devlin, and I plan to make certain you work hard every night showing me just how much you do love me."

"Shameless hussy, aren't you?"

"If you dress like a whore, I suppose you have to act like one," she countered.

"Uh-hmmm," Tully interrupted, clearing his throat.

Realizing for the first time that they had an audience, Rachel and Grey withdrew from each other's arms.

"Uh, Grey . . . Doc, this is Chief Sears. It seems we have him to thank for your rescue tonight."

Grey looked over to see the Marine Revenue officer standing nearby. Captain Jamal stood beside him, bowing and gesturing toward a cabin beside his own.

"Mr. Devlin," the chief started, "as harbormaster, this is rightfully your jurisdiction and I would be more than happy to turn this man over to you. But he tells an interesting story. Shall we put ourselves through it, or would you like me to take him into custody?"

Grey's blue eyes sliced through the Arab's haughty expression like the sharpest blade. Having heard his dealing with Frank Ballard, he would have liked nothing better than to throw him overboard. "I'm most tempted," he said, "to feed him to the sharks." He held a protective arm around Rachel. "But after all that's happened tonight, what's one more delay?"

Jamal, disarmed and apologetic, bowed toward Grey. "Blessings upon you, honored one." He nodded to Rachel, acknowledging her with one glance. He was caught and he knew it. "And my most humble apologies to you, lady."

Looking back to Grey, he continued. "It was my misfortune to accept those men aboard my vessel, for that was not my intent. If you will allow me to express my worthless reasons for anchoring my ship along your shore . . ."

Jamal was falling over himself, humbling himself before the man who controlled his future. But Grey listened.

"I know my situation is grave, but I am in the hands of Allah, for He has sent me to you."

"Get on with it," Grey ordered.

"I come here to return an important man to his home. By order of Mahmed al-Raschid, Sheik of Dobhara. It is Allah's wish that I do his bidding. This man I bring had the misfortune of entering my country as a hostage of mansellers, but he has proven his worthiness by saving the life of the sheik's eldest son."

The captain turned and, pointing to the stern, uttered an unintelligible command to one of his men, now guarded by a Revenue officer. In response, the seaman opened the door adjacent to the captain's quarters. A tall, frail-looking man, dressed in fine robes and baggy trousers, stepped out onto the deck.

He was heavily bearded and by lantern light his face was indistinguishable. Curiosity forced the small group forward. Jamal stepped toward the man, with arms outstretched, his loose shirt waving around him like a flag. "At last, sire," he greeted the man, "Allah has brought you home."

The man looked from Jamal to Chief Sears, a smile growing on his lips. Slowly he scanned the others until his eyes rested on Rachel.

"Daughter, can it be you?" the stranger asked.

At the sound of the raspy voice, both Rachel and Tully gasped. "Papa?" "Doc?" they cried simultaneously, their question a confirmation of an apparition that couldn't be. As incredible as it seemed, Doctor Theodore Thomas had returned home. The man held out his arms.

Rachel covered the last ten feet between her and her father in the blink of an eye. "Oh, Papa," she wept, "I can't believe it. It really is you."

Rachel collapsed into her father's arms, nearly swallowed up by the folds of his colorful robes. "There, now child. It's all right. I'm home now." He backed her out of his hold a bit. "Why, it really is my girl." He swept her hair back from her face. "Look at you, you're all grown up."

Rachel, oblivious to her state of undress, continued to stare, incredulous, at the man before her. "Papa, I can't believe it's you."

"It is I, child, I assure you."

"But how? I thought—"

"I know what you thought, but I'm back, and for the moment that's all that matters." He pulled her close once more before releasing her.

Until now Grey and Tully had waited, rooted to the deck behind Rachel, both hardly believing the vision they beheld. Rachel stepped from her father and pulled the two of them forward.

Doctor Theodore's gaze lit immediately on Tully. "Taithleach, my old friend."

Tully opened his arms and Rachel's father stepped into them, hugging his old comrade as if to let go would be to lose him forever. Finally withdrawing from the old seaman's hold, he looked at Grey, his dark, brooding eyes quietly resting upon him. His gaze then caught his daughter's as she clung to Grey's arm.

"And this would be . . . ?"

Grey stepped forward and thrust out his free hand to the older gentleman. "Grey Devlin, sir."

Before he could say more, Chief Sears intervened. "Doctor Thomas, Mr. Devlin here is the harbormaster and, if I might add, the best thing that's happened to this port in a long time. It's a long story, but he is our real hero tonight."

From the outer perimeter of the group, Jamal's voice joined in praise. "And a most worthy husband for your daughter, sire." The Arab's head bobbed his approval like a buoy in a storm.

The elder doctor's gaze swept over Grey a second

406

time while he still clasped Grey's hand. "Husband?" he asked.

"If your daughter will have me, sir . . . and, of course, if you approve."

"From what I can observe, I have no reason to object. I would be pleased to have you as my son-in-law." He offered his smile, so much like Rachel's own.

Rachel hugged Grey tighter, beaming at the two men who meant more to her than anything in the world. "Oh, Papa, Grey, this is truly the most wonderful day of my life."

"I hate to interrupt," Captain Sears interjected, "but Mr. Devlin and I have some unfinished business with Captain Jamal here." He acknowledged the rest of the group. "My boat is prepared to return the rest of you to shore."

Grey turned to the Arab trader. Jamal stood silently by, avoiding his gaze and the exuberance that so easily called attention to him. His hands were reverently joined as though waiting for Allah to deliver him from the hands of the infidels.

"If you please, officer," Doctor Theodore interceded, "Captain Jamal has done me a great service tonight. We had only just anchored when those criminals boarded this vessel. The captain ordered me to remain in my cabin in order to guard my safety. Nothing more."

"But, Doctor," the chief protested, "this man has the reputation of a jackal."

"Sir, this man has saved my life and seen me home unharmed. I ask that you allow him to return to his people. You have searched his ship and found nothing amiss, is that not true?"

"I must admit, sir, everything looks in order."

"Mr. Devlin? This is your territory."

The relief Grey felt at the outcome of tonight's near disaster overshadowed some of the bitterness he felt toward the Arab trader. He hoped that by releasing him it didn't also overshadow his good judgment. "I expect you to sail with the morning tide. Until then, remain aboard ship."

Rachel stepped forward and thrust the camel's eye into Jamal's hand. "For your despicable behavior I should throw this to the bottom of the ocean." In spite of the fact that she still stood in a whore's dress, she mustered all the dignity and sophistication becoming of her true station. "And you call yourself a follower of Allah."

The captain looked down at the treasure in his hand. "But how—?"

"It fell out of the figurehead when I touched it." She felt color rise at the admission, for suddenly she felt little more than a thief.

Jamal looked startled. "Lady," he said, "you bring this ship honor by your truth-telling and by your bravery." He bowed and scanned the deck, clearly uncomfortable at gazing into the uncovered face and cleavage of a woman. He closed his fingers around the stone. "Please, accept this unworthy token for the hardships you were forced to endure. It is but little payment, but Allah will be pleased." With a reverence reserved for the prophets themselves, Jamal turned to Rachel's father. "You shall both be long remembered."

* * *

After the patrol boat moved away from the clipper and Rachel sat ensconced between her father and Grey, she couldn't believe her good fortune.

As the boat steamed back toward port, she thought about how close she had come to being shanghaied as her father had been. She thought, too, about another night when she and the ''brides'' had nearly sent Grey away from Astoria forever.

If she'd not sworn to take up her father's crusade, to seek revenge against the people who'd kidnapped him and countless others, she'd probably never have met Grey Devlin. How empty her life would have been.

After all they'd been through, it was still difficult to believe they were all alive and headed for home. Rachel's future seemed as bright as the winking lights of Astoria as they drew closer to the wharf. For a brief instant she felt the acute loss of her mother and wished that she would have lived to be part of this glorious future.

Nearing the pier, her arms linked with her men, she fingered the camel's eye in her palm and thought about the risks she had taken since returning home in the name of justice. It would take weeks to explain to her father how she had taken up his cause, and some things she wasn't sure she could ever tell him at all.

Suddenly she broke into giddy laughter, while the others stared at her as though she'd taken leave of her senses. A ruby, she thought, clutching the gem tighter in her hand. As valuable as a king's ransom.

All that money for the Women's Aid Society.

Epilogue

A slight afternoon breeze swayed the fern baskets on the porch and floated in through the French doors of Sarah Ballard's home, cooling her guests after the long, sultry morning at church. Now, as her company gathered in her front parlor, Sarah flitted among them, refilling glasses of cold lemonade.

Rachel sat on the camelback sofa, showing off her goddaughter to all who stopped to chat and watching Sarah out of the corner of her eye. To imagine that, in three months time, her friend had survived a fragile and difficult pregnancy, the imprisonment of her husband, and the scandal of divorce. The woman looked happier than ever, having regained her health and her family's estate.

"I think you could use some refreshment."

Rachel smiled up at her husband and gratefully accepted a filled glass, then shifted to allow him room beside her. With no hesitation, Grey reached for the baby and cuddled her in his lap. The infant settled peacefully in the crook of his arm, yards and yards of christening dress spewing over his knees. Covered in white lace, he still looked perfectly at home.

"You make a wonderful godfather," Rachel whispered to him. He only smiled, his face flushing slightly, before changing the subject.

"Look at her." He nodded toward the baby's mother. Sarah moved throughout the room, along with Agnes, offering plates of sandwiches. "She looks positively radiant."

"She's making up for years of lost time." As am I, Rachel thought, considering the joyous change of events in her own life. From a lost and lonely soul, trying to heal herself, she had emerged with a future she'd never thought possible. She had the husband of her dreams, her father was back, and their combined practice was thriving.

"Thought you might like to know," Grey added, "I'm expecting a ship up from San Francisco tomorrow with new equipment for Camp Ross. It should all be in place by the end of the week."

"Wonderful. Mr. Ross will be thrilled."

"No more so than the day Sarah asked him for a dollar and handed him back the title to his land. I never will forget the look on that old man's face. I thought he'd have a stroke."

"You needn't have feared. Both Papa and I would have revived him. Speaking of whom . . ." Rachel scanned the parlor, ". . . where do you suppose he's gone?"

At that moment, Sarah made her way across the room. "If you're looking for Dr. Theodore, I saw him and Tully head for the library. That old salt was challenging him to another round of checkers."

"I don't believe it," roared Grey. "He never gives up, does he?"

"Don't mind them," Sarah chastened. "Besides, that library is finally being put to good use. Nothing but good things to come from that room from now on."

Rising from the sofa, Rachel stood and gave her friend a tight hug. All these years, she thought, that Sarah had been in trouble with no one to help. But in spite of her situation she had remained brave. Now, at last, she had found her reward.

She had a new life with her tiny daughter and tales to share with anyone who would listen about how she had helped Grey and Rachel bring about her own husband's downfall. This, indeed, was the Sarah Collins of old, full of life and laughter.

Community, Rachel thought. This is what life was all about. To have one's family and friends around, to be accepted. She thought back to the first months after she had hung up her shingle, when no one but Opal and her girls had accepted her for who she was. Just as she had accepted them.

In knowing the "brides of the night," she had looked beyond their scandalous lives into their hearts, and she had found a special goodness. And then came Tully.

The rest, she pondered, was a series of events not to be believed. It would, in fact, make a wonderful story to pass down to her own children. Perhaps someday, Grey would write it all down. No one could read a story the way he could.

Author's Note

When we headed to Oregon with the idea of placing our heroine, Doctor Rachel Thomas, in a rough and tough logging town, little did we know that our original idea would be thrown out and a whole new story born. But after countless interviews with the people involved in the state logging industry, we still couldn't find the spark that would make our already special character more special. It wasn't until we stopped in the port city of Astoria, on the Columbia River, that Rachel informed us, "My place is here . . . this is where I want to be."

So with her looking over our shoulders, we dug through historical records at The Heritage Museum and the Clatsop County Library. After talking with several Astorian citizens about their town's colorful past, we knew we'd come to the right place. And so we brought Rachel home—to take up her father's medical practice and his crusade.

We set her down in the middle of the boarding houses, gambling halls, and saloons of Astoria's skid row section. In the seventies and eighties this area was

413

known as Swilltown, where agents known as crimps procured unsuspecting citizens for outbound ships. For "blood money" these shanghaiers would routinely deliver drunk or drugged loggers and farmers to sea captains eager for crews.

Our research introduced us to so many entertaining stories on shanghaiing, we couldn't begin to tell them all. Such as the one of a woman who ran a sailors' boarding house and sold her own husband to a captain of a sailing vessel for one hundred dollars.

Or of Bunco Kelly, the best known crimp in Portland, Oregon. He once supplied a captain with a crew of corpses that he'd discovered dead from drinking formaldehyde in the basement of a mortuary—next door to the basement of a liquor store, whose supplies they had presumably intended to tap. Kelly got them aboard the ship and told the captain they were "dead drunk." On another occasion when Kelly was up against a deadline and needed one more man, he appropriated a wooden Indian from in front of a cigar store, wrapped it in a blanket, and took it on board. "Dead drunk" was his explanation again.

We borrowed the tale of the Methodist minister, Reverend Grannis, who was almost shanghaied out of his church. This did happen, but in the year 1889. For our own purpose, we gave the Reverend a fictitious name.

Last but not least, we'd like to introduce you to Doctor Bethenia Owens-Adair, the first woman doctor west of the Rockies. Having graduated from an eastern medical college in 1880, she returned to Oregon where she gave herself unstintingly to her practice, often rowing up the various streams in the night to take care of emergencies. She was the only physician in a considerable district immediately south of Astoria and was the real inspiration for our story.

Of course, Grey Devlin is a figment of our imagination, but the right man to tame our spirited doctor. By the way, Rachel just smiled her approval. We hope you, too, will approve of their love story.

Biography

When Atlantans Ellen Lyle Taber and Carol Card Otten met through Georgia Romance Writers, they discovered amazingly similar backgrounds. Raised less than two hundred miles apart in the deep South, they were both painters, had sent children through Auburn University, shared a love of history, and had admitted Trekkies for husbands. Even their custom-made wedding bands were alike. When, through their critique group, they found complementary writing styles, they decided to collaborate—and Tena Carlyle was born. The result was *Captive Treasure*, published by Zebra Heartfire in 1992. Their second Zebra Heartfire, *Runaway Heart*, was a June 1993 release. Also look for two more upcoming Carlyle romances—tentatively titled *Shady Lady* and *Wyoming Wildflower*.